Man

Music

Manhattan Music

a novel by

Meena Alexander

mercury house
san francisco

Published in the United States of America by Mercury House, San Francisco, California, a nonprofit publishing company devoted to the free exchange of ideas and guided by a dedication to literary values.

United States Constitution, First Amendment: Congress shall make no law respecting an establishment of religion, or prohibiting the free exercise thereof; or abridging the freedom of speech, or of the press; or the right of the people peaceably to assemble, and to petition the Government for a redress of grievances.

Mercury House and colophon are registered trademarks of Mercury House, Incorporated.

Printed on recycled, acid-free paper and manufactured in the United States of America.

Designed by Thomas Christensen.

Library of Congress Cataloguing-in-Publication Data:
Alexander, Meena, 1951–
    Manhattan music : a novel / by Meena Alexander.
       p.   cm.
    ISBN 1-56279-092-7 (alk. paper)
     1. East Indian Americans—New York (State)—New York—Fiction.
  2. Women, East Indian—New York (State)—New York—Fiction.
  I. Title.
PR9499.3.A46M36   1997
813'.54–DC21   96-53344
                                                      CIP

9 8 7 6 5 4 3 2 1
FIRST EDITION

Not one,
not two, not three or four,
but through eighty-four hundred thousand vaginas
have I come,
I have come
through unlikely worlds,
guzzled on
pleasure and on pain.
Whatever be
all previous lives,
show me mercy
this one day,
O lord
white as jasmine.

—Mahadeviyakka, Vacana to Shiva,
translated by A. K. Ramanunjam, *Speaking of Shiva*

Acknowledgments

I am grateful for support that was offered me as I wrote this novel: from the MacDowell Colony; the Arts Council of England; the Asian-American Renaissance. Friends in different places, in different ways, all so necessary, helped me on: Catherine Byron, Erika Duncan, Jessica Hagedorn, Walter Kendrick, Karen Malpede, David Mura, Alastair Niven, Susie Tharu, and I send them my thanks. My gratitude to Anne Dubuisson for her faith in this book; to Thomas and Carol Christensen for their care with the manuscript. Parts of the novel first appeared in the anthologies *Charlie Chan is Dead: An Anthology of Contemporary Asian-American Fiction* (New York: Penguin, 1993) and *On a Bed of Rice: An Asian-American Erotic Feast* (New York: Anchor Books, 1995). Jay's poems were first published in *River and Bridge* (New Delhi: Rupa, 1995/Toronto: TSAR Press, 1996).

Manhattan
Music

Overture: Monsoon Flood
(Draupadi)

Know her to be my second life/alone, speaking little.
   —Kalidasa, Meghadutam

What drew me close to Sandhya? Perhaps it was the way her hair fell over her face and she pushed it back with her hand, quickly, against high cheekbones.

She was alone, afloat in the city and I was someone to confide in, or so it seemed. At times, her own life seemed a dream: "As if I had picked up a pair of colored glasses from the pile on Nampally Road and set them to my eyes."

"Where was Nampally Road?" I asked.

"In Hyderabad where I lived," she replied. Then she sketched out a pile of used glasses, shifting, unstable, an old man had stored on the sidewalk. Imagine secondhand spectacles, on an old cloth, in a huge mound on the sidewalk. When she picked up a pair and set it to her eyes, the iron-colored leaves on the banyan tree started shifting.

I think she needed me.

Born in America, I must have seemed the epitome of newness, all she might one day be—leather jacket, Benetton sweater, short black hair, subtle eyeshadow, the lot. She asked me simple questions, the what, where, who kind of thing, and in response rhythms flowed out of me.

I was the one who was native but she made me play the foreigner, the woman who was permitted everything. Over coffee, fruit juice, bourbon, we met. How soft her questions were. I started speaking. Necessity drove me on.

Yet I felt our lives were poles apart, driven hard by place and circumstance. My ancestors were scattered from British sailing ships, dark bits of ground pepper flung onto plantations in Trinidad, Fiji. Bonded laborers from India scratching the dirt of the New World. Men used hard, and women, too, cane leaves cutting into their wrists. Papa and Mama migrated to America, settled in Gingee by the Hudson where Mama gave birth to me.

Sandhya's people, on the other hand, seemed never to have budged from the Indian subcontinent. Her veins were etched by centuries of arranged marriages, dark blue blood pouring through. She could point to a plot of land bounded by granite walls and name ancestors who had owned that land for generations. By fields swollen by monsoon flood she imagined her great-grandmother afloat in a black canoe. Then too, she remembered the cemeteries where her grandparents were buried, the houses that had held them, the rites under which they were married. But memory swelling like black water threatened to drown her.

Would she see her face in that flood, the delicate nostrils, the high cheekbones, the long-lashed eyes?

Who would hold up a lamp so that her eyes, darting like twin fish, could see themselves seeing?

Sitting

A sharp sound, and she felt it like music. Sandhya shifted her weight on the wooden bench at the edge of Central Park. A tinkle, perhaps a pebble striking glass. Then she saw him in the middle distance, a small man, as dark as she was, balancing on a bicycle. The street was curiously empty and allowed her full view of the assortment of mirrors tied to the back of his bicycle. No wonder the metal vehicle was wobbling. The man put out his foot to steady himself. One of the mirrors, the longest one, had streaks of gilt at the edge. She half raised herself from the bench, as if wanting to look into that flat gleaming surface, see something that was hidden from her. Where had the mirror come from? Was it torn from an old house at the edge of the park? Was it being carried to a junk shop somewhere on the lower edge of the city? As the bicycle moved on, she settled back onto the bench, feeling the cold wind on her neck. She raised her hand up and drew her scarf close.

There was that sound again, rougher now, as if flesh were slapped against metal, the sound the wheels of the subway made slowing at Union Square, the metal body of the train pitched closer to the platform edge. When was it she had got off the subway right behind Stephen, then let go of his hand to stand staring at the enclosure: a cage of chicken wire guarding twin sculptures, two metal chairs, bolted to the ground, their large proportions making them curiously childlike? The chairs were painted red and blue, their backs ornate in a fantasy of feeling. Stephen called her name, once, twice, as Sandhya tried to put her hand through the chicken wire that protected the art work. She wanted to shove forward till she could sit. All she wanted to do was to sit ever so quietly, waiting. She wanted her feet soldered to the rough tiles, in the middle of no-man's-land

—after all, what else was the subway at rush hour? She tried to imagine a figure seated across from her in the other chair, but the most that she could make out was a formless thing, something fashioned of mist, or smoke, hovering over ground.

Then the scene shifted all around, like a curtainless theater. Above her head she glimpsed the blue vault of the sky, herself a child of six crouched in a sandy courtyard, wiggling her toes, staring ahead at the white sheet stretched tight. Under the sheet the gawky feet poked out. She drew in her breath, it was the puppeteers and she was crouched in Grandmother's courtyard. Now the sheet was quite still and behind it shadows started their slow dance. Tiny figures with swords raised, a man on an elephant, the creature clumsy with the strings the puppeteer was tugging. Then a minute chair was pushed forward. "Why, a chair," Ayah laughed, seeing the rickety thing made out of palm stalks, but it was set in the center of the sheet and quietly, her knees hardly jerking, came Draupadi. The child knew it was Draupadi even before Ayah said so. The mulberry tree in the courtyard was stirring with wind, and the strands of hair pasted onto the puppet's head started blowing wild. As Draupadi was lowered into the chair, the puppet master started his recitation. Words Sandhya could no longer summon up about exile, about being unhoused, and the long years Draupadi waited. On and on the voice went, till a tiny figure bore down on the seated woman, his sword raised. "*Aoiou, aiou,*" the child cried, as the puppet, forced off the chair, raised her leather arms and started to dance. "Her dance will go on, till the end of exile," Ayah murmured, pulling the child close. But it had started raining after that and the play ended quickly. Brushing the raindrops off her nose, the child ran into the house, after her mother. "Amma, Amma," she cried, wanting a few pieces of silver to press into the puppet master's hands. Perhaps he would let her see the Draupadi puppet, show her how to lower her into the chair, then raise her, body quivering, in a slow dance.

T he bench was growing colder. Sandhya felt drops on her face. Where was she? The street in front of her was suddenly crowded. She noticed leaves dropping off trees, people bundled into coats and scarves blurring into each other. She thrust her feet into the damp ground and felt the rim of a soda can. As she thought of getting up, her hand closed over a plastic card in her bag. She drew it out gingerly, and tried to wipe the surface free of the mistiness. It was laminated poorly, and the image was hardly sharp. Still the resemblance was there: the narrow nose, lips slightly apart, hair blown back as if the woman were holding onto the mast of a ship. Working her fingers over the surface of the card she tried to reach what was buried under the gleaming plastic, under the dark skin and floating hair of the image—a dark face, drowned in hair that blew free, blurring flesh into background. Still the lips of the woman in the green card were parted in surprise, at the immigration officer who stood dressed in something dark, so energetic, cheery—"Welcome to America. Be happy here." Sandhya clutched at Stephen's arm. "Smile dear, smile." He stood behind the camera, an Irish man, Stephen said later, though she hadn't known and all these ethnicities confused her so. But she tried to smile while bending her body back to let a group of old women dressed in black robes, hair knotted in head scarves, pass by her. They were babbling in Portuguese. She recognized the language that she had heard from Marika, her Goan friend in Hyderabad. The sounds flowered in her ears so she hardly heard Stephen: "The gates of America are open wide," Stephen murmured to her. "We'll live here, Sandy, we'll be happy, I promise you." And he had flung down the leather bag from Nainatal, set his arms resolutely around her, and kissed her full on the lips.

Why couldn't it all be simple after that, a play, sensible and short? Wasn't that the way life was meant to be, after all? But nothing felt right. It was as if the sheet against which the figures danced was all askew, the puppeteer having neglected to pull it tight. Neither gestures nor words came out right. As she walked toward the bus stop, a thought gripped Sandhya. Supposing she were to swallow the green card, ingest that plastic, would it pour through her flesh, a curious alchemy that would make her all right in the new world? She gazed at her two hands, extended now in front of her. What if she could peel off her brown skin, dye her hair blonde, turn her body into a pale, Caucasian thing, would it work better with Stephen? Stepping carefully onto the sidewalk she pondered the version of beauty she had gleaned from the old movies that found their way to Hyderabad—Marilyn Monroe, though she was far too sexy to emulate, she who made the cats crawl on the hot roofs of the city, made helpless men cry "Zindabad Marilyn!" Someone like Michelle Pfeiffer would be better, her *filmi* body curved just right as she flung her blonde hair over her cheek, held tight to her purse, lifted up her stockinged ankle, showed off her heels.

Sandhya sighed, tried to focus her thoughts, brushed hard against a clump of rose bushes. She picked herself free of the scrawny thorns at her side, and in a trick of the mind tried to visualize crisp red English roses set in a bowl. "Rosenblum," she murmured, trying to hold on to the bloom-ing part of her married name. Then she thought of paler tea roses by the edge of a well-trimmed garden, in a misty part of early summer. Could one come by such summers in Manhattan? She did not know. The most she had done this chilly morning, with Dora safe in daycare, was lounge on a bench at the edge of Central Park.

With the muggers and looters about whom she dared not think. With the young mothers and their babies—the little things gulping at the air al-ways comforted her, so like her Dora had been. With the winos, lank hair falling over their eyes. With the wealthy ladies and their lap dogs yapping so that all at once the air under the yew trees was filled with sharp dog cries, and Harlem in the middle distance when she turned her head lay roasting like an oyster, its nascent pearl dissolved back into shimmering air. It was a heat haze coupled with the lack of ozone.

"Be careful when you go out walking," Stephen had warned her. "You need to learn your street smarts, Sandy. Watch out till then," and he chucked her gently under the chin.

"Rosenblum," Sandhya whispered out the name again. She shared it with Mildred from Hoboken, Mildred with her streaked hair and twin children with freckles and knock-knees, her living room furniture all cov-ered in plastic. With the housemaid from Trinidad, whose skin is the color of my own, Sandhya thought, having seen Esther in her tight white frock arranging cups on the table, laying out bagels and vegetable cream cheese as Mildred fussed with the strawberries and made furious signs to Stanley to pass the hot blintzes she had specially prepared for Stephen and his new wife. Sandhya had liked the warmth of the blintzes. One had split sud-denly, oozing a sweet substance. It was a dish brought over from another world. She thought of the steerage the Rosenblums had come in, packed tight, suffering the cold; the immigration officer on Ellis Island tugging head scarves off the little girls to check them for lice, cold wind on their cheeks in the photograph that Stephen's mother held up for her. And as light fell oddly on the crumpled edge of the photo Muriel said in her high-pitched way: "Never forget you are marrying into this, Sandhya." Then patting the photo hard, she added, "But you know this is the land of op-portunity!" Sandhya swallowed hard, eyes fixed on the pearls at her mother-in-law's throat, the aging skin, the fine lace collar. "There, there, eat up your ice cream," Muriel continued not unkindly: "You should just know what all this is." "Oh, Mother," Stephen protested, "Let her be." But Sandhya swallowed the thick chocolate that coated the ice cream and sat at attention next to a bowl of orange roses, in an oak-paneled living room that gave onto the river, thinking, "'Rosenblum' is what I am now, this bloom, this life, these roses."

She thrust her hands into her coat pockets. She stood waiting for the bus. Somewhere from the edge of the barrio she heard young men cry, a pack of them, racing down the road. She almost panicked but held her married name in her head as if it were a talisman, thinking, if worse comes to worst, Stephen will find me, he will pick me up, bring me home. And what of Dora if something should happen? Sandhya's mind stopped, as if at the rim of a nothingness, a green park massed with trees and shrubs, scrawled by sunlight. When the bus came she got on, found a window seat, and sat staring out at the gulls that flocked to the dried-out lake. The gulls were white with flecks of brown on their wings. They circled the rocks, they settled on the trees. Through the bus window she watched them. Something in her needed to slip free. What did it have to do with Stephen, the part of her she sensed to be in his grasp?

Sometimes at night when she gave in to his tender, roaming lips, she felt as if the flesh and blood that bonded her together were dissolving into a rarer atmosphere. As if what made her a creature of smell and touch and taste had ebbed into an element altogether alien, the scope of Stephen's own soul. Afterward, washing in the morning, she slapped her cheeks, her belly, with cold water, trying to get back to a sharpness that could define the world for her. As the bus jolted, she grabbed the seat in front of her. What was it? Why was she so anxious? Was it because of the dreams that poured into her night after night so she felt like an unborn thing, a puppet with no play to be in?

H er dreams gave her little respite. They took her to another country. Always it was the same place, the exact same time. That fragile flash of light before the sun rose, the sky still peach, stained with gray. She was a young woman, in her early twenties, sitting next to Gautam by the riverbank. They had their feet in water that eddied, dull, still, cool to the skin. Her shinbone, shining with river water, was so close to his larger, more robust ankle. He took off his glasses and polished them. He glanced at the hair blowing about her face, then looked away, his gaze fixed on a darkening horizon that perpetually drew him, so that some part of his conscious mind, some tiny jot of him, was forever turned away from her.

In the distance, across the water from the riverbank on which they sat, was the onion-shaped dome of the Public Hospital. Four towers flanked it in traditional Hyderabadi style. It had the air of a mosque, but there was no muezzin, no calls to prayer. The lines of the sick and dying seemed to grow longer each time Sandhya passed by on her way to work at Sita Travel. Those waiting to get into the hospital cast shadows on the dried-up earth, almost indistinguishable from the silhouettes of the ashoka trees planted by the last Nizam.

Now Gautam was closer to her. He was stroking her hair with one hand. The other hand was clutched around an unlit cigarette. She leaned back against a rock. Each hair on her head seemed to tingle with the circling motion of his fingers. The sun rose. The moon set. The cries of the night creatures ebbed away and the river water that bathed their ankles turned warmer, grew pinkish. Was it dawn already? Or was it the blood of a horse or camel, throat slit, and cast into the water further upstream?

Nothing left of him, not a tremor, not the imprint of a heel. It shocked her then, the realization that she had known somewhere all along that he would vanish.

A child cried out. It was Dora, who had crept into bed between her parents, a nightmare working its way out of her. Sandhya sat up still shaking from her dream and cradled the child in both her arms, feeling the small body relax a little in her grip. But Stephen's leg was bent over her thighs and as she tried to move with the child, he grunted and turned over. Quickly she rose and, wrapping the small child in a blanket, made her way to the rocking chair in the small living room. She turned it toward the window with her foot and sat there, gently rocking her child, gazing at the damp gray sky over Manhattan.

The stretch of sky grew lighter, and against the flat rooftops a single water tower, carved of wooden strips, bound round with metal, took on color and density. Sometimes lovers lay there, sunning themselves. Sandhya had seen one intrepid pair at the very edge of the roof, feet dangling, as if river water coursed beneath them rather than a seven-story drop onto black asphalt. But now all she could make out, as the chair rocked back and forth on its curved slats and the small child slept in her arms, were dark lines of roof, the stocky water tower, and a strip of sky, growing brighter, gray turning to pale blue, and then a rosy flush all over the visible horizon as the sun burst free.

Again and again Gautam came to her in dreams, only to torment her by vanishing. She tried to put him out of her mind by turning to Stephen, who slept by her side. She rolled over on him, stroked him gently on the belly, till he grew warm with the pressure of her hand, and aroused, set his mouth on her shoulder, then lowered himself, licking her nipples, his hand rolling downward, searching her out. And she, feeling the small hairs on Stephen's chest, the curve of his thigh, the heat on his penis as he thrust into her, grew to desire the man by her side, covering her. She forgot the dreams that had grown so ungovernable.

Afterward, her arms around her husband, a rare sweetness filling her body, Sandhya rested her neck on his soft freckled arm and lay back in the silence of the night, listening to Dora, back in bed in the tiny cubicle that served as a child's room, breathing softly, with the slight arrhythmic breathing that had so scared her as a new mother. Dora's heart was all right, the doctor had told her so. There was nothing, nothing amiss under that fragile rib cage that had grown in depth and strength, bent under her own breastbone.

But one night Gautam came to her eyeless, headless. His arms and legs were cut off. She knew it was Gautam because of the red checked shirt he had on. Because of the shape of his neck where the blood had congealed. The mutilated torso had washed up on the riverbank. Other arms picked it up. A man turned to her, offering her the body.

"Do you want it?" the voice asked in Hindi before the man turned away puzzled, as Sandhya choked, sitting on the very rock where she had been once, twice, so very many times with Gautam.

"Look, do you want it?" the voice asked, louder now.

She looked up and saw it was Gautam offering her his own cut-off torso.

"Gautam!" she cried out. "Gautam!"

But the head of the man offering her this precious, mutilated trophy faded into thin air, and Sandhya's voice, unable to stop, went on and on, sobs shaking her, till Stephen woke and clutched her tenderly to his breast.

"Sandy, what is it, darling, what is it?"

He held her tightly and stroked her hair. Holding onto his arms she buried her head in his chest. Stephen had married her and brought her to America. She would live here, she would learn to forget.

It was dawn already. Across the Hudson the houses of New Jersey were packed tight, swarming on the cliffs, and the river glowed in a heat haze. Sandhya slipped her shoulders loose of the shawl she had used, surprised at the blurred light over the river. Once upon a time those cliffs on the other side were outcrops of rock and shrub and tree, red slashed with green and brown, grass blades thrusting into the North American light. Now there was this haze of exhaust fumes and smoke from the factories of New Jersey. Where was New Brunswick, where Sakhi lived? How far across the river could one see?

She picked up the postcard she had laid on the windowsill and flipped it over. Mouthed out the scrawled line:

"Who can we look to? Not angels, nor men ..."

It struck her with a familiar air, not that she could have said where the line came from. Poetry surely. But there was a sharpness there, almost as if a twig had grazed her cheek.

On the postcard was a picture of the Berlin wall, torn down, thick with graffiti and, given the spotlit scene, obviously taken at night. Her cousin Jay had penned a brief greeting and the line of poetry. So he was in Berlin. Sandhya found herself hoping that he would come to New York. She would write to him, ask him to visit her. She must sound composed in her letter, lest he feel there was some problem in her marriage. A new marriage, surely it still was that, with one child and five years of living together.

She turned her face downward, right by the window ledge, trying not to be distracted by the sheer fall beneath. If she held her eyes straight, she could make out words: NORTH AMERICAN MOVING AND DISPATCH. At night those words were picked out in red and blue, the colors of the Empire State Building, that grand edifice her sister Nunu wanted to come from halfway round the world to see. It was distant though, in terms of city space, way downtown, past the McDonalds and Pizza Hut and the three blocks of elevated subway tracks.

Once Sandhya had tried to figure the precise height of the subway tracks, counting metal bars and railings, using imaginary men six feet tall, one on the skull of the other, the scarf of the highest flapping, bald head holding up the invisible rail tracks. Four men, she reckoned, the topmost crouching, twenty-two feet, give or take a bit. Beyond the tracks, the neon sign for the moving company jutted out of an ugly brick silo used for storage, filled with bits and pieces of human lives, particles of solid waste if one looked at it another way. The building itself was a stone's throw from the meatpackers and wholesale dealers of beef and mutton whose hooks hung from the darkened doorways she passed in the car, as Stephen drove so swiftly. The sky above the jagged buildings was flat, an indistinct coloration. In odd moments though, the grayness turned silvery, shimmering.

"Perhaps heaven is colored like that?"

She had whispered this so softly Stephen hardly heard, but she saw his hand tighten on the shift stick.

"What did you say?"

One hand clutching the seat belt, she shook her head silently.

Now out of the other window the sky was clear, just a few clouds floating across the Hudson. She jumped the initials on the neon sign to-gether—NAMAD. A vowel shift and it could make sense, NOMAD, a creature of restless passage. She thought of herons in the paddy fields of Kerala, wings outstretched, circling water, marking out the emptiness of the sky. Bird flesh shorn of gravity. To ease the disturbance within her, she did something she used to do as a small child. She stamped her foot so hard the flesh on her leg trembled. Her bare calf scratched against the captain's bed that doubled as a makeshift sofa in the living room. The rough cover in maroon and burnt crimson had always pleased her, but the coarseness hurt her exposed calf. How delicate her skin was, and how rarely she left her legs bare. Even after three years in America she felt naked somehow if her legs showed. In public she always wore a longish skirt or some manner of trouser. She stepped forward rubbing her skin where it hurt and stared down at the odd angled building, visible through a window on the far side of the room. The Cotton Club, always empty, even late at night, its architecture smooth, freestanding, with angles flung around curving walls, a windowless space. An imitation of an original that no longer existed, was that what someone had told her? She didn't know, yet sensed the metropolis survived by filling itself with ceaseless multiples, strange mimicry, and not just the Campbell's Soup cans Stephen had taken her to a museum to see.

And wasn't she part of it too, holding a subway token just so in her hand, copying the woman next to her so that the bronze coin slipped smoothly into the slot? Buying and selling came into it: the shampoos on TV, smooth hair glowing over shoulders, flicked by an invisible breeze; magical colors painted on lips; shimmering tights; perfectly shaped bras; all coordinates of longing. What would her cousin Chandu say if she admitted this to him? He would enjoy this insight.

"Free enterprise, the salvation of the world," he called it, "Free enterprise needs subways tokens, no, Sandhya? How else would you get to the stores?"

And he would laugh, a glass of gin and tonic in hand, throwing back his handsome head, his well-starched collar gleaming in sunlight.

Where was Chandu now? Where was Jay?

The transparency she assumed in the world, so that thousands of miles subsided into the flare of a moment—he is so far away, but I can call him and if the connection works, I can hear his voice, he'll know I'm speaking to him—reverted into a mockery of space, a black hole of longing.

Something caught her eye. She leaned forward, pressing her palms against hard glass. There, traipsing along the edge of the Cotton Club roof, was a boy. A teenager really, blue jacket blown apart in the high wind off the Hudson, his Air Pump sneakers shining in the sudden sunlight. What was he doing, walking unsteadily across the flat roof? She pressed her face against glass, staring out. He looked up suddenly, waved at her. God, yes, yes, he was waving. Suddenly the boy raced down the narrow stairs into the clear space of the New Khalsa gas station.

The station was owned by a Sikh family, and sometimes a small circle of men huddled outside in the cold, their turbans clearly visible. Before the dark fell, blue lights lit up the gas station across from the empty Club. Looking down she felt a great desolation. Once, standing like this she had pulled Stephen forward, so he could see too.

"Straight out of Gingee," Stephen remarked, referring to the small town where his uncle Ernie lived.

How odd that their friend Draupadi too should come from there. Perhaps she had seen Uncle Ernie, run into him in the Soda Shop.

"Same style of gas station. Classic American, like the old diner we went to."

Trying to prick her interest, Stephen added: "Where you had that pumpkin pie, remember?"

She nodded, feeling dull suddenly, wondering what was the matter with her. She had been sleeping badly, very badly indeed. It was as if there was something she couldn't forget. Something that made her screw her eyes tight. She needed a sack to shut it all, a silken drawstring to tighten over a body.

Where was it now? She thought of the dark cropped stone of Banjara Hills in Hyderabad, the dried riverbed, Madhu's house with the whitewashed walls, only a cook and an *ayah* there. Wanting to re-lease her old school friend, at least for a few days, from the cramped two-room flat in which she lived, Madhu had called Sandhya:

"We'll be out of town for two weeks. Stay here, my dear, you'll be doing us a favor: you'll have food, drink all you need, even wear my saris should you feel like meeting someone other than that Gautam of yours.

Why are you so secretive about him? Why does he never take you out? There's a screening of *Tristana* at the Film Club. I love Buñuel, don't you? Take him out, do something fun with him, have him meet us."

But Sandhya, accepting the generous offer of the house for a week, had kept silent about her friend. How could she explain to Madhu, a woman whose life revolved around the Secunderabad Club and the golf course, anything at all about Gautam, her secretive, penniless love whose rare words stole her soul away. Gautam who was so gripped by the dream of social equality he spent all his weekends in the jungle somewhere north of Hyderabad, though he never spoke about it openly.

Their love was confined to public places, cafés, the public garden, the road around the railway station where he bought her roasted peanuts or *chai*. But she wanted more. She wished he would put out his hands, hold her face, stroke her cheek, as he once had done. Then go on, do more.

For her weekend in Banjara Hills, Sandhya took a few saris, a pair of jeans, then added her loose *kurtas* feeling they would be perfect for the cool, vine-covered courtyard in Madhu's house. I will stare up at the light pouring through the vine leaves, I will do nothing but watch the light, the drops of dew on the grapes, the leaves, the knotty stalks, she told herself as if she were a child again, preparing herself for a visit to Aunt Sariko-chamma. Her aunt had migraines, fits, attacks of swooning. She had led a difficult life; the children knew this. Their aunt could not tolerate children, loud voices, bursts of gunfire, so Sandhya had schooled herself not to chatter away, but instead to consider the leaves of the grapevine, freckled with gold points, spreading through the inner courtyard, the blades of light in the banyan tree.

The first few days in Madhu's house passed uneventfully. Sandhya enjoyed the tandoori chicken grilled just right, the *pomfret* and *vindaloo* the old cook prepared each night. Her daylight hours were consumed with reading *Eve's Weekly* and old Mills and Boon romances, her evenings with watching the new Star TV, which offered the latest version of "The Bold and the Beautiful." At night the old *ayah* would come in and sit with her and together they'd watch the blonde thing with the six-inch waist fall in love with a fashion designer, a longer, lankier version, it seemed, of the youthful Shashi Kapoor. But the fashion designer's father fell in love with the blonde thing too, unheard of in Indian TV. Breathless, sensing disaster down the road, the *ayah* turned to Sandhya and cried:

"If only we could give them Lata Mangeshar, a song and dance, it would help, no?"

"The Americans don't sing on their TV," Sandhya informed her, "but they have good coverage: presidents, nuns, Jehovah's Witnesses, all that. But no singing Kanthamma, I can't imagine why not. Someday I shall go there and find out why they don't sing on their TV."

It pleased her to hear the old woman chuckling at her joke.

It must have been about three or four days into her stay that Sandhya felt she ought to step out. It was cooler and the stones outside the walled compound looked less steamy, the dried grass more inviting. She put on her old *kurta,* slipped her feet into sandals, and announced to the *ayah* that she was going for a walk. The old woman did not try to dissuade her, but it was almost new moon night, the memsahib should know that it wasn't safe. All right, Sandhya proclaimed, but right now it was broad daylight and she would just go a little distance down the road. Perhaps she would see a passing goatherd or Hamid the barber, whose children cried out to her for lollipops as she passed on the way to the bus stop. Perhaps the sweet shop would be open and she could step into the dark coolness.

It felt oddly quiet, no children around. The *Hindustan Times* had come that morning, but Sandhya had promptly flipped to the astrology section toward the paper's end. As a result she knew nothing of the outbreak of rioting in the walled city, one community against the other as the paper put it, its self-censorship technique ordained by a government that prohibited mention of Muslim or Hindu in violent outbreaks. So news of riots read like gobbledygook, and ordinary folk who got the paper had no clear sense of what was happening. Who would tell them that RSS jeeps went through the village with cassettes hooked to loudspeakers blaring sounds of rioting? That frightened Muslims gathered together, only to be beaten at the entries of small doorways with steel-tipped sticks? That what resulted in multiple deaths—and certainly innocent Hindus lost their lives too—was reported in the national press as small-scale, practically random violence, identities of the victims buried in the white spaces of newsprint.

Once outside the compound, Sandhya started walking fast. Her sandals felt uncomfortable. She should change these white sandals, she thought. Her big toe always stuck out and gathered in heat from the ground. She found the road steeper than she recalled, with big clumsy boulders looming in her way. Some were immense, shaped like giant fists, broken tree trunks, volcanic cones, and she wondered what massive shake up at the earth's core had thrown them up like that, the Indian earth vomiting up boulders so that ever after poor people who lived by what had once been a river, and now was only a dried-up riverbed, should stop and

wonder at the natural desolation in which their small children roved, in
search of what they could find, an odd job here or there, a bit of money
carting goods into town, cleaning a house for a rupee or two, gathering
up scraps a kindly lady might throw their way, though a lollipop or two
could hardly fill an empty stomach and guts hurt from that spun sugary
stuff.

Climbing down she lifted her *salwar* so as not to get it caught in a stone.
Setting her foot down again, she struck something odd. Instinctively she
knew it was not wood, it was cooler, more akin to her own body's
smoothness. Dark as her own skin, an ankle. Her gaze rested on it and
moved upward, fascinated: a thigh, and below the belly's smoothness,
naked genitals, heavy, limp. She saw the chest too, the rib cage visible
through the skin. A poor man, so little flesh on him, the worn throat,
the short stubble rinsed with gray, and eyes. It was the eyes that made
her cry.

She felt a sharp pain in her weak ankle as she started running, scraping
against boulders, wanting only the sight of another human in all that
emptiness. She ran where the force of gravity drew her. When she re-
gained her senses she found she was at the base of the valley, all the way
down in the dried riverbed. The soil was an odd bluish color and the rocks
smaller, finer, as if rinsed by centuries of water. To her right was a huge
striped rock, painted that way in honor of Shiva.

That poor man I saw is dead, I must tell someone. Get home. Tell
Ayah, wash all this dust off.

The clarity of her thought surprised Sandhya. Breathing irregularly,
she started to walk, noticing small scrubby bushes to her right, their leaves
the color of hot ash as it blows in sunlight. No color, she thought. She
climbed steadily for a few minutes in the direction of the house and was
comforted when its white-painted walls came into sight.

Then she saw a man running toward her. A small man with stubble on
his cheeks and a tinge of gray in his hair. He was running surprisingly fast
in spite of what seemed to be a hump on his back. She would stop him, tell
him about the death she had seen down the road, he would help. An ordinary man, coming to ask me the time, she thought as he drew closer. He
doesn't have a watch, he needs to know the time. She glanced at the watch
her father had given her for her birthday, a Favre Leuba he had bought in
the Geneva airport, a simple silver thing, clasped lightly to her wrist.

When the man was so close she could have touched him, Sandhya panicked. Something in that drawn face told her she should run, as hard as she

could. She was almost within reach of the house when the figure, so like the dead man she had left by the wayside, was on her, grabbing her body. His mouth wide open with the dreadful alcohol stink, panting. He threw her to the ground and sat astride her. He was thin, she could feel his hump-back, his cheap clothes soaked with sweat. He couldn't have been very strong, or was it drink that broke his resolution, for when she raised the stone that lay to her right and aimed it at his head, he stopped short, eyes wide with fear. I will strike him, she thought, if he tries to rape me, I will hit him between the eyes with this stone. The thought, which seemed perfectly natural, filled her with an energy she did not know she had, and she pushed hard to save herself. In the few seconds after she got her legs free, she started stumbling, up through the rocks, the stone still in her hand.

She walked into the house, but there was no one in sight. She entered the living room Madhu had furnished with Gujarati laquerwork and soft Kashmiri leather. In a daze, Sandhya inched toward the chair, set the stone down softly at her feet, and let the numbness invade her. It was as if nothing had happened. She noticed the stone was beautifully smooth, that it had a blue vein running through it. She even found herself feeling sorry for the desperate man who had tried to attack her. Then low moaning sounds came and she noticed the light from the TV. Ayah must have been watching "The Bold and the Beautiful" and for some reason stepped out. How long she sat there utterly stiff, hands in her lap, the stone at her feet, staring at the TV, Sandhya could not tell. The next morning, the old woman entering the room found her seated in the same posture, eyes fixed in an unseeing stare.

The glare forced Jay to shut his eyes. It was hot and close in Manhattan, much as it might have been in Hyderabad. Dense smoky air, leaving one breathless. Rashid el Obeid, a friend Jay had met in Berlin, drove him over the Triborough Bridge in a rusty Honda. Through the open window Jay breathed deep, the fumes, the sweet rotten air. He gazed out at a jagged burnished skyline, the Chrysler building, lacy bits and pieces of stone and glass, sharp plunges into air, buildings stacked so high, with windows sheening in sunlight. He wondered how it was such massed verticalities could support the delicacies of flesh New Yorkers were famed for: rare steaks, Nautilus machines, Rockettes at Radio City Music Hall. Frank O'Hara had lived here. Sandhya lived here, somewhere. He had misplaced her address.

"Look up *Rosenblum* in the phone book," Rashid advised. "There may be hundreds, thousands. Look up *Stephen Rosenblum*. That's who she's married to, you said."

Jay, his eyes fixed on the metal grilles, the cut-up windows of Rikers Island, barbed wire clearly visible all around, mumbled: "Never met him."

Rashid grunted in response, moving the old stick shift. Conscious of Rikers looming to their left, he said: "Maximum security. Did you bring a bit of the wall for me?"

Jay laughed: "I faked it. I have a bit of Hyderabad stone and a shard of glass."

The thought that Sandhya was sitting in one of the rooms in an apartment block not far from the prison or strolling down a city street sobered him. She had chosen to cut herself off from her old life. Should he speak of Gautam at all when he finally met her? What would he say?

Jay knew that things had frayed between those two well before Gautam was first taken into police custody in Hyderabad. Over a period of several months Gautam had deliberately withdrawn from Sandhya. He did not turn up at four o'clock at the public gardens as they had planned. He avoided having coffee with her. He even stopped carrying her books as they walked toward the library. Once she thought she glimpsed a hardness in his eyes, something utterly unrelated to her. A crack in the known world. She trembled without knowing why. It was not that they had made plans for the future, but she had always felt that she loved him, that Gautam returned her love. The thought of his withdrawing from her was unbearable.

"Amma wants to arrange a marriage for me," Gautam once said to Sandhya as they walked down the street, discreetly in the manner of young students—no grand show of lips or hands or thighs in public, just quick smiles, a touch at the wrist. He stood at a slight distance from her, under a neem tree, and Sandhya could see his black hair floating upward, merging into the neem bark, as if his hair were an outgrowth of that local vegetation, part of nature, indubitably a part of her.

"Amma has someone in mind," Gautam added, "from her own village. How can I hurt her, Sandhya, after all she has gone through?"

He seemed to be pleading with her. But Sandhya did not trust his words. She stiffened as she walked by his side. She sensed he wanted to be rid of her.

Two or three months after he was released from prison she still knew little of what had happened. Gautam refused to speak of the matter to her. Once, chancing on each other by the railway station, they wandered together to a coffee shop, trying to make conversation. That night Sandhya fell asleep biting her pillow. Her teeth punctured the striped cotton, and cotton muffled her cries. She did not know the precise details of what had come over him, nor did she ask. But the sight of Gautam's lean body, scarred hand trembling at the edge of the broken glasses he fiddled with, was more than she could bear.

"Let's get some new ones," she had suggested, trying to be practical, cheerful, a manner that came to her with great difficulty, but Gautam refused. When they said good-bye at the coffee shop, she had no idea she would never see him again.

The first time he was imprisoned, Gautam was a sympathizer of the People's War Group; that was all. His experiences in a jail cell made him care less about the wind and the birds and the sunlight, about Sandhya, too. Or perhaps it was despair that had eaten into him, corroding his flesh, the delight of his senses. Had Rajan become like that? Had too much resolve turned his heart to stone? His old roommate Rajan was arrested in an outlying district after a local landlord, notorious for his cruelty, was murdered, his severed head displayed on a pewter plate in front of the Shiva temple. There was no public proof of Rajan's involvement, but all his friends knew he was involved, however indirectly, in the planning.

"We will flush out violence, we will purify the land," the Inspector General of Police promised in his elegant diction at a press conference. The theme was "Cleaning House" and many foreign journalists were invited. It was clear the backbone of the nation was weakening, people would have to be taught how to behave. The Inspector General was clad in immaculate khaki and surrounded by bodyguards with walkie-talkies imported from Taiwan.

The following day several hundred radicals were taken into police custody. "A Precautionary Measure," said the headlines in the local newspaper. Gautam Reddy was one of those arrested, and from the start his friends feared that there was little hope of having him released quickly. He survived for three months till, weakened by repeated attacks of malaria, brutal questioning, and the incessant damp in his cell, Gautam died. The day after his death his widowed mother was summoned to the police station. Her son's body, wrapped in a prison blanket, was handed over to her. She crouched by his body on a pile of cold stones, and found she had no tears left. Her body was all dried out with its pain. Later, after the simple cremation, she wondered who she should tell. Which of his friends would come close to her now?

The afternoon of Gautam's cremation, gripped by a sense that her own life had fled, Sandhya left Sita Travels early and walked to the public gardens. She stared at a flock of gulls circling the lotus pond, glimpsed the dead body of a cat half-buried in the rose bushes.

Kanyamma did not know of Sandhya wandering aimlessly, a few miles away in the public gardens. Gautam had kept Sandhya a secret. When Sandhya returned to her rooms, she had made up her mind to accept the job that Sita Travels was offering her in Delhi. Perhaps she would meet up with Jay, who by then had already left Hyderabad.

From Delhi, through his friends in the PUDR, Jay had tried to keep track of Gautam. He went on marches to protest the fate of political prisoners, he wrote editorial pieces in a local newspaper, mentioning Gautam by name. But nothing budged. Jay focused on photography. In the months that followed the anti-Sikh riots, his photos of young children—mouths open, eyes enormous, fragile, children who had witnessed the stabbing of a parent, the rape of a sister, the lynching of an older brother—won him acclaim. Singled out for particular praise was a photograph that looked as if smoke had been rubbed all over its surface. It showed a deaf and dumb boy pointing out a tree in Sultanpuri from which two weeks earlier his father had been hanged.

Fire had been set to the dying Sikh's ankles and knees. The child clinging to the man's feet had his face and hair singed. The boy's hands moved like twin birds, quick, quicker than thought, mimicking the tree, the hanging man, the shooting flames, his own body clenched to his father's knees.

The child's neck hung limp. Jay's photo caught two small hands outlined against the field, maimed birds poised for flight. The eyes of the speechless child were enormous, gazing at what looked like the shadow of a broken tree. The photo was taken at three in the afternoon, in one of the rehabilitation camps run for children who had suffered in the violent aftermath of the assassination of Mrs. Gandhi.

"Three in the afternoon," Jay titled the photo. It ran in the *Illustrated Weekly of India*. It was picked up by *Life Magazine* and stood as an icon of childhood innocence violated. Sunlight that blazed into the lens rendered the entire image smoky, as if a fire had burned over a film of water through which the child's gesturing body was visible. Jay felt as if he were gazing through a bit of Gautam's broken spectacles.

The photo brought him several invitations, some more enticing than others. By then the news of Gautam's death had reached him and Jay knew he wanted to leave Delhi. He accepted an invitation to Berlin and arrived just as the wall was falling. The sound of jackhammers punctuated his dreams, and the wild euphoria that coursed through Berliners eluded him entirely. Something mad chanted in him: A city divided will never be united. He saw Turks huddled in bars, their houses invaded by gangs of neo-Nazis. He saw an Algerian in a quiet Berlin square racing away from skinheads. He chased the gang, camera in hand, but came up with nothing.

In Berlin he made love to Nathalie, who worked as a volunteer for the Green Party. He twined his fingers through her dyed black hair. Exhausted by dreams, his camera idle, he fell asleep night after night, his head between her breasts. In Nathalie's house he met Rashid el Obeid. Rashid invited him to New York and he accepted instantly.

"Have camera, will travel," Jay quipped to himself as he climbed the steps of the rickety Misrair plane that was to take him to New York. His body shook in flight. He felt that he was on the brink of an agitation in all his parts, visible and invisible, a swirling, turbulent state that would not be pacified. Nothing of home or motherland pierced his thoughts, for such notions were alien to him. Inside the plane he looked at his two restless hands and thought of cut blossoms, swirling.

She was bent over the kitchen table, hair aswirl in the breeze from a fan. He could not get that image out of his head. His cousin Sandhya Rosenblum doing her own kitchen work. But, of course, that's what America had brought her to. Jay touched her gently on the shoulder.

"Okay, Bachi?"

She nodded, two grains of rice on her palm. He touched the delicate shapes of white; the grains left two shadows on her flesh.

"So, what are you planning?"

While Jay had intended the question in more general terms, Sandhya took up the issue quite literally.

"Rice and sambar, I think."

It made him smile.

"Grandma's recipe?"

She nodded, pouring the rice grains out onto a flat dish, picking out the black husks, the broken bits of chaff. At her elbow, next to a box of child's crayons, he saw ridged green okra she had washed and slivered, tops and tails cut off. So he spoke to her, not of the rice fields by their grand-mother's house, not of Gautam and the city of Hyderabad. A new life absorbed him. His part-time job at the ICP helping with exhibits, pro-cessing photographs, had allowed him to make new contacts and paid just enough for board and lodging and food. Jay spoke to her of the Humphrey Bogart movie he had seen, all over again, in a broken-down theater, the skin of the blonde woman weaving a shadowy, irresistible image, Marrakesh of the mind; dyed hair and pierced flesh in the East Village; the coffee bars of Soho; a reading at St. Mark's by many voices, Frank O'Hara's poetry of flick-flac surfaces, words emblazoning the trash heap of the century. He would stay as long as his visa held, he told his cousin, and then he'd try for another.

As he spoke, Sandhya felt the grains of rice slip out of her fingers, splat-ter onto the pine wood of the dining table. She sensed her fingers grow-ing warm with excitement. How could Jay do this? Exchange one life for another? She felt an odd bitterness fill her at the lot she had chosen, her life as a woman thrusting her almost into the very role her mother would have picked for her. She heard her mother's voice and a scene from the past floated up.

"Arranged marriages are the best, Sandhya. How could you doubt it? Look at all these messy divorces in our cities!"

Sandhya had grunted, walking away from plump, sleek Sosa, whose silk blouses were perfectly tailored to her matronly girth, whose earlobes were scented with the rosewater she sprinkled on them each morning. Sandhya had kept her bond with Gautam a strict secret, and Sosa had no clear sense of how her daughter lived her life in Hyderabad. Sometimes, though, Sosa saw a shadow draw over her daughter's face, a hint of melancholy that she attributed to the impossibility of Sandhya, dark and gaunt as she was, finding a man on her own. Once they had a quarrel that mother and daughter both tried hard to put behind them.

As they sat on the veranda Sosa pulled out her little black book, the one filled with names of eligible young men. Then she drew Sandhya into a necessary conversation. They had started with the organza sari the new deacon's wife had worn to church. The inappropriateness of it, Sosa felt, the embroidery excessive for Sundays. And where might she have got it from, on her husband's salary? Her brother, of course, the one in Dubai, must have sent her the funds.

"And that garish house the brother is building, right by the paddy fields on the way to college. Have you noticed?"

"With red pineapples and green lions on the terrace?"

Sandhya laughed, joining in with her mother's disdain of the bizarre excesses of Middle Eastern money. They relaxed for a moment into an unusual camaraderie.

Then Sosa launched in:

"People like us really must do their duty. Keep up the family lines."

She leaned forward and stroked her daughter's hair. Sandhya, sitting two feet away from her mother, was gazing at the sunlit leaves of the gooseberry tree, a reverie filling her. Two months earlier she had met Gautam, his eyes intense with longing, his arms thin, scarred. She couldn't keep her eyes off him as he sat across from her at the café table, Jay between them, chattering away.

Her mother's touch jarred. Sosa so rarely touched her daughter; she wanted something from her, Sandhya was sure.

Sosa tapped her elegant fingers on the little black book. She sat up as straight as her plump torso would permit.

"At least two young men would be excellent for you. One is the Kuriakose boy. He has an MBA from Stanford and the family line is impeccable."

Sandhya felt her body growing hot, glowing like the bark of the gooseberry tree. She tried to speak to her mother, but all that would come out was a hoarse cry.

"Mama!"

Sosa misinterpreted the pleading she sensed in her child's voice. Perhaps she had struck a nerve there. The Kuriakose boy would be an excellent match. Too bad she hadn't had time to speak of the Kandathil lad, public school trained, St. Stephen's College, top-ranked in the Foreign Service exams.

"So?"

She smiled at her daughter, struck by the odd stiffness in Sandhya's posture. The child was poised at the edge of the parapet. It was so long since she had really looked at her daughter. There was a butterfly just behind Sandhya, a softly whirring thing, delicate yellow and darker gold on the wings, a creature risen from the lilies Sosa had brought from the hills just three weeks earlier. Rare tiger lilies. Sandhya, with her back to the light, against the softly moving life of the garden, butterfly, and bough, stippled with sunshine, seemed cut out of porous stone. Sosa clenched her hands in her lap.

"*Mol*, please!"

She couldn't bear it, she thought, if her daughter sat there, unmoving. It struck Sosa suddenly that apart from her husband's hot words, and how rarely he had shouted at her in rage, three perhaps four times in all their married years, it was Sandhya's silences that she feared the most.

Sosa drew her ankle out of the folds of her beige cotton sari. She thrust both hands against the white chair. She would walk the two feet to her daughter, she would hold her in her arms, fold her into her own flesh, perhaps even sing to her. What else could a woman's life hold but marriage? And a good marriage was one of the few ways to avert loneliness, the dreadful fate of women left to their own devices. Just as she started to rise, Sandhya, with a little cry, jumped off the parapet and raced into her grandmother's bedroom.

After the old lady's death, the room was left just as it was, rosewood bed, small desk by the window, dresser with a curved mirror tilting at the light. And that's where Sosa found her daughter, staring at the mirror. How large her eyes were. Sosa stood behind her daughter, one hand reaching out for Sandhya's shoulder.

"The Kuriakose boy. I've spoken to his aunt already." Her voice was soft, but resolute. Very little could have prepared Sosa for the storm that took hold of her daughter. Sandhya banged her fist against the rosewood dresser, and when her mother caught hold of her wrists, she tore herself loose. Trying to shake some sense into her, Sosa moved forward, grabbed Sandhya's shoulders. Raising the pillow she clutched, Sandhya pulled away and started striking her mother. First she hit her on the broad belly, hearing the fine cotton of her mother's sari hiss in protest. Then, filled with shame and rage, she struck her mother on her face, rushed into the bathroom, locked the door, and proceeded to strike her own forehead against the window ledge. Bits of dark wood ripped free. The limestone plaster started to scar. There was a dull pool of blood when it was all over.

With the help of the maid, Sosa forced the door open and discovered her daughter standing by the window, head bloodied, the window ledge a mess. She tried to put out her hand to Sandhya, but drew back sharply.

All that mess, thought Sosa. All that bloodied mess. Was this what a woman's life could come to? But she kept the ponderings tucked inside her and gave brisk orders to the maid to clean up the window ledge, pick up the bits of the pitcher that had smashed at the base of the huge pewter urn in which well water was stored. And all the while she stood behind her daughter, not able to touch her.

Finally she murmured something inconsequential, gathered some of the cool water in her own palms, and splashed it on Sandhya's forehead, watching as the bloodied crust dissolved and streaks of brownish red trickled over Sandhya's eyelid. Nothing, nothing more could be said, but in her own intrepid way, Sosa decided to try again later. A decent interval of time had to pass.

That night in her white bedroom, the walls newly painted, the curtains freshly laundered, Sandhya pulled out the tattered notebook in which she had written down her thoughts. She was a schoolgirl then, but the lines were sharp, written in black ink, the letters lopsided in passion:

"If you want me to live as a woman, why educate me?"

"Why not kill me, if you want to dictate my life?"

"God, why teach me to read and write?"

She closed the book gently and put it under her pillowcase. As she left the room her forehead ached and her fists were oddly distended with bruises from the window ledge. Over dinner that night Varki was concerned about the ugly swelling on his daughter's forehead, but mother and daughter had an unspoken pact between them. Her eyes large with unspilled tears, Sandhya gazed at her mother, who passed the fish curry to her husband and murmured, "She hit her head, poor child, against the granary ledge."

"What were you doing there?" her father asked in surprise. He had raised his voice somewhat, in spite of himself, then noticed his daughter's lower lip trembling.

"Sandhya?" He blurted out her name in a mixture of concern and surprise. She kept her face down, still gazing at the fine plate she was eating from. A few grains of rice clung to the edge of the rim. As she wiped them off with the side of her hand, she felt her father's eyes still on her.

Jay stared at the rice grains on the table, then at his cousin sweeping them up with the edge of her palm, dropping them back into the bowl. She straightened up, looked at him. He noticed the fine lines on her forehead, a few hairs on her brow, graying. She was thirty-five now, still young, of course, but how ill-suited she seemed to her new life, hardly knowing how to conduct herself from one moment to the next. Almost as if she were reading his thoughts, Sandhya lowered her hands into her lap and murmured in a flat voice:

"Let me take you to see the Statue of Liberty. Or Ellis Island." She sat very straight as she said this, her thoughts brightening with the simplicity of the gesture: "Why not, Jay, it would be such fun!"

She was pleading with him, but he shook his head.

"Not even the Empire State Building?"

"Now that, perhaps, if you could throw in a gorilla."

Suddenly she seemed to relax, and he wondered at the tension in her, all that energy and nothing to do with herself.

"So let me help you with the rice then!"

"You?"

"Why not? I learned to cook in Delhi, you know. All those months when I was taking photographs, I would return home after work and cook rice and dal for myself."

She stood up and let him carry the rice into the kitchen and then watched intently as he ran water over the grains to wash them. She watched his hands change under water into the hands of a child playing in a bucket of well water, sunlight on his head and on the fine skin of his hands; above the metal bucket and kneeling child, the blue sky of Tiruvella.

"Remember how we used to play by the well?" she asked him and he nodded, carrying on with his task. He left before it was time for Sandhya to pick up the child from daycare.

It was early afternoon and as the elevated subway sped past the apartment blocks, the storage spaces of Manhattan, Jay felt as if his sight were blurred with a slight smokiness. As if rice were boiling too hard on a woodstove. As if fire were lit in water. Where did those lines come from? He murmured them out loud but no one stared at him. The jolting of the metal cars covered up his words:

"*If fire is lit in water ...*"

How did it go? He fumbled about in his mind. As if a book of an infinite number of pages were turning in a slow wind, the lines suddenly clarified:

"If fire is lit in water, who can extinguish it?"

"If fear comes from the Protector, who can protect us from that fear?"

Those were Nagarjuna's words. Where had he heard them? Had he seen them etched on stone in Nagarjuna Konda where the sage had lived? Were they cut into the wall in the old city where voices, male and female, cried out in Bangle-Seller's Lane? Did they come from a book he had seen on Sandhya's mother's bookshelf, a collection she had inherited from her father and left untouched while she devoted herself to more practical pursuits? He felt the inexactness of the memory and the struggle to retain it both dissolve into the cramped space of the subway car. Then it was the shock of arrival as the brakes took hold and passengers thrust bellies, thighs, fists, shoving themselves out. Sandhya, he thought, as he stumbled out. He had a sudden image of her, bent over the rice bowl. He must go back and see her. Talk to her about Gautam, about Stephen. Why had she married Stephen? He almost dived back into the subway car, but it would have taken him quite the wrong way. So Jay stood on the platform, in a mass of travelers, and slowly rubbed his eyes. He saw a small child, oddly familiar, boy or girl he couldn't be sure, sitting on the bench next to him. Jay rubbed his eyes, feeling as if a thin smoke had filled them.

The breeze from the park blew in through the high window, stirring Stephen Rosenblum's hair. Summertime, and with the lime trees in bloom, it was as if the champak had blossomed too, and fragrances, real and imagined, wafted toward him. Then a slight hint of smoke, as if something were burning. Twigs, old fencing from the park? The park volunteers were cleaning up the area by the old river wall. Just like them to start small fires. He clenched his fist, drew himself up with a jerk, shifted his mug of coffee closer. Some of the brown liquid splashed against his thumb and he wiped it off on his sleeve. Where was he? He was all alone in the apartment and the book that had first drawn him to India lay under his hands, a tatty brown volume from Uncle Izzy's library.

His mind moved to his wife, her hair blown about her face as he had first seen her. It was odd how that image stayed with him, Sandhya's face with the sunlight flickering on it, those great dark eyes, the hair blown about the mouth. Sometimes he felt he hardly knew her.

The book was different. He had read it from cover to cover with great care. How the old man had come by it, he didn't know, perhaps he had bought it for a few cents at a library sale in Newark, or from a peddler on the sidewalk. It contained a whole set of travels eastward. In it, Stephen had learned of Columbus's obsession with traveling east by the westward route, the earth turned into a golden pear, and the closer one got to the stem, the nearer paradise came. He read of Marco Polo's travels eastward, the European who actually "discovered" India, and what a foolish word that was, as if the ancient kingdoms were waiting for the Portuguese admiral and the gifts he brought the Zamorin of Calicut: striped cloth, four red hoods, six hats, four strings of coral, sugar, honey, oil, and finally, to crown it all, six ceramic basins to wash in. Entering the great Shiva temple in Calicut, Marco Polo was convinced it was a cathedral, and the dark goddess transformed into a shining manifestation of the Virgin Mary, the Divine Mother who had kept watch over his voyages and could seal his monopoly on the spice trade.

All this Stephen read, gripped with the appalling wonder of the armchair voyager. Toward the end of the book he came upon the tale of a Russian called Afanasy Nikitin, a peddler of stallions who made his way to India from Tver, a town in Russia. The young Stephen, who knew some of his ancestors had come from Russia, fancied himself in the unknown Afanasy's boots. In 1466 the man sailed down the Volga, surviving the dangers of Turkistan, passing through Baku and Bukhara, till he reached Hormuz. He and his horses, all fifteen of them, white and honey-colored wild stallions, were loaded on a ship to India. Nikitin landed in Gujarat quite penniless and was forced to sell his last stallion for small measures of millet and meat. Southward he wandered till he found himself in Calicut. Clearly it had been no part of Nikitin's design to land in Calicut, gateway to the Indies. He was beached there, a vagabond, forced to search out sheltering spaces. He adopted Muslim ways, for he had forgotten the liturgies and holidays of the Russian Orthodox church of his upbringing. What kind of man was he now? Nikitin was filled with anguish.

What struck Stephen most closely was that even as the Russian adopted the Muslim name of Khwaja Yusuf Khurasani, and dressed in Indian style, his soul bubbled with a turbulence he could vent only in poetry:

> O Lord, which way can I turn?
> In Hindustan, must I burn?

While he particularly appreciated the rhymes of "turn" and "burn," it was the confusion in the man's soul that moved Stephen. That all too human sense of having lost one's way. He had heard it often happened in the middle years.

The figure of the Russian voyager stayed with him and Stephen felt there was some obscure connection between the fate of the fifteenth-century peddler and his own. Trying to think it through only landed him in greater confusion. He himself had arrived in India almost by accident, if truth be told. The cheap ticket he had bought for a holiday in Athens he had been forced to cancel due to the pressure of work. But four weeks later the ticket still held good, and paying a little more, he converted it to a round-trip to Delhi. He had prepared for his Indian travels by reading up on intermediate technology and the multiple uses of livestock, cattle in particular. He also knew a few phrases of Hindi that he taught himself from a phrase book. Landing in Delhi, he quickly took the advice of friends at the American Consulate and escaped the heat of the plains by traveling up to Nainatal, a hill resort filled with surprisingly gentle slopes and trickling streams of water. It was there he met Sandhya, and just in time, he thought, for he had felt himself on the brink of the turbulence Nikitin knew. This in spite of the fact that his own return ticket was lying safe in his suitcase. What was it about India that overturned the soul, thrust him back into his childhood, forced him to start afresh? He still wasn't sure.

When he was very little, his grandmother who lived on a side street in Newark had told him about the tree of life. It was spoken of in the Torah, she told him, a tree of many branches that stood by the golden river of life. The roots of that tree could be found in all the nations of the earth. All of the earthly languages, the old lady assured him, were written on the leaves of that tree. "Languages, too, that cannot be written," she told the child. "As the west wind passes through the leaves they whisper in tongues unknown to you and me."

Hands wet with the dough, she sang him a little ditty she had made up, of all the languages she thought the earth contained. The melody remained in his head. His grandmother's humanism was rich enough, cryptic enough for Stephen. He understood the distaste of native peoples of North America at being called Indian, merely because Columbus had thought them that. What a barbarous fate they had suffered, having their languages destroyed, their earth parceled out into federal reservations. He wondered what the Indians of India thought of Columbus, if they bothered at all. But now that he was in Nainatal, securely in the landmass the fifteenth-century Spaniard was searching for, he decided to breathe deeply, go on long walks, soak up the sunshine, even look for a bookstore in which he could find a tree book or the book of Indian birds written by Salim Ali that his friend at the consulate recommended so strongly.

He found Sandhya under a tree. On their second meeting he found her under a tree so massive that its leaves, raised directly into the sun, seemed cut of gold. She was standing there, her black hair blown over her mouth, calling, calling him, or so he thought. He approached in great eagerness and she, pleasantly surprised, invited him to join her in the shade, where a few smooth stones could provide them with comfortable seating.

The first time they had met it was right by the hotel, a small secluded place, just two stories high, with rocks in the garden, a stream running through, and packs of mountain goats traipsing through the flower beds. At the foot of the mountain near his hotel, in a small tea shop, he had found her. He entered and was sitting alone, rubbing his chilled hands together, when the young women passed, Sandhya and six college friends, chattering away loudly. She had a green sweater on, he still remembered that. Perhaps it was the green that first caught his eye, the nubby wool of the sweater lit by her shoulder-length hair. She was laughing loudly, a tinge too loudly, as if there were something within herself she feared. It was the febrile quality that drew him.

Gail had that. Something on the brink of being ignited, a candle, a firebomb held in one hand, but then snuffed out with the other. Gail had stuffed her delicate breasts into the lawyer's regulation black suit and made her way high up in the realm of contract law, torts, mishaps of the flesh. It still hurt the way she had abandoned him, or so he still insisted on calling it. He thrust the thought out of his head. In the manner perfected in his Columbia University days, strolling down Broadway, staring into crowded cafés, he balanced his scarf around his neck. Each hand noosed in a bit of the brown woolen stuff, he cleared his throat, then stood before the young women, bowing slightly, palms held together in greeting. He was quite close to Sandhya. He could have touched her thick green sweater if he had extended his hand an inch, tangled his thumb in her hair.

It all happened very quickly, or so it seemed in retrospect. The women beckoned to him with their fingers and shook their delicate wrists on which glass bangles shimmied and shone. "Aao, aao, come, come, sit at our table." Decorous as ever, he inclined his head slightly in acceptance. He directed all his speech at Sandhya, who was flattered at the attention. She flung her long hair back, sat up straight, a flush working its way into her cheeks. He tried out his Hindi and was rewarded by quick laughter, praise, question upon question: "Where are you really from? Where did you learn that Hindi?"

The conversation quickened: Hindi, English, bits of French that one of the young women had learned in convent school and wished to try out. What they construed as the glamour of their meeting hung over them all, a man from New York who had traveled to Nainatal. The boundaries of the world seemed to shift and open, the dream of one world realized. He struck the young women as utterly trustworthy, a gentle stranger, someone to be indulged as a pet might be. And he in turn was amused by their antics, pleased to be included in frivolous pastimes. Only Sandhya seemed to sense something different in him, a seriousness, a loss that underlay his laughter. On their way out of the tea shop, they fell into step, side by side.

He invited her for breakfast the next day and she arrived, hair carefully combed back, fastened with pins, giving her the air of a young missionary lady, someone so serious that irony seemed impossible. He felt she was playing something out. The next day she came for breakfast again, at his invitation. They dined on masala-scrambled eggs, toast made moist by the glass dome that trapped heat and turned it into droplets of water. They drank coffee and lime juice. Her hair was loose now and hung over one shoulder, blowing in the breeze from the garden.

She hung on his every word, his tales of cousin Sigmund, who had bought the franchise on Burger King stores in Newark and spent his extra cash buying up slum properties in the Bronx, Uncle Eddie, who kept a shoe store in Maine and spent hours waxing his mustache, Uncle Izzi, who played the violin to such perfection, but was forced to work as an insurance salesman. He turned to his own research on development and intermediate technology, the topic he had turned into a thesis for his M.A. in International Affairs.

"What was the topic?" Sandhya quizzed him.

"The balance of global power, the implications of intermediate technology for the Third World, the uses of livestock in dry pasture lands. Consider, for instance, how we might use ghober gas. You've heard of that, haven't you?"

And she had nodded quickly, unwilling to hear more, wanting to pass on to another topic. He told her about Afanasy Nikitin, the tale he had read as a child. He quoted the stanza with the line: "In Hindustan must I burn?"

It made sense to Sandhya, Nikitin's lines. Her friend Smita had burned. She had burned dreadfully in Hauz Khas, in her newly married home, and the women's group had gone over and demonstrated in front of the house, for everyone knew the kerosene stove had not fallen accidently on Smita. For months her in-laws had been trying to get more dowry money, and Smita's father, pushed to the brink, borrowed as much as he could, but was forced to stop. And Rahul was cruel to her, Smita confided in Sandhya the one time they had coffee together at Nirula's. Perhaps she should run away, she asked her friend, and Sandhya had stared at her in bewilderment.

"Where will you go?" she finally responded.

"To my parents, but it would be humiliating for them in the village."

Smita stopped and Sandhya, putting out her hand to touch her friend, was alarmed at the heat in her flesh. Was Smita running a fever? She could not tell. It was in the papers several months later, the half-charred body of Smita rushed to the hospital with a police report of accidental burning by kerosene stove. Shortly thereafter Rahul remarried.

She could not tell Stephen all this, at least not yet, but she repeated the words of Afanasy Nikitin, "In Hindustan must I burn?" much struck by the sensitivity of the man who had quoted them. He had the soul of a poet, this Stephen who had traveled all the way from America to meet her.

Back in the youth hostel, in the long room with the seven cots laid out next to each other, Sandhya shut her eyes. Her friends sang out the latest

Lata Mangeshkar songs from the movies they had seen, mimicking the gestures of the hero punching the bad guy, over and over, at the edge of the high rocks of Simla, bang-pow-bang-shub-shub-shabash, till the hoarder of black money, complete with gold waistcoat and diamonds in his teeth, fell over the edge.

Sandhya shut her eyes tight, covered her ears with her hands. Her head hurt a little. How gentle he had seemed, how kind. It rose in her, a desperate longing she could not affix to anything. She wanted to talk to him, be near him, tell him about Gautam, but what could she say? As if sensing her need, her friends turned to the old movie songs from *Pardesi* about the Russian traveler who came to India and fell in love with a lovely dark-haired maiden. "Champa!" he cried out to her in a soul-stirring Russian accent, and the songs rang out, her voice low, plaintive, answering his, across the mountain slope. But soon the Pardesi had to leave and Champa sang out her pain, across a hillside rough with the stalks of wild rose bushes. Sandhya felt a tear hot at the edge of her eye. She let it remain there without wiping it off. As it rolled down, the tear dissolved at the rim of her upper lip, by the mole that Gautam loved, that Gautam said made her look so beautiful.

She shivered a little. She drew the sheets over her face. As the cool cotton slid over her mouth, it came to her with great clarity: she wanted Stephen to open out his pale freckled arms, to hold her, to take care of her. The voices around her rose and fell and the cries of the vendors of *chat* and *behl puri* poured in from the courtyard. Sandhya felt her body torn with its excitations, tiny electric impulses racing this way and that, her skin tingling as if in anticipation of Stephen's touch. She felt a shudder of delicious anticipation, and slid lower still into the sheets, tucking even her hair in, so her whole body was shielded in the white cloth.

She would give herself to him and he would love her. He would lay his pale nakedness down next to her, roll his cool freckled skin over her. She would be his wife. She would give him a son. The thoughts, which did not seem daring in themselves, merely necessary steps to straighten out her torn life, seemed in retrospect to have occurred in strict sequence, a way of conducting a woman's life. He was a stranger to her, but a kind one, and what more could she ask. She would arrange her own marriage, leap over the terrible wall her mother had erected; foil her parents at their own game. Married to Stephen she would be quite beyond their power. She felt the blood surge to her forehead, and the welt, under the cover of her soft hair, pulsed hard, the blood rushing through. She thought of her mother, a glass of lime juice in her hand, relaxing on the veranda. Perhaps it was raining there now, that gentle Kerala rain. More peaceful now, Sandhya shut her eyes and slept.

The following morning in Stephen's room, Sandhya sat stiffly in an arm chair. Through the rough metal grille at the window she saw a stunted fir. It was growing out of a split in the high rocks. Suddenly, she burst into tears. Stephen knelt before her and scooped her up into his arms. Within four weeks they were married by the Special Marriage Act, which had been designed by the British specifically for intercommunal marriages, elopements, unions that had resulted from abductions. After their marriage he gathered a bouquet of delicate flowers, whose names he did not know, white and pink flowers he had found by the waterfall, and handed them tenderly to her. And he thought of poor Afanasy Nikitin. Had he not met Sandhya he would surely have gone mad, Stephen thought, burning like Afanasy in Hindustan.

There was family at home to notify. Stephen sent a cable to his mother, who sent one back in reply, congratulating him.

"What else could I do?" Muriel asked her friend Dorris over a long cool Campari, as they played Scrabble together in Muriel's Riverside Drive apartment.

"His life is his own, God knows. And after he split with Gail ..."

"I never did like that Gail," Dorris spluttered, her voice hoarse from her addiction to Russian Sobranie and her winters in Palm Springs. Gail, ridiculous chit of a thing with those black suits she wore!

"Where in the dickens is she now?"

Muriel shrugged her shoulders in response and picked up the metallic letter *S* from the edge of her Scrabble board. It was enamel, covered with black-and-red cloisonné work, part of the fine set she had picked up at an East Side boutique. She held it in her hands and stared at it.

S oon after they settled in New York, Stephen took his wife to visit Ellis Island. The visit was prompted by the renovation of the immigration facilities on the island. The newspapers were full of it. Stephen could not resist a sense of pride in the fact that the broken fixtures from the contagious hospital, where one of his great-grandmother's sisters had been interned, were tucked neatly behind plexiglass.

They saw a stovepipe, a blue-painted bed frame, a bit of an ancient toilet bowl, a sign THIS WAY UP with a red arrow pointing skyward, all arranged as if the passerby might enter through the immaculate show into a past so cleft from its indices of dirt and disaster that the magnitude of dislocations the immigrants had suffered might be cast afresh in a time without before or behind, well-lit and clearly palpable.

But what if the fragments were heaped up and viewed by a fallen angel, the poor creature blown backward into the future, wings clenched tight, passage irrefutable?

How reluctant Sandhya had been to enter the boat crammed with tourists from the four corners of the globe: Japanese, Nigerians, Australians, Danes, even tourists from the United Provinces, which was what Stephen privately called the broken-up Soviet Republic, substituting for its new name that of the state in the Indian subcontinent he knew best.

There was a dazed look on Sandhya's face as he pushed her forward. She hung onto the rails, staring at the acrobats, three black men who leaped over each other's shoulders. They were wearing T-shirts with patterns of the American flag. The youngest took a burning brand his comrade held up then, legs set firmly athwart a third man's shoulders, leaped. As he landed he thrust the fire brand into his mouth. The crowd gasped as flames poured out where a tongue should have been.

Granted the showstopper, granted the mood of the crowd set to throng onto the rocking boat, putting up in fairly good humor with the calls from the acrobats—"Dollar bills, please. Five dollar from the Japanese, sure they have mo, mo"—why that look? Hadn't she begged to be taken to visit Ellis Island? Finally he tugged her along so that, putting one foot in front of the other, Sandhya stepped onto an old Peruvian woman's dress and had to apologize in that convent-educated way of hers, "Sorry, sorry, ever so sorry," in an accent that, coming from so dark a face, raised eyebrows. Stephen was forced to put his annoyance aside and take the manly part. He drew her forward, past the Irishmen with their blue caps and baseball insignia, past the bawling children.

She seemed quite distant all through the boat ride. Was it because so few Indians had come that way? He did not ask, but tried to illuminate the scene with a running commentary, lively with anecdotes about Great-aunt Ewa who, let out of the contagious hospital where they had held her because of a rash on her right cheek, dreamed forever of the red arrow on the sign pointing upward, thinking it was meant for the angel of death, who was supposed to pass over the house, not stop.

Thrusting his thoughts onto happier things Stephen pointed out white yachts in which the wealthy took their pleasure floating on the blue waters round about Manhattan. The yachts were visible from a partially open window of the museum next to the exhibit with the bits of the old toilet bowl.

Once he lost her. He panicked, racing about the museum, even into the room with anti-Asian images, "Jap Go Home" and the like, which he hadn't wanted her to see, the flat caricatures, the Asian Exclusion Act written up in big type next to the letters THIS LAND IS NOT YOUR LAND. Surely she couldn't have entered that room? Down the escalators he went and found her leaning against the wall, staring at an enlarged image of a Moroccan or was it Algerian in djellaba and turban, eyes moist with the light blown into the lens, a young man, brought into Ellis Island. What wind had steered him here? She seemed to be staring, but not really seeing. He caught her by the hand and was so relieved he felt himself on the brink of tears. For the first time in their years together her sense of lostness had seeped into his own soul, dissolving the clear walls he had constructed to make himself feel at home. She seemed uneasy at seeing him.

"Come, Sandy, come," he whispered, leading her out.

On the boat, on the way back, he pointed out the lady, the stone folds of her gown draped over the massive six-pointed star on which she was placed, the site below swarming with tourists. In the clear air, even the lamp was visible, with a flock of white gulls floating over it so that their wings made a blurry halo. He pointed out the lamp to Sandy and she stared at it, biting into a crabapple she had picked off the ground, right by the boat. A curious habit of hers, he thought, picking fallen fruit off the ground like that, a village habit surely. But then she had gone to the washroom and cleaned off the dirt and held the green speckled fruit in her hand, biting hard into the crisp flesh inside.

In the months after their Ellis Island trip Stephen started to worry. At odd moments in Greenwich he gazed at rows of numbers, and found himself wondering what Sandhya could possibly find to do now that Dora was in daycare for the good part of each day. Sandhya was growing thinner he could tell, there were circles under her eyes and he sensed that something was gnawing at her. He did not dare ask outright. What could she have said in any case? If he had thought of it further he might have admitted he was scared of what was lurking in her. He held to a firm approach.

"You have choices, my dear," he said, straightening himself on the couch: "The whole of New York City lies ahead of you. Do something: volunteer work with the Hadassah, Mother will help you, or my cousin even, though it's hard for her to come all the way from Hoboken. How about the soup kitchen at the Presbyterian Church, except," and he bit his mustache at this, "I would be a little worried about you there. But it is a church, closer to home, eh?"

And he smiled encouragingly as she sat, needle in hand, hemming Dora's dungarees. Then, trying to draw courage for the difficult conversation ahead, he looked straight at her: "You have a green card, Sandy, you could try for a job. Something like Sita Travel?"

He softened a little at the memory, then drew himself straight.

"They're setting up something across the road, Harold tells me. How about that: Sandhya Rosenblum of Tascot Travels, badge and all."

He touched her under the chin gently, with his forefinger. He had to lean over uncomfortably to execute this spousal gesture, for Dora was squatted at her mother's feet, busy crayoning a yellow duck. For some reason Dora paid little attention to her father that evening and Sandhya was grateful. Otherwise she would have had the hard task of tearing the child away so Stephen could ease himself out of his overcoat, sit on the captain's bed, take off his hat, his shoes.

"I'll put the kettle on," Sandhya said, getting up, half-hemmed dungarees in hand, edging her feet over Dora's back. It came back to her how on hearing Stephen enter, the scrape of the key in the lock, slight jangle of the Maharashtrian cowbells she had hung on the doorknob as a signal of entry, she had felt her whole body stiffen. Now it seemed even the corners of her mouth hurt with the effort of trying to smile back. Their trip to Ellis Island, the discomfort she had felt in the museum, made things much worse for her. It was as if he were proposing a past she might enter, but her flesh resisted. Staring out at the cold waters, she felt her thoughts turn to the early days with Stephen, memories of shared emotion on the cool slopes of Nainatal, the freedom he seemed to offer. Now she couldn't even speak openly with him, locked as she was into a world she felt she had not chosen.

There was a longing in her to go out, into the streets of Manhattan, saunter freely on the sidewalks, past the stalls of fruits and vegetables, past the scrawny lime trees. But she felt she did not know what to do with her arms and legs or how to adjust her torso in order to speed past a gang of teenagers, their baseball caps bent back, trousers lowered almost to their crotches. Once, she had raced past a group with a boombox and a man slightly older than she had yelled, "Indian?" noticing her dark hair, her brown skin. She opened her mouth, but felt the hot wind from the elevated subway blow her words away. A Chinese woman was looking out from the door of the take-out restaurant. A thin woman in a polka-dot dress, she had kind eyes, and if the need ever arose, Sandhya decided, she might take shelter under the bright signs that advertised rice, pork, beans, the Chino-Latino quick cuisine a favorite in her neighborhood.

Later, buying a cauliflower from the sidewalk, she tried to bargain in Spanish but found herself unequal to the task. She tried to imagine her mother on this very street, silk sari tucked tight into her waist. It might have worked out for Sosa with her bright, sassy words, her winning ways in the marketplace where she went each Sunday in Tiruvella, two maids, baskets in hand, escorting her. Sandhya rubbed her eyes. The figures in the street were blurring. It was a Latina woman right there, in a pink dress. She certainly had Sosa's coloring, her girth, but this wasn't her mother, and the man with the beret was waiting for his money. Sandhya paid and then retreated, bartering sense for memory, her inner life so sensual, unstable.

This was the world Stephen had brought her to, but he himself was oddly absent from it, and Sandhya felt that there was no way she could draw on his experience to help her live her life. Bred in the late sixties, Stephen's liberal vision offered him a sense of equality that buckled under the weight of his wife's life. She should take America head on, he felt. Her difficulties in the street would surely ease. By his light, Jewish immigration had laid out the groundwork and now Sandhya Rosenblum could benefit. But often his resolution wavered, and the truths he had discovered for himself wore thin when stretched over his wife's dark femaleness. Then, too, his daily work took him to Connecticut, a realm of arcane order and cleanliness, it seemed to Sandhya. And when he was at home they hardly went out together, what with the heat in summer, and Stephen's exhaustion at traveling so far from home each day. Each weekend though, they did D'Agostino Supermarket, fifteen blocks from their street. Sandhya loved to watch her husband speed through the aisles like a small boy on a go-cart, his trolley primed to topple the cheapest, most "natural" cans off the shelves. She found herself following behind, trying to pick out the few goods she recognized, Marmite, Johnson's Baby Powder, Ovaltine. The baby powder was just what Dora needed for her prickly heat, she was sure of it. But too nervous to quarrel with Stephen over the brand name—he frequently objected to anything but the generic brand—Sandhya tucked the can under an unwieldy packet of pads she had picked up for her own needs. At the checkout counter he'd be too preoccupied, she hoped, to notice. Why, she might even be able to sneak a few moments with one of the glossy magazines on the far racks, the stars in lurid colors, parceling out fate. She made her way to the checkout counter, peered into the magazine:

> Aquarians Alert, this week a new Romantic Interest will enter your lives. Be aware though, of the difficulties of reconciling your bank book and the callings of your heart. Watch out for ankles and kidneys, weak points while Saturn is in transit. Best for those who can float free, yet return to their moorings.

She had just completed reading when Stephen approached, his concentrated look never wavering. The child, tucked into the front of the trolley, her dress a splash of vivid orange, waved her arms in her father's face, filled with delight at the new game. Sandhya helped her husband tip out the contents, lay out milk and meat and broccoli, then the canned goods, some Goya beans, cereal for the morning breakfast. Her eyes lit up when she saw the frozen *samosas* he had picked up as a treat. She slid the pads and baby powder over quickly and saw his eyes narrow. But Dora was in his arms, her mouth filled with a graham cracker, and he chose not to make a fuss. In the street later, he said:

"You know I hate that, Sandhya. Buying that brand-name powder."

But she shook her head and stared away, glad that she felt so very little. They were right by the Leprechaun Bar. The door swung open, and she gazed at its dark, misty interior. The polished wood glinted and she felt as if a hidden river were flowing. The outside of the bar was covered with brilliant mirrors and for a moment she was forced to shut her eyes from the glare. Then she caught sight of the three of them, husband, wife and child: Stephen with his kind, bewildered mouth, his soft hair rumpled, and next to him, her own bodily self, eyes disappearing in all that light. The child swung by her dimpled arms between the two parents, a weight, a precious burden. The brown plastic bags filled with food, suspended on the free arms of the two adults, vanished at the base of the mirrors. The glare from those mirrors stayed with her.

"Tell me about the man," she said later that evening, "who lit up his room with so many lights."

Stephen stared at her quizzically over the *Times*, checking out deals on apartments in the city.

"Lights?"

She backed down. It was something Gautam had told her, a book with a man in it, keeping the bright lights burning in his room, so he could exist, so he could be. A black man in Harlem, not so far from where they lived. And she didn't pursue the topic when Stephen leaned forward:

"Hey, look at this, Sandy. Not bad, eh?"

And he pushed the paper toward her with a picture of a brownstone in Brooklyn, the sidewalks patched up, lime trees at the edge of the quiet yard.

To keep things on even keel, she kept returning to her childhood home, a house with a red-tiled roof and a sandy courtyard where the mulberry bloomed. Each summer, gradually using up the savings Stephen had put away before his marriage, she made her return. Dutiful daughter to the core, she would carry back with her the long list of items her mother requested: rubber rings for the Moulinex blender; deodorant; vaseline tubes; yeast in jars; eau de toilette with a light jasmine scent; American lace to attach to nighties; 38B cup bras, three in black, three in white; dried figs from California; dried tomatoes from Colorado; pistachios imported from Iran since the Afghani source had dried up in India; several packs of Wilkinsons blades for her father; three cassettes of any kind of music by the New York Philharmonic, at least one symphony to be conducted by Zubin Mehta and bearing on its cover an image of him, baton in hand; and (if possible), her mother had added this in parenthesis, light synthetic material not even available in Bombay, in beige or pale green, suitable for living room curtains. And so the list went.

Sometimes as she went shopping she felt her belly might rip open with all the stuff she was putting into it: indigestible sterilities of objects no landfills might take, ready to be packed in plastic sheeting and borne with love across the oceans, across the landmasses, and placed in Sosa's hands.

But her own digestive system was too delicate and Sandhya felt faint from the bright lights in the stores, the masses of pistachios and almonds in their cellophane bags waiting in the small kitchen to be packed into the suitcases Stephen had bought at a sale in New Jersey, suitcases with bodies unzippered, half-filled. But it was worth it all, to see the pleasure on her mother's face, her father's sharp gaze as the gifts rolled out. Or was it really her libation to the gods of guilt, household deities who might swarm up in sleep and catch her by the throat for leaving them, nick her in the thighs and draw blood?

She always took Dora with her and her parents were delighted to have their grandchild come from across the seas. In her grandparents' hands, Dora grew thoroughly spoiled, every whim satisfied, every call drawing an immediate response. And the gifts Sandhya carried were put to visible use. It pleased her to see the fabric she had brought three years before turned into curtains, draping the elegant living room windows. Though the transportation of the gift had discomfited her, she could rightly feel she had added something to the ancestral home. And her father always wore the shirts she took him, pure Egyptian cotton, finely tailored, for he was a man of refinement and appreciated those things. For Stephen L.L.Bean seemed best, and for her too; or in summer, shorts from the Latino Discount store where the shoes were heaped up in piles outside and sold for $3.99 a pair, and shorts under $10.00 hidden in a mound under the flimsy bras and synthetic panties in lurid greens and purples that she didn't quite have the temerity to touch.

So, with bag and baggage, Sandhya made her returns and struggled for a poise she was sometimes hard put to maintain. Having Dora helped her, she had no doubt about it. With the small child in tow Sandhya could be a mother, and surviving in transit lounges was rendered entirely more bearable with a resolute vocation such as motherhood with its pressing requirements granted her. Her sexual body, too, was less troubling then, for with Stephen, and this was something that had taken her years to acknowledge, she constantly felt as if she had to overcome her body, rise beyond it in some difficult, inescapable way.

That this elusive sense remained with her even during consummation was something she had learned to accept in her conscious mind and cope with, much as she coped with dislocation, and her several homes. There was a stoical grain in Sandhya that she had inherited from her father. She felt that certain emotional strains had to be borne in silence in the interest of preserving a difficult world.

Recently, though, the emptiness was growing in her. Something Stephen did not know about and could not touch, a gnawing hunger, a desperation even. The closest it came to being eased was when she held little Dora in her arms and rocked her, or when the child ran her hands through her mother's hair, or clung to her thighs in a delicious burden of touch.

Subway Song
(Draupadi)

I've wired the entire ceiling, every inch of it.
And not with fluorescent bulbs, but with the older,
more-expensive-to-operate kind, the filament type.
  —Ralph Ellison, Invisible Man

The summer before I met Sandhya Rosenblum the sky burned blue above me. The love I sought bound me tight, close. I rode the subway that summer up down, down up the length of Manhattan. Once, riding hard, jolting, I gripped the metal bar, then found a seat. I had my litho tools clutched to my chest. In a plastic bag I had a bit of rope I picked up at Pearl Paint, a roll of chicken wire found in a dump by City Hall, some canvas too, and pencils and rough draft paper.

I was pressed next to a saxophone player with green antennae, shimmering sequins on his suit. Hot, wet, summertime. Boobooboo, shuu-shuushuu, he kept going. I clutched my litho tools, took in the antennae bobbing on a man's head. Perfect outfit for the underground. Fifth circle. What would Columbus have made of this? No memories there. Doors clanged shut.

"Black bitch," someone said under his breath.

I stared at my hands, held my head proud. Looking the other way I saw a small stick figure waving its red paws—jammed tight against a track. A new poster:

LA VIA DEL TREN ...

The young man sitting across stared at me, puckering his lips. He opened up a newspaper to shield himself.

Front page, bottom right-hand corner. "Five Dead in Derailment As

Subway Nears Union Square." A train jumped the rail from four to six. Metal carriage split. Five dead, over a hundred injured from the impact of the collision.

I could feel the heart jolting against my ribs, Bertran de Born next to me, swinging a head in his hand, swinging his dead eyes to make a light.

Imagined ends in a world without grace.

"Christ, Christ," it was some guy from Crown Heights saying: "No warning. Nothing. I thought it was the end of the world. People lying in a daze, bleeding."

It could have been me trapped there in pig-metal on my way to visit Rashid in his white room, to set my cheek on the new pillows he picked up at the futon shop.

I had started complaining about my neck. It hurt from bending over to mix the concrete I needed for my work.

"I love your brown neck."

He kissed me in Arabic, making a word as he kissed. A little roughly. I loved that.

"Halati," he crooned.

I started complaining about my neck. "It hurts. Rub it for me, Rashid. Please. Pretty please."

That neck might have been torn off, just where he loved to kiss it. Rashid of the rounded lips and the delicate hands with blue veins running.

"I am New York, you are New York," he sang at me through his coffee cup. Then his mood changed, abruptly, as it often did:

"They killed me once," he said, looking at me dead straight. This was after we made love with the new pillow under my ass. I was raised as the princesses were raised in pharaonic days, pillows of down under brown asses. As Cleopatra was raised.

"They killed me once," he repeated. "Then wore my face many times."

"Whose?" I asked, wiping the tears off my cheek.

"Samih al-Qasim," he replied, "poet of the Occupation. I met him once."

"Beirut?" I asked.

"No, Gaza. Eyeless," he smiled at me.

His black eyes spread into his face.

He stood by the window in Brooklyn utterly naked.

I had the morning paper. My tools, too. A bit of rope I wanted to use for my installation. There was a tall tree behind him, a green tree waving its new leaves in the spring air, a tree visible through clean glass. And a flagpole. A red, white, and blue flag. If only Papa could see me.

"It's just a bloody circus. That's all it is."

My own voice rose in my head and I did not know what to do with it. Or with what was not voice, just unmitigated body.

"Circus," I kept muttering.

"What's that?" he asked.

I quieted down. Pretended to look at a tree, a stone, water trembling behind us.

"Shall we sit?"

"No, no." He was uncomfortable with people around, even with the shadow of the tourist from some Slavic country with a camera dangling helplessly from a shoulder.

"Let's walk on a bit."

Through rough grass with odd nettles scraping our ankles we strolled to an elaborate arrangement of seats. On one side was a disused monument, something round, bald, gray with graffiti, the scratched-up stuff New York is full of. I stopped and said:

"This bench do? Or can't you bear these faded American monuments?"

"Why so symbolic?" he snapped. "Can't you stop it?"

I started laughing as he stared at me. I kept on laughing and then it started to hurt my ribs.

Over now. The shit pile of history. I shall never visit Beirut with him, walk down the Hamra. Nor dream of Alexandria where he walked by the waters.

I shall never go to Brooklyn with him, lay my naked body on a down pillow. Nor rendezvous by Columbus's cold statue, stroll in Central Park. No more.

B itterness made me sore. But love was to come, go, right after my subway ride, at the AIDS show at Franklin Furnace. I had made a figure out of scrap wire and condoms, diaphragms for the lips. Molded eyebrows out of the congealed gel of an Orthotube—the stink-smell I can't stand. The figure was blank-faced, breastless, neither male nor female. Then I gave it two extra hands, goddess style. Wanted to find a sword for one of the hands to hold, a lotus for another, but gave up on that thought. Hung a rope instead, loosely round the neck.

Spray painted the whole thing in orange, dazzling orange that shimmers in the dark. Set a wooden case around it, cut with a peephole, so figure and rope shone out.

Arrayed myself in Great-aunt Loulou's old cloak, the one she wore when KKK men threatened her with death and she spat at them. Added brilliant orange beads to my dreadlocks to match the rope.

Stood there with a sign, next to the dark box with the hole in it. A hand-made sign I carried:

CHOOSE YOUR BLOOD. THIS IS AMERICA.

Under it very carefully I wrote my name, all in capital letters, my attempt at autobiography: DRAUPADI DINKINS FROM GINGEE NEW YORK. The cloak was tattered in parts.

Next to me an old gramophone played Nancy Sinatra's *You Only Live Twice.*

The music made me want to weep. A Thai woman did that piece and on the spindle she pasted cutouts of bikini-clad prostitutes, bottoms twirling. The moral of this piece, Sikrit explained to me later, is we are bought and sold for dollars. She started to explain this to Rinaldo when he came in. I noticed the muscular strength of him first.

The other side of me was Rosie's work. A shot of a vulva, delicately open, labia lipped out, clitoris showing, all the fragile softness of it, hair cloaking what would otherwise be too tender for sight. Under the blown-up photo a sign:

READ MY LIPS BEFORE THEY'RE SEALED. Rosie, a white woman, stood by, placard in hand, raised high: OUR BODIES SHOULD BE PLAYGROUNDS— NOT BATTLEFIELDS: DOWN WITH MADNESS IN WICHITA AND ELSEWHERE IN OUR LAND.

In smaller letters: ON MAY 23, 1991, THE SUPREME COURT UPHELD THE FEDERAL GOVERNMENT'S RIGHT TO DENY FUNDS TO CLINICS THAT PRO- VIDE INFORMATION ABOUT ABORTION.

"What this have to do with AIDS?" Sikrit asked, nudging at me.

"It's okay, gal," I signaled. I could tell she was much struck by the piece.

On her front Rosie from Milwaukee wore a plastic blow-up of the image, so magnified labia rippled as she moved in her tight leotards. She held up her hands for Rinaldo to see. I was watching quite closely. Her hands were black with fingerprint ink.

Other pieces, too.

Simon Escobar, my next-door neighbor, did The Virgin of Westbeth.

He and his lover did it together. Bought the statue from the *Botanica* in the Bronx that Simon's aunt frequents, put twisted metal in it. Plastered it with images of gay couples, Latino and Chicano, Asian-American, African-American. Made a skirt for the virgin with condom packets. Around the black virgin's neck a rosary, each wax bead sculpted out as a tiny skull. Her eyes were bloodshot, the mad virgin of Westbeth. She too had dollars round her neck. A hell of a lot of dollars there. The two men, Simon and Juan, knelt in front of her.

There were a few Jehovah's Witnesses protesting outside. I think they had the wrong building. In the afternoon a few trickled back, saying:

"The end is approaching. It is the Lord's will."

I took a break, still wearing the cloak. I felt ill. When I returned I saw Rinaldo, his shoulders rippling under his coat. He looked at Rosie and her labia for a bit. Then walked over to me. Stared at me long and hard.

"Aha!"

"Yes?" I was quizzical.

"America?" he said in his Italian accent. I didn't know about Fiat cars back then.

Stood straight. Set my shoulders back as Miss Howe, my teacher in Gingee, ordered me when I was struggling to get over Jimmy O' Flaherty: "You and I are colored women," she pronounced, "we must set our shoulders back."

I threw my left arm over the wooden box: "Take a lookie," I invited him.

But he just stood there, raised his eyebrows.

"Yes, yes," I muttered, "I too am part of this show. This is America."

"No, no."

I understood. It was the bit about choosing your blood that threw him. Earlier I had thought about having a spot of the real stuff on the label and writing MISCEGENATION in big letters, the whole superimposed on David Duke's face, but the silk screen didn't work out right.

I understood that Rinaldo was foreign, that he needed an explanation.

"I was born in Gingee, most part Indian, part African descended from slaves, pride of Kala Pani, sister to the Middle Passage. Also part Asian-American, from Japanese, Chinese, and Filipino blood: railroads in the West, the pineapple and sugarcane fields." I straightened up, my voice growing hoarse.

"I also have a smattering of white—low European—in me. Hence the slight pallor, I suspect."

He smiled broadly at this.

After this speech I breathed hard. When I went out he was there, conversing with one of the Jehovah's Witnesses. He had just flown in from Naples, I heard him say.

"Come, come?" he asked, smiling, arms wide open in all that cold.

"Fire! Fire!" the Jehovah's Witnesses were yelling.

I require, dear Rinaldo, love that's made of fire.

You came toward me, cheeks flushed, whispering, "Come, come."

Touch, I was all touch for you, Rinaldo.

"Why do we make love, Draupadi?" you asked.

We were in my white room. It was summertime and the flies danced in the polluted air, high above the piers where Melville strolled.

"Because we know we will die," I said.

"And animals?" you asked.

"I don't know, I don't know that."

I looked down at you, the black hairs curling on your thigh, your hands pulling up the condom, its transparent stuff rolling bit by bit up your cock, and I longed to put my mouth on it, kneel over you, my black hair over your thighs, my face in those strong thighs of yours, trembling now, trembling with it all.

Last summer who knew I could write down such words, be such a creature as I am?

Stirring

Jay saw his cousin staring into the shallows of a silver dish her mother had given her on the occasion of her marriage, a dish Sandhya had wrapped in a torn silk sari, wedged amidst her folded petticoats, and borne to North America. With her index finger she was touching tiny grains of rice, setting them in some mysterious order. The grains clung to her finger, minute white insects. Her eyes swarmed with their reflections. He felt a sorrow welling out of him, watching her in that way. She needed to go out, Jay decided, without Rosenblum. Needed to meet others. So it was that Draupadi Dinkins entered Sandhya's life, part of a whirlwind that was to blow through the brittle order she was struggling to create for herself.

One afternoon, Sandhya was standing in her bedroom, combing her hair. She heard a sound at the doorway and turned, brush in hand. A little cry of delight came out of her lips at the sight of Jay, but who was that woman behind him? Sandhya craned her neck and, looking for an instant in the mirror that hung on the bedroom wall, saw a woman, almost her double, gazing earnestly at her. For an instant in the clear, well-lit mirror, their two faces blurred into each other, as shadow might into substance. Then Sandhya stepped forward, Dora, who had crawled off the bed, clinging to her skirts. The child suddenly broke her hold on her mother's thigh and ran to Stephen who, ever the gracious host, was hovering about the doorway, inquiring as to their needs:

"We have Scotch," he said, "and some soda. Gin too, and tonic. What'll it be, Jay? And for you?"

But the visitor, who had a fuzz of black hair and was dressed in a curious ensemble—silk blouse, leather skirt, and what seemed to be a wisp of tulle tossed about her neck—was too intently staring at Sandhya to reply.

"Draupadi," Jay introduced her.

"Yeh, Draupadi Dinkins," and the visitor extended her hand.

Sandhya was fascinated. How did their visitor come by such an Indian name? "What a pretty stole," Sandhya murmured.

Draupadi nodded, struck by the sari Jay's cousin was wearing. Did Indian women always wear saris? And what power of will did it take to swathe those six yards of fabric around the body?

The four adults settled for drinks in the living room that overlooked the river and, after some prodding from Jay, Sandhya spoke of her desire to go shopping, buy a few American clothes, a coat even. Stephen, discussing the prospects of war in the Middle East, inclined his head courteously.

"Of course, my dear, with Dora in school, you have all the time in the world!"

"And where did you grow up?" Sandhya asked Draupadi.

"Gingee."

"No!"

"Sure. Right on the Hudson. North of Claverack in Columbia county. Dad settled there. Remembers as much of Trinidad as a snake would its shed skin. Left when he was just three. All sorts of blood flow through him. Indian, black, a spurt of white, some Japanese too, from Great-grandma."

And Draupadi stopped, wiping her face. The Scotch was getting to her.

"There's a Gingee in Tamil Nadu to the east of where I come from," Sandhya said. "No, Jay?"

"Possible, never heard of it though."

Drawn from his discussion of Iraqi aggression, Jay was noncommittal.

Draupadi bent forward and touched Sandhya on the knee:

"We have it all here in New York State, I swear: Milan, Rome, Delhi, and Gingee, too. Just wait till the snow falls and you'll see, driving north, place signs sticking up through a white blanket."

Stephen, who seemed quite taken with their visitor, asked about her line of work. Sandhya sat utterly still as Draupadi spoke of the piece she had conceived: a mixed-media installation about Columbus, a man who had an imaginary India in his heart. She was taping music. Dvořák's cuckoo from the New World Symphony would play in the background as people walked through.

"A loop," she said.

"What's that?" Stephen inquired.

"A piece that plays on and on. But I'll cut the cuckoo cries with the latest rap pieces."

It struck Sandhya that Draupadi was nervous talking about her work. Perhaps it was one of those things that would never come into being. Like an architect with unbuilt houses. But Draupadi's voice cut in:

"Jay tells me your mother was born in Calicut? Right where Vasco da Gama came, cap in hand, to greet the natives!"

"And you're writing lines about this?" Stephen cut in, not giving his wife the chance to reply. "Will you give us a few lines?" So Draupadi Dinkins, never one to let an opportunity pass, nodded her head and began:

> Back against the kitchen stove, Draupadi sings:
> Christopher Columbus, your soul's my battlefield.
> See! Great Garuda has rainbow-colored wings!

Stephen squirmed in his chair and even Jay had a hard time suppressing a laugh. Only Sandhya and Dora were filled with awe at the voice that poured out. What seemed to the others a curious lack of fit between the words never troubled either of them. Dora put out her plump fingers and tugged at the blue tulle around the singer's neck and Sandhya sat very straight and asked:

"You wrote it yourself?"

Draupadi was refreshing herself with an ice cube, passed it over her neck and dropped it back in the glass, then nodded.

"And you'll take me shopping?" asked Sandhya, her voice almost a whisper.

"Of course, honey," Draupadi assured her. "Of course."

Later that day, back in Westbeth, in the studio cluttered with clay and wood she had laid out for her installation piece, Draupadi stared out of her window. Down below on the pier by the gray waves she could see lovers, arms entwined, two men, both in gray windbreakers. One started leaping over a broken flowerpot, the remnants of the plant sale that was held every weekend. He was waving his arms, making wild gestures. The other, seemingly fatigued, walked with a slow plod, head held high. When he turned, Draupadi drew in her breath sharply, seeing the sunken features of an AIDS sufferer. She leaned out the window and waved her bit of tulle at him. Heartened, the man broke into laughter and waved back. "Lady at window, eh?" he called in a hoarse voice, and Draupadi leaned

out and sang her song to him, the unfinished one that began with the
kitchen stove and moved on:

> She steps straight out of Gingee, a parrot in her hair,
> But oh her throat is bare, very bare.

The lines had come to Draupadi the previous night and she scribbled
them down in a species of automatic writing she neither questioned nor
fully understood. Surely some of it had flowed from her reading on the
cult of the Draupadi dancers in Tamil Nadu. There she discovered a
mythic heroine who often bore a parrot, symbol of the soul, perched on
her shoulder or her wild hair. Then, too, Peter Brook's production of the
Mahabharata at BAM had much inspired her. She tried to imagine a real
parrot on stage, on the actress's arm. But what if it suddenly squawked,
broke free, flapping its wings in the dark theater? Crossing art with the re-
calcitrant actually might be too hard, she decided.

When Jay visited her a few days later, she shared her thoughts with
him. Given the coincidence in name, Draupadi felt she had some kinship
with the heroine of the *Mahabharata,* though what she wasn't quite sure.
Then, too, she was the great-granddaughter of a woman who had come
as a bonded laborer to Trinidad, worked in the cane fields in the swelter-
ing heat. That was her bond with India. India owed her and she would
draw what she wished from that world, rework the language, pack it with
lore. Syncretism was part of her being and it might work for her, over-
coming the barriers she felt she had faced since childhood.

But Jay was puzzled. Quite gently, a lump of chewing gum in his
mouth, he faced her:

"But is this your past?"

"I want to make it up," she argued.

"But why call the *Mahabharata* your heritage?" he quizzed her. "Why
not the *Iliad* and *Odyssey* also?"

And for once she had no answer. The shreds of memory she got from
her grandmother didn't add up to the wild glory of the epic. All she had
were whispers, shards of songs, torn phrases, and could they add up to a
heritage? Still, as a human being, she felt she had a right to anything out
there. And what came from India was closer.

"But in what way?" he pressed her, irritated by what he thought of as
her hallucinogenic vision of myth.

"Is that Draupadi as close to you as Billie Holiday, for instance, whom you love so? Why not take your blood from there, redraw the map?"

Draupadi disliked his arguments. They seemed coy, insidious: "Hey, toss out that gum, Jay. I'd much rather you smoked." Then in a quieter voice she added: "I feel I do have a bond with Billie Holiday."

But he demurred, chewing hard, pressing her about the singer. Draupadi Dinkins wasn't lying about the connection. One of her great-aunts had worked the coat rack at Café Society, the nightclub where Billie Holiday often sang. And this, Draupadi told Jay, with more than a little bravado, she took to be her truest bond with American culture. Indeed, Lady Day's songs made Draupadi dream of a new world. "All the colors of the sun," she told Jay, who had gotten rid of his gum by now, "painted onto human skin—the target of desire—mingling."

Jay listened quietly as Draupadi moved on to speak of her difficulty with Sandhya. She was lovely looking to be sure, but straight out of India, something seemed lacking in her. A poverty of sense, an inability to coast along on the winds that might blow from just around the corner. Was she lost? Or was Sandhya what one might call a realist? Draupadi shivered at the word her father had dinned into her.

Waking early, setting up the bottles in Dinkins's Soda Shop, cleaning off the tables, Himanshu Dinkins had counseled his daughter to be a realist. The same word had cropped up that clear fall morning, when he stumbled home from the shop in Gingee, his hands bleeding. During the night, a group of skinheads had tossed bottles into the Soda Shop, heaped garbage and spent condoms by the window, and Himanshu was forced to pick up the tawdry bits in his bare hands and to clean out his shop front. Draupadi saw the helpless rage in her father's eyes as Maya, her mother, bandaged his hands. On and on she bandaged them, packing clean white cloth over the wounds till in the end his two hands resembled the appendages of a mummy. Never, never, swore Draupadi, would she follow her father into his line of work. She would leave Gingee.

The School of Visual Arts in the City gave her a way out. She arrived at the height of the brouhaha about identity and fell right in, the fragments of her past, real and imagined, swarming into her art. She read Emerson and Thoreau. What the former had said about art as a mirror carried through the streets had moved her deeply, so too his counsel to his readers to forget the past, fling memory away, live in the eternal present like the roses. And *Walden* she carried about with her in a side pocket, haunted by the double shadow the writer glimpsed one winter's day, a substanceless being on the shoulders of the other, one crouched on the ice, the other up on the grassy hillside. Soon enough she put away these works of high Romanticism in favor of a more apocalyptic literature, one that wedded the ferocious indignities of racism in America to the possibilities of a radical liberation.

Then, too, parts of the globe, places she had no experience of, flowed into her. She met Rashid el Obeid, an Egyptian scholar who had started in the city as a post-doc fellow at Columbia, but in between jobs was making do as a doorman at Westbeth. She succumbed to his black hair, the lure of his arcane knowledge. It started with Turkish coffee in her apartment, which he prepared. They met, more frequently each week, till finally she had drunk so deep of passion she felt she could not live without him. But quite quickly thereafter it went badly, and the little note Rashid pushed under her door announcing their breakup hardly surprised her. She had been expecting it, almost. Far better than the broken glass on a shop floor her father had to deal with, she mused, in an odd, pained conjuncture of thought, staring out the misty window.

What hurt though was the sudden emptiness in her arms, nothing to hold onto. Even work was hard. She would stand then and gaze out of the window at river water in waves, sullen indigo tips forming and parting, pale waterbirds wheeling over. Surely they had come from somewhere far away, perhaps Mount Fuji.

It was Rashid who had whispered to her at what she now saw was the height of their passion: "Somewhere in the distance is Mount Fuji."

"Why Fuji?" she asked.

"Don't you know Basho's invocation to the snail?"

She shook her head, thrust her elbow into a mound of clay she had left on the window ledge. Then he murmured to her:

"Climb Mount Fuji, O snail, but slowly, ever so slowly."

Still, her responses to the note were quick, frenzied. Draupadi stormed over to the bar at the edge of the block, drank herself into a haze, spent the night on Tom the sculptor's floor. Hard floor. Tom held tight, rocking her. "Gone," she whispered to him. "Going, going, gone."

Draupadi turned back to the window. The two men she was watching had walked away and in the middle distance the waves on the Hudson were streaked with white. She could make out a fine mist that spun over the waves and clouds tinted with mauve in readiness for the sun's going down. She stepped back from the window and decided quickly—she would take Sandhya Rosenblum shopping. She would do that for sure. Why, the woman was just her age, no less, no more, and hungry, Draupadi sensed that. There was an emptiness in Sandhya's soul she felt she understood.

They met the very next day at the corner right by the Korean grocery store. It was warm and the sun made the plastic on the green plantains shimmer. The sun made Sandhya want to pull off her long *salwar* and dance in her bare legs all over the sidewalk. Draupadi stood by her in a miniskirt, a straw hat shielding her face. Then, just as Sandhya turned to the wooden stall to pick up a glistening black plum and sniff it, the rain came down. In a few minutes the streets were full of water. Holding onto Draupadi's arm, Sandhya let water splash on her ankles, her elbows, even her cheeks. She was laughing like a child, walking with this near stranger down Broadway. They were right by the entrance to a subway when the rain stopped, and a crowd pushing out of the mouth of the underground surged over them. Sandhya felt the blouse being tugged off her body. She turned in panic but saw it was only a cart pushed by a vendor, its over-loaded top thrust high with bric-a-brac caught on her sleeve. "Subway bro-ken down," Draupadi muttered as she held onto Sandhya's arm. They coasted forward, pointing out the young things on their platform heels, the matrons gesticulating, men and women mouthing English, Spanish, Haitian Creole, whatever came first. Sandhya thought she saw her mother in front of her, sari pulled tight around her hips, Marya the maid following behind her, basket in hand, as they did on market day in Kerala, but the image dissolved. Sight sharpened onto a hand pinching a small child's cheeks and the child grimacing, tugging at her pink balloon.

"So glad Dora isn't with me," said Sandhya, "I would have had to carry her on my shoulder," but Draupadi didn't seem to hear. As they passed in front of D'Agostino Sandhya gesticulated with her thumb, and the two of them coasted in. Why she didn't know, but they ended up right in front of the toothpaste rack. Freed of Stephen and the child, Sandhya stood there, rooted in the aisle. Toothpaste blew her mind, its infinite variety.

"So many kinds," she whispered to Draupadi, who nodded, then turned away.

It was as if she were in a theater, and her desire, faced with the multi-ple, glittering items before her, could slip and slide freely. Finally, with Draupadi coaxing her on, Sandhya selected a toothpaste she wanted with multicolored letters: *C* red, little *r* dark blue, *e* burning turquoise. Draupadi followed her to the checkout counter and Sandhya counted out dimes, nickels, getting the sum just right.

"Where did you meet my cousin Jay?" Sandhya stood at the door of the supermarket, tucking a penny back into her purse. Her hair hung damp over her shoulders from the sudden rain.

"A party Rashid took me to."

"Rashid?"

"He was my lover. Jay knows him, you know. Met him in Berlin."

They moved toward the subway. Draupadi had two tokens out. Sandhya stood at the dark steps, the mirrors in the Leprechaun Bar winking, casting back two crooked figures, dark women, windblown, at the edge of an underground passage.

"So, you met Jay at a party," she said softly. "Do you think he's happy here?"

Draupadi did not answer. She guided her newfound friend down the steps, pushed in the two tokens, thrust Sandhya ahead into the train. They shoved through elbows, packages, bellies, heads rammed low and close. Draupadi pointed Sandhya's hand toward the overhead bar so she could hold on tight.

"Happy? What an odd question."

But Sandhya Rosenblum did not hear. She seemed so set on her own thoughts. "This man Rashid," she asked Draupadi. "What does he look like? Is he Indian?"

"No, Egyptian," Draupadi murmured. "Anyhow, it's over." And she turned to the window, the letters in the dark tunnel spray painted over darkness, glowing sites of desire.

That night, standing in the kitchen cutting up the thick stalks of the swiss chard Muriel had picked up at the farmer's market in Union Square, its leaves thick, swollen, like the spinach that grew wild by the wellside in Tiruvella, the image of her shopping companion returned. Draupadi standing in her miniskirt in the middle of the aisle of Sapna Saris ("Dream saris, yes, it means dream," Sandhya had told her), yards of multicolored fabric glimmering over her arms. The more the saleswoman unrolled, the more Draupadi wanted to drape over her wiry arms, her head, till she stood in the aisle, the variegated fabrics, silks, and chiffons making an unholy mixture over her body.

Mrs. Mathai, whose husband owned the shop, was making chitchat with Sandhya, their hometowns in India were quite close, just a river and a bridge separated them, and a few acres of palm groves. She stared at Draupadi in shock. "Who is she?" Mrs. Mathai whispered in Malayalam, and Draupadi caught the gist.

"Am I Indian at all?" Draupadi asked the astonished shopkeeper, then started laughing. "Tell me, who am I?" Her hands fluttering in embarrassment, Sandhya had to usher her friend out. They found themselves at the subway stop, but the quest for a coat was quite forgotten. After a brief ride they exited into the steamy afternoon heat, quite close, Sandhya felt, to Dora's daycare. She offered to take Draupadi in, show her the brightly painted room, the slide and swing, the sticky warm faces pressed close, tiny Dora in the red dress she had made racing toward her. But they were somewhere else entirely and Sandhya's map of Manhattan seemed useless. Draupadi, her arm around Sandhya's shoulder, drew her into a side street, off upper Broadway.

They came upon a man with a saxophone making music with his mouth, dark skin ballooning, precious music afloat. The musician was dressed in red silks, shirt, scarf, and cheap black slacks, shiny shoes with fretted leather work. Sandhya wanted to stop, watch the veins on his forearms where the sleeves were rolled up. But Draupadi pointed at a building that stood half-broken against the skyline.

"A house dismantled," she murmured. "I lived there once."

It was an old residential hotel for the poor. They were pulling it down as part of a neighborhood gentrification scheme. The threshold was a gash, the main door destroyed, the eastern wall jagged, the dust of a thousand broken bricks pouring out. Sandhya saw windows with ledges blown off, a splintered floor suspended in air. For all that she knew, it could have been a war zone.

"You lived there once?"

"Three days, when I had nowhere else to go. Look there."

Sandhya followed Draupadi's pointing hand and saw an old black woman kneeling on the sidewalk at the edge of what had been the foyer. The woman's flesh was bound with bits of cloth, soiled from overuse. Her torn skirt was held together with a pin. In spite of the heat, the old woman had on a woolen vest, to cover her nakedness. Three plastic bags finished up her costume. They were tucked in to cover the bare flesh between skirt and waistcoat. Paper bags, mouths yawning, stood on the sidewalk, some stuffed with fragments of clothing and food, much of it picked off garbage heaps. Back and forth, forth and back the old woman rocked. Keening sounds rose from her mouth, struck the damp air.

Sounds in a language Sandhya felt she could almost understand. And the old woman, what was she: African-American, Somali, Ethiopian, Indian, who could tell?

Days later Sandhya turned to Stephen: "Alexandria Hotel it's called, ever heard of it?"

"Might have passed it on the way to Hebrew School," he said, then cautioned, as her face brightened up at the shard of recollection they might share. "This was years ago, mind you. It probably wasn't called anything like that."

At night the old woman's keening came back to Sandhya, mingled with ritual rhythms, liturgies of the past, herself as a child kneeling at the icon of a black Christ, head bowed, parents on either side beseeching the Lamb of God for mercy. The next morning when Sandhya returned to the street the old woman had vanished. Where she had knelt was a strange processional. Bits of furniture were being borne out by two men: a sofa with black and blue stripes on the arms, an ancient armoire with the paint peeling, a pitcher with a broken lip that no one would ever wash from. A few yards away in front of a packing crate stood an old Haitian peddler. Sandhya moved slowly toward him, staring at the crate. On it a few of his belongings were laid out for sale. Two paintings caught her attention, one of a marketplace, the other a sugarcane field, both peopled with children. Sandhya touched the rim of the sugarcane field, struck by the turquoise sky, then found her gaze held by a tiny black doll made of string.

The strings were cunningly wound over a wooden frame, and when Sandhya lifted up the little thing, all of two inches long, she found that another identical doll detached itself from the back of the first and hung loose. Red threads and a few strands of gold held the two dolls together. The man put out his hands and she saw the dark lines on his palms.

"They looked as if they had been cut in with a knife," Sandhya told Draupadi later, a whole year later. "As if he had laid the wood in his palm to cut the dolls. Marked his flesh."

With palms splayed apart, the man made the dolls play. When one twitched, the other twitched, not the identical arm or foot, but its counterpart, left hand to right, right foot to left, mimicking a nervous motion.

"How much?" She had to have that doll.

He put up two fingers and Sandhya Rosenblum took two dollars out of her purse and gave it to him. She slipped the dolls into her purse, then noticed Draupadi way over on the other side of the street, speaking to a man in a red shirt. Sandhya crossed the street quickly. Her friend hadn't heard her call, but she would make her way over to her. The man had dark hair, but was balding slightly. He was gesturing with his hands. There was something about his eyes, his cheekbones, that drew her. He was Indian, surely, Punjabi perhaps. She crossed the street, holding her purse tight to her side.

"Ah, Sandhya," Draupadi said, "allow me to introduce you."

Sandhya smiled and watched in delight as the man gave a little bow. His manners seemed so European.

"Rashid el Obeid," he said to her, extending his hand. "I'm a friend of your cousin Jay. And Draupadi too knows me."

There was a pucker to his lips as he said this. Touching his hand, Sandhya Rosenblum felt a curious warmth fill her. Somewhere, in the middle distance, over the sounds of an approaching bus, she heard the mellow tones of the saxophone. The man in red silk was approaching, his music twisting sunlight, till it hung in threads above her head and she was forced to crane her neck, gaze upward at the shimmering light. Staring at Sandhya Rosenblum, who stood at his side, Rashid caught his breath, marveling at her taut, dark beauty.

For the next few weeks Sandhya went about her daily life in a mild state of agitation. When she lay on her bed, after having her morning coffee, she felt her heart pounding, a sparrow caged in a cupped palm. She caught herself in the kitchen about to pour milk into the frying pan instead of oil. Or unpacking the cheese to slice for meat curry instead of the customary onions.

The face of the man she had seen on the sidewalk kept returning. First she saw the back of his neck, then his hand, holding her own. That shirt he wore, it was the color of flame. He was talking to her, and when he turned his back, his right shoe was in a puddle of water. He raised it sharply, dashed off the water on the sidewalk. She had to see him again. But Draupadi had broken all links with him. When she mentioned his name on the phone, Draupadi sounded slightly irritated.

"I'm returning his books to him, including *Season of Migration,* you know, that Tayib Salih book."

"No, no," Sandhya murmured.

"Well, I'd never heard of it either till Rashid gave it to me. Part of it's set in a village by the Nile, the other part in London." Her voice trailed off. "That day in the street, he asked me if I still had it."

"Doesn't he have another copy?" Sandhya asked. Her fingers fiddled with the string dolls she had set above the fridge. She tried to make them extend their feet, dance a little.

"He says he wants to teach it in his post-colonial course and he's misplaced his other copy. Thought Zahir might have carried it off. Then this morning, guess what, Mama called."

"Your mother?"

"Yeah, from Gingee. Wants to come out and visit."

The very next morning—it was Sunday with cheap international rates—Sandhya dialed her parents' number over and over again; rewarded finally, she heard her mother's voice on the other side, warbling as if the syllables were mouthed through water.

"So, how's Appa?" Sandhya asked. There had been worrisome news in the last letter of chest pains her father was suffering.

"Those pains are all gone. It's the mango season and you know how he loves to pick the fruit himself. Comes in with his hands all smelling of mango juice. No, *mol,* its just that he's started coughing a lot."

"Coughing?"

"It must be all the dust from the construction."

"I didn't know you were adding to the house."

"It's the new water tower. Didn't I tell you we needed one, right at the edge of the courtyard? We have the best architect we could find," Sosa said proudly." He was trained in the United States, California-side, and now wants to work on indigenous forms of architecture."

"What does that mean?" Sandhya didn't want her voice to be so abrupt. Except this was just the sort of man her mother might have tried to get her to marry a few years ago.

"Tiles, I suppose, and sloping roofs. Courtyards, windows cut in teak. Adapting the Kerala style to the contemporary age."

"And those bright pineapples built with Dubai money."

Her mother started laughing at the other end:

"No, my dear child, no pineapples. So what are you up to now? And how's Stephen? And my little grandchild?"

"They're all fine, Mama. I even tried an American dish with some swiss chard Muriel gave me. Listen, I wondered if you could tell me how to make *meenvevichethu.*"

Sosa was pleased, Sandhya could tell, and directed her to the *Best of Kerala Cookery* to double-check details—the book included not only traditional fish curries, but also sweets such as pineapple upside-down cake and Scottish pudding—and then led her through the necessary rituals. The marinade needed an earthenware pot. Did Sandhya have one? Well, she could make do with the new Pyrex dish she had purchased from Zabar's. And the Le Creuset casserole? Yes, that would be just right for the slow cooking the fish needed. The black balls of tamarind that Sosa had sent through Sakhi in the spring, yes, that would be fine. Be sure to let it sit though, in boiling water, till the juices soak out, Sosa cautioned.

So her mother's voice, calming her, led Sandhya through the details of the meal she was to prepare; fish curry, dal, sambar, thorun, rice, golden papad were all on the menu. Putting down the phone, Sandhya breathed deeply, then sat on the couch by the window, making up the guest list. Stephen would be pleased, she knew, would want her to have a dinner party.

S o Sandhya Rosenblum had a dinner party. It was just the sort of thing she was raised to do. No servants, but she could shine at the chosen tasks. The moment she stepped in the door, Draupadi realized that her new friend had plotted and planned for days in advance. How else to or-chestrate all the fresh herbs and savory yogurts and that fish, delicious smelling, not Mexican, or Caribbean either. Draupadi's own mother, stuck in the small clapboard house behind the Soda Shop, had relied on instant foods, hamburger, mash, that sort of thing, running to Trinidad goat curry only as a last resort. But here was the stuff of dreams, a cuisine subtle and elaborate, the fruit of seemingly endless labor.

She found Sandhya standing by the counter, dressed in green. Her hair was tied back, low on her neck. Light from the window marked out her cheeks. She moved to the counter where objects clarified, a mixing bowl, a pair of child's scissors, a metal spoon, a blender ready to fall apart, three bowls with the fish mark on them, the kind you pick up in Chinatown for a dollar-fifty. Sipping at the Scotch Stephen had pressed on her, Draupadi squinted a little as if with the effort to concentrate. "Sakhi's coming," Sandhya murmured. Was she a little nervous, Draupadi wondered, or was it just all that cooking?

"All the way from Philadelphia. Remember, I told you about her. Her husband, Ravi, can't make it. Had to go off to Germany. Some deal or the other. And Jay."

But Draupadi cut in. Scotch in hand, she quipped:

"Consider the roses!"

"Roses?" Sandhya looked puzzled, then gave a little smile not wanting to offend, rubbed her hands against the green dress. Above her head were pots and pans neatly hooked onto a white metal grid picked up at Zabar's the week before.

"Since you took me shopping, I've been out on my own." She pointed to the pot rack behind her head. The kitchen was adequate. Enough space for two adults to push pots and pans, make do. Enough for one dimpled three-year-old to shove peanut butter down her throat. Hanging above the rack, a bunch of dried thyme, mixed with sage, knotted up and hanging from a pin. That caught the light, and Dora's hair as she trotted in, looking for her mother. Sandhya did not notice the child; she was bent over the stove, ladling chilis out with a spoon, tossing mustard seed into hot oil, mixing in turmeric and *garam masala.*

Draupadi heard her own voice rise. It must be the echo in the small kitchen, she thought, but her voice sounded disembodied, unreal, a poor performance:

"I meant roses. Sandhya, we're women of color. Think of what Emerson, our household philosopher, said. Be like the roses, cut off the past, frisk it, skin it, live in the present! You can't keep on cooking all wonderful Eastern food."

She meant this little speech as a joke, but Sandhya kept her face averted. She was hurt, Draupadi sensed, so putting down her glass she touched Sandhya on the cheek. "I'm so sorry, my dear, I didn't mean it like that. It's great all this food. Perhaps I'm just a bit jealous."

Sandhya dabbed at her eyes and brought out the cookbook. In that tiny kitchen Draupadi found herself gazing at a cover image, two women in white Kerala saris kneeling under a palm tree by a quiet river. A silver tray with coconuts and fresh chilies rested at their side.

"So would that be home?"

Sandhya nodded. "They're all dressed up. As if for a festival. But the palm tree and river, that's Kerala. Hyderabad, where I worked for the Travel Agency, is quite different, much drier, much more built up. It's an old Muslim city, a kingdom of quite a different sort."

Then the mustard seeds started popping and Sandhya had to turn her attention to the pan. There were loud voices in the living room and Draupadi wandered in. Saw Jay in the corner. And that woman in brown, her hair drawn back into a long plait, must be Sakhi.

"Sandhya, where's my dear Sandhya?" Sakhi was calling out, her arms raised, ready to topple off the captain's bed. Draupadi felt her breath tighten. Rashid was sitting by the window. Had Sandhya invited him? Or had Jay just brought him along? She made her way forward, casually, conscious of her tight leather skirt, the mound of hair she had pinned up, now slipping down her neck. That was what he'd been, her free fall, and now she had to cut loose.

"Ah, Mr. El Obeid; fancy meeting you here!"

Rashid looked straight at her, whispered, "Draupadi," a slight inflection to the *r* in her name. Then Sandhya burst in, the child clinging to her skirts, and in her arms the fish with its cover of cariapatta leaves. The scents of tamarind and garlic filled the room. Rashid rose quickly, offering to take the dish from her, set it on the table, and Stephen, eyes narrowing, watched from the corner. But Sakhi was engaging him in conversation about the situation in Kuwait.

"So many Indians there, from construction workers to college teachers, bankers, surgeons. This terrible war, it's an Asian war, you know."

And Stephen nodded, his mind on the sudden animation in his wife as she handed Rashid the fish and swept her hands through her hair. How alive she seemed all of a sudden, Stephen thought, and was pierced by a tenderness for his wife. He had done right, just right, bringing her here. He would buy her that rice cooker she had set her heart on, for Hanukkah. Her eyes would light up. She would kiss him on the cheek, the nose. But Sakhi broke into his reflections, muttering something about domestic violence in the South Asian community. The lack of resources. The things that woman talked about. What did he know of that? He swung the conversation closer to home and said firmly:

"Connecticut is in trouble, you know. Unemployment to the hilt, stocks falling, brokers stripped to the skin in swimming pools."

"Eat cake," mumbled Jay. "Eat apple strudel," as he strode out of the room. He needed more ice in his glass, more bourbon; he needed to think about the bit of lens Gautam had pressed into his hands, over a year ago, made him promise to give Sandhya. And all this while it had lain in Jay's camera bag. Right now it was burning a hole in his pocket. What had possessed him to bring it this evening? With Sandhya so taken with Rashid el Obeid, what was he to do?

Jay stepped sharply into the kitchen, picked up a sponge, and wiped the counter. From his pocket, he pulled out a handkerchief, unfolded it, took out a thick piece of glass. The light from the sink shone on the lens and the surface swarmed with silvery reflections, men and women and angels, dancing in the molten territory of longing. Jay touched the edge of the glass with his index finger. It was cool to the touch. He lowered his face, as if doing homage, touched his cheek to the glass. He saw a shape there, dark, amorphous, a shadow of the past cast by the visible present. Where was the past, who did it belong to? He had no answers to the questions but felt that, lacking a past, the present would be sucked of its sense, made void.

A scene returned to him, the New Mysore Café in Hyderabad. He was sitting with Gautam underneath the fan. Seeing his cousin enter the dark room in her thin cotton sari, a pile of newspapers in her hand, he had waved. Sandhya had moved quickly toward the two men, seating herself between them. But Gautam seemed hardly to notice. In minutes he had wandered away, into the kitchen. Leaving Sandhya alone, Jay was forced to go in search of his friend. In the kitchen of the New Mysore Café, Jay saw pots simmering, griddles gleaming with half-cooked *dosas*. He glimpsed Gautam's dark brown shirt against the table where the cook's assistant was chopping a pile of fresh coriander. Gautam was bent over, listening to the lad. They were old familiars in the café and often Gautam strolled into the kitchen to have a conversation with the cook and kitchen boys, taste the rasam or the sambar, take the temperature, as he put it.

"The people are all around us," he murmured to Jay, with an impish grin. "We must know what they're thinking, saying."

"So what are they saying?"

"It's hard to get fresh coriander in the city now."

"Coriander?"

"They're stopping the trucks that bring vegetables from the south. Setting up roadblocks. Even setting fire to the trucks to create the semblance of anti-Hindu violence."

"Come, my cousin is waiting. You'll like her."

Jay put his arm on his friend's elbow and drew him out of the kitchen. Back at the table, they sipped the coffee the waiter had brought and Jay saw Sandhya gazing at Gautam with that fixed shining look. It was just a few months after that first meeting that Gautam was taken into police custody, to emerge emaciated, malaria-ridden, his eyeglasses smashed by the police. He came to live with Jay.

For two weeks, till his friend could get him a new pair of glasses, Gautam was confined to the one small room and balcony Jay used on the outskirts of the city. When smoke from the factories across the river wafted toward him, Gautam gagged. He reached out for the nearest wall or tabletop to steady himself. He felt his guts cramped with the memory that skin and fatty tissue still retained of cigarette after burning cigarette stubbed out on his navel.

"Who are they?" the voices kept pounding. "Who, who? Tell. Who are you? What is your code name?"

"My name is Gautam, Gautam Reddy. Reddy," he repeated. "I was born in Hyderabad."

"What is your PWG name? Your accomplices when the train was firebombed? Women and children burning in the metal compartments. Think. Think. Remember. Can you remember?"

And the cigarettes stubbed into him, pain so pure his brain stopped. Then the burning eased, and hurt poured all through his flesh. But questions began again, accompanied by beatings, electrodes attached to his genitals, the sharp rod up his anus almost rupturing his kidneys.

In odd moments of lucidity, as he crouched in the damp cell, hands chained behind his back, palms clamped together, Gautam tried to think of his mother, the gentleness of her, that shy laugh she had. But it was years since he had seen her. He had kept apart to protect her. Just once in the cell he had tried to invoke the god Ganapati, whose carved stone icon he had kept in a drawer in his old room. He recalled smooth black stone etched with diamond shapes over a belly forever pregnant. Ganapati had his glowing trunk upraised. To be held there, in Ganapati's trunk, his whole life written over again. How would that be? It would be peace to be wiped out and written over again with a god's broken tusk. He wept at the thought. Tears he could not wipe away flowed over his face.

Then Sandhya came to him. He struggled to open his eyes, to reach out his hand, grope toward her. But his eyes were sealed tight with blood and dried mucus and his hands hung limp in the manacles. She returned to him time and again, her long lashes wet with river water, not sorrowful or anything. He was surprised to hear her giggle a little, as she had done when a gull swooping by so low splashed her with cool river water. Then a segment of smooth, scented skin, about the size of the burn on his navel, a fragment of her skin from just above the right breast, hung before him, weightless.

Trying to coax his friend back to what he thought of as the ordinary world, Jay stumbled about Hyderabad. In his right pocket was a bit of glass from Gautam's old spectacles. The police had returned his belongings in a brown paper bag, the broken spectacles together with one stained shirt and Gautam's private notebook, its innards ripped out. Jay cradled the inch-long fragment of glass in his hand, wrapping it in his white cotton handkerchief. It was his hope that someone, somewhere, could match it up with an existing pair and so give Gautam a way back into the visible world.

On Nampally Road he found Optical Palace. Jay squatted on the sidewalk and the old man who ran the eyeglass shop set the shard of glass at his feet, picked through the mound of old spectacles he had so carefully amassed. After fifteen minutes of squinting through odd bits of glass, his fingers lit on a pair of green frames with flecks of brown. With his free hand the old man picked up the smashed lens and adjusted it to his eye, removed it again, matching it with the older intact lens.

"Do you mind if I take a photo?"

The old man posed for him, the broken bit of glass in his right hand, recycled frame in his left, both raised to the sunlit air as if in prayer.

In the photo the old man's face was pursed up, squinting like a small child, white peaked cap a little askew on his head.

He had caught a shining instant, Jay thought to himself years later, scrutinizing the image. And a moment caught like a live dragonfly clasped in a child's palm, wings still sieving sunlight from a stream, lets us live. Live and breathe.

Back home he found Gautam bent over his torn notebook, drowsy with fatigue. "Close your eyes," Jay commanded his friend, then placed the green spectacles over the bridge of his friend's nose. "Open, open," he cried, as if they were both children, "Open Sesame!"

Gautam slowly opened his eyes. Through the speckled glass of an ancient pair of spectacles a man on Nampally Road had found for him, he stared at Jay's face. As he tilted his head, a white bird clarified in the middle distance, its claws dug into a telegraph pole.

"See!" cried Jay, as the two friends embraced and Jay brandished the bottle of beer he had picked up on his way home. Over rice and leftover dal and beer, over fresh green chilies, sliced and salted, Jay read out lines from a page in the book he had borrowed from the American library high on a hill.

His voice rose as he read, trilling over unfamiliar words, racing over exotic images with a verbal excitation he had not felt in a long while, a clear varnish of feeling, reflecting the unreal. His motives were simple. He wanted to take Gautam out of himself, make him laugh:

"*Extended vibrations,*" he began. "*Ziggurats ZIG I to IV stars of the Tigris-Euphrates basin. . . . Busby Berkeley kiss me you have ended the war by simply singing in your Irene Dunne foreskin.*"

Tears dammed behind the new spectacles still on his face, Gautam started laughing. He laughed so hard the small wooden table threatened to topple over. Gautam's arms were clenched around his chest.

"I would like to meet Irene Dunne," he said as he coughed through tears.

"Irene Dunne, enter my war," I would say to her. "Remember that girl in Bangalore, buying sweets at Spencer's? With a frock on and big ribbons in her hair. That's how I imagine Irene."

He stopped, for his chest hurt with all that laughter. He reached into his pocket and handed Jay the broken bit of lens his friend had brought back to him.

Then his voice sank to a whisper. He looked at the thick shard of glass and Jay heard him say, "Give that to Sandhya. Please, when you see her." Jay had taken the lens, wrapped it in a muslin handkerchief, set it on his window ledge. It had traveled with him to Delhi, Berlin, New York.

Now, hearing voices approach the kitchen, he picked it off the countertop, folded it back into his musty handerkerchief, and swiftly, as Sandhya entered with Rashid, a sprig of fresh coriander in her hand, he thrust the little package into his trouser pocket.

"Coriander!" she said laughing. "Remember, Jay, all those piles of fresh coriander we would buy in Hyderabad? I was telling Rashid about it. Cairo too has coriander, he tells me."

The scent of the tiny crinkled leaves rose through his nostrils and Jay, leaning against the counter, shut his eyes. Suddenly he felt the whole earth was turning.

She was turning, facing him, shining into his face, thought Draupadi in a daze of liquor, watching Sandhya with Rashid. Then she saw them dance around each other, plates laden with food, and sensed the first excitation she herself had once felt, a raw fragrance, a lure such as animals put out, camouflages ready to be flung off as hunter and hunted get to ease themselves in, blood pounding in the soles, the skull.

She felt she had never seen Rashid so excited in public, and perhaps it was all the Scotch she was having. Draupadi could have sworn that several languages spilled out of his mouth: Arabic, French, bits of Greek, German from his philosophical studies, phrases of Hindi, even his perfect British English, though this last, which might have served to contain his agitation, almost washed away, a bridge to which no one clings as the wind rises. She noticed, too, that Sandhya was looking out of the window, pretending not to listen to Rashid, who had taken to addressing Stephen:

"Now you must admit that were it not for the new internationalism, the whole Rushdie business would not have blown out of proportion. Faxes, e-mail, CNN, the whole lot. Why, some of the death threats, I was told on good authority, came via fax. If TV in Lahore hadn't carried what began in Iran, and then if Bradford hadn't carried the news, things might have been very different. Islam is getting a bad name in the West, not of course that I'm a believer. Just a cultural Muslim if you wish."

Stephen felt himself getting hot under the collar.

"Now, of course, I'm not a believer either. Who is, these days?"

He looked about helplessly, as if summoning his wife to his aid, but Sandhya was giving Sakhi the details of how to get to Zabar's from Penn Station.

"But that's not the point, is it?" Stephen was marshaling his wits about him. "Human beings need something to believe in, and these new societies, what do they give? No wonder the Indian ideal of secularism is breaking down. And there's militia training, I hear, in the Midwest. In the United States we have our extremists too, you know."

He was spent after that little speech and didn't bother to listen to his guest, who was putting on quite a performance: about the book he wanted to write on post-colonial identity. New York City of course was the perfect location in which to put such a narrative together. And mightn't one argue that varied languages altered the structure of consciousness, made one better equipped for life in a world of multiple anchorages such as New York presented?"

"Surely one can live an ethical life with just one language," Stephen murmured, the Biblical story of the Tower of Babel vivid in his mind.

"Quite so, but what of the Muslim immigrants in Europe, in America? Who will learn their languages?"

Stephen found his thoughts in tumult. Issues related to language made him feel delicate, vulnerable. They pointed up his failings. He sensed that the ability to learn languages was a gift one was born with, lacking which there was little remedy. The phrases of Yiddish he had gleaned from his paternal grandmother had proved burdensome, threatening to flood him when he traveled in North India, and some simple response in Hindi was required, like: "More tea, please" or "How much for those mangoes?" It was as if the pressure of another tongue set up a counter-world, a chaos that rimmed around the fragility of his spoken English, which at such times turned rigid with the precision he attempted to force into it. But he was drawn to the soft, orotund syllables of his grandmother's speech, and a more natural life it seemed to him had sprung from her hands, her mouth. The fumes of her kitchen seemed a haven from the cutthroat competitiveness of the New York he was flung into, the world he had to return to time and again.

"Like playing tennis without a ball, eh?"

Rashid sat up and laughed and Sandhya, who had forgotten the question, trembled in her agitation. Though she managed to restore a quietness in her demeanor, the thought of two rackets striking an invisible object excited her in a way she could not have explained. She felt Rashid was enormously learned, pressured from within by the multiple speeches that jostled in him.

As for herself, unable to read or write her mother tongue, Malayalam, for she had been brought up within the boundaries of a new India, where regional divisions were not considered overly important. She had fallen back on the Hindi of her school days and the English that people of her class mixed in with whatever Indian language they spoke, the polyglot nature of their sentences a sign of breeding. Stephen's American English pleased her, accents most soothing to her ears, signaling an intactness she felt she could never aspire to, his language undeterred by border crossings into other, fraught territories. This belief was bolstered in her by what he told her quite early on: that had his grandparents remained in Poland, he would surely never have been born. The thought of the boxcars, the mechanized death camps that European Jews had faced, filled her with terror, and she was suffused with gratitude for his survival, for his grandparents' percipience in leaving for America. He seemed so whole to her.

The word *whole*—which she had discovered for herself in a rare reading of Coleridge, something her B.A. Final teacher in Delhi had counseled her to do—worked well during her brief musings. She found it in the fat prose book: "The poet brings the whole soul of man into activity." Now the fact that woman was not mentioned didn't worry her a jot. What took hold of Sandhya was the notion of a whole soul, something that had previously never touched her, not even in the compulsory churchgoing her father forced her to. Indeed, the three or four hours a week of Syrian Christian worship in the churches of her childhood only served to bruise yet further her sense of purity in the self. The doctrine of the religion of her birth, Christ spread-eagled on the cross, the bitter blood drops on his brow, the fierce stain of evil, nothing of this granted her the clarity of spirit she longed for. What could make one "whole" was good; what tormented and splintered was bad. She glanced furtively at Rashid, then turned back to her husband. There was something in Stephen's delicacy, an innocence as she felt it, that still held her.

Watching her old lover, Draupadi felt very tired. She thought she might distract herself by talking to Dora. The child was tottering about, rubbing her little fists into her eyes, almost asleep on her feet. But no, there was

Sakhi drawing her onto her lap, offering to take her to brush her teeth, and there was Stephen turning to her, in such serious fashion:

"So what do you do with yourself, Draupadi, these days?"

He persisted. "I know you do your art, the performance pieces, the mixed media you told us about. But can you make a living at that?"

She shook her head, about to plunge into details of the legal copyediting she took in to make ends meet, the part-time work in art galleries, hanging up exhibits, making sure the art works arrived on time. But suddenly Jay burst into their little circle. "The bombs!" he cried. "The bombs have started to fall. American bombardment." And for a moment she felt there was something comical in the way he gesticulated, moved his body. But hearing him, they all fell quiet and even the steady munching of the food stopped.

"Think of all those innocent people caught in the middle," Rashid broke in, grim.

"It depends which middle, doesn't it," offered Jay, at which the conversation turned quite abruptly to the Iraqi attack on Kuwait and the American response. Sandhya felt as if she were stranded in a field full of wild grass, with four companions playing badminton without a net, the game veering wildly, the target caught and struck, the blue sky flashing. So she sat there, her hands in her lap, and wondered out loud about what would happen to her Uncle Reji, the cardiologist who was working in Kuwait.

A week later, when Draupadi visited, Sandhya told her in detail about Uncle Reji, who had had to flee Kuwait: "Masses of money. He had to flee with his wife when the Iraqis invaded. Good thing the children were in college in India. Uncle and auntie took a desert road as far as they could, abandoned the car, got into a truck with some Pakistani workers and ended up in the dry land outside Amman. There was barbed wire all around, in that transit camp."

Sandhya sat on the brown quilt, her hands poised at her side. Watching her, Draupadi wondered if she should say something about Rashid. How she still dreamed of him sometimes, how he never wanted to live with any one person, was plagued by restlessness, how his cousin Zeinab, his first love, still haunted him. But she kept her mouth shut. Of course, Sandhya would be the authentic thing, as far as Rashid was concerned. True Third World. In her agitation, she spilled a little of her coffee. Sandhya kept on:

"There were bombs all around, where Uncle Reji was. Amma told me on the phone. I got such a clear line."

"Whose bombs where they, do you know?" Draupadi asked softly.

As if a disquieting thought had come over her, Sandhya got up hastily, poured Draupadi more coffee from a gleaming pot, offered her a plate with little samosas on it. They were bought, she confided, from the frozen food section of the supermarket.

"Imagine that," Sandhya said: "Frozen *samosas.*" Then shivered as if with thoughts of desert nights when even *samosas* might freeze.

"I got a very clear line last night," she added. "Amma told me that neighbors from my father's village have a daughter who lived in Kuwait. She was eight months pregnant when they fled. She gave birth in the sand, in a transit camp outside Amman. There was very little water to wash her or the baby. He lived, a male child."

She looked tearful as she said this. Dora waddled in and Sandhya drew her close.

"Well, we're safe in Manhattan!" Draupadi reassured her. "Safe and sound, and you have Stephen to take care of you."

"He's in Connecticut all day, you know that, don't you?" She said this in a low voice, through the child's hair. Then, looking down, she murmured, clearly enough:

"Sometimes I remember things. I try not to."

Would forgetting free her? An image shone in puddles of water, in the plate glass of grocery stores as Sandhya walked the streets of Manhattan in search of fresh coriander or okra. But whose face was it? The features wavered in water, in glass, and she was filled with unspeakable longing. Gautam was dead, Jay had told her that, even showing her a bit of glass from his old spectacles. Why had Jay done that?

"You have a fine husband, and a lovely child," Jay added. It was so unlike him to talk in that way. She had touched his wrist then, and he smiled at her in melancholy fashion, as if he knew something she herself were not aware of:

"Be careful, Bachi!"

"Of what?" She had asked her question more than once, but he just shook his head, begged off, saying he had a photo assignment, something in Lexington, in the Indian neighborhood.

"Local scenes, that sort of thing. Draupadi tells me you took her to that side?"

She nodded, then let him go. As she searched out vegetables, or the tiny bananas that Dora relished, trying to make the shopping fill up her whole day, it was another face that overlay Gautam's. Sometimes the features merged, one into the other, eyes and mouth blurring. She lost herself in the play of luminous light and did not notice the Chinese woman waving at her. When she glanced up, the woman was looking at her curiously. Next to her stood a man, her husband perhaps, who was about the same age as Sandhya's father.

She sensed she was cast adrift in a world neither of her parents had prepared her for. Had her father ever known passion in his life? Certainly not for his wife, though there was a feeling of duty there that could not be denied. Somewhere in the world, wasn't there a woman Varki had loved? In England, perhaps, where he'd gone as a student just after World War II, or in Karachi, where he was posted just before Indian independence? Someone whose hands, whose face moved him almost to tears, whose name became for him a litany of longing. A Helen, or a Hadiya? Sandhya stopped short, she had almost walked off the curb, into oncoming traffic.

That night, before she fell asleep, she drew out the tattered notebook from her teenage years. She had wrapped it in muslin and borne it with her to America. She stared at the pages she had scrawled two decades ago.

"If you want me to live as a woman, why educate me? ... God, why teach me to read and write?"

The rage in her seemed alive again. It fused with the live blood pounding in her head. Who was she now? Would she be able to live her own life, feel her way through? She knew she wasn't cut of the same cloth as Navleen, her cousin who had joined the Foreign Service and was posted to Finland, or even cousin Nilufer, who had started her own interior decorating company in Bangalore, both modern, independent women. But in spite of her own fears of solitude, she couldn't prevent her feelings and she hated to be dictated to. No wonder her mother had been so scared, sensing her rage. Once a woman knew how to read and write, the world was open. "Use your mind," her grandmother had counseled her, "and then you can live your life." What did it mean?

She thought of grandmother Eliamma at the edge of the veranda, staring out at the well. Ayah had taken Sandhya to the well, cautioned her on how dangerous it was for girls.

"For boys, too?" Sandhya had asked, but Ayah had insisted on the special danger for little girls. When Thoma's sixteen-year-old daughter was found dead in his well, the rumors stared flying through town.

"How plump her belly was."

"It wasn't the water that filled her?"

"Two months pregnant at least. Perhaps three."

"Oh, the poor soul, her eyes dark as bees in all that sodden flesh. Her skin whitened with water. And her red clothes floating about her."

"Three whole days she lay in the disused well. They had to grip her by the throat with grappling hooks."

"The men were scared to go down, in case there was an evil demon."

Ayah had gripped her by the elbow, taken her back to the edge of the well: "See what I was telling you?"

Little Sandhya stood on tiptoe, conscious of her grandmother seated on a stool in the middle distance. On tiptoe the child stood, staring in. But it was not the plump, sodden eyes of Thoma's pregnant daughter she saw. In the midst of the dark pool, welling up from the earth, Sandhya saw her own face. Her own two eyes gazed back at her from cool water, and her chiseled nostrils quivered and reformed. A dragonfly coasted by, from the guava tree, skimming air, and the image broke.

"Ayah, look, look," Sandhya ran crying to her *ayah*, who was discussing the new cockerels with the first maid: how ferocious they were in the pen, how their claws glimmered in the twilight, how new chickens might be expected.

"I saw, I saw!" Sandhya cried out, stumbling on the gravel, but Ayah was not listening. So she ran into the kitchen and buried herself in her grandmother's soft-smelling lap. An ancient lap that smelled of rosewater and eucalyptus and soft, white cotton covering the crinkled skin.

"There, there," her grandmother Eliamma murmured, holding her excitable grandchild. Sandhya's grandmother had married into a landowning family a mere ten miles away from the village where she was born. And her life had been conducted, or so it seemed to the child, in strict accordance with all the proprieties. When she died at the age of seventy-five, she was buried in the ancient churchyard where her husband's people had lain for centuries.

One clear afternoon, sipping tea with Draupadi in her living room, Sandhya described what she could of her grandmother's life: the sweetmeats her grandmother would prepare with jaggery and fresh coconut, the ripe mangoes she sniffed, spending hours bent over the baskets the servants brought in, choosing the best for the household.

"Did she ever leave your grandfather's town?" Draupadi asked.

"Not that I know of," Sandhya replied. "She never left the compound without escort. And the *manthrakodi*, the rich brocaded sari her in-laws draped over her head on the wedding day, that very same sari lay over her face, her head, when she was borne out on a bier."

How quiet Draupadi kept. Staring at her friend's impassive face, Sandhya wondered if Draupadi were working on a performance, casting her in it, casting all these Indians who were adrift in the new world. But would her grandmother ever find a place in Draupadi's imaginings? And what would Grandmother Eliamma think of Draupadi, if they were ever to meet? She would want to annoint her head with coconut oil, braid her hair, dress her in red saris, and Draupadi might love it. And Sandhya and Draupadi could giggle about it, like schoolgirls on the way to the well. But Grandmother was dead, her soul afloat in a dark river where the canoes of her childhood plied their way, a river winding through paddy fields, past old teak bridges. Born within sight of the river, she was buried in the churchyard just inches above the floodwaters.

And here she was, the eldest granddaughter, sitting in an apartment in a great metropolis three continents away, living a life that had no ready pattern. And all she had at hand were scraps of space cobbled together, morsels of time, scooped up like burning flesh. The borders she had crossed had marked her very soul. Now she was a tattooed thing, thought Sandhya Rosenblum. And who would find her beautiful?

W hen Rashid called to invite her for lunch, Sandhya allowed herself to be surprised. Deep down she felt she was falling into the life that was meant for her. At night she dreamed of a well, its cool waters glimmering. In the morning she was in a panic about what to wear for their meeting. She shifted between choices: the green linen dress she had picked out from Bloomingdale's, with Draupadi's help; the beige *khatau* sari her mother had given her; a fine pink *kurta*. The look in his eyes when he first glimpsed her rounding the corner, entering the restaurant, would be reward enough.

As bombs fell in desert lands, the lovers met in Chinese restaurants, ordered hot and sour soup, the lunch of the day. Once Rashid read out something from his notebook to her. He was working on a larger manuscript, but this was something he wanted to share with her. He took her ideas seriously, wanted her response—she could hardly believe it. As he read out the lines she lightly skimmed his hand with her palm, touching the rim of his left thumb. She noticed the black mole on it. As she nibbled spicy prawns in garlic sauce, he read out the *hadith,* first in Arabic, then in English translation:

"The Messenger of God said: Man should not say 'Time be damned' for I am Time. I send the day and the night and if I wished I could seize them." He gazed at her face as he read and Sandhya felt herself growing breathless. The waiter, hovering with the teapot, decided not to interrupt.

When she spoke to her mother over the weekend, Sandhya found she could not respond as quickly as she might to the questions about Dora's dance classes, the new tablecloth, the price of fresh vegetables. Something else gripped her inner world, a turbulence she could scarcely spell out. The thought of Rashid took root with an intensity she could not have predicted. He, in turn, overwhelmed by his emotions, threw caution to the winds. He would have her, he swore, whatever that took. And they would try their best to keep the world from knowing.

After weekly lunches in small, out-of-the-way restaurants, Rashid drew her to Zahir's for tea. But something dangerous was at hand and he would have to make sure Sandhya was not mixed up in it. Rashid had heard Zahir whisper of a circle of acquaintances, men who imaged themselves soldiers in the army of God, secret agents in the cause of purity who were ready to blow up buildings, bridges. Rashid could not be sure from the phone conversations Zahir conducted as he paced in the kitchen how serious his friend was. But he felt breathless as he watched the short, squat figure, outlined against the kitchen window. As to why his friend, who was raised in a liberal, Westernized household, would be drawn to such moral desperadoes, Rashid could not say, unless it was the craving for excitement, danger in action raised to a requirement, an addictive impious desire.

But Rashid tried to put all this out of his mind. He needed Zahir's friendship, the warmth, the room in Brooklyn. Rightly or wrongly, he felt that there was a trust between them deep enough for him to dissuade Zahir from any desperate action. Then, too, Rashid felt his childhood friend was growing dizzy with the long trips he took, his brain softened by dreams of world unity in the oddest places: as he was bent almost double in plastic chairs in airport lounges; reclining at ease on elegant leather in cocktail bars; back erect, dining on grilled quail at the Grand in Brighton, its facade just fixed after the IRA attempt to bomb Mrs. T. and her cabinet. Zahir described to Rashid his experience in Brighton. He had set a morsel of bird flesh to his mouth and, staring out across the balcony at the gray seas, imagined a lovely woman calling him. But as he bit into the meat, a disillusionment awoke. All he could see were the pleasure palaces of Brighton rocking in cold water, old piers dissolving away, grand ceremonials of glass and metal, isolate, unreachable.

When Sandhya agreed to visit him in Brooklyn, Rashid spent hours preparing Zahir's room. He laid out fine cups from his friend's hoard, twirled incense under the teapot so the tea would glow with the milkiness of rich fumes, a trick he learned from watching the cooks in his grandfather's house near the Nile. He laid out plates and forks and white napkins for her. He imagined her lips touching the white fabric his cousin Zeinab had sent him one summer, linen squares, a delight for the eyes, a four-cornered field ready to be filled with the beloved's touch. He pulled out the table in Zahir's front room and smoothed down the quilt his friend had laid on the bed. He saw Sandhya, her dark body outspread, coming, coming to him.

What was it about her that moved him so? Perhaps it was something about her mouth that made her seem young, naive, not really comprehending the language spoken around her. At times he felt he needed to drown her in his mother tongue. And the fact that she comprehended not a jot of Arabic bothered him not in the slightest. As he sang to her, she would murmur back sounds in her mother tongue, whose lyric delights would sweep him along. Shutting his eyes, he imagined himself on a boat on the Nile, the tall rushes, the dark soil of Upper Egypt cut from him by rushing water. Both he and Sandhya were foreigners in America, they would cradle each other. He would cast her afloat on the Nile and with her, he would sail on the Ganges.

She entered his dreams, her features merging with those of an Egyptian child he had known decades ago, when he was seven and she six and they played on the terrace in Cairo. Cormorants from the salt marshes south of Alexandria clustered on the balustrades and men bearing huge bundles of cotton and crates of sesame bound up with ropes cried out from the streets below. He heard the cries of very poor men. Later, the sounds shifted to marches of revolt on the dry, palm-lined streets of Cairo.

Rashid stared at Sandhya, who sat on the bed in Zahir's room. He was trembling, filled with her touch, her smell. Sandhya's right hand, a little cold as always, rested on the pillow he had plumped and set out for her. Her legs were out straight, but then her limbs relaxed again, and she ran her hand through her hair. After his tongue had filled her lips, yet again with a delicious warmth, she opened her mouth carefully:

"I never thought I could love like this."

"What do you mean?"

He moved closer, sitting carefully between her parted legs, her thighs pressed around his wider, rougher ones.

Suddenly she felt shy.

"Have you ever done this before?"

He shook his head, mutely.

"Like this means in Brooklyn. Naked in Brooklyn."

She started laughing, not knowing what she was saying.

"You mean by the side of a kitchen in Brooklyn, no clothes on?"

"Of course!"

What she had meant to say and was too frightened to think out loud was that she never thought passion would enter her life like this, through all her body parts, brain, spine, vagina, anus. Just ten minutes ago he had turned her over, pulled her knees under her so that she faced the window, looking for all the world like a tottery brown cow in her grandfather's compound.

He leaned over intently, trying to put some cream in her and then move his penis in. But it was too tight, it hurt her, and she cried out. He stopped, troubled at her response. Then, picking her up with his deft hands he rolled her over onto her back, parted her legs, and slid his hot self in.

"I can't bear it," she cried, biting into the pillow when he was done.

"What?"

He lifted up her face, tenderly. Wiped the tears with the back of his hand.

"I don't know," she lied. She had no idea what she was saying or why.

"The past," she said. "I can't bear the past."

All she wanted was for the sweet pleasure that had filled her earlier to return, flood her again, cast her down into the wet clay basin of her own life.

He was serious now. Sitting astride her, his elbows bent over her sides so that his body bridged hers, and she felt herself starting to flow again. He didn't know what to say, just looked at her lying beneath him. He started to say something, then thought better of it, and instead set his mouth so that it lit on her shoulder and made wet butterfly patterns over it. Then he slid into her vagina again, in a sudden swift move she could never have predicted. She lay beneath him, simmering with delight.

As he served her tea, he suddenly took up the broken leg of a chair that Zahir had left on the floor. Then added to it the piece of a wooden Nubian sculpture, and a worn metal grille, carved with fine fretwork, dislodged from the balcony. He juggled the pieces in his hands, set them together in a free floating form, supported by his hands and knees.

"Sandhya," he said, "the past is a rough instrument we have to play. People like us have to make up the past from little bits and pieces, play it. Imagine strings running through, playing it, *halathi!*"

She smiled, that unbearably sweet smile, at the term of endearment he used, but after she left he recalled something in her eyes that disturbed him.

Back home, Sandhya Rosenblum washed out her mouth, hands trembling at the edge of the sink, almost dropping the dinner dishes. That night when she sank into bed next to Stephen she was naked, hoping that something would be kindled in her husband, something more than the slender disinterest that ran through him when she moved her own hands over her back, over her shoulder blades and the neck she had bared for him, hoping against hope that he might take her, even brutally from the back. No wonder, she thought, in her half-sleep that night, I cannot bear the thought of women he has wanted, for there is something in him I cannot touch.

"I never really knew you, Stephen," she wanted to say, "never really," but the thought stopped in her, for the heat of Rashid's cheek seemed to burn into her. She heard a curious atonal music from the street outside, metal scraping wood, and when she shut her eyes, she saw Rashid's face again, moist, as if awash with river water.

That night Rashid had a dream: There was that little girl again, crouched by the banks of the Nile. She wore a white dress, curiously unstained, but her feet were in the mud. There was a monstrous-looking male squatting by her. It ambled away, lay on a rock, shut its eyes. The girl came up to Rashid.

"Stab me," she whispered. "Please stab me with your knife."

Rashid was horrified. He backed away onto dry earth. Edged into a thorn bush, scraping his arm.

"Please, please, stab me," she insisted, coming closer to him, raising her white skirts off her ankles.

Rashid, pressed hard against the thorn bush, heard Zahir right behind, urging him: "Go on, do it. She's asking, don't you see?"

The girl came even closer. Her voice changed, a harsher note in it. She pointed to the monster:

"If you don't, I'll wake him up."

The threat scared the lads. "Go on, you," they pushed at each other with their fingers and fists. Finally it was Rashid who took action. After all, his marbles had dashed Zahir's into a gutter, his date pits made the best sling balls, his reeds broken from the riverbanks made the sharpest swords.

Stepping to the side, the boy drew out the little penknife his uncle had given him. First he stabbed her on the black matte of her blown hair, then her toes and palms, working slowly inward into the delicacy of her torso. Watching him, Zahir joined in, pulling his djellaba sleeves back as the work grew sweaty, frantic. And still the girl cried out:

"More, more!"

Finally the two boys dropped down, quite worn out. They fell into the mud at the base of the river, smiled sweetly, and the girl let her long hair, once tangled under the monster's head, blow in the wind.

"It was good, I loved it," she smiled.

Rashid stared down in horror at his own hands holding the little brown penknife. She added:

"It's the only way I can have revenge on him."

Then, quite unaccountably, she vanished. The very next morning, he told Zahir.

"Too many dreams," his old friend muttered, brushing his teeth. Then rinsed out his mouth and spluttered. "Not Uncle Mustafa's daughter, was it?"

Rashid sat up very straight. "Of course, that's it. Remember what happened to her? I never saw her after that summer. Years later I heard she was missing at the edge of Beirut. And then that awful business in Cairo."

Zahir, who had completed his toilette, was wiping his face with a towel. He stopped short:

"I met Hassan yesterday. He had a plan afoot. Want to hear about it?"

Rashid, his mind still haunted by the young girl's face, how like Sandhya she had seemed, hardly heard him.

"You didn't listen," Zahir accused.

"Well, what were you saying?"

"Shh, listen. Hassan from Khartoum, you've never met him, is now in Jamaica, Queens, that is. After much difficulty he has got himself a driving license and now drives a car for a VIP you've heard of, the half-blind preacher."

"So?"

"There's more. Hassan and a group of others have been collecting chemicals. Want to hear more?"

Rashid shoved his coffee cup into the sink. Opened the hot water faucet, felt the hot water hissing on his palm. Suddenly he said very loudly:

"Not if it's a bombing spree your friend has in mind."

"He suggested the Holland Tunnel."

Rashid sat up in shock.

"You're crazy, Zahir. They did that business in the Café du Nil. Remember? It's always innocent people who get hurt anyway."

He stopped, the image of a girl's mouth, vivid, the mouth bleeding at the edge, a tiny trickle as the child, full-grown now, in a white blouse and pale green skirt, lay unnaturally bent over a metal chair in the sidewalk café, right hand folded over a stone.

"Remember? She was abducted in Beirut, then came back to Cairo and was killed."

His voice choked as he turned to Zahir but his friend, busy fixing toast in a beat-up toaster, bent over the frail, glowing wires, was no longer listening.

Thereafter, their conversations avoided incendiary topics. Once, out in the park in front of the brownstone, Rashid tried to talk about Sandhya. "I feel I'm falling in love with her," he confided to Zahir.

"Don't be an ass," Zahir tapped him on the shoulder. "It's okay, for a while, remember. But she's a married woman. Move on, old chap." Then, seeing the hurt look on his friend's face, he murmured, "Okay, so she's beautiful, you have it bad. What about Zeinab then?"

"What about her? There's nothing more between us, you know that."

"And that Trinidad woman, Draupadi?"

"We parted." Rashid was sullen, his head swimming with the complications of love. He knew Sandhya had a husband and child. There were limits beyond which he shouldn't go. He needed to control his feelings, turn his thoughts to his book, scribble a few notes, do some research. Perhaps with Sandhya to inspire him, he would read Gandhi's *Autobiography.*

Later in the afternoon the two friends returned to the park, a bottle of wine, some leftover plums, a cloth rug in hand. Carmen, Zahir's new woman, was with them. "He needs cheering up," Zahir mumbled, pointing to his friend.

"Hey cutie, what's up?" Carmen leaned forward, mussing up Rashid's hair.

"Okay, okay," Rashid muttered, backing away.

"Hey, look at that thing," Carmen cried, pointing at the flag flying at half-mast, a seagull perched at its tip, clawing the tough cloth.

"Met this chap called Hassan. Code name, Chutput," Zahir leaned forward, whispering. "He majors in chemistry at Rutgers."

"Majors?"

"Sure. Haven't you been to college? That's Chutput for you, your all-American lad. Bang, bang!"

And Zahir, perhaps to get Carmen's eyes back on him, ripped off his pink shirt. Clad in nothing but his shorts, he did a little dance, whooping back and forth:

"Look, I am holding machete, I am on native ground." He sang this while Carmen, who was filled with wine, clapped and clapped her hands shaped like gull's wings, the tips smeared with plum juice.

Later that night, Rashid watched Zahir lie on the bed, his hands clenched. He looked up, cocked his head. *"Alouette,"* he hummed, a bitter smile on his face, and he sang out, in a low, guttural voice, the words of their childhood song:

> *Alouette, gentille alouette*
> *Alouette, je te plumerais.*
> *Je te plumerai la tête, et la tête, et la tête*
> *Je te plumerai la bouche, et la bouche, et la bouche …*

It was dark outside in the Brooklyn street and streetlights shone in. Rashid saw the pallor of his friend's face, the taut muscles working. He could tell that Zahir's mind was wandering. Clutching his pillow to his chest, Zahir drove his jagged route into history:

"When Flaubert on his Egyptian journey faced Kuchuck Hanem, what did he cry out? Okay, okay. Let me change tack. I shall be the Lord Mayor of Portsmouth for you."

And Zahir leaped off the bed and started strutting around the room, pretending to be the dignitary:

"Do you see this crescent and star hung on my neck? Bow, bow low. How do you like Portsmouth, by the way? Is it not an indifferent town, at the edge of a parched island? I have my hair permed every other month, tinted auburn so it gleams in the sun as I climb the decks of the H. M. S. *Victory.*"

Zahir gave a little bow. "Now, my dear, now we've lost the Orient, Egypt, India, all that—I wear this star the Lionheart brought back from fighting the infidels. A group of wogs came to visit: for their benefit I pointed to the pure obsidian of the crescent that hangs over my heart."

"Here, stop, Zahir, that's enough," Rashid begged, for he saw his friend down on his knees at the edge of the bed, vomiting out the words.

"Without meaning, that's what," he spat out. "The words of Kuchuck Hanem. Sex only. Her smell, her bush, her throat where the amber hung. Swear you will *abeille* for me. Swear, swear."

Rashid could not bear it any longer. He shook his friend, hard, by the shoulders: "Zahir, stop. Stop, this is Brooklyn. We're in America now. All that stuff's over."

He hauled his friend up by his pajama sleeves and tried to knee him back into bed. But Zahir was serious, a zither strung into tangled chaos, his voice low, as if nothing had hit him.

"Have you seen me like this before?"

"No, not really."

"What did you feel when Baghdad was bombed?"

"What sort of question is that?"

"Come on."

"I thought I would lose my mind."

"How long did it last?"

Rashid was resting on the worn sofa. Perhaps by speaking from the heart, he would restore his friend to some sanity:

"To tell you the truth, it was worst in the metal elevators at Hunter College. The whole place seemed deserted and I had the metal elevator to myself. As it moved up, I felt a pounding at the back of my head. Right there." He pointed to his skull's base.

"Alouette, gentille alouette," he heard Zahir sing out of the corners of his mouth, the song Mme. Lefort with her rouged lips had taught him.

And as if that old tune returned him to the steadfastness of place, the only possible resort in a time of torment, Rashid turned to Zahir. "Brooklyn," Rashid said to him. "We are in Brooklyn."

Staring out at the clear streetlight, the indigo of the night that might have been painted in with stormy Nile water, Rashid heard his voice repeat the place name, like a talisman: "Brooklyn, amigo, Brooklyn. But Zahir was seated absolutely still, his head against the white wall, his feet straight out on the bed, waiting for an impossible end.

S andhya Rosenblum felt it could never end. Over and over, carrying loads of laundry to the washer one flight down, making peanut butter and jelly sandwiches, scrubbing out the kitchen sink, she played out the scenes of their encounters. Rashid took her to a white room. She saw the wooden stairs again, the balcony with the wrought-iron trellis marked with the shapes of gingko leaves. Rashid bought plums for her. He washed the plums carefully and dried them off with a kitchen towel, piled them in a bowl with markings of royal blue. China so delicate, marked with the jut of a wing or claw.

She tightened her skirts with both her hands. Feeling a little funny, she pointed her toes as best she could, pirouetting. Bent over the bowl, he turned to look at her as she stood, right hand clasped over hipbone. For the first time he noticed that she was exactly the same height as he was.

"I want you." His voice was perfectly low. He did not say her name. She thought she heard him say it but needed to be sure.

"Want?" She moved to the balcony. The grillwork on the tiny balcony was marked in textured iron. Inside her rose the memory of his hands, and then the sweet, delicate taste of his flesh inside her, sounding over her thighs as if a globe of water covered with a transparent membrane had brushed lightly against her.

She kept utterly still. The memory was fragile. It was her great safety, against him, against the storm his hands would soon release in her. "Whose room is this?" she asked. "I mean who does Zahir rent it from?" But he preferred not to say. "I want to live with you. Forever and ever." She felt herself mouth this, but the words did not come.

Rashid was speaking about an old man from Nubia he had seen as a child. She did not listen very carefully. She looked at the leaves. The air was humid, almost like India in the weeks before the monsoon struck and the leaves were splayed apart.

A few weeks ago, from this same spot, she had heard the cries of the man from Eritrea who was brought into the United States on refugee papers. The man had spent four years in the squalor of the camps on the outskirts of Khartoum. The Blue Nile burned his eyelids raw, heat glinting off the brassy hood of water. The White Nile by the Sunt forest, acacia branches scratched like a mound of hair over the blistering sky, no help at all. Mud made his ankles sore. Once, twice, wandering by the water, the man tried to stuff half-dried acacia leaves down his throat, gulp some water, but started to choke.

He entered America, his head bound up in rags against the cold, and in this very street, not far from the subway stop saw sunlight spurt against the metal railings of a park. Water from a burst hydrant splattered his feet.

Later that day, as Rashid led her away from the house, holding her by the hand, Sandhya caught sight of the man in cast-off clothing. His whole body was swaying. She turned to look at him more closely, but Rashid drew her on. She could not make out the man's words. His cries seemed torn from inside him as if someone had stuck a finger down the delicate passage of the throat and plucked the tender flesh, made music by taking that frail membrane, stringing it on an oudh, and playing.

When Hamza el Din plays the oudh, the waters of Nubia burn, as if angels were descending, casting golden crowns into the waves. Can Hamza el Din make sense of a poor man weeping? Or is the mind of the great musician set on the rhythms of a young lad sitting atop a water-wheel, rubbing sand into the shadow made by his knee. Is his mind fixed on a child who knows nothing of angels or djinns, who has learned not to fear the sun?

She raised her hair off her neck and the sun burned into her shoulder. She could not tell if it was the sun or the memory of his hands, rubbing, rubbing into her. "Rashid," she cried, turning to him where he stood, watching her. The cry was torn out of her.

So that they could be all alone, with nothing between them, Rashid took her to a white room.

The white room enclosed her and there she saw the grave of her father. She saw prints on the walls: a man with an erect penis. A woman with the lips of her vagina parted. A love apple with pinkish skin such as she had seen growing on a tree in Tiruvella, except that hairs grew out of it. SANDHYA, it said in big letters, under the love apple. She saw a drawing of a subway that spiraled into the blue sky. And next to it, a sign: MURI / THE ROOM. Then the walls fell away to reveal the turquoise sky and she saw the graves of both her parents.

The graves were simple gray stones engraved with crosses and dates that blurred in her head as the rain that poured down. Rashid was standing between the two graves, utterly naked. At first his face was turned away, so that she saw his legs, his thighs, the pallor of his buttocks. Then he moved a little to the side and stared down at her. His face was utterly still. She could not understand why he was staring down at her with a little smile. But from her wet belly and the sari that threatened to clamp its folds over her bent knees and ankles, she sensed she was on the wet earth. There was mud on her belly. She was crawling on the earth. "Appa! Amma!" she cried out to her parents, her voice sounding as if it did not come from her body at all.

Another India
(Draupadi)

Sorrow concealed, like an oven stopped,
Doth burn the heart to cinders where it is.
— *Shakespeare,* Titus Andronicus

Sandhya never met Rinaldo, she only heard of him through me. And in any case, by the time she and I became really close, Rinaldo and I had broken up. It was Rashid, my other man, who entered her life, stole her heart. Perhaps that was why I needed to tell her everything about me, make up a story. The words were hard, heavy at times. And often, when sitting on my futon, listening to me, her eyes wide open, she looked as if she were dreaming. Or was it just the light that struck the Hudson reflecting off the wooden piers and the drifting clouds, lighting up her face? I know she wanted to make a home in America, but it seemed so hard at the time.

"Home is where the heart is," Rinaldo whispered to me. It sounded like a quote from the letter Columbus wrote in 1502 to the *Banco di san Giorgo,* after his terrible third voyage:

"Though my body is here, my heart is constantly there."

Did he have an imaginary India in his head? Where, where, I want to ask my love. Where is that place held in the head, the unreal air whose sweetness sustains?

Columbus dreamed another India. He carried it in his head. Heard herons singing as angels might, saw sea spray turn into glowing pearls. Noticing that natives held swords by the blade—they knew nothing about sharpened metal—he sensed they would make good slaves. They would bring him gold, frankincense, myrrh, as the three kings brought the Christ child.

India was the land my great-grandmother fled. A woman with an ille-gitimate child she clambered on board a ship and offered her services in the New World Columbus found. They took her on as a bonded laborer to work in the cane fields, took away her name, gave her a number. Her male child died on deck, fever racking his tiny frame. She saw her mother standing utterly still in the doorway of the mud hut, sari pulled over her head. She saw her father walk away into a field filled with pepper vines, never once turning his head. She saw the merchant who had drawn her into his room with the fine red and gold *dhurri*. She saw his plump hands, his nails. They were all ghosts now. She stood in the rain, on deck, as they lowered her child's body into the waters. She did not wipe her face.

In the cane fields of Trinidad they gave her a new name. "Dropti, Dropti," they cried after her, and she accepted it. "Ah, Ah," she shouted back in reply, *"Nyan ah,"* it's me.

When I hear the calypso singer on the tiny radio in the kitchen in Gingee crying out, *"Dropti, Dropti, India girl of pepper curry, hurry to me!"* I think of Great-grandma in the cane fields. She came running through the canebrakes. The leaves, green and gold, massed around her head. Their edges were sharp, they cut her hands, her cheeks. She came running hard, her sari damp with sweat. Great-grandma ran right through me. There was blood on her hands from the cane leaves, blood on her side from the overseer's whip. Her story works in me.

When they speak of India I hear a woman's breath in an island canefield, the hot sun on her head, arms held before her as she races down a narrow dirt track.

I was born on the fourth of July in Gingee, a stone's throw from the Hudson. Fit to weep at the sight of tall ships, sail after sail. Did Columbus come this way, legs held apart with muscular force, arms ex-tended, ready to be filled with the burden of the new world?

Born in Gingee, in a damp hospital bed, the building subsequently abandoned to realtors from the city who gutted it, putting in hotshot kitchen fixtures, revolving grills for chicken and quail. And where doctors scrubbed down, in the corner by the broken sink, and a whirlpool bath, video center in plain view of the glass door, Nautilus machine, the works.

Born to the only daughter of Suhasini of Trinidad and Tobago, not knowing which bit of blood came from what island side. Great-grand-mother, Indian by way of Fiji, sent over to work on the plantations. Father, Indian with Japanese blood in him and a dash of white. His mother, part-black from Kentucky, with a streak of a native nation. Grandpa changed his name from *Dineshwaran* to *Dinkins,* thinking it sounded easier on the ear.

Why they named me *Draupadi* I cannot tell. What did they know of the goddess born of fire, wife of the five *Pandavas,* she who rode an elephant, was humiliated in the court of kings, survived a battlefield, lived out her life in exile, then raced into the wind, atop a tiger, a lotus blossom in one hand, a sword in the other?

Why couldn't they have named me *Dorothy?* That name would have hung better on me. As it was, I was the only Indian kid in a school filled with poor whites and blacks, the whole mound of us whistling in the wind, waiting on freedom.

Freedom for what, I never thought to ask.

I ran away to the pond by the edge of the railroad tracks in Gingee, thinking: If I jump into this muddy water, I will surface in India. No one will tell me apart in India, even if my hair is streaked with water weeds, my clothes all damp and sticky. No one will mind my name there, a child called after a goddess blessed with four arms, five husbands, she who was born of fire and endured exile.

G rowing up was hard. Mama standing at the kitchen window, gripping the bars, her knuckles bloodless. She stares at my back as I ride out with Juan Carlos into the bright lights of Albany. Juan Carlos has hair jet black as Papa's used to be. "You and me Indians," he'd say. At that time I knew nothing of what it meant to be Indian in that way. I had never heard of Doña Marina, who translated herself for Cortés, that plucky go-between. What Juan Carlos murmured somehow comforted me.

Papa never seemed to notice my affairs. He was busy trying to get a loan from Uncle Alex of the motel business. It was a bad year and the Soda Shop had its shutters down half the time, like so many other stores in Gingee. "Young flee into the Defense Industry," the *Gingee Recorder* printed under a photo of a man who looked much like Jimmy getting into a battered car with a mattress under his arm. In the corner of the photo were the chimneys of a factory. I pointed it out to Juan Carlos who didn't seem to care. Then he too fled Gingee.

Uncle Alex started visiting. Seeing his bald head didn't help Papa any. Uncle Alex stood by Mama in the kitchen as she cut okra, *baingan,* spinach, her fingers raw with the chill of it all. Gently he handed her a towel, whispering, "Come Maya, come."

And she would lift up her eyes and gaze at him. I had never seen any-thing quite like that. Her hands extended in front of her like twin birds, brown birds caught and caged that he rubbed so tenderly.

Her hands were her great delight. After scrubbing the dishes, Mama rubbed Lovelight cream on her hands. It had a pinkish hue that sat ill on her skin, so she hid her hands in gloves. Even at night she wore gloves so the cream would not rub off, moisten the sheets she shared with Papa. Once peering in at night I saw them lie like mummies side by side. I smelled the collagen cream she daubed over her cheeks as if her flesh were in perpetual rehearsal for a better life she might step into someday. Lying by Papa's side I saw the creams, gloves, tight dresses she forced her body into and wondered why.

"What else can a woman be," she asked me so plaintively, "What else?"

Somehow I felt she was thinking of Alma, Juan Carlos's mother, who threw over both husband and daycare job, then took up gunrunning somewhere south of the border. Alma wrote Mama a card from Mexico City with a big mural by Diego Rivera on it. "Love and Kisses, your Alma," she signed it, with a heart, arrows running through.

Mama buried the card in a pile of plastic bags from K-mart lodged in the damp space under the kitchen sink. Sometimes, after staring out the window at the Lupo's garage door, Mama would sit at the kitchen table and write. Once, she gave me the letter to post. She was sending it to Uncle Alex. Why, I wondered, why?

Years later, after Uncle Alex had moved away to D.C., Mama visited me in Westbeth. Rinaldo came by, and how she took to him. They were, of course, almost the same age. He bent delicately over her hand and set his lips to the spot where her vein pulsed. As he straightened up, I saw him glance at the fake pearls shimmering round her neck. I felt something crimp in me. He sensed my difficulty and looked straight into my eyes. It stopped then, the sorrow that was rising up.

I have the memory of his hands though, holding hers, making a yeast-like sorrow, a particular heat.

Trapped in her own life, Mama was filled with desires for me. "Look at that lovely dress in *Gingee Bride.*" She pushed the catalog over, its cover emblazoned with a bride decked out in a willowy outfit, cheeks flushed. The bride looked like my old Barbie. I asked her straight: "And how's Uncle Alex doing?"

I felt bad for a long while after, for Mama's lips puckered and her hands, all of their own accord, did a fandango in her lap. I wondered how it was that a man bald and bleary-eyed with working the accounts in Best Western Motels could move her so. Years after he moved away, her eyes filled with tears, as if from onion juice her own mother had spilled, a knife working into the heart of bone, a ghost-blade held in a woman's fist cutting at the silence of story.

When did I first figure out that something was on with Uncle Alex? Perhaps the funds he raised from the new waterbeds in the motel paid for my art school in New York. I tried to savor the thought. And there was Mama gripping the kitchen bars, staring out into the cold backyard. She had just heard that Alex had bad liver trouble, that his wife, Shaila, was coming from the islands to take care of him. The two were moving away. How would they meet, Mama and Alex, those two whom fate had joined outside matrimony?

Would they ride the monorail in the Catskills Game Park late at night when Papa was at the till? Or watch the tiger huddle in its cage, those mid-semester lovers approaching the end? What did Alex whisper in Mama's ear? Did he touch her neck with his wrist, kiss her there? Did she cry out, "Alex, what shall I be without you?" Is this what love makes of us, a great dissolve? Delight risen in the gorge, excitation of skin, pore, and muscle, all threatening death to the fragile *I* bunkered down in fears that vanish at the touch of a hand, the kiss of soft lips. Yet at the toss of a head, the fears return, blades sharpened, bloodthirsty.

And Papa? He was going down, down, a mist winding round his eyes so that, even if he were to cut off his own head and swing it, no light would come as it came to Bertran de Born in that fiery darkness he was flung into.

"**N**o more. Bonded laborers we shall be no more." Papa muttered in my ear. Then shifted me on his knee, over the shiny patch worn down with use. I was seven then, with two tight braids Mama smoothed with oil.

"Born in America, there's nothing you can't be," Papa added. "Make yourself up, child."

"Dinkoo" they called him, mounding up trash into a heap in his backyard, trying to drive him out of Gingee. He held tight, cleared it all out, the bits of broken glass, spent condoms, burned styrofoam that had held cheap coffee, tasteless tea. Mama helped him bandage the cuts on his right hand, then fed him mulligatawny. How quiet he was at first, then repeated to me, "Born in America, you can be anything, Draupadi."

At high school they taught us a play by Shakespeare about a woman with her tongue pulled out and hands cut off. She had a lovely name, Lavinia. I got a line from that play I held to:

"Sorrow concealed like an oven stopped ..."

It went on about burning a heart to cinders.

I thought of Papa, quiet as a mouse, clearing up all the trash from behind the Soda Shop. How tired he looked in the fall when the leaves drop like ash from the elms and the crimson maple starts its flaming. I crept down to the water's edge with Jimmy O'Flaherty. Jimmy of the snub nose and delicate freckles. I let him touch me all over, thrilled at his touch, opened my eyes wide as he lay by me on a pile of woodchips. Saw the eagle swoop low over the Hudson River. Jimmy wanted to go into the air force, only the boot camp bit scared him. "It's free, it's all free," he whispered into my ear. I loved his thighs with the reddish hair growing on them, his strong knees.

Closer to the river, closer to the pond by the railroad tracks, I let him hold me. A pile of coal protected us from sight. It was summertime. The lights were fading all along the river, the shapes of trees and rocks and bushes turning pink with the sun's going down. I tried to melt into Jimmy's arms but an old tramp came by. His hair was black as coal; his skin mud colored. As he shuffled close, I could tell he wasn't really old, it was the clothing and the wide, staring eyes. His bag wobbled on his shoulder. He waved his stick about in his hand and, spotting me, cried out, "Indian, Indian!"

Jimmy scared him away.

"Who was that?" I asked finally, straightening out my skirt, brushing the coal dust off my thighs.

"Yasunari. A Jap interned during the war. Crazy guy. Draws pictures with a stick in the dirt."

"Why?"

"He's wild, that guy. Didn't scare you, did he?"

I shook my head. Later we saw the dust churned up by Old Man O'Flaherty's truck. I tried to hide behind Jimmy, but had no luck. He leaned out the window and yelled at us both. The following evening Jimmy's dad visited the Soda Shop on the pretext of buying something or the other, a pack of matches, soap. He leaned his belly against the till and yelled:

"Keep your girl away from my lad, Dinkins. Don't want none of that Paki stuff. Jimmy's going in the Air Force, hear?"

At dinner, my knee still sore where I hurt it on the coals, I faced Dad. He kept very quiet. But I knew from Kusum who cleaned the floor that old O'Flaherty had been round again.

Next morning, eyes red with weeping, Mama came into my room. Did the thrash of a wet sari on my thighs help her any? I kept my mouth shut tight. I watched her race away to the kitchen, where she chopped up okras quick and fine. Her little finger, too.

Papa made her do it, I thought, come into my room like that. I kept clear of them both. Took my Barbie doll into the bathroom. Locked the door. Touched my breasts where Jimmy had set his hands so gently. Then, in a rage, as if a switch had been thrown in my head, I scratched myself hard. I ran water in the faucet, dropped all of Mama's Avon talc in. The stuff smelled so sweet going down the drain, the stuff she patted on to whiten her skin.

Jimmy, oh Jimmy, I wept.

He would not look at me in the lunchroom or by the lockers the next day. I held Barbie under the tap and smeared her with *kajal*. I watched her turn black. I tore a strip off Mama's favorite sari, the one Grandma gave her. A pink silk strip I tied over Barbie's lips, her mouth. I sealed her eyes with wax.

Somehow this came back to me. I was doing a performance piece at the Museum of Natural History, right under the shining bones of our long-lost ancestor Lucy. The piece was called "Women of Color Whirling through the World." Sandhya came to visit me backstage. She gazed at me as I sat on a stool rimming my eyes round with *kajal*. Later she told me the glittering black outfit I wore reminded her of a Hindi film tunic, the kind bad girls in bars wore. The tunic was made of strips of sequined cloth stitched together, a body suit, under a tight black skirt. As I worked around my eyes with *kajal*, rimming round the sorrow of flesh, I felt her breath so close. Glancing up I saw her mouth poised over mine in that odd mirror. Suddenly she tugged her scarf from her neck and bound it over her lips. Nervous, I dropped the *kajal* stick.

"Good women, good maquillage," I quipped.

Dropping the scarf, she asked, "Where did you get that *kajal* stick?"

"Lexington, the Indian store at the corner of Twenty-ninth."

She nodded as if something had eased up inside her. The scarf was hanging loosely round her throat.

"I have one just like it," she offered, pointing at the *kajal*, "I bought it in Hyderabad. Perhaps yours is imported from there."

I shrugged my shoulders. I had to get on with making myself up. Body paint, undies, leggings, scarves, pins, brooches, buttons, the stays we make, mimicking eternity.

Where nothing cramps, where time becomes the body.

"Beautiful, so beautiful," she whispered behind me. I should have taken her longing in, but her helplessness scared me. Watching her in the mirror I powdered under my eyes so the makeup would blend in without harsh bounding lines.

To survive the darkness I fled the clapboard house in Gingee, the Soda Shop, the railroad tracks. Then, embroidered ancestors aplenty. There was Great-grandmother Draupadi, who escaped rape in Fiji.

But what did I really know of her life? It was hard to tell from the mumbled account Mama gave.

Grandfather Hari on Mama's side became part of the revolt on the good ship *Komagata Maru* docked outside Vancouver. His brother Kishan, a member of the Ghaddar party, threw bombs at Lord Chelmsford in Bombay, then landed up in a San Francisco jail. Great-uncle Chander, earthing himself in the Imperial Valley, took for his wife a Mexican beauty who sported tight black skirts. Gold crosses swung between her breasts. There was Great-aunt Ethelamma who, rumor had it, worked the coat rack in Café Society and saw Lady Day. Heard her croon "Summertime" against the cold frosted window. Ethelamma's daughter Simi passed food to the Black Panthers and sprayed her hair with chemicals to turn it kinky. Another daughter, Dakshini, lived out her days with a medicine woman on Hunter Mountain, learning those ancient ways. Vijay, a cousin three times removed, rode with the cowboys in Montana; his brother Varun hid out with the Weathermen in Greenwich Village, hands stinking of chemicals.

But even I felt it was flimsy. Who would share this footage of invented passage? I was trying to people the North American continent, but what sense did it make? I felt like a jot of black pepper sneezed out by an irritated god, flung into the flat, burning present.

Going

The sky was brilliant, blue. It hurt Sandhya's eyes. She came home from shopping, hung up her coat on the hook, reached into the paper bag. She drew out the plums she had bought for a dollar-ninety, dark rich plums. She set them aside on a metal plate and stared at their luminous skins. Her thoughts all a blur, she reached in for the carrots. Fresh carrots, she would scrape off their skins, top and tail them. Then purée a few for Dora. She and Stephen would have carrots for supper, cooked in olive oil. They would sip wine, then have some of the meat she had cooked in coriander and turmeric the night before. Perhaps then they would sit by the window and some of the breeze from the river would blow over them.

The phone rang so loud she trembled a little with the thought that it might be Rashid. Someone was speaking to her in Malayalam. A pricking of emotion at the nape of her neck.

"Ena? Ena? Ara? Ara?" she asked, as the flickers of sounds vanished. She felt the panic rise in her, heard the caller speak again, quite clearly now:

"Your father's collapsed. Can you hear?"

She reached over, set the knife on the tabletop, its handle facing outward. That way it couldn't hurt anyone. She touched the phone line and tiny shreds of carrot skin clung to the phone. She did not have the sense to wipe her fingers dry.

"A snake, it crawled in by the kitchen veranda. Sandhya, can you hear? He had to kill it. There were only women in the house. A house full of women!"

"Where is he? Where?" she felt her own voice rising.

"In the intensive care unit. Call your mother. She wants to speak to you."

When Stephen returned that night, he found his wife on the kitchen floor next to a pile of uncut carrots. The child sat by her mother, dabbling her fingers in a cup of milk. Sandhya's eyes were swollen with tears. Stephen helped Sandhya up, then picked up the child quite tenderly, washed and cleaned her and sang her to sleep. A few hours later, when she had recovered a little, Sandhya turned to her husband. Over the bunched bedclothes, the pillows bent to the warm shapes of heads, elbows, she spoke to Stephen:

"If Appa should die, I'll never forgive myself."

"Don't be foolish," he whispered.

"Who was that on the phone? Your mother?"

"No, Sarla. She was the one to call me."

"The cow lady?"

"Aha."

"The lady famous for her milk cows. She was impressed by my credentials, the only one, too, in the whole of Tiruvella."

Sandhya pulled the bedclothes about her. Sarla's voice came back:

"We could hear your father crying out, '*Jesu, Jesu.*' Your mother rushed out into the mango grove crying for help. Three men carried your father into the car. His feet jutted out of the window. The driver drove with headlights on, in broad daylight, your father's feet jutting out through the car window."

As Stephen spoke she heard a serires of loud pops, gunshots or a car on the street below. She couldn't tell. She huddled in the bed. Soon it would be midnight, time to reach her mother half a world away. In the days that followed Sandhya learned of her father's decline, the blood disease they had diagnosed six weeks ago, which her mother had kept secret, the heart attack he suffered while killing the snake. Each night she hung on the kitchen phone, dialing the numbers over and over again, heart beating as she heard the click-click-click of the international line. Tiruvella was not on the main line so the satellites that beamed directly to Madras or Delhi couldn't work their magic. The relay lines were notorious. She shivered in the cold, waiting for someone to pick up, imagining the room in which the black phone rang, windows with muslin curtains by the beds her parents used, photographs of her grandparents with the background painted blue and wispy pink, so that the seated figures seemed suspended in ether, their saris and dhotis floating away into eternity. And her grandmother's embroidered shawl, it still hung on the chair in the bedroom.

Walking the cold streets, or shopping in the supermarket, Sandhya felt stretched so thin she feared she might die of the sheer transparency needed to be in two places at once: crossing the sidewalk in Manhattan, even as her soul was in Tiruvella, in an unseen hospital room where her father lay. Sometimes, though, when she held little Dora in her arms, the comfort of Rashid's touch, and it was a whole month now since she had seen him, awoke in her. It was a fragrance, a turn so elusive it could scarcely be figured in speech, releasing her.

So she sat, tangling her fingers in her daughter's hair, eyes locked to the open window that gave onto a bit of blue sky. Then it was left to the small child—with her sticky hands, her cries for cocoa or an apple or a doll that had disappeared under the pile of toys in her bedroom—to draw her mother back.

Stephen tried, but felt that he could not really help his wife. He only knew that her father's illness, or something else, had drawn her away from what he thought of as their shared life. Often she wore a haunted look, sleepless, lean. It was as if a mistress of maquillage at Saks had painted pallor on Sandhya's skin, though her coloration still burned outward. So his brown-skinned wife bore herself upright into the sunset, as if burnt by moonlight, he told her, standing at the prow of the steerage, coming into Ellis Island. He said this to her because he thought he loved her, but the statement did nothing for Sandhya, who was worn out from trying to live two lives, and so clung to her father's illness, letting it draw all the buried pain out of her soul.

A month after that first call, Sosa called her daughter in New York. "You should come, Sandhya. The doctor says you should be informed. Your father is very weak. He has a lung infection now and it's not clear whether the antibiotics are working."

The calm in her mother's voice astounded Sandhya. It was as if she had stepped into an icy waterfall and been startled into life. She was needed, she had to go. It no longer made sense to stay. She would go alone, Dora would stay behind.

Muriel stepped in, offered to pick up the child from daycare and keep her each afternoon till Stephen returned from work. Dorris and she never started their Scrabble games till well after seven in the evening, and all she would miss would be a round of soap opera on a dull afternoon, or the utter silence of her apartment where she sat sipping gin, the *New Yorker* open in her lap. Clearly Stephen was in trouble and she had to help.

Sandhya needed a ticket. Jay took her down to Tanjam Travels near Grand Central Station. Inside the art deco building it was just cheap paint with posters of Konarak and Madurai pasted on, images of Indian stone, centuries old, mechanically reproduced over and over again. Jay stared at a poster of the Sun Temple that featured a large ad for the latest five-star hotel—AC, private generator, TV, VCR, video.

"A ticket, I need a ticket," Sandhya said to the travel agent in English and Hindi, adding in her mixed up Tamil, "Ticket *venam.*"

Venugopal Pillai, with his shiny hand-painted silk shirt and slicked-back hair, took one look at her and gulped, "Sandhya, Madam, Sandhya Rosen-blum," as he returned the passport she had extended to him.

He had a ticket all ready for her. He noticed her palm trembling a little, he noticed that. Five years in the ticket business and no one quite like Sandhya—reeking in just that way of Diorissimo, her shirt tucked into blue jeans, covered in a silk stole, hair teased and wild—had come his way.

"It's her father," Jay explained. "The emergency quota worked, eh? We spoke to Tanjam Amma."

"Yes, yes, Tanjam madam called."

The sounds of a burglar alarm four flights below them in the packed street almost blotted out his words. The travel agent was making squawking sounds as the check changed hands.

That night, in a flurry of baby foods and torn silks, and a final frantic phone call to Rashid, who could not be reached, Sandhya jammed herself into the plane. In unaccustomed fashion she traveled light. There was a slight gush of tears as she parted from Stephen and Dora. The child did not seem to realize her mother was leaving her for quite a while.

L̲ater Sandhya could not recall the plane ride, not even what she wore. It was the entry into the airport lobby, carrying her small overnight bag, that stayed with her. A smell of raw wind in the coconut palms, the acrid stuff the Arabian sea brings in over the seawalls. Scent, the most elusive of the senses, summoning her. Not homeward, that would have seemed too grand a way of putting it to herself. Rather, it was an accustomed life, rounding back through the corridors of memory, a landscape so blurred one is hardly even conscious of it, soft limestone marked by running water. Feet damp with sweat she slipped into the Ladies' Room and tugged off her tights and shoes, put on the leather sandals she carried with her.

Her cousin Chandu, dark, well groomed, his blue cravat tucked in around his neck, was waiting with car and driver. With windows raised and the air conditioning on, the world outside was quite inaudible. She must have slept through the long, hot car ride, for when she awoke she thought she heard her own heart beats, magnified, saw Chandu's mouth open and close. Now he was mouthing, "Mission Hospital," once, twice, to make sure the driver understood.

At the red-pillared doors, she shook the dust off her hair, her feet, and walked briskly into the hospital, past the patients peering through the open doors, past the nurses wheeling metal carts with bottles, swabs, rolls of cotton wool. She turned sharply to the right, reading room numbers: 4, 6, 8, 10, 14. Chandu was somewhere behind her, keeping watch. Doors were ajar to catch what little air there might be. On and on she walked through the corridor till she came to 18.

There was clear light in the room. Cooler air blew in from the windows that faced a parcel of open land with rough grass. Crows clustered in a grove of mango trees. Further away there was a sprinkling of coconut palms, and flowering trees with scarlet and ocher bloom, petals glistening with heat.

The walls of the hospital room were painted a light blue so that the inner light took on the quality of limpid water. When it stormed, the blue turned a vivid indigo, as if the roof had been blown off and the darkness of the sky entered. She stopped at the threshold.

On the left, sitting on an upright wooden chair, with his back to her, shirtless, was an incredibly thin man. Bending over him, her hair blown loose, grayer and a little thinner than before, was Sosa, who rushed forward to Sandhya with a little cry and embraced her. Under her hands Sandhya felt her mother's body, her mother's cheek pressed to hers for an instant, but all the time the daughter's eyes were on the man who, turning slowly toward her, heard the cry, letting his ears do the work before he gathered the energy to shift his body around in the chair and face his eldest daughter. Letting go of her mother, Sandhya took a step toward him and he leaned against her, his face gaunt with the illness that had brought him to the brink of the grave. Tenderly, she held him against her.

She cradled his head in her hands, a thirty-five-year-old daughter come from across the seas to see her dying father. When she released him, she saw him reach for the fine cotton towel that hung, Kerala-style, on his shoulder, saw the motion of his hand as he lifted it up to his eyes. It was then that she noticed the tears in his eyes, the fine light stream down his cheeks. He wiped away the tears.

"Sandhya," he said, trying to smile, regain himself, "Sandhya."

She gazed at him through her own tears, unable to say anything, amazed at being there.

That night she felt she could not bear to leave her father to return to sleep at the old house, just a five-minute walk away. "You go, Amma," Sandhya said to Sosa. "How long is it since you slept in a proper bed?"

But Sosa shook her head, motioning toward Varki. "He wants me to stay, don't you?"

Her father nodded. Later, out of Varki's earshot, as mother and daughter stood in the corridor outside, Sosa explained that part of reason Varki wanted her to remain was out of deference to his daughter's feelings. Suppose he needed to use a urinal in bed, or had to struggle toward the bathroom?

"I am a grown woman, I have a child, I can do all that. Please," Sandhya begged, but her mother insisted.

So Sandhya contented herself with the stone floor, on which a finely woven mat was placed for her. That night she lay between the metal beds on which her parents lay. Through the palm weaving of the mat she felt the coolness of the floor and thought: I am lying here in Tiruvella, my birthplace. I am lying in room 18, in the Mission Hospital, in G Ward, G for Genasseret, probably where Christ did some miracle I knew about once, but have long since forgotten, my childhood faith quite lost, I am lying here between my two parents.

Forty-eight hours ago I left Kennedy airport.

And in her head, for the sake of some clarity that might eventually help her piece her life together, she thought out all the places the plane had stopped at, as if she were a schoolchild counting an abacus, moving the shiny beads under her fingers. So the place names slipped in her head and the act of flying across borders took on the rigor of the fine metal rod that held the beads in place.

I flew here from New York, Sandhya thought, beginning where she could. I came through London, two hours stopover; one hour in Istanbul. A ten-hour layover in Bombay, with a change of plane and then into Thiruvananthapooram, where Chandu met me with car and driver. Then a four-hour drive to the Mission Hospital to see Appa.

And it came back to her with a shock, how she had first heard the news of his illness. She shivered at the cool stone floor she could feel through the mat, through the everyday street clothing she wore. She who had traveled so long had been unwilling to undress, to accept her mother's offer of a nightgown. Now she opened her eyes wide, trying to adjust to the half-darkness. There were lamps set in the hospital corridor and a slit of light coming from the bathroom door. She balanced her chin on her elbow, raising herself slightly to look at her sleeping father's face. His cheekbones were so fine, the brown skin stretched taut over the seventy-year-old forehead miraculously unlined, delicate mouth, eyes with the long lashes so lovely. She had not seen a face so lovely, she thought, as that of her own father, wasted from the inside, the flesh subsided and the skin stretched over the hollow spaces creation had carved out. But how vital he was: the sharpness of his mind, in all that wasted flesh, took her breath away.

Just ten hours earlier, but it might have been a lifetime away, she had sat in the window seat of a plane that circled over the turquoise waters of the Arabian Sea, the ribbed coastline of Kerala, tiny black fishing boats poised like stick insects on the blue, frothy breakers visible against white sand, red soil, tiled rooftops, swaying palm trees.

What was a house but a prayer, a pivot of rock and tile and white-washed wall, a barrier human hands put up, to keep the elements at bay?

And she was praying all the while, O God, to a God she did not believe in except in uttermost need, O God, keep him alive. But then it changed and it wasn't to God anymore that the words worked in her mind, but to her father. The voice changed too, as if it had become wind, the wind that made the breakers splinter like lace, a hundred, no, two hundred feet beneath her, where but for the stout metal capsule with wings she would dash down to death: *Wait for me, wait for me, please, Appa, please wait for me.* And it was the pleading again, the child in her, once more, one last time.

"How swiftly." The words turned in her and where did they come from, those remembered words, as the plane swooped lower over the ocean rim, and the spume from the water rose like white flags raised by invisible hands, and through it shone her father's face, eyes shut. *How swiftly the blown banners turn into wings, things dark …*

She sat up, she rubbed her eyes. Her father had raised himself from the bed and was fumbling for his slippers, his two feet reaching down onto the floor, inches from where she lay. "What is it, Appa?" She was up as if sleep had never touched her. "My slippers, that's all."

"Shall I turn on the light in the bathroom?"

He nodded. "Yes," he said, "yes," whispering with the effort of making the breath come and go again in his worn body.

So she got up as her mother slept on, tired out after three weeks in the hospital, and she turned on the bathroom light, helped her father in, and waited outside. When he was done, she helped him back, then picked up the glass and poured in the Horlicks as he wanted, three heaped spoons, adding the filtered water from the flask they had brought from the house. She stirred the paste in with the spoonful of sugar he couldn't do without, poured in more water and gently set the glass in his hands. She watched him drink it up greedily, almost like a child, his body desperate for nourishment. She sat upright on the mat, watching him. This is what she had come for, to be of help, to be of use. He had waited for her. He knew she knew he had held out for her, waiting.

That night as she lay on the hospital floor, Rashid came to her. A shimmering presence, a breath of wind, all along her back. She felt as if her clothes had rolled off her, she felt him enter her, through all her pores. When they parted company, this ghost and she, the air turned cool as monsoon mist. She was fearful she might cry out his name in sleep. If her parents heard, what would they think? As she turned over, clutching the sheet her mother had given her, gripping it tightly over her breasts, she felt that this was the only way she could keep herself whole, with her father dying so slowly in front of her. Greedily she let herself go, thinking of Rashid's delicately shaped mouth sucking at her flesh, the warmth in his palms flowing into her nipples, down along her ribcage, then lower down, all the way to the very rim of her footsoles. So that instead of wanting to be freed from what she was, which was how Stephen so often made her feel, her weight, her skin, even the smell of her, all subsided into a precious earthly gravity. It was as if she were being given scent, taste, texture, so that in all the localities she inhabited, however cut apart from each other, she might be made vital through desiring flesh.

And these thoughts, if these indeed were thoughts, blurred in her and she felt that Rashid's coming to her in this way was something spiritual, and all over again she felt herself trembling on the mat as if he had actually touched her.

Looking up in the bluish light that poured into the room just before dawn, she saw her father stretch out his hand for a cup of water, and she felt her sight blurring. She got up hastily, picked up the metal cup, and set it gently in his hands. She lay down again as quickly as she could, for she felt her legs would dissolve under her in all that intensity of feeling.

She woke at the crack of dawn. She opened her eyes in the pale orange light that blew into the room, inhaled the scent of the *gulmohar* flowers waving on the trees by the railway track, the sharper scent of crushed mango leaves. A herd of goats was passing outside, bundles of cut branches on their backs. She turned to her father and thought she saw him repeat the gesture, his frail hand stretched out for a cup of water. When she lay down on the mat again, for her father motioned her to lie down, she felt her gaze dissolving in the sudden sunshine so that the figures before her turned indistinct, faceless: her father on the bed, her mother dressing, winding the six yards of the sari round her overweight waist, tucking the ends delicately into the waistband. Finally Sandhya got up and stood with her back to her parents and looked out at the trees by the railway track, at the banners she had failed to notice the evening before, strung out for the tenth national election.

It seemed to her that in the sudden pre-monsoon wind some of the banners dissolved into blown wings, parti-colored blown wings.

When things started to fall apart for Sandhya, after her return to Manhattan, the image of wings predominated. An angel, blown backward by a great wind. Everything she saw became that velocity, a swift corrosive motion, silvery fire.

"Wings, *WINGS,*" she wrote in the tattered journal Stephen found in her room. She had started writing when her sense of things skewed and often the most she could do was walk the streets of Manhattan, stand in traffic islands, or stare into the windows of the new shops that had opened on Broadway.

Looking in at the plastic mannequins set in the new clothing store, she saw their suits and jackets emblazoned with the words "wings" in neon colors, and knew that only if she could put her hand out through the glass, she might be saved. She considered tapping the glass with a bit of metal she had found on the street, making a hole, enough for a finger or a knuckle to pass. But she gave up when two cops stepped forward.

The letters she saw as she walked down the street started spinning. Slowly at first and then in a rush, Sandhya bowed her head, as if she were starting to ascend in the metal cage of a kamikaze machine set up in a fairground. Then English alphabets, bright and jittery, started to spin into the wild incandescence of Malayalam. She opened her mouth wide so she could swallow the hybrid syllables spinning by. Passersby gave her odd looks, the well-dressed woman that she was in her designer jeans and silk blouse, clutching her head in front of the plate glass of the new store, bending over as if doing obeisance to a terrible goddess.

But no Kali was in front of her, with gleaming arms and chain of bloody skulls. Only a plastic mannequin, with a brilliant smile, teeth glossed in the makeover she received at the factory, where bodies were manufactured in the thousands and shipped all over the United States. Who knew how long that industry would last, before the factory shut down and parts made up in Korea or Taiwan—thousands of blonde heads, it was still felt that blondes sold better—were posted back to the motherland?

In her mother's garden she could breathe deep, feel the warmth of her own flesh. She felt she knew every inch of outspread land, three acres fenced in: mango groves, papaya patches, golden clusters of laburnam, orange blossoms of tiger lilies perked into fans. Even the heat haze that had driven her indoors—as a child she sought the cool kitchen floor and curled up on the tiles, her tongue greedily licking the innards of a fresh coconut—could not exile her now from these acres of wild grass and flowering trees.

Dressed in a fresh cotton sari, Sandhya Rosenblum stood in the shade of the guava tree, her umbrella by her side, basket of fresh coffee and food all ready to be borne the half mile to the hospital. They took turns, mother and daughter, at Varki's bedside. Sandhya relieved her mother each morning so that Sosa could bathe, have a nap, arrange for the servants to prepare dinner before she returned to her husband's bedside. In the evenings, Sandhya enjoyed the quiet in the large house, the courtyard echoing with her footsteps. She would sit sipping tea by the mulberry, breathing in the fragrance of the glossy leaves where silkworms used to roost. No one would interrupt her in the courtyard unless her cousin Chandu were to return from Quilon or Ernakulam and burst in on her quietness, a glass of hard liquor in his hand, exhorting her half in jest, "Join, come join me, Sandhya." But she always refused his offers. Once she had said to him, "Now if Nunu's life were different, she might have joined you for a drink," but Chandu, for some reason she could never figure out, had taken that as a cruel joke, poking fun at Nunu's troubles, though that had hardly been what Sandhya intended.

Sandhya stepped back, rubbed her eyes with her hands, then straightening, glimpsed hundreds of black shells littering the gravel. Was she seeing right? Tiny snails glimmering with lacquer, the tips of their hard spirals phosphorescent in sunlight. Where had they come from? Surely not all the way from the river, or even from the small canal newly dug by the side of the bridge? She heard odd scraping sounds. Wings swept over the ornamental palms, past the incense tree. Forty, perhaps fifty crows, drawn by what sign she could not tell, had descended on the migratory snails.

With expert claws the crows tilted the shells, used beaks to ferret out the soft, moist life inside, gobbled up their prey.

She heard an odd whimpering in her ears, almost as if the helpless snails were exhorting her. If she weren't wearing a newly starched sari she would have raced down the gravel path, scooped up what snails she could, poured buckets of water over the nasty crows. But already, in a matter of a minute or so, the driveway was littered with the empty snail houses.

"Bhaskaran, Bhaskaran," she cried, and when the man came running from the rubber trees, she pointed at the remnants of the carnage. "Bad sign," he muttered, "Christ in heaven, how did they get here?" And he pointed back to the pond by the cowshed where the snails had started their migration toward some impossible, promised land.

Walking to the hospital calmed her. Sandhya decided she would say nothing to her parents, lest what she had witnessed be taken as an ill omen. If they asked why she was late, she would make up some story or another, draw Nunu into it if need be. But her parents, seated across from each other in the hospital room, nibbling freshly cooked *vadais* served on banana leaves, seemed not to notice. Her father had the radio turned on, something about a lightning storm that had struck the Kerala-Tamil Nadu border as Rajiv Gandhi was campaigning for reelection. A member of the Legislative Assembly had been injured by lightning right by his car, which was parked at the edge of a mountain pass. "Pre-monsoon storms," Varki announced, when she asked him about it. "Nothing to worry about where we are. We'll all get a good night's sleep, Sandhya," and her father had smiled at her.

In spite of her father's predictions, she had a hard night. Of course it was the phone call that shook her. Left to herself she might have been calm, concentrated on trying to forget those poor, helpless snails. But around midnight the phone rang, harsh, insistent. She forced herself out of her grandmother's rosewood bed, where she had taken refuge, raced into the living room. Then, cradling the receiver, she gazed out onto the driveway. One or two shells, missed by Bhaskaran in his cleanup, still lay on the gravel, pale inner passages transparent with moonlight, cavities all emptied out. She wanted to say something to Stephen about the snails, but he sounded so far away, bent upon maintaining his poise in that other world. He put the child to the phone and Sandhya murmured anxiously:

"It's Mami, darling, Mami," but Dora refused to speak. Stephen came on, clearly in charge now.

"She's fine. I miss you, though. When are you coming back?"

"Things are still a little hard here."

"Of course," he said. His voice sounded uneasy.

Sandhya held on to the line, hoping against hope to hear her child's voice.

"Sandhya?"

"Yes?"

"When are you coming back, I asked."

"They need me here."

"It's been a while."

Then, as if he felt this were too blunt, Stephen tried another tone, light, witty: "New York is waiting, you know! Bye bye, honey."

She put down the phone and, gathering her nightclothes about her, walked barefoot onto the veranda. Her mother was sleeping in the hospital, and the servants on the other side of the large, airy house could hardly hear. She set her knees on the marble parapet that ran the length of the house, gazed up at the moonlight in the *gulmohar* trees. The light had worked its way through a thicket of branches, then held to the leaves, so that all she saw seemed afloat in midair, parceled out into a thousand pools of radiance.

She gave herself up to the light, to the simplicity of the garden that drew her in, allowing her skin to be lit by moonlight, illuminated flesh cajoling sense, the snake of eternity, fragile as molting guava bark, rampant. But then thoughts of her married life crept up on her, an unkind disturbance. Stephen's call, even as it had comforted her with thoughts of his kindness toward her, for that is how she phrased it to herself, made her seem so arbitrary a creature. The physicality of her estrangement could not be denied, but that it should work into a spiritual uneasiness bewildered her.

Returning to Tiruvella, being needed as a daughter, she felt she had shed a second skin, an itchy nasty thing. She could breathe a little better, but the aching love for the child she had given birth to swelled inside her, made her feel tender, vulnerable, all her joints stretching to hold the child again. But to be Stephen's wife, how precarious it seemed, fraudulent even, matched only by the pasteboard face she forced on herself when greeting Mother-in-law Muriel. And out of Sandhya's mouth came a soft litany of "yes" and "no" that had even her gruff mother-in-law perplexed.

Only in the fleeting moments when she thought of Rashid, his hands, his small mouth, the slight irregular curve of his chin, did something of a finer self return, and it seemed to her then that his touch alone could save her from the cruel mesh of hands, elbows, knees she had fallen into. Longing to keep hold of her lover's image, she turned toward the garden that massed all about her, a profusion of flowering shrubs and fruit trees, the circular path winding around the incense tree whose bark glistened in moonlight. She stopped by the well, by the guava tree she had climbed as a child.

Were those his lips in the cleft of the tree, its skin mottled in moonlight? His hands were surely hidden in the crook of a branch, the mess of leaf covering it, his thighs, two smooth branches curving over her. Quickly, she set her hand to her mouth to stop herself from crying out, for she came upon a live snail worming its way into the orchid roots. She picked it up, gently set it into a puddle that had formed by the large patch of wild mint growing on the other side of the well. Then, slowly, she gathered her forces, tilted her face upward to the moonlight. The silver light wove into her, like the soft strands of her grandmother's hair dropping from the maid's comb. Kneeling by her grandmother, Sandhya had loved to wind the gleaming strands till her small thumb turned a silvery casque fit to trap the stars. *"Theru, theru,"* the old lady whispered, holding out a copper bowl for her fallen hair, and Sandhya was forced to relinquish her treasure.

The night was still, just the odd cry of a myna bird, a dog barking, and every now and then, a handful of crickets rasping against the steady hum of buses on the road to Mallapally. She shivered in the sudden chill. Back in her grandmother's bed, she felt as if she had a slight fever. Her legs were tight and cramped around the calves. She pulled the sheets over her face, shut her eyes. Someone was calling her name. She heard it again, a man's voice coming from a large room hung with paintings where music thickened and rose. The man held a thick, tubular instrument, pointed skyward, his cheeks puffed out, rosy. The child clutched her mother's hand.

"Mole, Mole, va, va." It was the *nageswaram* man calling her, but Sosa dragged the child away, toward the teak gallery in the Sri Chitra Palace, away from the man with his chest heaving, music pouring from him. Seated on an elephant, as he surely should have been, it would have been hard to tell him apart from the majestic beast, its trunk reared, the human

passenger doubling the haughtiness of animal flesh as the sun vanished behind the pearl-colored clouds and peacocks cried out in the palace gardens.

Suddenly it grew darker. The soft light seemed to have vanished. Sosa stopped in front of a painting. The child stared at it, the bottom frame level with her eyes. Behind her stood her mother, bulky, dark, preventing flight. Outside, the man with the *nageswaram* played on and on as if summoning guests to an invisible wedding, on and on as if his heart would burst. The child stood stock-still in front of the Ravi Varma painting, then, shifting her weight from foot to foot, she gazed at the details: a caged lady whose long hair dripped in black. Her sari, painted in thick dabs of white, shimmered like river water. In her right hand the painted lady held a knife. At her feet lay a mound of snail shells.

"As if the rivers of the east had turned to blood, were pouring down the human form," she heard someone say behind her mother.

"East?" someone else queried.

"Yes, Ravi Varma must have felt it."

The child turned to catch the faces, but the couple had moved on. She tried to free herself from her mother's hand, race away from the caged lady, find the man with the bursting instrument. She longed to bury her face in his lap, grasp the bony thing out of which a restless music flowed. But her mother held tight to her hand.

Then the landscape shifted. The palace walls fell away. Sandhya was walking very fast, leading her mother. They were far from the palace now, in a green landscape where the paddy grew, and river water turned turbulent under the bridge. Sandhya was walking toward the mango trees by the churchyard wall. Her bare feet marked the muddy path that separated the paddy fields and she walked on the flat of her feet, so she wouldn't slip. Sometimes though, when the path dipped by the paddy beds, she felt the river had risen, was almost in her eyes. She had to make it to the mango trees where the fishermen stood, waiting. Something was happening behind the churchyard walls, people gathering in a great silence. Then she realized that her mother was no longer with her.

"Amma, Amma!" Sandhya cried. But no one replied.

With a jolt, she drew herself up in bed, started disentangling her hands from the pink satin ribbons her grandmother had used to hold down the mosquito netting. Seated upright against the pillows, she rubbed her eyelids with her knuckles, blew tangled hair off her mouth, opened her eyes wide. It was only air, with the curtains blowing. In a blur, she saw the checked curtain swirl over the window bars and sensed, rather than saw, the sky's warmth at dawn, its blue bowl upturned on her. Then the room composed itself, the edge of the bed, chair, window ledge. She raised herself on an elbow. Perhaps Chellama would come into the room with a cup of hot milk. Or even her mother. As the sheet slipped off her shoulders, she stood up, feeling the cool tiled floor under her bare feet.

Slowly, shrugging her shoulders into a thin cotton gown, Sandhya made her way through the darkened bedrooms. Passing by way of the courtyard she entered the unlit pantry. The shelves were all around her, packed with utensils her mother used, ladles cut of metal or coconut husk, earthen mixing bowls, spoons cut of teak, sharp bronze knives, tiny silver forks. Eyes shut, she ran her fingers over the rows of Complan and Horlicks and fortified milk powders her father needed. His stomach was so frail, he could digest so little, laid up in the hospital bed. All the food had to be taken from home, twice, thrice a day. With eyes still adjusting to the half-light, rearranging the density of the objects on the shelves, she turned to the far corner, to the old white fridge her parents had purchased in Pune and brought with them to Tiruvella when they retired, seven years ago.

In front of the fridge a small figure was kneeling.

"Oh God, the head, where will they find the head?"

The old woman was weeping. Loudly, much too loudly. Why hadn't she noticed earlier?

"Oh God, that poor poor head."

Sandhya moved quickly: "The head, Chellama, what do you mean? Whose head? For God's sake tell me, whose head?"

She knelt and clutched the thin figure, her old *ayah* wrinkled now, the flesh on her arms sagging with muscles that had atrophied, hands gripping the fridge door. The old woman ripped the door open and pistachio nuts, dried raisins and figs, little vials of saffron Sandhya had picked up at the grocery store and carried to India in her luggage, all spilled out, a stream of nuts and dried fruits and shining tubes filled with delicate yellow shreds. With one hand she raised the old woman and with the other struggled to pick up the rolling condiments. She gave up the effort, shut the white metal door with a clang, rubber on corroding rubber, then squatted by the old woman who could not stop blubbering:

"*Ende Jesu, Jesu Christu,* the head, the poor bloodied head, blown up child, blown into little bits. Bloody little bits."

When she had calmed the old woman, Sandhya splashed water onto her own face, then went into the dining room and turned on the television set. The early morning broadcast started up with a low hum, relatively little static. The announcer's voice was low, mournful. Late last night ex–Prime Minister Rajiv Gandhi had been assassinated, at Sriperumbadur. As she listened carefully, Sandhya heard the moan of sirens coming from the back road. She stood at the doorway and saw four bicycles, two autorickshaws and a single jeep, all with loudspeakers held by Congress Party workers, black armbands in place, a slow, heavy convoy winding forward in a processional. They were announcing the *Maranam* of Rajiv Gandhi. Over and over the names of the three Gandhis were intoned. The great Mahatma topped the list. Then the Nehru family, mother and son. All three gunned down. Most recently, though it hadn't been a gun. A bomb of some sort, a body bomb a woman had tied to her own waist, that blew a forty-six-year-old man into tiny bloody bits.

A time of danger. Sandhya Rosenblum knew that was how she must think of time present. She leaned forward at the table. Already the cook had arrived in the house and was weeping bitterly, filled with conspiracy theories about the Janata Dal or the BJP. News of the LTTE made little sense to her. Sri Lanka seemed too far away to her, much further than Delhi. As Sandhya sat at the table, the wind from the garden blew the hair about her face. An onlooker would have thought her ten years younger, a lean young woman, waiting somewhere, at the edge of a platform or airstrip, where the pre-monsoon wind blows. From the back of her mind a bit of angry awareness seeped in: the monsoon never comes to Kerala in May. The rain never falls that early. Her waiting was too soon, too anxious. When the rain finally came, it would dissolve the tiny particles of the man blown up in Sriperumbadur. Thoughts splintered about her in a little halo. She turned her head to the right and out of the open door saw dust whirling around the incense tree whose glossy leaves hung in a shining umbrella. A hot wind started up, beating at the ornamental plantain leaves, twisting the wild corkscrews of the crotons with their scarlet-and-orange freckled leaves. Why did I have to come back, come back here at this time? She stared across the dining table at the man who sat with his back to her, his eyes glued to the TV set.

"Chandu," she called out, but he didn't turn. The music from the TV was too loud. Chandu, she wanted to say, Chandu look at me, here, turn around. She sat in the polished chair, holding herself erect and still as the hot wind blew in through the open doorway, raising the sand in the courtyard. How like Jay he looked from the back. He was four years older, though, and a few threads of gray showed in his head. "Chandu," she called again. He didn't turn. She stared out at the courtyard. It was hot, filled with sand. She saw the new water tower shaped like a dovecote, thirty feet tall, built by an architect whose dreams of Tex-Mex architecture in the hills of San Rafael made him overly sensitive to large structures, and in his zeal he designed a water tank out of all proportion to the two-hundred-year-old house built in the old Kerala style, with tiled roofs, long verandas, Dutch doors, and courtyards.

The tank cast a shadow on the mulberry plant that stood in the sandy courtyard, right by the window of Nunu's wing, a bedroom with a dressing room and bathroom attached. Nunu, my only sister, Sandhya thought. She was probably lying there staring out of the window, breathing in, breathing out, as if all of time had contracted to the pulse of breath. Was she willing her body to be a part of nature, like the goldfish in the fountain in the back garden or palmyra leaves swirling on the tree? Was Nunu sobbing? Sandhya strained forward, till she was sitting in a ramrod position. Then she blew out her breath, saying, "Chandu, Chandu," yet again, crooning the syllables as if to comfort herself, till the man across from her at the round table, facing the TV, narrowed his eyes and stared at her. There was something in his gaze that made her nervous. Why did he look at her so?

Chandu's cool voice cut in. With the TV down, Sandhya heard every vowel.

"All this Chandu-ing. *Bolo?* So his body got blown up into little bits."

"Not quite little bits."

She was feisty now, facing him, turning around in her chair.

"All right, all right then, face blown off, guts slipping out of the *salwar,* the Tamilian—that MLA, Janaki something-or-the-other, crying out, 'Rajivji, Rajivji,' I'll know him by those shoes. Shoes, sneakers really, with a big logo on them. LOTTO LOTTO!"

Chandu snorted, an odd intake of breath, as if the words had caused him some effort. Then he started laughing. There was sweat on his forehead, just beneath the thick glossy hair. Looking at him, Sandhya suddenly felt hot. It was just like when they were children: he got to it, always, bang-bang-bang. She wiped her face with the end of her sari and listened to his voice going on.

"Only the nostrils left. Imagine that. Only the nostrils left on the front of his face. That's because of the suicide bomber, Shalini-Shalu-Thanu, whatever-her-name, last seen before Sriperumbadur hundreds of miles and an ocean-crossing away, riding a bicycle in the green plains of Sri Lanka, NALAYANI painted in yellow on the mudguard of her bicycle. Did you know that?

"Now this thoroughly contemporary woman, precisely the same age as you, my dear cousin, this Shalini-Shalu-Thanu whatever, caught us, the Indian people, on the sly. She bent to do obeisance, bent down, mind you, low to touch his lotus feet. Then, bang-bang."

He waved his arms in the air. He pumped his knees up and down on the stone floor. The old table, which Sandhya's grandmother had acquired with her wedding dowry, its legs squat, teak top and sides covered in lace, masked over in plastic lest the turmeric sauces drop through and stain the fabric, that ancient table on which he had sometimes lain as a baby, creaked with Chandu's energy.

"Stop it, Chandu. Stop or I'll drop something and then Chellama will come running out and you'll get no tea. I swear. No *chai* for you. No *vadai* either."

"Okay, okay."

He seemed content to let the little speech pass unapplauded. He pushed the chair back and moved his well-built body forward to turn the sound on the TV up a little.

The image of the overweight vina player dressed in a white sari caught the light, and the lilting, melancholic air, Doordarshan funeral music, seeped into the white-walled room. Sandhya focused in on the strings, on the fingernails of the vina player. How absurd they seemed, little welts of brightness on a screen. Yet they made the music come and go, they plucked the strings, and the soft flesh beneath the nails caressed the wires into those electric leaps of melody. She shivered a little, thinking of flesh: flesh in sneakers, flesh that reached out, flesh caressed, flesh burnt, flesh blown into tiny bloody particles.

The whole of the next day the TV screen was filled with the state funeral. Doordarshan was doing a continuous shoot. Every two hours, to offer a respite from the electronic vision of May heat in Delhi, packed crowds moving through the dust haze risen above the Imperial Delhi Luytens had laid out, the music came on. Sandhya bit her lip. She was glad that it wasn't the singer of *bhajans* who held the hour. That voice, those words, imploring Krishna to come closer, always reduced her to tears. Whatever the occasion, there was always a terrible distance between the singer and the beloved.

If he saw her, hot tears slipping out, and where could she hide, Chandu would feel he had won. Won outright. It didn't strike her as odd that she still thought of winning or losing with him, first, second, I got it first, that sort of childish thing. Once he had plucked out a frog from the lotus pond and, as if in afterthought, started tormenting it till she gulped out, *"Ila, ila*—no, no," covering her eyes with both hands but peeping still through parted fingers as the hard pebble struck a quivering green foot and the webbed thing tore soundlessly.

She never made to move his arm away, or stay his hand. She watched, coward that she was, crouching on black rock.

What was it he had said the other day?

"New York has made you soft." That was it.

"Sandhya, Sandhya mine, New York City has softened you up. No iron left in you. Just tepid Hudson water."

And he brushed his hand against her cheek, just to make her realize it was a joke, paying absolutely no heed to her protests. So she raised her voice:

"You don't know what that city is like now. Killing fields, that's what. Asphalt, barbed wire, a demilitarized zone."

But her voice sounded tinny, unreal, even as she spoke. What did she know of those burned out blocks except in the eyes, the tight mouths, of those she saw on the subway, or at the edge of the sidewalks in the safer reaches of the Upper West Side where she lived. Except, there too one heard gunshots, and stabbings sometimes occurred even in the daytime. How could Chandu be expected to understand? It was ten, no, twelve years since he had taken his MBA at Columbia and since then he had never been further west than Berlin, where his chemical business took him each year. Fertilizers, wasn't that what he did, with some import-export God-knows-what on the side? Nothing too illicit, she hoped. Suddenly she felt she couldn't think straight anymore. All the thoughts in her head were crossed and the future tangled up in the plastic bomb that ripped through a young woman's flesh, tearing up our once and future leader.

That was what the inane old man they had brought on as a talking head kept repeating as a mantra, "Our once and future leader." Though what kind of future he had in mind, Sandhya could not imagine, or what the state-run TV station thought it was doing bringing an ancient processional on, chatting, chatting away about Nehru and Mrs. G. and Rajiv's charming childhood, and how this alone was India, this pasted-up, marked-down nation, its handsome leader bloodied, blown into the fragments any schoolchild in Saberkantha district or Quilon district could see on the local TV.

Catching Chandu out of the corner of her eye, Sandhya noticed he was fiddling with the wires behind the TV, black wires that linked up with the antennae on top of the house, wires they had to disconnect when it stormed in case the electricity tore into the set. It troubled her a little that she was alone with him in the house, the many-roomed, multi-verandaed house, heavy, sustaining itself without their help, stone floors, rosewood ceilings, delicate windows with carved shutters, double doors, Dutch-style, opening with the wind.

Why was it no one else was in the dining room, in the southern quarters, this side of the courtyard? Who could she cry out to? Who would hear her? Her mother was in the Mission Hospital down the road, in Room 18, where her father lay struggling to breathe.

She drew in her breath sharply. It was then that she heard the voice, high-pitched and clear, calling her. Nunu, she thought, Nunu. The name came to her with a little shock. Something suppressed, catching the light, a burble from a nostril left loose, a snitch of raw breath. Her little sister Nunu. Locked. That was it, locked in as was her habit. Though if you knocked gently, she might open the door a crack and peer out.

"Might as well do to myself what they do to me" was her explanation when Sandhya had asked her about locking herself up, and the response had a logic, a clarity that sat ill in the tangle of weeds and flowering shrubs, jagged spikes of the ornamental palm that jutted by their faces, as the two sisters reclined on white wicker chairs they had drawn out into the garden one fine summer's day.

The habit hadn't left Nunu. She seemed to have refined it though, locking herself up in her bedroom with the set of intricate bolts she had asked the carpenter to install. In Nunu's room were ancient posters of Pat Boone and Cliff Richards, and above her bed a poster of a contemporary evangelist who sported a fifties hairstyle. A Tamilian who operated out of Texas and went by the name of Pirabhakaran, selling the Gospel in honeyed notes to black and white and Indian alike. Under the image it said in bold lettering:

"Rainbow-hued Pirabhakaran calls you, in the Name of the Lord Jesus, Savior of the World."

Each of the letters in the legend was a different color, bright primary colors, fit to please a preschooler. Pirabhakaran—who looked like a cousin once-removed of the Rev. Al Sharpton, same plump cheeks, same dandy forehead, mustache shaved into a fine Dali-like line—had dressed himself for the poster photo in a Western coat of many colors: stripes rounded over his belly, buttons ready to burst, a lurid rainbow of synthetic stuff, printed on glossy paper and shipped all over the globe for subscribers to *Multi-colored Gospel,* the evangelical tract that his Society for Present-day Believers produced.

Nunu, her eyes glassy from the pills she took to keep her on an even keel, led her older sister into the room.

"Look, look," she said proudly. "They sent it to me, special delivery. Do you like it?"

"It looks American. Who is he?"

"Pirabhakaran, a convert from an outcaste community. Tamilian. They keep it quiet in America. They speak of him in the magazine as one of the last of the lost tribes of America."

"Native American, you mean?"

Nunu stared back at her sister, taking in the tired face, the hair that had fallen free of the band in which she had set it. Her own hands fluttered over the handloom skirt she wore, bunching up the fabric.

"Well, black, really. A black man from the lost tribes of America."

"Ahh ..."

Sandhya gazed at her sister's dilated eyes and kept her silence. In her own mind she rejected the jovial rejoinder that had come to her: "He must be a Malayali really, not Tamilian, all that enterprise." Her heart wasn't in it. There was no need to say anything. And why should she need to put out her armor so soon, buttress herself against her sister? It was two years since they had last met.

The fan worked the air in the room into little ripples that touched the edges of the posters, the sheaf of papers, the little blonde dolls Nunu had placed all in a row by the windowsill, their acrylic hair blowing. One of the windows was open a crack and Sandhya could see the tips of the mango leaves, dark green cut with lighter-colored veins, leaves she had brushed against, leaves she had once bitten and tasted. The green globe of fruit and then the curved chin of a new mango swung next to the leaves. Sandhya started to put her hand out, to touch Nunu, and found her own fingers trembling. She clasped her hands back behind her.

"How is Appa? How? How is he? You saw him, didn't you?" Nunu's voice tripped up and up. Obviously she too found the silence hard to bear.

"You stopped at the hospital, didn't you? Tell me."

She gripped her older sister roughly by the forearm. Sandhya shrank back, startled at the strength in Nunu's pale fingers. Then she eased herself down on the unmade bed, slowly passing her hand over her own face, wiping her forehead.

"Yes, yes," she said gently. "Yes, yes."

Then, since she could bear it no longer, she craned her head to look away at the stub of the mango tree outside, bark coated with dirt:

"He's so thin, though. Skin and bones."

Abruptly, Nunu pulled herself up and walked away, taking jagged, irregular steps. She posed, arms akimbo, by the poster of Evangelist Pirabhakaran.

"My sister." Nunu's voice sounded mocking in Sandhya's tired ears, an echo of something she could scarcely catch.

"My New York sister, foreign returned."

"I came for Appa, you know that," Sandhya said softly.

She laid herself down on her sister's bed. Outside she could hear the Kottayam bus passing, the milkman crying out, the crows tearing their lungs out. And under it all, the lilting sounds of a new film song, turned very low, from somewhere across the Pamba river.

"I've come home for Appa. To see you and Amma, too. But because Appa was so sick."

She shut her eyes, utterly exhausted. *Home is where, when you go ...* she thought, but the thought remained unfinished in her head.

The sand-strewn courtyard, with its brilliant light, hurt Sandhya's eyes. She forced her eyes open again as sunlight tore in, flooding her. There was nothing in that courtyard, not even a torn white sheet left over from the traveling puppeteers of her childhood. Somehow the momentary blinding offered relief, a small certitude in a landscape filled with nothing but itself, a crater, a ripped-up desolation.

Suddenly, she and Chandu started running, across the courtyard toward Nunu's room. Nunu was inside the room, they were sure of it. But what was she doing there? When the door finally opened, in response to their banging and cajoling, all Sandhya and Chandu could see in the half-darkness, apart from the curtains blowing and the fan turning slowly, was Nunu standing at the door, her blue-eyed doll in her hand. One of the doll's legs was mangled, torn.

"Are you okay?"

"Is everything okay?" Sandhya heard herself repeating. All she got was Nunu's twisted little smile. "Those snails," she heard her sister say. "The

crows really got them, eh? Nature's cruelty, Sis. That's why we need God."
Nunu's fingers moved restlessly through the doll's bleached white hair. "I
saw those crows," she added, needlessly.

Sandhya could not bear to look at her sister's face. She turned her head
sharply away. Through the open window she saw a piece of sky drifting
between two blossoming trees, a powder blue, unreal substance. And
then her sister's door slammed shut, and Sandhya was left in the dim light
of the adjoining bedroom, next to Chandu.

Later that evening, Chandu, perhaps to distract her, brought up details
of the chemical sales he had in mind, including some deal that he wanted
to make with Ravi, cousin Sakhi's husband. Perhaps they could start an ex-
port of Kerala goods. "What?" Sandhya queried, trying to distract herself
from worry about Nunu.

"Rubber, coconut products. Coir, that sort of thing. Surely there would
be quite a market in the States for coir rope and matting? In any case, Ravi
is fairly well-placed in ATT and has business contacts there. How is Sakhi
doing, by the way?"

Not waiting for his cousin to respond, Chandu answered his own question: Sakhi was involved in some feminist stuff. He said this sniffing the air
about him, his handsome nose jutting out, as if there were something just
slightly off about the notion. "Like jasmine that's gone overripe," he explained to Sandhya, who sat without opening her mouth.

"After all, my dear, what are women for but to fill us—by which I mean
the male species—with their exquisite fragrances?"

When she remained still, hardly seeming to listen, he added: "Twenty
to one, I bet that Pirabhakaran Nunu's so taken with has his group of feminine adorers, women who cater to him. No harm in that, is there?"

At this, Sandhya turned away, her face a mask. Watching her walk out
of the room, Chandu thought how finely she was shaped, and how she
was wasted on that American chap whose name, quite inadvertently, he
kept forgetting. Someday he would meet him, and Pirabhakaran, too.
Little did Chandu know that just a month later at the Maramon
Convention, packed with Christian evangelists from the world over, he
would wander out into a tea shop and come face to face with
Pirabhakaran. A conversation would start up between the two men on
the subject of America, with Chandu listening in disbelief to Pirabhakaran's grand plan of burning up the garbage dumps of New York City.

The next step would follow: shattering glass from New York City's sky-scrapers into tiny fragments.

"Rapture Returned" was what Pirabhakaran called the scheme, and Chandu could not get that phrase out of his head. He was to think of it as he stood by the Maramon River, gazing down at the swiftly flowing water. Soon hordes of Christians would come to cast themselves into the river water. Then they would show off their glistening bodies in the light, crying out in ecstasy at the new world.

Poet's Café
(Draupadi)

And when you came toward me, your face uplifted,
it really was transfigured by fire, wasn't it?
  — *Jean Genet*, The Balcony

While Sandhya was in India, I got a call from Anthony. "Dream up a performance piece," he said. "Something that involves crossing borders. Set it by a riverbank. Imagine us all, black, white, yellow, brown, stripped down, leaping into water."

I laughed gently. "Not quite in the mood," I told him. But he pleaded with me and I agreed. I needed work that could keep me, body and soul.

Things were hard with Rinaldo. And though I hardly saw him, I felt he was the only home I had. There was a heat in my calf muscles, an ache in my guts I couldn't control. I stood for hours staring out of my window. Rough water and sky entered my soul.

I imagined the air Melville breathed, different from the acrid stuff outside my Westbeth window. Ahab taking shape in Melville's brain, the monumental whale of desire sharpening its teeth. I exiled myself in dreams of a man racked by longing for islands, chartless dreams where trees with live heads of women sway in the wind, and men in concupiscent camaraderie chuck each other under the chin, then swarm into oily piles of ambergris in celebration of the all-American thing.

I made notes on a scrap of paper. I thought of making up a song, "Ooh, America, my newfound land …" But the voice stopped in me.

The copy of *Walden* I pinched from the high school library in Gingee caught my eye. I thought of HDT, who refused to pay taxes to a government that had undertaken the task of being "the refuge of liberty" and yet kept a sixth of its population enslaved. I thought of Harriet Jacobs, who wrote under the name of Linda Brent, a woman escaped from bondage, hidden in a tiny hole in the attic, peeping at her children. Oh, the longing to touch them, hold them in her arms. Oh, the longing for freedom!

This great Leviathan, America, surely it's our fantasy of freedom that makes it come alive, chewing off arms, legs, ears. Sackfuls of sleep it guzzles, this new Kaliya setting up whirlpools of death.

I thought of CC, duped by the dream of Cathay, the route eastward to India, the surface of pacific waters working particles of salt that shimmered till cormorants turned into angels.

Late at night I started writing, sipping clear water to take away the hurt in my head.

I made it all up in the present tense.

I race up the stairs at Poet's Café. Tongues shoot out of my head. Anthony stares, dreadlocks askew, then wipes his eyes. Mago with his Bwango Band: "New York Salsified," he cries in delight. The Fifth Avenue matron brought in by her gigolo screams as Anthony, squinting to see if Mago's microphone's in place, trips over her knee, his "Free South Africa, Then Free Me" T-shirt tight over his chest. She bobs and her blue hair sprouts over Mago's mouth.

The crooner with the hennaed hair and orange silk suit—they brought her in from Arthur Avenue where the Mafioso roves—cries without stopping. I imagine her words:

> Draupadi, syncretic buhuhu
> Where have all the maidens guhuhu

I beckon my soul sisters forward, three of them, one Black, one Anglo, one Hispanic-Asian. They start swaying, arms linked, singing the words I had made up the night before.

"Dottie and her sisters, all exiles, heads flaming! Listen to them roar!" Anthony cries out through his microphone.

I performed for them all. For Simon Escobar and Juan and the woman from the Literacy Program in the Bronx; for the Fifth Avenue matron and her gigolo; for Anthony and the group of kids from the barrio who were turning themselves into a "Postmodern Unit for the Propagation of Poetry in our Streets." I performed for lovers twined round each other, men whose mouths sprouted perfect mustaches, others whose lips turned the color of ripe pomegranates such as Cavafy might have kissed in the darkened alleyways of Alexandria.

I performed for the young woman who woke up crying, "Mother, Mother, I am burning!" and her dead mother rushed out of the East where the sun rises and put out the flames that were eating her child's breasts, thighs, the purple blotches on her arms from the HIV turned fiery.

One of my dancing sisters turned into Tawana Brawley, wrapping herself up in plastic, smearing excrement on her dark skin, tarring herself, setting white feathers on her flesh like the white men did to her foremothers. Then she crept into the plastic garbage bag. "She was put there, whether her own hands did it or not," we sang, arms linked, swaying.

Then another song turned in my head. A song of Paradise House:

> Gimme, gimme, go-go, Dottie sings at the shelter door,
> I shall live in Paradise House for ever more!

I started crooning it, doing a double take in my head, figuring out how I could use that song for the show at Lincoln Center I was trying out for, the outdoor bandstand with the lime trees all around and the Race-Ethnicity-Gender-CrossTalk thing everyone's so hot into. Except it's our flesh that's crossed, wires and all. I know this as I hang the locket with Mama's picture in it round my neck and feel the lace under my armpits drenched with sweat. I am making up my own act, rehearsing it as I go along, and it's all I have.

Music thickens. Mago with his Bwango Band comes on crooning "Congo Boys, Congo." He turns to the girls: "Say Pwango, girls, say Pwango." The girls, one touching fifty, lean up, wiggling their breasts, shirts decked out in squares of black and blue. They grind their hips, put out their hands, and the marimba calls.

Anthony's eyes screw my back so tight I walk dead upright. I know through the muscles in my back, it's a wise muscle that knows, he's trying to get himself off the lapdog's leash. "Come, come tonight," he hisses. Then the wind blew and door flew open: Santosh Blissji, the singer, entered wrapped up in silks. He blew me a kiss and suddenly I longed for Rinaldo. Wanted him bad. I was sick of his voyages, to Italy, Brazil, Peru, wherever Fiats are sold.

No peace then. I had to put on my skintight thing, do my solo. Lights dimmed. I stepped forward, clad in a brown body suit mimicking skin, embroidered in satin fakery.

A flute player from the Forty-second Street subway stop started up. And the player of the Indian cymbals cut from conch shells and rosewood. I moved slowly, started using the words that came to me:

Old CC, just listen to me. It's my rega thing, I am making it up like Apache Meridian might.

This country of ours, this America is a wild riderless thing. All the presidents know it and the presidents' women too.

We need autobiography else the blue expanse would drive us mad. Think of the dead bodies of Apaches, the broken bodies of slaves thrust underground. This is how we reach the blue expanse, the sublime vacancy?

HDT saw that space. Staring into water he longed to escape.

If I drove a horse and cart through the woods and put a man I loved into the right side and a woman I loved into the left, I would be flush with water.

Or would I sink, hoisted by so much body weight, the flood of Walden pond letting me through?

We emerge, not wet at all, into Asia.

It is an Easter thing, this rising into Asia.

In India I stoop, I drink the pure water of the Ganges. My hat slips to my nose. I hook my arms through the arms of the man and woman I love. We dance south, into the sea.

O Thoreau, tax-evader, inspirer of Gandhi, who inspired Martin Luther King Jr., make a blessed ring for us with your dancing.

I stopped, took a break to wipe my chin, run a comb through my hair, fix my bra straps. I practiced moving my arms in a low swirl as I imagined dancers in India. I continued:

Ladies and Gentlemen, watch me as CC writing a letter to Ferdinand and Isabella of Spain.

Dear Lord and Lady, you have driven the Jews out of Spain, and driven the Moors out, too. Now give me leave to sail westward to India.

I shall spike that loose fish for Christendom, and return, souls aplenty drawn behind my boat. I'll bring sackfuls of pepper, trunkfuls of gold.

It was the Pope who replied:

Blank space, snare it, old CC. Only all heathens there. You must plant our flag where you can.

I stopped, breathing hard, then went on:

Columbus struck America and called it *India*. It was India to him till the very end, when mad, bound raving to the bottom of his boat, he was shipped in chains to Spain. "O India, *my newfound land,*" he cried. "*My kingdom safeliest when with one man manned …*"

He would have said more except that, unable to bear his ravings any longer, they were forced to gag him. Then old CC heard music in his head, played by creatures with silky black hair, dwellers of Hispaniola whose beauty had dazzled him. He could not believe those were the half-human, half-bestial creatures he had once been led to expect.

I stopped, shut my eyes, took in the applause, stepped back, dizzy as if India were all around. I might have slipped and fallen except that Anthony stuck a drink into my hand and called on my dancing sisters. He guided me to my seat so that I could sit a while before my Harriet Jacobs/Linda Brent piece.

I had told Anthony I needed help, so he brought on this new guy, John Ray. The man had wandered in, in search of work. From someplace in Pennsylvania, said Anthony. I was not so happy when I saw him on the outside of the cage I was to use. A thin man dressed in camouflage garb like he was part of some militia. I choked, clipped on my mike, and closed the cage door.

They put me in an attic to save my life. I could hardly breathe. I had a tiny hole to peer through.

I shall never bow down to Dr. Flint, that cruel man.

I started coughing and Anthony, seeing my trouble, walked over quickly to help. "Try something else," he whispered. As if on cue, John Ray, that gaunt blond man, made his own thing up.

He stuck his fist into the cell door and offered me an orange.

"Who are you?"

"Who?" I stared at him. He had no lines there.

"I said, 'you.' Hear me, girl?"

"Call me *Draupadi!*" My voice rose.

"Dropti!" He started laughing at that. "Funny name for a girl with black hair! Come over here, Dropti, Dropti!"

I lost my nerve, held the cage door tight. I was glad I had the bars between us.

He made up a new name for me. "Bette," he called me. "Bette, you Asian cunt. Come over here, slow, take it slowly now." And he held his hand out with a lump of sugar in it as if he were beckoning a mule.

I stood up very straight, gripped the bars of the cage. "Draupadi!" I cried out loud and clear then, with my hands free, I did a little dance. "Call me 'Draupadi!'"

Out of the corner of my eye I saw Santosh Blissji clapping for me.

Later, perhaps even a whole week later, I returned to Poet's Café. I was sick and tired after a phone call from Rinaldo. He called from Dhahran airport. I could hear the luggage carts, the voices booming in the background. The performance space was empty now but I needed to touch those walls again. The cage was standing in Poet's Café. Anthony must have felt it looked good as part of the decor. I sat with my back against it and the feel of the bars comforted me. I sat there and wrote to my love.

Poet's Café, I put at the top, *Avenue B*. So he would know where I was. Not Bellagio or Perugia or somewhere grand and old world, but right here in our North American ferment:

> *Rinaldo dear,*
>
> *You told me once that your reading of Nabokov drew you to America. Not irrelevant perhaps is that the nimble genius of butterflies, White Russian fallen from grace, confessed in print he had to invent America in order to make* Lolita *that work you so admire.*
>
> *And did you have to invent me in order to live here, Rinaldo? I need to know. No more calls, chéri. I cannot stand those voices in my ear.*
>
> *I have a "Fuck the Fathers" program in my head, do you know, Rinaldo?*

I thought of tearing my composition into little bits, then smearing lipstick on the bits. Instead, I found a scrap of wall. I stood straight, a lean young thing dressed in black, scrawling with black-cased Revlon:

Rinaldo dearest,

Lest we forget. You picked me up when I was a young thing and got me into the Paradise House program. You are an old man with a hot cock. Spit on you!

Draupadi

Dear, dear Rinaldo,

Down with sorrow. Up with fucking. We are all here in the present perfect. I should not be addressing myself to you any more. My thumb up your ...

Your Beloved (She who has no name. Who stood in a cage. Whose skin is no color. Queen under each hill you ride your super special Fiat over.)

Draupadi

Stoning

She had chosen life in the new world. Sakhi Karunakaran put out her foot and prodded a stone. It was hard to move, and her toe hurt. She drew back sharply. Perhaps there was a base to the stone, perhaps it extended hundreds of feet into the depths of the continent. On smooth bits of it, buried now under topsoil, native peoples might have etched a sacred knowledge. She could have a petroglyph under her feet. And there she was, with her little picket fence, in the town of New Brunswick, living off the fat of the land. No, not in a mobile home or trailer, rather enjoying all the spoils of this country. She breathed hard. Watched the car speeding out of the driveway past her. Waved at her neighbors and was struck by the profile of the woman in the backseat, so like Sandhya, a little lighter in coloring perhaps, but those same high cheekbones. The Costas's niece, she thought, edging away from the hard stone, toward the trickle of water that ran over the curving cobblestones she had set in place just a year ago.

There was a slight mound in the earth and the trickle ran around it, ending up in a patch of mint. The soil around the roots absorbed all the water. The stalks of mint were etched with scars from ice and snow, winter wounds, but underneath the hard nubble the new green leaves were starting to push out, tiny whorls of green. Sakhi wished she could stop, put out her fingers, smooth them against her cheek. What a long time it had taken her to learn to plant her own garden.

She had never worked soil into her hands as a child. But on long summer holidays, before the monsoons fell, when heat rose from the green trees, making it hard to breathe, she and Sandhya had watched the gardeners carrying bucket after bucket of water to Sosa's precious orchids. In the late afternoons her aunt would take the car and driver and vanish into the hillside, fifty-odd miles away, returning with bushels of the fleshy, fragrant flowers to replenish her stock. The back of the car was all covered in soil, and Sosa's sari drenched with moist earth, but no one seemed to care. Afterward the girls would stand by the well as Ayah washed the mud off their arms with the sweet-tasting well water.

Born within a week of each other, Sandhya and Sakhi had been taught to regard each other almost as sisters. Their mothers, who lived twelve miles apart, had shared detailed news of their pregnancies: morning sickness, the first flutter under the breastbone, tiny, racing heartbeats. Then came the painful contractions, and after giving birth, the sheer delight of infants, their cries, the regularity with which they drank milk and excreted, their first steps. The two women also shared other bodily sensations, how heavy their breasts felt, whether the nipples were sore, the special blend of oils needed to ease that soreness. They did not speak of the enormous welling satisfaction as the child suckled, the sheer pleasure it gave, though perhaps this was understood in the warmth of their conversation, the slow laughter that spilled out. How had it happened then that the cousins had gone their very different ways? Sandhya was always drawn into difficulty, while she, Sakhi, stood at the edge, watching. Helping if she could, running away if she couldn't. And Nunu. Sakhi paused, drawing in her breath. Where was the letter Nunu had sent weeks ago? It had begun on a fairly friendly note, but turned bizarre soon enough:

The mangoes are thriving. Black pond snails attacked the garden. But the crows from the mango trees got them first. My sister, Sandhya, has changed a lot. She tries to make sure I take my little pills at night, but I threw them out the window. By the way, Sakhi, I hope you don't mind my saying this, but why live in America? Don't you know it's the country of high garbage? Soon they will burn all the garbage, Dr. P. says. Have you met the Rev. Dr. Pirabhakaran? He believes in Rapture. All the worlds will end soon, he says. As in Apocalypse.

Sakhi had tucked the note away in a drawer and never written back. What could she have said to Nunu? Of course your sister has changed, she lives in a different world now. As for garbage, I recycle whatever I can. I have a small garden here and do all the work in it myself. The reference to Pirabhakaran, the charismatic religious leader, she wouldn't touch. All of that religion made Sakhi nervous. If only human beings could keep their heads straight.

She tried to imagine Sandhya and Nunu walking in the Tiruvella garden. But those flower beds and carefully manicured lawns had all fallen into disrepair. The crew of gardeners had vanished. There was barely enough money to keep the white walls painted, tiles on the roof in good trim. Perhaps if the house were to tumble down entirely, they would all be forced to live in the forest. If all the houses were to tumble down!

Impatient with her ponderings, Sakhi stared at the stone, its inch of granite risen, impenitent, through soil. She stamped her feet clean of dirt and tried to focus her mind. She would have a hard day ahead. Day by day, Sakhi's caseload as a social worker was increasing—more calls for help with children forcibly kept out of school, married women being beaten up. Some ordinary root of evil in the human heart. Was that what it was? The thick knob of the mint in her garden came to mind. The gnarled central stalk, then the fragile newness bursting through. She could live for that newness if she had to.

She stooped and plucked a few stalks of mint to take with her to work. She would set the leaves in a glass of water and breathe in a little of the intoxicating fragrance. A few hours later, cleaning out her desk, she found a scrap of paper. A single line caught her eye.

"It's lovely to think of you back home." It was a letter she had started to Sandhya. Sakhi's gaze took in the rough ending of the sentence she had penned. The word "home" scrawled as if the hand hadn't quite wanted to acknowledge it. "Home," where was that after all? Was Tiruvella, where her parents lived, "home" to Sandhya? Or New York? Sandhya had married Stephen and crossed a border with him. Surely marriage meant setting up a new home? Sakhi tried to the get words right from an American poem she had read as a child. A poem about an old woodcutter, a family retainer perhaps, who had returned unexpectedly and the householder and wife were debating what to do with him. Something about home and having to "take you in." No one could turn Sandhya away from Tiruvella, that was for sure, though who knows, if Nunu had enough power, she might try.

Her hands in her desk drawer, turning over a pile of paper, Sakhi cast her mind back to her dead mother. An unhappiness used to come over her, like mist over a summer morning, bathing her in a simmering melancholy. Shobha was in her early forties when her gloom seemed worst. She would sit by the edge of the bed, in the small house in Trivandrum, her long hair flowing about her, unable even to comb it. So Sakhi, who couldn't have been more than eleven, would call for the maid. And under the tender combing Marya gave her hair, her mother revived a little.

"I want to go home, Marya," she would whisper to her maid, who responded: "Amma, Amma, where can you go?"

"My parents are dead. I need a change of scene. Should I go to my brother in Tiruvella?" Shobha would ask this as the shining strands of her hair were worked into a gleaming sculpture on her head, and the maid, fingers wet with coconut oil, stood over her stiff form.

Quickly Sakhi got up and worked her way to the coffee machine. The image of her mother filled her. That melancholy, where had it come from? Was it caused by a keen longing for love? Shobha was unhappy in her marriage, but that was something a woman was brought up to expect. Why had it affected her so? Was she too frail to deal with her husband and his harsh political friends, their drinking, their dreams of business expansion?

Returning to her desk after some chitchat with Martin, who asked after her old casework, and Rhona, who had a hurt hand, having strained it riding a moped in Greece, Sakhi found it hard to concentrate. Sandhya slipped into her thoughts. There was a helplessness in her cousin that put Sahki in mind of her own mother. She should throw that unfinished note away. After all, Sandhya would be back home soon. Home. She was using that wretched word again. Sakhi shook her head and turned back to the files on her desktop.

It was late at night by the time she drove back, grateful the highway was deserted. Entering the front door, she threw off her coat, worked her way upstairs to the bedroom. Almost before she knew it, she was sound asleep. A good two hours later Ravi came in, ran the water in the tub, hoisted himself into bed. Sakhi thought she heard him mumble something about having a drink with Jay; too many drinks with Jay; they were debating the terrible assassination of Rajiv Gandhi. She sat up, rubbing her eyes, and held his hand. It had shocked her too, that news, but she tried to put it out of her mind as best she could. She slipped back to sleep and by the time she woke up, Ravi had left for work.

Glad to be alone, Sakhi pulled on a sweater and an old pair of trousers. She stood on the porch and brushed her hair aside, squinting into the sunlight. Her hair was long. She normally held it back with a simple ribbon. Blue was what she preferred and she bought blue ribbons in the store, six for a dollar, just as she bought tights and knee-highs all in black so if a ribbon or sock got lost, the whole accoutrement would not dissipate into unnatural eccentricity. She was wearing only sandals and stamped her feet to warm them. As she moved forward into the garden, her right foot hit another stone. This one was loose, she could sense it, but it was half buried in green and instead of stooping to pick it up, she was content for the moment to leave it unturned. Sometimes she would let things be, just where they were, a stone, a fallen sweater, a scarf on the bedroom floor. At other times she worked her way toward a quick, petulant order, which might give a sense of a well-ordered household. Yes, there is someone here who notices the small things out of place, a pin, a hairbrush, and sets them back where they belong. So she pushed the loose stone with her foot, quite deliberately, bent over, tossed it toward the white picket fence Ravi had just painted. The stone landed with a thud, scraping the paint. Nothing that would show, but it seemed to her another sign of the general decrepitude, a world where so few troubled themselves to make room for others.

But what of feelings that welled up? Intense feelings. Was that what was happening to Sandhya? Sakhi felt a pang of hurt. Why hadn't Sandhya written? Jay had received a postcard from her. He had come by, bearing a wild strawberry he had grown in a pot on his windowsill. A tiny thing, bright scarlet, half the size of her thumbnail. Sakhi had cradled it in her hand, filled with wonder at the bright flesh, the tiny hairs stuck on like burrs. So what if Sandhya had something going on with that man Rashid, as Jay had hinted. When Sakhi had met Rashid at the dinner party, she found him utterly charming. She tried to follow his line of thought when he launched into a description of post-colonialism, something to do with the aftermath of European rule, new global villages, telecommunications. In spite of his pedantic language there was an energy about him she found attractive. Had that drawn Sandhya? Would Jay know?

She sighed deeply, how people changed! Jay had taken photographs in India, powerful, painful images that opened people's eyes. Why had he stopped taking real pictures? The things he did on Lexington Avenue didn't really count, so he told her. Now he was scribbling lines of poetry that didn't quite work and reading them out to Ravi, perhaps to Rashid, too. Not that she had anything against poems, but Sakhi felt they were seen by so few people. It was not like there were *mushairas* or *kavi sammelans* in America. The audience for those printed stanzas was so small. Pictures, on the other hand, could be published in magazines, newspapers. Hundreds, thousands of people could see them and be moved. Jay had done that with his "Three in the Afternoon" and the other photos he had taken after the riots.

A car passed on the road by her fence, its radio blaring. "Making up, breaking up," an old song Sakhi had heard in Madras and more recently in the East Brunswick shopping mall. The Beach Boys, wasn't it? She hummed the tune. How fitful human emotions were. Still, people got married, in the hope of some permanence. But all around them, those who married were getting divorced. Look at the Hayakawas three doors down, or the Powers, plain spoken people from Vermont. Or even the Mukherjees, who would have thought it of them? And it wasn't always that there was another human being involved, sex or the steamy side of things, which is what the mind always jumped to. Perhaps these divorces were just another sign of human beings saying, "Yes, I have some control over my life, yes."

A minimal sense of control and the pleasure of beauty, what else was there? Would she consider leaving Ravi? Would she stay if he came with a wild strawberry in his palm, a tiny prickly thing, all red and bruised, saying, "My dear, I plucked it for you. On my way home from work in Edison, New Jersey, I got off the highway and turned into that grassy patch I see so often. Got down on my hands and knees, leaving the car door open, and found this tiny thing, and plucked it for you." Sakhi stopped. It was hard for her to imagine Ravi doing this. He had coarsened, grown duller in his time at ATT. Of course he had done very well, rising to a fairly good middle-management position. But the act of getting there had consumed him. What of the small joyful impulses that had made him come running to her, off the bus, all those years ago in Madras, arms filled with jasmine flowers for her? How young he had looked, how happy. The soul needed pleasure, or else it got bruised. She felt this, but how could she put it into words for him? She too had changed in America, no doubt about it.

The decision not to have children had been hers, and he had respected it. It was hard on him. She could tell by the way Ravi played with the Mukherjee's boy Tarun, showering presents on the child, lollipops, little cars with wind-up keys, the kind he had had as a child. Or with Dora, Sandhya's daughter. How good he was, taking her on his knee and singing her songs while the child played with his little finger or stood on his lap and twirled her fingers in his hair. But even if they had children, might it not have come to this, the mute way in which they brushed past each other in the mornings, not knowing what to say, because so much had already been left unsaid? The small betrayals of trust. Nothing major so far, but the little things added up.

She herself had changed in a way that she could not have predicted. Needing something clearer, firmer than Ravi could offer. The winds that blew into her face from the world outside held voices crying out to her. With so many others to be accounted for, their pain, their need to be taken care of, what she might have thought of as her self had altered radically, even perniciously some might argue, in the search for a greater good. Now there was scarcely time for the little patch of mint she had planted in the yard and hadn't bothered to weed and trim. Bushelfuls she used to take into the kitchen to make mint tea for Ravi, herself, their friends.

She bent down and set her hands to the green fragrance. It grew wild in East Brunswick, as it did in her grandmother's house in Tiruvella, in Nagercoil too, where Ravi's parents still lived. Straightening up, she set her back to the fence, right where her husband had painted the wood, and its coarseness against her back comforted her.

Her mind moved to Sandhya's husband. Stephen seemed such a kind, decent chap, but it was as if Sandhya had shut him off in a rage. Perhaps it was the difficulty of marrying a foreigner, the burden of giving birth in a strange city. Perhaps it was the jumpiness of the city that had worked into her cousin, forcing her away from Stephen, into the arms of this other man. But could cities have that power? The thought of Manhattan made Sakhi tremble. All that crime, guns, rape, even in the subways, everyone heard of it. New Yorkers had the Empire State Building and the World Trade Center. Still, what good did it do to live staring down from an immense height at poverty and pain crawling on the ground, human beings drugged out of their minds, stabbing each other, shooting, for absolutely no reason except that nothing made sense and there was no reason to stop oneself. She thought of herself as a moderate sort of human being, but at times the idea of an overcrowded metropolis made her feel faint. She pressed against the fence. She had to admit, though, that on her infrequent visits, she rarely failed to enjoy the city: its sheer robustness, the quickstep of the marginal folks crowded in there, competing fragrances rife in the polluted air.

Sandhya had grown attached to Rashid in Manhattan. But why had things fallen apart with Stephen? Sakhi grew uncomfortable with her thoughts. Perhaps there was something in her cousin, some intensity of perception that Stephen simply did not see, could not feel. The thoughts seemed too close to home. She turned back to a memory of the Manhattan skyline, jagged, piercing the air, the sun red on that winter afternoon, floating like a blood orange beside the Empire State Building. They didn't get that grandeur here. Back against the picket fence she gazed at the strip of road, then the swath of green broken by the white walls of the grocery store, the livid orange roof of the new Howard Johnson's. She loved East Brunswick. She would live and die here. The simplicity of that faith had sustained her when she went to be fingerprinted, then stood in the long line of people pledging their allegiance: other Indians, Dominicans and Russians, and Chinese and Koreans too, all come to this large, ample-breasted country, *Americamata,* which fate had drawn her to. She would rest here. The thought consoled her. She felt nothing of the guilt so many of her compatriots bore in switching passports, as if they were mortgaging one world for another. She was Indian, she would live and die that way. No one could change her skin, or say to her: your parents are not buried in the churchyard in Tiruvella; your in-laws never lived in Nagercoil. Nor have you ever spoken Malayalam. Surely it is the greatest of illusions that it is your mother tongue. None of that would happen.

Rather, responding to what this life, this ceaseless metamorphosis of spirit, required, Sakhi had become an American. It was what she wanted, given the way she had lived, so simply and well, all these years. Fifteen years since they had come to East Brunswick, bought the house and fixed it up. They had very little money at the start, but they persisted. She had her job as an accountant and Ravi with his M.S. from Madras had done well, starting right away at ATT. She had learned to drive on the highways, to navigate her cart through the supermarket, adjust her feet to shoes and socks in winter and the endless layers of garments the snow required. No, it didn't come naturally, wearing all that heavy clothing. She knew this, having observed young mothers in the church she sometimes attended. They had to hold their children down, forcing young legs and arms into snowsuits to prevent frostbite, pneumonia, sickness by exposure to cold. Human beings learned how to survive, and in surviving, they changed. The thought did not hurt her.

But how swiftly things moved. When Jay visited, the conversation had turned to childhood play. "The train game!" he said, turning to her, his eyes shining. And they remembered the chalk hill by the Tiruvella house that summer long ago. Sandhya, too scared to slide down, had stood by a neem tree and watched them. Once Sakhi had pulled her so hard that Sandhya had slipped down the hill and hurt herself. So they just let her be as the train game went on. Not minding if she cried out on seeing Uncle Itty's long shadow, clumping along, down by the paddy fields. They didn't pay any heed, for Jay and Sakhi were calling out to each other the long list of trains they had seen on the tracks that ran by the paddy fields. Trains that connected up the shining breadth of the new India: "Kottayam to Kanyakumari," "Kashmir to Koddaicanal," "Cuttack to Cuddalore," and the real names spilled over into childish play as wind and wet chalk clung to them, turning their young bodies into speeding spots of delight. As they slipped down the chalk hill, faster and faster, Jay pressed on with the train game while Sakhi, who was older, but more timid, flagged. "Come on, come on now," he cried, "Tirunelveli to Trishur. Make it all *T*'s, Sakhi, please please," and he raced round the far side of the chalk hill where Sandhya stood, her hands clapped over her ears as she watched Jay working his tongue over sounds that all blurred into one shining, incomprehensible whole.

S andhya Rosenblum was in the car when the stoning took place in that New Jersey mall. How could he have forgotten? The odd look on her face, the shame, as if it were her fault that the teenagers, cruising by in a red car, had cast stones at her. She had ducked, avoided direct hurt, then wanted to conceal the whole thing from her husband. "It will hurt him so much," she had begged her cousins. "After all, he brought me here." What a funny attitude to take. Ravi couldn't understand it, but there was always something a little fragile about Sandhya and a sense of shame, as if she were fit to be punished, though for what she herself didn't seem to know. Of course, they'd told her husband. Stephen's face had gone all white and he had knelt by her, and murmured, "Poor, poor Sandy." And she just sat at the edge of the chair, a slightly bemused expression on her face, ill at ease, to say the least. Like a crane in a rice field, hobbling on one foot. Now if only Sandhya had married an Indian, living in America would be easier on her; Ravi truly believed this. In her present state it was as if she were cast out by the community. Where could she make a place for herself?

There was something on the road ahead, a pothole. He braked hard. The sun was beaming down. Ravi shut his eyes tight, then squinting, moved out his hand to pull the reflector down. He forgot about Sandhya. He was grateful to be driving, quite fast, through the streets of East Brunswick. It gave him a sense of accomplishment, of power even. Yes, that was what it was, the feeling of getting things done. Not like the bewilderment that flooded him as he sat in the bar listening to Jay's poems. Jay had drawn a sheaf of poems out of his pocket and thrust them in his face. What a thing to do to another man! Seated upright in the car, Ravi shook his head in dismay. There was one about a bench with lots of funny words stuck together. A second poem made an impression on him. "Against Something or the Other." What, he could not recall.

A poem, almost raunchy he thought, about a woman tearing her Kancheepuram sari into a G-string and doing a dance on the table at the West End Bar. Crazy! In spite of his five bourbons Ravi was shocked when Jay told him the woman he had in mind in the poem was Sandhya.

"No, not our Sandhya," he had protested weakly.

"Sure," Jay replied. "She needs to tear up all the saris old Stephen bought her in India. She might be better off then."

Then in a serious vein he added: "I think she's in quite deep with him. I don't think going back to India will help her." When Ravi asked after the anonymous "him," Jay clammed up. In the blur of drink he had thought about that as carefully as he could. Was Sandhya having an affair with someone? But it was Sakhi's face that floated into his mind, and quickly he pushed the thought away.

Ravi could feel the car humming beneath him as he crossed a bridge over a stream, and the sound of running water was in his ears. He was grateful for East Brunswick, the clarity of the streets where they leave you alone. The lights of the newly furbished bagel shop glowed in the slight mist. Perhaps a heat haze was coming on. He held onto his steering wheel and thought about his boss Manikam. Rumor had it that Manikam was shortly to be posted to London. All Ravi knew of London was the transit lounge at Heathrow, but he imagined fog over the houses of Parliament, British gunboats he had heard of as a child, and then suddenly he imagined children pouring out of a red double-decker bus, onto the bridge, racing into Westminster Abbey. Children all colors and shapes, rather like a UNICEF calendar come to life, except they were dressed in identical workaday clothing. Their mouths wide open, singing. One of those children—his heart almost stopped—surely one of those children was his, a small girl running apart from the fray.

Suddenly it started drizzling. He clutched hard at the wheel. A piece of fabric on the road, dark, balled-up, almost halted him. He pulled into a gas station, the East Brunswick New Khalsa. He saw the daughter, Sonali, in her red *kurta*, come out the door and stand in the rain. He thought he saw a banyan tree behind her and the clear skies of the Punjab, without massacres there, no blood where millet should bloom, no stones in the mouths of dead children. He saw himself holding Sonali's hand, racing across the street. Suddenly he felt a wet mass pushing against his thigh. It was the pile of *vadais* Manikam had given him, left over from a wedding his wife Saroja had catered.

"Give them to Sakhi," old Manikam said. "She'll enjoy *vadai*, no? *Thaire vadai.*"

Ravi had smiled his thanks. Now he rolled down the car window and young Sonali approached him.

"*Aaou, aou,*" he said, smiling at her. She stood there so shy. Still in the car, he passed the foil pan out to her. "Please take these," he said, "give them to your mother. They are good *dahi vadai.* You'll enjoy them."

What a sweet child she was. She accepted the pan, hesitantly holding the gift of food in her hand. The wind was damp on his face as it blew from the small wooded area. He blinked, then pressed the accelerator down. Damn, he had forgotten the gas. She was still there, watching him, Sonali with her *dupatta* flying about her face, holding the *dahi vadai.*

A gift, it was so long since he had brought his wife a gift. There was so much rage in Sakhi, he could not understand it. Where did it all come from? Perhaps it was the stoning incident that sparked it off. She had gone with Jay and Sandhya in search of Indian shops and spices. On the way they stopped in a mall. Sakhi was dressed in a sari. Five youths, she counted them, from the working class Italian neighborhood drove by in a fast car. They had rotten tomatoes, a pile of stones.

"Don't stare at me like that, Ravi. Yes, real stones, my dear, and they hurt me. Sandhya ducked, that's how she escaped the stones."

One had hit Sakhi on her right breast, and the nipple, to which she applied all manner of medicament, grew swollen, and remained bruised for weeks. But the shock was worst of all, the moral shock. Two stones struck. "Paki," they yelled, then, "Hindu," one after the other, as if the words were interchangeable.

"Neither of which," she told him with a wry grin, sitting in the bathtub, "suits my flesh very well."

"But what is flesh, or black hair?" she asked, tossing hair off her face. Then, "Ouch, ouch," for her breast hurt and she tucked flannel over it as he brought her hot tea in the tub.

But the tenderness the stoning episode brought out was brief, for Sakhi, in the weeks that followed, was eaten up by emotions he could not understand.

"Stoning," she said to him one evening as they came in the front door together.

"They said when we were girls we would get stoned in the marketplace if we went out without escort, or showed our bare arms. Half-clothed women get stoned. It stayed in my dreams. I longed to hide my whole body in a *burkha,* only the eyes showing. Such safety in coverings. Women are at risk, all over the world, you know that, my dear, don't you?"

"My dear," he thought. "She called me that."

And it was with a pang that he realized it was only force of habit that led her to use the term. She was so intent on trying to teach him, to take him with her into this new world lit by anger. Whereas he wanted to touch her, hold her hand, stroke her hair, draw her closer to him. Then that book came UPS, or did Jay bring it along? He wasn't sure. Something Jay's friend Draupadi wanted Sakhi to see. Sakhi had laid it under his nose, so he could hardly focus on the white cover with the three ships. A chap called Bernal Díaz standing by a ship, pontificating. The drawing made the chap look quite ridiculous. Sakhi read out the words:

"These Indians, they don't know an island from terra firma, they are such savages." And then, she added, a slight smile on her lips: "Words of the fifteenth century Spaniard."

As she read out the passage so solemnly, he felt a pang of sympathy for his wife, who was taking it all so personally. Every time she heard the word *Indian,* she started up. Now she was threatening to give up the accounting business that had helped them to set up, and devote herself to antiracist, antisexist work, as she put it. Not that he had any aversion to it, but why bring it all together like that? All these oppositions. Resistances, she would have said. What of their shared life, he wanted to ask. What of that? It hurt him too much to think.

The next day, when Ravi passed the New Khalsa gas station, Sonali was nowhere to be seen. The skies had cleared and the field of wild grass immediately to the right shone with tiny grass blades the color of bright honey. He could make out a pile of neatly laid rocks and a mother and small child with tousled brown hair sitting still beside it. Seeing them in that bright field he felt the delight of light and air and sensed for an instant an eternity at the borders of which he sometimes hovered. His childhood had given him that.

But there were red lights and he came to a quick halt, watching intently as a family crossed the street. White, working class folks. The father with blue jeans eased down his belly, the mother in a pair of culottes, the two children clutching bags, all moving down the road, closer to the forests. He tried to imagine what their life might be like, the raw meat shaped into patties, cold milk for the children, endless rounds of the televangelist Tom Tamburn crying out, "Love, love," while the telephone number was rattled out so that money might pour into the coffers of Tamburn, Inc.: Salvation on the Rebound. Then another voice cut into his head. He heard Jay in the bar holding forth: "The fear of the present that late capitalism instills in us is ground down into the pennies in the small child's hand. The phone line rattles into the future, foretelling instant cash. Consider the background sign: BELIEF IN GOD BRINGS WEALTH, SPEND AND RECEIVE. But

Tamburn was shouting into the microphone and the woman's hand placed according to instructions was trembling against the screen— "Harder, harder, that the grace may pour down ... Pour down your grace"—and suddenly the shot cut to Tamburn's Rolls Royce parked next to dark green trees in midsummer, a whole forest filled with rippling green, the camera closing in on the *RR* discreetly set into the back of the polished metal body while strains of "Amazing Grace" poured out.

Ravi shook his head hard. He was hearing voices, seeing things. Mercifully, the family was past. He trembled, thinking of the future. And perhaps for the very first time, his thought moved to others quite unlike him: workers for the Asiad games, bused into Delhi from distant villages a whole year before the athletes arrived; stuck in insanitary little hovels, hundreds died from cholera and dysentery. And the bridges and highways built with cheap concrete started collapsing soon enough in the monsoon rains. He thought of a small child in the marketplace in Sriperumbadur, standing near the unfinished statue of Gandhi. The bomb blast that killed Rajiv Gandhi had smashed part of the plaster nose, the wire glasses fitted to the low-cost image of the father of the nation. He thought of an American solider fitting his body into army fatigues and gas mask on the sands outside Dhahran, biting back prayers that his four-year-old left behind in Oregon will not shiver as the wind blows, rattling the windowpane.

These fragmented ponderings so disturbed him, Ravi was forced to stop the car. It made no sense to keep driving. He sat for a long while at the edge of a field where wild strawberries grew. But though he opened the car door, and set his two feet on the earth, he did not stoop down and pick any of those small, scarlet berries. He let them grow, in the wild American grass whose fragrance was still new to him. He breathed in deeply, tugged off his polished brown shoes, plucked off his socks and when he felt some peace flow in from the earth, through his bare feet, he decided to go back home.

Back home, resting in the green armchair, Ravi felt feverish. He took out a white linen handkerchief and wiped his forehead. If only Sakhi were with him now. He would give anything for a cup of warm tea from her hands. That strawberry, why couldn't he have picked it for her? If only he could ask her to shut her eyes, draw the blue ribbon out of her hair. He would watch the dark mass flow onto her shoulders, and when she opened her eyes, Sakhi would find the tiny strawberry in her palm and give a little cry of delight. "Sweets to the sweet ..."

Where did that come from? Some line he had studied in school, surely. It bewildered him, for the voice that was uttering it had grown harsh. No, it couldn't be, could it? John Ray, the new janitor at work, come in off the streets of Manhattan, they said. Hired on some ATT plan to employ veterans. The man with dirty-blond hair seemed to be fixated on Ravi, lying in wait for him, even outside the corporate dining room where, of course, a janitor had no business being.

John Ray, it was him again.

"The angel John, the archangel who took human form and had visions of the end," Jay quipped when Ravi told him of his discomfort with the janitor. But that voice. He was drunk in that bar, and there was John the janitor. A scene from work flooded into him: John Ray was on his hands and knees. He was blocking Ravi's entrance into the men's room. There he was, down on his hands and knees, ostentatiously scrubbing away, his green T-shirt dripping with soapsuds.

"How goes it, John?"

"Yeah?"

"Nice day?"

"Sure." The man paused. "Know Shiva?"

So that was what it was about, his religion. But John seemed a most unlikely adherent to Shaivism. Still, Ravi thought it best to merely nod his head and seem unfazed.

"Know Shiva, like Shiva lights?"

"Shiva lights. You mean special prayer lamps for Shiva?"

He was trying hard to talk to the man. Surely anyone could see.

"Sure, sure," and John got up, towering over him. Ravi noticed how red his hands were with all that scrubbing. John was saying something to him:

"You thought I meant new cigarettes, eh, Virginia Slims sort of thing. But I meant: Out by the Mekong is where I saw the lights, on the ship cruising back and forth. We were shelling Commies from the ship. Went in there after the flood, to rescue the their idol. That's who. They had their little villages, neon Shiva wheel, and in the middle a laughing Buddha. Plastic kind. Like the dashboard Jesus. Seen it now?"

Ravi shook his head. Mercifully, John was back on his knees. But he looked up, tilting his head on strong shoulders, and went on. Why does he need to get back on his knees to talk to me, Ravi thought, and it struck him that the man might spring up again any minute. But he was talking into his bucket, every now and then glancing up at Ravi as if he had known him from another life:

"Know Verdi village, right there, not far from your home country, too? I got her in the ass. Called it *Verdi,* but it was bloody green once the shelling started. Brown bits too. I dragged her down by the wheel and butted her. That's for that, you too. We had an Indian with us. Forget your native tribes, I said to him. You's American now. Bang, bang. Right, left, center. That's what I taught him. Back on the reservation, keep it up. Okay, okay? You too?"

John's voice slipped and he returned to the soapsuds. Was he out of his head? There was some psychiatric trouble in the background, old Vietnam vet. That's what the company had said. When he mentioned it to his boss, Manikam, later, being careful to leave out all reference to the presumed proximity of Verdi village to India, the old man was angry. "I told Kleinhazzer in Personnel there would be trouble. Would he listen? No."

It was days later, watching Sakhi move in her fluid way about the kitchen, picking up the oil, the mustard seed, the chili powder, that the rest of John Ray's talk returned:

"Powder, that's what we use for Shiva lights. Know that? Powder in the horseman's eye. Not your religion, I know, but read it." The man was counseling him, Ravi felt, and let the kneeling figure go on:

"The number is exact. The elect. The powder means he can't see a damn. Not a bloody damn. After I left Kentucky, I had a spell in the Big City. Full of signs. Numbers glued to lampposts. I tore one off and stuck it to my palm. Made a fist over it. Numbers are prophetic, right? Took me to Avenue B in Manhattan. That café filled with drink. Found a cage. A woman in it. Stuck her an orange. Looked Indian. Sure looked Indian. Right? Like you?"

Ravi started backing away.

"'Are you saved, Bette?' I asked her. On and on she went, growling. That wild music!"

Ravi heard his own voice as he backed away, to his office.

"Saved?"

"Uh-huh."

It was clear the man would not leave him alone. The voice filled the hall, rough, rude, homegrown:

"Your kind, that woman. Keep singing your song, I told Bette. Music never broke cage doors!"

The house of her childhood with its whitewashed walls and sandy courtyard marked the center of a luminous geography. Sandhya had known it since her memory began, the red-tiled roof, lightning rod now set about with TV antennae and, by the wellside, grasshoppers, small red ants and, in the cottonwood tree, cicadas trilling. All this was etched into her and she did not want to travel far during her stay in Tiruvella for fear it would blur. Nor did her daily strolls make her stray from this clear center. She almost never went as far as the riverbanks where the swirling waters bound for the lagoons closer to the Arabian Sea might have put her in mind of her own troublesome desires.

The landscape of childhood seemed to allow entry into a simpler world. When small excitations of the flesh occurred, she had thrust the carnage of pond snails firmly out of mind, she took them to be part of encircling nature. Even the assassination of a political leader, terrible as it was, could be seen as part of a life where eruptions of violence, even when they occurred, were intermittent and far from the norm.

The thought of New York was confusing and returning seemed forced on her, part of a course of events she could not avoid. Yet to swerve now might cause danger, rupture a marriage whose complexities she did not have the wits to name or the resolve to openly acknowledge. In any case, her longing to see Dora again was growing.

There were consolations: her father was back in the bedroom with the high teak ceiling, windows swathed with muslin curtains. Her mother was less fraught. Sosa's hands had ceased quivering as she combed out her hair and she had even pulled out a pile of her old silk saris to give to the *dekchi wallah* in exchange for pewter plates. Other, finer saris Sosa had given the maid to take to the new drycleaners who had opened in town, and one or two she pressed on her eldest daughter. "My dear Sandhya, you never know when a good *kancheevaram* sari will come in handy." Sandhya didn't have the heart to refuse.

Nunu, however, had become harder to deal with, her brief conversations with Sandhya taking the form of fantasies that Nunu now harbored: of climbing to the top of the new water tower, there was a slight metal ladder attached to the side for use by workmen, and singing out the praises of Pirabhakaran's new doctrines. Fortunately the ladder was removed on Varki's instructions and somehow or the other Sandhya managed to calm her sister down.

A few weeks after her father's return from the hospital, Sandhya sensed it was time to go. Stephen was sounding tense on the phone. She herself was growing cramped in the house of her birth. When the time came Sandhya hugged her mother, bent over and kissed her father tenderly on the cheek. "See, you're all right now, Appa, I came back for you. We'll meet again soon," she said, and before the easy tears could slip down her cheeks, she picked up her two small bags and got into the car. Nunu was lying on her bed in the back room and wouldn't emerge, even when Chandu, who was escorting his cousin to the airport, yelled, "Hey, Naomi, where are you? Your sister's leaving." Sandhya waited a few moments then, unable to stay any longer, slipped away.

In the airport she felt a bitter emotion course through her, as salt might in water. She saw the palm trees dance rhythmic, green, brushing the sky, heard the voices of passengers and felt she understood very little. The plane was poised on the runway, its tiny wheels glinting. She stopped short, unable to budge, somehow managed to slip off her sandals. The shock of the hot runway against bare feet roused her. If no one were watching she might have knelt, touched her lips to that black knobby substance, hard as iron, over which planes raced before launching. Then the energy of transit took hold of her and cautiously she walked over the runway, climbed up the tilting metal steps. Airborne, she saw the spray of the Arabian Sea, foam and water blown against a blue bowl of sky. She knew that something within her had changed.

Back in the city Sandhya inched back, closer to her lover. It was as if proximity to Rashid absolved her of the need to choose how to live. Then, too, their intimacy could thrust the messiness of the world aside, or so it seemed for a while. The question of moral courage, voicing the truth of what she really felt, never arose. This would have been alien to her, raised as she was to a femininity where desires were to be kept hidden. The notion of resolve, charted out by what one might call an inner voice, or even a delicate governance of will, would have seemed far too disruptive to what she had fashioned as her way of living. So Sandhya Rosenblum groped her way forward, in odd, inchoate fashion, binding what she could to a fragile self-awareness. Needless to say, the distance between her and Stephen grew. They wandered apart, each seemingly content to let the other be. But underneath something boiled, a dark root of rage, sulfur to the tongue, threatening composure. This incipient danger was well veiled, the hood snapped tight over the eyes, the brown hawk prancing on the hand.

Sometimes her child seemed part of a life she no longer needed. And it was hard for Sandhya to refigure herself as the one who must coax and cuddle, wash and dry and heal. Dora, on the brink of turning five, seemed oddly jittery in her mother's presence. One afternoon the child used her crayons and made a plane with silver wings, an odd wobbly thing, thick-bellied. Two stick figures, one big, one little, were going up the steps. There was blue all around, sky, air, but in one corner of the picture stood a dark jutting thing.

"What's that, darling?" Sandhya asked.

"A subway, Mami, there's a subway."

"In the sky?" Sandhya leaned against the fridge, a cup of cocoa for the child in hand. Dora nodded solemnly.

"That's the subway through heaven. We'll go on that to see Appa-chen." Heart pounding, Sandhya held the small child close to her, then set her on a little metal stool and watched as Dora sucked greedily at the tiny marshmallows in the hot cup. "More?" asked Sandhya. The child shook her head and the picture, which was set at the edge of the kitchen counter, fluttered to the floor. Sandhya stooped, picked it up.

"Before I put it on the fridge," she said to Dora, "will you draw something more for me?" The child waited. "A flower, darling, draw Mama a flower." Sandhya watched as Dora picked up the red crayon and made a flower with four petals on a brown stalk. In a child's desire for order, she drew a flowerpot to hold the stalk. The single blossom stood underneath the spiraling subway line, a vivid reminder of longing.

Then came the days when the news from home turned bad. Her father, who had gained so much strength, was slipping into a decline nothing could prevent. Every weekend she called him, spoke in slow measured syl-lables, gave Varki all her news as she thought of it. She even mentioned a few details of the political world, the mobilization of soldiers, the local protests against the war, and felt the pleasure of his responses. He was hungry for her news and wanted to hear more than the cut and shape of Dora's new clothes.

But when she was with Rashid, Sandhya let herself slip, sank her be-wildered consciousness into what she felt was his strength. In spite of how little she really knew him, she longed to dive into his past, be stung into newness by him. At such times Rashid's touch, his taste, filled her. His scent was in her nostrils. The roughness of his palms moved her, the soft-ness of his fingertips. He held her hair in his right hand, the whole of her body cradled on his thighs. Her long black hair swinging its heft through the circle of his hands, he sang a song in Arabic. How she loved it, those sunlit landscapes sparked by his voice, sights and sounds that promised to release her.

She tried to imagine his mother, and what he was like as an infant. He showed her a photograph. Rashid, about a year old, seated upright in his mother's lap, wary, frowning a little. The child's feet were bare, toes flexed. His mother's right hand was held firmly over the tiny foot as if to stop it from kicking out. How lovely the woman was in that photograph, with her two black braids and her downcast gaze. The embroidered bedouin robe she wore covered her knees and ankles. She was dressed up for a festival with jewels on her forehead, and earrings that cast a tiny shadow in the image. How still they sat, mother and child. How did they begin? Where did they part?

Abruptly, Rashid took the photograph from Sandhya and set it on a table by the bed. He looked at her directly:

"There was something desperate in me as a child."

She did not want to listen to him, for she felt the gentle, rhythmic rise and fall of his ribs, the aftermath of desire, a sweetness uncoerced. Surely this was how she was to be always, her head on his belly, the black strands of her hair falling over his navel, covering too that most tender part of him, limp now, with a freckle on its upper rim. To give it a name, "penis" or some other, would have been beyond her. She had never learned such words in her mother tongue, her upper–middle class background, with the Victorian ethos of her nationalist grandparents forming shield and buckler. The best she could do was listen to the raucous talk of servants, where the pleasure of bodily parts was freely evoked, jokes exchanged, curses spat amidst the evisceration of chickens, the ordure of goats, the gutting of fresh fish, the cleaning of cow dung.

She felt Rashid's palm on her right shoulder, then his thumb working into the muscle that so often hurt when she lifted Dora up. She wondered at the memory of pain entering into the delicacy of a room shielded by rain-drenched trees, the clear sunlight about to break through.

"Because of your father?" she asked, thinking that might be what he meant.

Slowly she drew her wrist across the pallor of his belly, where a few hairs curled, wondering at the darkness of her own skin and how it lit his up. The fragile, concupiscent harmony they made was surely not bound to any conceivable permanence. Or could it be?

He was speaking of his mother. Had Sandhya forgotten that his father had died when he was so very young?

"No," she said, "I have not forgotten."

"Mama went out to the market, taking the maid with her. We had no incense, for tea you know, so that the cups could smoke over it. She was out for a long while."

As she listened, Sandhya curved her knees over his side, so she made a bridge over the pour of his body. She tugged hard at the thin sheet Zahir had left behind. The sheet was dappled with the sunlight that filtered in through elm leaves, poised on delicate sprigs of stalk. Stalks that also held thin brown birds whose cries punctured the far roar of traffic.

Her mouth felt dry. It was all that kissing, she thought. There was a glass of water by the table and, raising herself on an elbow, she sipped from it. She loved Rashid's stories. Perhaps now he would speak of a walk by the Mediterranean, or the sudden sighting of a gawky secretary bird in the swampy lower garden, or a camel broken from the herd driven to the slaughterhouse. She wanted something strange, previously clenched inside him, unfurled gently as a gift for her.

"I was in the bedroom. The bedroom I used was almost bare."

"Did you have your own bedroom?"

He nodded, asking her in turn: "Didn't you?"

"No, never."

How could she tell him how odd that would have seemed, cruel even, a young girl put in a room by herself in the large house in India. The parents would have been severely blamed.

Sosa, passing through New York for a brief visit when Dora was six months old, had been shocked to find her grandchild sleeping alone in a crib in the small makeshift study that was tucked off the kitchen. Promptly she bundled up the sleeping child and bore her into her own room. The following morning, right after breakfast, she delivered a little sermon on the errors of letting children sleep on their own:

"Put them in by themselves now, and they leave you at eighteen. Is that what you really want?"

Sosa was pleading with her new son-in-law, the curious child-rearing practices of Westerners filling her with a momentary despair. She appealed to her daughter,

"Why, Sandhya *mol,* you never slept alone, by yourself in a room, till you went to Hyderabad. Why, why?" And she had clutched her grandchild to her bosom, determined to give it what love she could.

Rashid was sitting up, tugging his shirt over his neck. Watching him,

Sandhya felt an emotion, fluid as a light wind through elm leaves, dropping her down, turning her over and over as if her body had scarcely any weight to it. Soon he would pull on his trousers. She in turn would push arms, neck, hips through blouse and skirt and they would be forced to part.

She waited for him to go into the kitchen, put on the black, half-burnt kettle. She waited to hear, "Coffee, Sandy, remember *Gahwa. Gahwa, wala chai?*" But instead he said:

"I had my own bedroom: it was large, cavernous almost." His voice was oddly hollow, coming from inside the shirt.

"Sparsely furnished, a small desk I used for my homework with a lamp on it, a bed set against the wall, and an immense cupboard I inherited from my father's father. That was it. Through the double windows I saw Nile water, heard the cries of the fellahin dragging piles of wood and metal up the path to the construction site that Uncle Yunus had set up."

Buttoning up, he seemed to hesitate. Had he forgotten about the tea? She was on the brink of offering to put on the kettle.

"It's very simple."

Something in his tone made her turn to look at his face.

"As soon as I heard the car with my mother pull out of the drive, I threw myself on the floor."

"Why?"

"I needed to."

"Was it cool on the floor?"

"Yes, of course, it was stone. Were your floors like that in India?"

She nodded, waiting for him to go on, puzzled when he didn't. Somehow the topic of the floor made her uncomfortable, though the coolness of fine stone lapping at skin and hair was something she had always relished as a child. A desk, which he could have used with a chair, would have seemed so much more ordinary.

"You used a desk for your homework?"

He gave a lopsided smile: "Of course."

"Perhaps you hated homework?"

"Nothing like that. I was reading the usual, *Robinson Crusoe,* and an abridged version of Melville's whale book, nothing about the whiteness of the whale in the version I read. I had thrown myself on the floor, remember? I rolled over on the floor, right by where the desk was."

"How old were you?"

"Seven, eight, something like that."

"I found the spot—the plug point. The lamp was disconnected. Wiped off my little finger and stuck it in. The shock threw me back. I did it again, and again. Once I was flung back against the bed and hit my head. I told no one, of course."

Later, they sat in silence, drinking the fine Earl Grey tea Rashid preferred. He had brought in a tray, with the two cups poised on its shiny surface, and a plateful of crackers. She watched him shift the glass of water, set down the tray, lift up a cup for her. She put out both her hands to receive it. The gesture calmed her.

She could sense that Rashid needed to talk on. His voice had a low, swirling quality to it, as if he were reaching through waters in a stream, bending low to capture the memories:

"Had a long stick, found it by the water's edge. Went on whipping it by the seawall. Mama, seated on the veranda, under a parasol, heard me. As I approached, she bent over quickly, over a piece of embroidery, and wiped her eyes. The sun was very bright, shining off the river. I could only see part of her face because of the parasol.

"'Nuha, Nuha.' She called one of the maids to bring out some sweets for me. She always forgot I couldn't bear the *konafa* that was her favorite, prepared in such large quantities in the house—crushed nuts, filo pastry rolled over, honey. You know it, don't you?"

Sandhya said nothing, so he added with needless emphasis: "As a child I disliked it intensely."

"I love *konafa*. I've only had it once or twice."

She whispered the words through her tumble of hair, not wanting to talk. Half of her mind was on his words, the other half on her jacket that lay flung over the back of the chair by the window. How shall I raise myself, she thought, pick up the brush, for I need to brush my hair even as he speaks of his mother. I shall arch my back just so he can see my spine.

Such thoughts about her own body and its taut, lovely disposition had never entered her in her lovemaking with Stephen, the only other man she had ever had. Her love for Gautam had never been consummated, and with his death sexual memory was knotted in her head with the barbed wire the Hyderabad police used to torture their victims.

With Stephen, the nervous tension she now felt was lacking entirely, but the lack, she thought, made somehow for a transparency, a greater innocence. When things worked out between them the atmosphere they breathed in remained clear and cool as running water. Often, though, it seemed as if there was no compelling connection between them, and their warm bodies lay firmly apart.

The desire Rashid awoke in her was an agitation in all her parts, a series of small fires lit in her muscles, her skin. How could she have lived without it so long? Feet crossed, intensely thoughtful, she gazed at him as she moved her head under the hairbrush she had carefully picked out of her bag. Too new in the ways of passion, she did not ask herself, "How long, how long will it last?"

He watched her as she sat, arm resting on the back of the bentwood chair, sunlight on her face, on the edge of her brow, almost turning her into a Coptic icon. His blue shirt was tossed casually over her shoulders. So she had not dressed yet. He was pleased. Normally she raced as if a hound dog were after her. The hounds of the God of Death, risen from my native Nilus, he once thought in an odd Orientalist turn, but his compassion had risen. When he looked out of the window, she was shaking as she ran past the *Forty Acres and a Mule* store, not even glancing at the long line of teenagers, the kids in Afros and blunt cuts, girls with huge hooped earrings and bright chatter, that normally held her gaze.

Sandhya went on brushing her hair. It was quite long and covered her face as she tipped her neck forward. He kept talking. A Cairo bedroom came back, uncanny, shifting backdrop, effacing the present. But the furniture in it seemed overly solid, collateral to any damage dreams might inflict.

"Once I threw myself into the cupboard. It was Father's, you know. Years later, in boarding school in Britain, I imagined bombs falling. Their bombs and the cupboard burning."

"I too was curled up inside a cupboard."

She said this softly. He heard her voice through the pile of hair. She was thinking: Burning, burning inside a cupboard, and nothing makes sense anymore.

After a silence, during which Sandhya sat up, her hair brushed and shiny, and looked at him steadily, Rashid said:

"I think the experiment with electricity came after that."

Rashid was seven when he conducted the experiment with electricity—stuck his little finger in the socket. Sandhya knew that age. She was seven years old when things started to fizzle and burn in her own head. It was the summer Uncle Itty, her mother's cousin, had come visiting from the Nilgiris. He had just had a nervous breakdown. "Such a brilliant man," Sosa whispered, "a taste of family life will help him." And Sandhya had watched as each evening, after dinner, Itty tore scraps of cotton from the cotton ball he kept in his bedroom and, stooping low, stuffed the wisps into all the plug holes in the dining room.

"So it won't leak out, Sandhya *mol,* so it won't leak out," he reassured her.

"Here, come and help me," and he had made her tear off bits of muslin from her old petticoat and hand them to him. It was Itty who, as part of his "Frankenstein game," locked her into a cupboard. First, however, he had done his best to explain the rules of the game to her. It was all to do with electricity. Mary Shelley had a story about a monster made of bits and pieces of flesh. Electricity made it come alive. And Itty had pointed out the great casurina tree by the fence, struck in a lightning storm, bark split down the sides, red flesh darkened by sun, broken up inside. It was the same force that could make life, said Itty. In the story, a scientist had given this creature made of bits and pieces of flesh jolts of electricity.

"Will you help me?" he asked Sandhya.

Thinking the game harmless, she had nodded, fearful though when he coaxed her into the rosewood cupboard.

"Cry, 'ouch, ouch' if you feel anything," he counseled her, as he poked bits of tamarind thorn through the gap in the cupboard door. "Little bits of flesh electrified, *mol,* like that creature."

She had shut her eyes, rolled tight into a ball to avoid the jabbing stick. And managed all right, squealing only when Itty wanted reassurance. Her nice pink frock was all soiled and Ayah had scolded her. Itty meanwhile, each time he poked a stick through, had trembled in excitement.

"There, there," he cried in his triumph, stopping only when Sosa entered the room, a pile of saris neatly folded in her arms, and put a firm stop to the game. Itty had been banished to the far wing of the house. Much later he came back and said how sorry he was he had locked Sandhya in. And to try and make it up to her he drew two paper dolls, one bent over the other. He colored them with burnt coconut husks and cut them out. Always good with his hands, he attached string and made the dolls dance on Sandhya's desk as she was doing her Malayalam homework. The vowels she was trying to learn by heart slipped and struck against each other; the feet of the dancing dolls, thin, tremulous, made a curious music the syllables she was memorizing could neither capture nor erase.

Later, subjected by Sosa to a long lecture on "Never behave like that again," Itty returned to Sandhya. This time, Itty blamed his actions on the

Communists: "I put you in the cupboard so you'll be safe, child, safe," he told her over and over again. Then, quite forgetting the "Frankenstein game," he quoted lines from Percy Shelley's sonnet:

> Graves from which a glorious Phantom may
> Burst, to illumine our tempestuous day.

Clearly it was a poem about liberty. But as Itty explained it to Sandhya and Sosa, the Kerala Communists were bursting out of paddy field and coconut grove all set to take vengeance on those who had forced them underground.

"They say it'll be a class war, child. So I locked you up to keep you safe. Sandhya *mol*, do you know what class you belong to?"

Her mother was no longer in the room. Sandhya had looked down in her confusion. Twanged her fingers in the strings that held the two paper dolls together. She loved them dearly, and tucked them into her bodice. She ran outside and saw the sun make double silhouettes, all of two inches long, against her own flesh. She held up the dolls, thinking this might quiet him down. "Class war," he insisted, running onto the veranda in his silk dhoti.

She shook her head.

"Have you read the poet Shelley?"

"No, no," she whispered. "No, no." And when he put out his hands, she set the little dolls on his outstretched palms, twanged the strings, and made them dance.

J ay was worried about Sandhya. Since her return from India, she was getting more tense. The ordinary tasks of the day, which had always seemed to afford her some pleasure, seemed tedious now. Draupadi too was concerned. "Go look in on Sandhya," she asked him. "It must be the news of her father's illness. Or perhaps it's something else." Draupadi had stopped there, unable to go on.

"Why don't you go?" Jay asked. "She's so fond of you."

"I have so much to do with this new performance piece, trying to pull it together, and in any case," and here her voice grew harsher, "she's not my cousin, is she?"

So Jay invited himself over to his cousin's place. Sandhya seemed surprised, but Jay explained that he was between assignments and needed to "cool down." Sandhya, in turn, was relieved. Her loneliness was starting to grow more acute, and at times she hardly knew how to get through the day.

Trying to distract his cousin, Jay launched into tales of Uncle Itty, the man who had never permitted his nephew to photograph him. Itty's dream, Jay told Sandhya, had been to study the Romantic poets. One summer, finding himself in London, their uncle had made his way to the Manuscript Room of the British Museum and asked for a manuscript in Mary Shelley's writing. They brought out a bound volume of the journal she kept at the time of Shelley's death. First came Trevalyn's scrawl, then Mary Shelley's upright hand, each telling of the poet's death. Mary wrote of her dream, of waters risen about her husband's boat.

"And then it happened," Jay said, moving his teacup closer to the windowsill, "just as Mary Shelley dreamed. You know that the monster in *Frankenstein* came to her in a dream, too, don't you?"

Sandhya, who was letting down the hem on Dora's little red dress, nodded. Jay explained how Trevalyn, who preserved Percy's heart when his body was destroyed—"After all, what could they do but cremate him after such a drowning?"—also gathered fragments of the poet's skull from the funeral pyre. These gray bits of matter were set into a glass urn, about an inch tall. The urn was embedded in the massive covers of a volume that found its way into the collections of the British Library. The very book that was pulled out at Itty's request.

When the keeper of manuscripts, an elderly man, had his head turned, Itty ran his fingers over the glass urn then, growing bolder, pried open the glass and shook some of the stuff into his handkerchief.

"Why?" asked Sandhya, the needle trembling in her hand.

"Who knows? One thing though, he tried to electrify the bits. Make new life. Mad old coot!"

Sandhya got up hurriedly. She didn't want to stick her finger with the needle, mess up Dora's dress. She had hamburgers to grill before the child came home. Following her into the kitchen, Jay continued with his tale of Uncle Itty who, having stolen bits of ash from the poet's skull, wrapped them tenderly in his white handkerchief and bore them off to Calcutta.

"He couldn't very well display them there, could he? For one thing, his nerve failed him—imagine our grandmother seeing those horrid bits of dried skull, with little wires poked through to electrify them!"

Sandhya let out a short, nervous laugh, a cough almost. Jay watched her as she moved over to the fridge, rearranging two black dolls tied up with twine. Haitian-looking, he thought. Not the sort of thing he could have imagined her buying. Perhaps someone had given them to her. Surely not Rashid. The thought made Jay anxious. He must talk to Rashid about all this mess. To hide his confusion, he pressed on with the story.

"Now, about our Uncle Itty, it was British India at the time, remember? They could have put Itty in jail. So the poor chap kept the handkerchief hidden in a drawer, knowing all the while that the fragile stuff was the relic of a revolutionary poet. Then, too, our Itty knew that students in Hindu College would love to get their hands on the ashes. Agitating for national liberty, they had read Shelley with excitement. Why, Gandhi had quoted the poet in *Young India*. Lines about non-violent suffering, from an overly long poem Itty was sure was called 'Lucifer Falls.'

"In fact, he quoted me lines!" Jay spluttered in excitement. His long narrative of a past, real and imagined, casting its pale light against the sharp necessity of time present. As he was trying to hold onto his teacup, his right elbow dashed against his cousin's wrist, a dangerous turn, since Sandhya was about to chop an onion with great concentration.

"Careful, Juju," she murmured, and he apologized and went right on. He didn't want to lose track of Uncle Itty, who had taken root in his brain.

"You must admit, my dear cousin, that insanity gives one an extraordinary certitude. Then too, Sandhya, one can read all this as a response to colonial education. Itty had got the title wrong. 'Prometheus Unbound,' I told our uncle, but would he believe me?"

"He wouldn't?"

She turned round slowly to look at him, her hand poised over a mound of hamburger meat. The way she looked at him, Jay was sure that Sandhya was on the brink of confiding in him. He wanted to stop, tell her not to touch that mound of raw meat, ask her what was on her mind. But she turned away abruptly, tucked her head, and looked down at the chopping board. She drew out a bit of ginger and started scraping it. Then she pulled over a tin full of rice and, hands coated with fine scraps of ginger, she poured out some rice and stared at it.

"Want me to help clean it?" Jay offered.

She shook her head. Her voice sounded thick, as if it came from deep down in her throat.

"So, what happened to Itty?"

"Well, I didn't know at the time, but Uncle Itty was already locked into his own head, beginning his descent. And shortly thereafter, unable to tell the voices in his head from those in the world, he took to walking the streets of Conoor."

"Just walking?"

"Well," Jay paused. "Sure you don't need help with the rice?"

The way she was picking through the grains made him feel nervous, sad somehow. Perhaps his voice would comfort her, though it was such an odd story.

"He hung signs round his neck, Sandhya. I guess his mind had fled. After all, he did that horrid thing with you, locking you in the cupboard. Aunt Sosa told me."

She looked up, her eyes shining with surprise. "Amma never told me she'd told you."

"It was that summer after you married Stephen. She was quite cut up about your going to America and just wanted to talk, I guess."

"Was Appa listening?"

"No, I'm sure he wasn't at home just then."

She nodded, reassured: "So what were these signs?"

"Quite something, my dear. Chandu told me, and I even saw one of them myself."

And Jay described how their Uncle Itty had hung the sign SHELLEY DASAN over his neck, writing out the words in all the colors he thought the rainbow contained. It was one of the pen names the Tamil poet Subramaniam Bharati had used, Shelley Dasan, meaning Slave of Shelley. "What greater glory," Jay asked his cousin Sandhya, who had returned to her slow labor over the grains of rice, "than to bear the name of Shelley, who believed, till the very end, even as his boat was overturning in violent water, that the world might be remade in imagination?"

Her vision contracted to Rashid's gaze. Her eyes, her breasts, her thighs gained substance and weight through his desire, his touch. She longed to be threaded through her lover as a burning thread through a cool, iron needle. Lacking him, she could not compose herself. As time passed, he did not return her phone calls. Once, without warning, Sandhya caught the subway to Brooklyn. The subway to heaven, she thought, imagining the rails poking out of the ground, skyward. She found the front door locked. Her frantic rings brought him to the door. Rashid looked unkempt, as though he had not slept for a long time. She felt their bodies tremble as she held him tight, his pajama top against her chin. Inside his room, she sat at the edge of the warm bed, tugged a little black doll out of her pocket. It was damp with sweat and he could see the red string tangled around its neck.

"For you, darling, I have the other one," and she pressed her lips to his throat. Gently, he pushed her away.

"Wait here," he called out as he dressed, slapping cold water on his face. The distance hurt her, he did not want to serve her tea, undress her, let her body succumb to the fever that lit all her parts. How smooth his face looked, almost as if she were gazing into a mirror.

He set the doll she had given him on a table by the window. Next to the doll was an empty bowl. Once that bowl was filled with plums.

"Rashid," she said, whispering his name over and over, a blunt talisman she hardly dared hang on her neck, hold in her hand, raise to her lips. "I've been having bad dreams."

He thought it best to leave the house. He led her back to the subway and they quickly found themselves near Christopher Street. They sat at a table under a lime tree. White blossoms sprinkled the cobblestones. Three girls in high heels, one had green platform heels, passed by. The huge wedges made her stalk, awkwardly, like a young giraffe.

"What is it, darling?" Rashid asked her, looking at Sandhya's smudged face.

She slipped her palm into his hand and held tight. She shut her eyes, wanting his voice to flow within her. But Rashid broke in: "See, I didn't call you back. But I've been worried. Zahir and his chemicals."

"Chemicals?" she queried, puzzled now. And Rashid, forgetting himself, confided in her. Listening, Sandhya thought it all sounded rather like a child's mystery: midnight schemes on how to procure vats of chemicals, a truck in which they could be transported, a safe place for storage, code words for the conspirators. But she felt too uneasy to laugh out loud.

Sensing her discomfort, he stopped short. Explained how he had cautioned his childhood friend. "'Remember what they did to people in Cairo. They'll do that to you too, if they can. Blow you up,' I said to him."

"They wouldn't do that, would they?" Sandhya's voice was taut, harsh.

"Who knows, my dear? Moral desperadoes, that's what they are. And not just them. Haven't you heard of the militia in the Midwest? Different ends, same means. Stocking up guns, ammunition, food. Wanting to wipe out people who are different."

He plucked the little doll from his pocket. She blushed suddenly, pleased that he had it with him.

"So, tell me about this creature."

"I picked it up, on the street. There are two of them, you see. I thought if you had one, and I ..." her voice trailed off, waiting.

"Like the monster in *Frankenstein.*"

"What?" She was hurt.

"You know that story, don't you. I thought you might," he added when he saw her face light up. "I was telling Zahir about it, just the other night."

"So tell me." She sat with her chin in her hands, in the light of the lime trees, thinking, I have never seen Rashid as beautiful as this.

"Well, the monster, remember, was made of bits and pieces of flesh, all gathered from charnel houses. But he needs electricity to live. Or was that only in the movie?"

She gazed at him, silently.

"I told Zahir that immigrants are like that. Our spiritual flesh scooped up from here and there. All our memories sizzling. But we need another. Another for the electricity. So we can live."

She waited, poised at the brink of her seat.

"The monster turned on *el doctor* Frankenstein when he refused him a mate, refused him love. El doctor, of course, was terrified of a new race of bits-and-pieces creatures, monsters peopling his world."

"Oh Rashid, what a story!" She found herself almost happy. She needed to hear his voice, needed his stories to make sense.

"My dear, there is another part to what I think." He was at his most professorial, too, she could see, sitting up straight in the chair.

"Better to have all the little bits than to cleanse, blow up, destroy. For that's the other option, isn't it? A hatred of all the parts of flesh that form us, wanting the pure blue, the perfect slate."

"And people like us?" she asked him softly. "People without that fierce belief?"

"We have to look for our love." He said this gently, his hand poised above hers.

But she was not satisfied, feeling there was something in his tone that denied her the comfort she sought.

"Rashid," she said, more loudly than she intended. She felt her heart pounding, as if this were her very last chance. "Rashid, I was cooking rice the other day. Washing the grains, letting water from the faucet run over my fingers. And I felt you and I should live together, make a house."

But he didn't let her finish. His hands were nervous, fumbling at the edge of the table, with the doll's leg. She noticed the tiny shadow the sunlight cast under the legs, the head of the doll.

"No, no, it's not like that with us, Sandhya. I can't, don't you see?"

"Don't you love me?" she asked, simply, hurt to the core.

"I do, but it's not that sort of thing."

He waved his arm to summon the waiter. Sitting in the awful silence that had descended on the street, Sandhya Rosenblum held up delicate wrists and watched the sunlight sieve through her fingers.

J ay's fingers were long and lean. He tapped them on the table, staring at the smooth brown markings on his skin. Under his left hand lay a piece of paper that had been shoved in under the door, a scrap of blue marked with an elegant scrawl:

"Salut comrade, home is where the heart is—another India!"

Then came a large *W.* and a local phone number. Warrier, so he was in town! Jay felt a sudden rush of pleasure. It was still early morning. He would have time to see his friend. As he set the kettle on the stove, memories of his meetings with Warrier returned. Born near Sriperumbadur, Warrier had spent some years in Cholamandalam before moving to Paris, where he made a living as a painter. His large orange and green canvases were prized by corporate clients. Jay heard Warrier's voice again.

"Set my painting in an office lobby and it is guaranteed to transport you. To an elsewhere! The French still have a bit of Mallarmé in them, particularly the monied types who need the green and orange visions I provide."

No, he wasn't cynical, old Warrier. He had once told Jay he would sit at the corner of the Champs-Élysées and beg if that would enable him to continue painting. "My life is painting."

So the price of being a visionary was to sell one's paintings to corporations! But what was he doing? Once again, he stared at the note in his hands, then abruptly moved forward, flung open a closet, and stared into the dimness.

When was it—perhaps a few days after Sandhya returned from India—Jay had picked up his camera, rolled it in a bolt of green silk his mother had given him before she died, set the bundle in the wall closet. One final time he had touched the silk, then stepped away sharply. The mental frame needed to balance his images no longer held together. Something had fallen apart. There was a sharp gap between what the eye saw and what the heart might hold. Composition seemed too contrived, its balancing act too finicky to contemplate. Making sense meant letting images hang together in a previously inexistent luminosity. Something, like the sheen of eucalyptus leaves he had known as a child, might have inspired him again, a tiny jolt of beauty so necessary to work. But that earth was so far, those sounds, those scents. His hands trembled as he thought of the hard form of his camera, the quick silver edge of composition. And now the shock of an explosion.

It had happened while Sandhya was there, in India. He had been no particular admirer of Rajiv Gandhi. But the man stood for a secular vision of India, despite all the pomp and privilege that went in his wake. To kill him was too awful, flesh shattered into tiny particles of matter. What had happened to the old visions of nonviolence, peace toward all men? He must ask Warrier what he thought. Could his friend have painted the scene in his old home town? Right by the scene of assassination was an unfinished Gandhi statue. Perhaps Warrier knew the sculptor who had started doing the old man's feet, marking out the toenails with his chisel. The stone form had fractured, ground down by the mass of people running in panic from the body bomb.

"Blown up into bloody little bits," Jay murmured as he moved restlessly in his room, touching the tabletop, the glass of water, the stub of the plane ticket that had carried him back from the Hague. It was hard to believe it was just three days since he had returned. The details of torture at the Human Rights Conference had been acid in an empty belly. He had rushed out into the streets for air. Did he no longer have the stomach to deal with man-made terror? He imagined his old friend Gautam, a tiny fly settling on his nose, in that other life. On the damp street, outside the conference hall, a hand had touched his shoulder, a woman calling out his name. It was a woman he had noticed before in the meeting. Her voice sent a sudden tremor through him, as if he had never heard his own name uttered before. He stopped short, blinking his eyes, trying to get rid of the accumulation of rain drops. She stood there, tall and silent, hand at throat, gazing at him. Surya was her name, from Jaffna in Sri Lanka. She had come westward to represent her women's peace group. Purani, they called themselves, as in the full moon, these believers in the nonviolent path.

As he leaned against his windowsill in Manhattan, the images of his meeting with Surya filled Jay. Slowly, he slid down to the floor and let the cool brick wall sustain him. Her gentleness moved in him, her voice a dark stream, splashing as she spoke of the killing of her friend, Doctor Rajeshwari. Gunned down as she was riding a bicycle on the way to work. They found her body lying by a well.

"Imagine killing someone because they oppose bloodshed," Jay whispered.

"It happens all the time."

"And those women raised to kill, the suicide squad? Like the one who killed Rajiv Gandhi?"

"Girls born in despair," Surya replied. "Brought up in villages where they cannot look straight at the full moon. They are taught to feel that the real hope is through bombs and grenades. Children of death."

He nodded, holding tight to Surya's hand. It had been brief, what held them together, a deep recognition flaring up. He invited her to New York, knowing there was no way she would accept. She told him she simply wanted to return to Jaffna.

"It's my home," she said, and he believed her.

So was that what it took to feel out a home, a landscape where one's blood flowed, a soil, a perpetuity? Sitting with Surya, hadn't he felt at home? He was aware of a delicate irony, pungent as lime juice on the tongue. The parting from Surya was bitter, sweet. Outside the airport the wind blew her hair all about his face. He told her what had happened to his friend, Ahmed, then felt there was nothing more to be said.

On his return he tried to call her. He left messages, but she never got back to him. Then, distracting him, came news from Berlin that Petra Kelly's body had been found, shot by her lover, or a double suicide, who could tell? Nathalie had left the Green Party, taken to the hills, carrying only a few clothes, a water bottle, and a copy of Bobrowski's poems. Over and over on the phone she read him "Oder my river" in a soft tearful voice. Her call upset him to no end. To make matters worse, things were not working out with Briana. There was a flatness in her that he was surprised it had taken him so long to see, a coarseness of sensibility that her physical beauty could only mask for so long.

Jay started wandering out alone. He found his way into a bar on Forty-second and Eighth. It was moist and dark inside, hundreds of bodies pushed together, mostly Indian. How could that be, so many young Indians all together? After long months of foreign living, it astounded him to see so many of his own people crowded together into a room. Then the music started up and the crowd pressed back. Against the gold screen stood the singer, Santosh Blissji, skinny as a cricket, the silks he had drawn across his flesh doing little to conceal the knobby bones and parched skin. But his song was a golden thing, it trembled and rose, and the voice propelled the body against the screen, jerking and shoving from posture to posture. Bits of rock, African dance, Tandava steps had been woven into his act. Then, in a sudden scuffle, no doubt deliberate, the golden screen was rolled off and a white movie screen unfurled. Jay saw images of bodies, multiple, magnified, edges blurred with terrific speed. Santosh in livid silks, his anorexic body turned hallucinatory. Then the voice started up. Santosh was humming into a mike, but this was a powerful godlike sound filling every nook and cranny in the nightclub:

Come dance with your brothers, your sisters too
This is the As-i-an Di-as-pora. Dance, dance, do, do.

The words pounded as the screen image fell into a shallow well. In jerky fashion, arms spread out, well water flattening to hold him, as amber might, arms and legs splayed brilliant in liquid, Christlike. Behind the well was a dark forest that suddenly lit up into a myriad of dancing arms and legs. And all the time the screen phantasm was falling, falling.

Isolated in real time, shrunk by the magnitude of the screen images with their swirling magic, the magnetic voice backed by sizzling castanets, oudh, vina, who could tell that Santosh himself was getting faint, that he tried to mop the sweat off his forehead with the end of his scarf, that his breath was coming in shorter gasps? But he kept on, revivified by the music and motion of "Diaspora Ditties." In a small airless room, right by the South Street Seaport, he had worked up the words in his head, tapping out the jerky, arrhythmic steps.

Jay knew something of Santosh's story. His parents tossed out of Idi Amin's Uganda, at the age of seven Santosh had landed in Britain. After teenage years in the bitter housing projects of Brixton, the bright lights of New York City summoned him. Santosh found himself a room in the Bowery, a lover who taught him how to cross-dress, a job in the bar, where his throaty voice poured out, bouncing off the rainbow-colored silks he swathed himself in, not least because his own body was drawing into itself fever, sweats, the unbearable oppression of dreams in which dancers lacking an arm or limb jolted in empty subway cars.

After seeing Santosh on stage, the words poured out of Jay. First in a whisper, then in a roar. He started jotting down phrases, images, all infused with a strong rhythm. He set the words back-to-back and lines started to appear. He carried these lines around as he went about his business, and in odd moments, started fine-tuning them. Portions of stanzas appeared in what he felt was a woman's voice. This excited him. He needed breath, he needed air to ponder this curious creation.

He set one in front of him and glanced at it. It was done, he thought, a

poem having to do with the new world in which Indians found themselves. He called it "Brown Skin, What Mask?" A little academic perhaps,
but he hoped it worked. Ravi had nodded Swhen he read it out in the bar.
The second, which he had written back-to-back with the first, was a weird
thing—that he admitted readily. It was about Sandhya. She was casting off
her sorrow, dancing as Santosh might have done, but in her own way, on
a tabletop, in the West End Bar. It might shock her, he feared. But of
course there was nothing in the poem to connect it overtly to her. Then
there were two more he was making notes on. One about an oil tank by
the river, the other about a woman squatting by a stove. That one felt like
a dream poem. He didn't know when he would get to write it down. How
fretful the thought of that poem made him feel.

Pulling on his coat, knotting the long uneven shoelaces, Jay decided he
would confide in Warrier, share the pain of giving up photography, the
rush in which poems came to him. He would whisper all this to him as
they strolled to the Whitney to see the show. His notebook caught his eye.
Jay picked it up and set it away in a drawer, under a pile of overexposed
film. Perhaps when he returned he would write a little more of the river
poem, and the way the George Washington Bridge arced over the water.
He needed to keep track of images, so they did not flee him entirely.

That was the best he could do—try and seize a border where newness
flashed by.

Jay's Journal

Stood in front of a painting by Basquiat.

"Teeth, Teeth," the words in the frame stuck in my head. Thought of a very old woman in Tiruvella whose skin was peeling off. She survived the "Lehelam"—the shootings, the stabbings during the uprisings in Malampura District. Ordinary people, Muslims, risen against the landlords.

Note: Ask Sandhya who the old woman might be. Talk to the old woman in Tiruvella if she's still alive. Learn her name. Learn to write it.

People kill for land. Who has the right to live in a place? Muslims must be pushed out of India, they say. Next it will be Christians, Buddhists, Parsis, Jews. Only Hindus are true sons of the soil. The fierce blade turned at surrounding flesh. Ethnic cleansing, they call it.

The terror in Jaffna, Surya shared. Her body drawing mine, across a shadow line. The horror in Bosnia. Rapes, unbelievable cruelty.

The sniper in Sarajevo, a Christian woman code-named "Arrow" shooting at the Muslims as they stand in a breadline. Watching bodies doubled in pain. Much made of this in the Indian newspapers. A woman sniper. What has become of the dream of a multiethnic state in Bosnia? Why do human beings need to kill so?

This guy with fatal crimson paints, rage laid out on canvas.

Another image picks up the savagery of a Negro policeman.

The gold glory of his Griot. Could have stood there and wept.

Took Warrier with me. We looked at the paintings together. Warrier was preparing to hang his work for his own show in Soho.

"What do you do in Paris? How do you live?"

He had left Kerala almost twenty-five years ago.

"Live? I paint and sell the paintings."

"Sell?"

"Sure, Arjuna. I have a gallery that represents me."

He stared at the red and black man, bleeding out of his fingertips. Must have wondered why I was asking all those questions. Later, Warrier and I sat and had coffee.

"Have you read Kumaran Asan's poem about the Mopilla Uprising?"

"What is it called?"

"'Duravastha.' Read it."

I can't read Malayalam, I told him, feeling quite ashamed. Only Hindi, English, French. I let him tell me about the poem: the celebration of the uprising of the oppressed.

All the body parts in Basquiat's work. I should make a work like that with the organs flying apart. A terrible centrifugal force.

"In Italian." I read the title. Why Italian, I thought, why not Mala-yalam? It's all available to us, pitched to the end point the century is coming to. Then I corrected myself.

It's hubris to think it will all end just because there's an angel in my head saying so. And how to make sense thinking you know exactly what you need, through TV, faxes, e-mail, the foreknowledge of lives pitched to the buying and selling of desire. Fate slashed headlong, time foreshortened.

It's all in the present, comrade, and we must probe with our nails, scrape with our teeth to understand.

"Warrier," I said to him.

"Ena?"

"Have you painted the Mopilla uprising?"

He looked at me as if he hadn't heard right. We were on the sidewalk outside the museum. His head was cocked a little, that handsome head of his, with the mess of hair, just a little streaked with gray.

"I know it's a while back in time," I said, "but it could serve to inspire us. The uprising the British put down, but it was also against the feudal classes. The pain of the subaltern risen. Well, have you?"

"Other things I have painted, Arjuna. This I have reduced down. My soul, though, make no mistake about it"—at this, he quaffed the drink he was carrying down the street in a brown paper bag—"my soul is a map of Kerala."

He always calls me "Arjuna."

I must return to Kerala, to Poonthera, where those riots were. To Ayodhya in the north, where all space contracts to the ruins of Babri Masjid, brown bricks powdered into brown earth.

Which is worse, the bombardment of civilian quarters, or this slow relentless hatred, wanting to drive entire peoples out of a land?

Perhaps I understand why Basquiat put down "Teeth, Teeth" in that relentless way.

Warrier's teeth are so white. Mine so chewed down, indifferent. Must talk to someone about words, clothing, the body, plate glass in which office workers are shut up. How little we understand. Is the world itself just a mass of little pieces? And to survive? Santosh needs his music, that torn disruptive thing, with its own majesty. What would Warrier say hearing him? Or Sandhya? The flow of the imagination: photos, poems, paintings.

Is that enough to house us? Human beings need food, clothing, shelter. And these must have their spiritual counterparts.

Paradise House
(Draupadi)

I call them by their English names: English, the rough basement.
—William Blake, Jerusalem

It was the year of our obsessions. I could not bear to listen to the TV. In the voice of a fighter pilot—"We bombed and bombed till the rubble rose"—I heard Jimmy O'Flaherty talking to me through water. "On Death's Highway," the voice went on, "enough twisted metal to be raised into a cathedral."

A bunker was bombed. I saw a girl, hair in flames, carried out on a stretcher. The flesh of her mother clung to her. Her face showed bones that came up through flesh, fusing together. I saw the burning door they bore her through.

I heard of men and women from Sandhya's village who were trapped in Kuwait, then fled into the desert. A woman gave birth in desert sand. Her legs were heavy, drenched in sweat. Did the wings of the wild locust stir in her throat as the child thrust out? He came out kicking, cord throbbing. His feet dipped into desert sand, a male child of the Indian diaspora. His mother called him Arjuna Kuruvilla. "Why that name?" they asked her. "Because he came out whole, into the burning sand," she replied when her wits returned.

It was the year the Soviet Union splintered and giant statues of Lenin dropped into Russian soil. Children came out of school in droves to stare at the dull eyes pocked with lime. All week the mausoleum in Red Square was filled with empty whispers. Pasternak's swan, Akhmatova's chain of linden berries burned in the humid air.

It was the year Rajiv Gandhi, campaigning for election, was blown into tiny little bits by a bomb strapped to a woman's waist and brassiere. She was a member of the LTTE Suicide Squad and held cyanide in her teeth. Why did she have her glasses on as she did the job? She needed them to see. Why did she bend so low to touch his sneakers with LOTTO embla-zoned on? As she rose, she touched a little button at her waist and her flesh exploded, taking him too.

"*Sthree ithe engana cheyunede?*" they kept asking, over and over again. "How could a woman do this?" As if a woman's hands are any different from a man's, her hate, her despair, the passion risen in her brain.

Rain, it rained all day and night in the hills around Sriperumbadur, where the suicide bomber did her task. In the alleyways, the gutters, the hovels, the rooms where prostitutes wiped their thighs clean and washed out their mouths with well water, everywhere they noticed the slow, fra-grant rain. On rivers and streams it rained, on bamboo groves and groves of mango and coconut.

It rained here too, the day Sandhya came into my room and I played Billie Holiday for her: "Summertime," "Strange Fruit," that sort of thing. But when my back was turned Sandhya picked up a hunk of rope I had bought for my installation. She drew it out to its full length, touched the rope to her lips. Much later, when we were both stronger, had learned to survive our own lives, I whispered in her ear: "Let me take you to Paradise House, old gal. It's still there, in the fairgrounds, in my hometown of Gingee!"

Grandma Suhasini loved the fairgrounds in Gingee, the carousel, the drop-the-ball-in-the-bucket-and-get-three-goldfish game. But her favorite was Paradise House. Of course, it was at Mama's insistence Grandma Suhasini came to live with us. I must have been fourteen, fifteen. Grandma had hurt her leg. She was finding it hard to manage on her own. "With all the crossings this family has seen, my mother must end her days in this house, nowhere else," Mama insisted, tugging at the kitchen blinds so the Lupos would not see her, bent low, carving up chicken livers Papa got cheap from the local Butcher Boy store.

So Grandma came over from Port of Spain. We picked her up in New York City and drove back home. She had a room of her own, all laid out in blue, which Mama insisted was her favorite color, like the funeral par-lor on Harry Street. If we can't do that for her, at least this, Mama insisted.

When her leg was better and she could limp around, Grandma drew me to Paradise House. Newly installed in the fairgrounds, it was a House of Mirrors painted red, white, and blue on the front, and left unpainted on the back—inside it was filled with mirrors. On a stool they had set trinkets: an old top, a handful of bells on a cord, three headless dolls, a string of glass beads, two photographs of unknown children set in frames.

Later, I was put in mind of the bits and pieces the English explorer Frobisher and his crew left on a North American island to trap Eskimos. On an island their Virgin Queen dubbed *Meta Incognita*.

The English captured Eskimos to take back with them. One was a proud and fierce man who bit off his own tongue when they got him. Another, a woman, whose tiny baby they wounded as they dragged her onto the ship. She sang to that infant all night, in the cool winds, singing out sorrow, tenderness, a mother's music, strung out in the barrenness of exile. The infant did not survive. The mother pined away, refusing food, drink.

No one could get their language from them.

I entered Paradise House with Grandma holding tight to my arm, but soon enough she knocked me loose. I heard her on the other side of the mirrors, singing:

"Ooh, Carib chile ..."

I found a set of plastic bells on a chair and tinkled them loudly as if at a ceremony. I heard a flurry of skirts on the other side, Grandma racing as hard as she could, bad leg and all, toward me. She was so relieved to see me she babbled in her island English:

Dance, dance to the *tassa*,
Give me Lata Mangeshkar!

She was a mad thing, my grandma.

The Englishman Frobisher captured the Eskimos to take their language from them. Take the natives hostage, learn their tongue.

Hostage to what? To immortal death who comes robed in colors so splendid no man can refuse. Death who bears on her tray severed tongues, cut roses, the souls of infants washed with cold sea spray.

Who would willingly enter the trick house the English built, feed off that bitter bread, stare into the bits of polished glass they left behind?

With Grandma Suhasini's help, I worked my way out of Paradise House. When we got back Mama was in the kitchen, staring out the window at the Lupo boys who were making mudpies and splattering each other.

"This daughter of yours," Grandma announced, "is a trickster, all right. Can work her way through the crookedest situation. Straight into solid glass she walks and it melts for her. Why, she may even end up in India. Now, did you ring some prayer bells summoning me?"

I nodded to humor her, not wanting to point out the many times I had banged my skull in so-called Paradise House for her sake. Or been on the brink of transforming into a dwarf, then a mountainous thing, akin to the bride Frankenstein's monster longed for.

As her arthritis grew worse, Grandma was confined to her bed. She could no longer make it into Paradise House. It grew in her head, those mirrors, that fantastic sloping roof made of luminous glass, the red, white, and blue frontage glittering with stars. She would babble about it all and the storyteller she saw squatting inside, his body mirrored in a thousand shards of glass.

Once as a fever came over her she clutched my hand and whispered words about a man whose skin was dark brown, who had a rippling brown bag of skin over his shoulder, who walked from door to door in Port of Spain peddling his stories. I asked her his name, but at that point she blacked out and I held her up and slapped her gently on the cheeks and fed her a spoonful of sugar water as Mama had told me to do. Outside the Lupo boys were firing their BB guns at crows in the cornfield and that sound helped wake her. Then, too, there was the sound of motorcycles revving up as they sped over the road from Albany, a whole crew of riders in black leather vests, their faces so pure and innocent.

Once one of them had shouted after me, "It's five hundred years after Columbus, Keep out Colored Scum." Naturally I did not want Grandma to hear any of that.

But hearing was hard for her, seeing too. She did not want to sip the sugar water anymore, nor mulligatawny with coriander in it that Mama made. Her skin grew soft and powdery, the color of the brown butterflies on our willow trees. Sometimes I felt that holding her hand too hard would make it dissolve into a fine spray, the kind that washes over the coast of her native Trinidad.

One summer's day she died, my grandma Suhasini, and Mama told me that the gods of her ancestors had come, swooping down from the rain clouds to take her soul away. We cremated her in the funeral home near the fairgrounds, then quietly, for he feared it might be against the American laws on hygiene, Papa took us all out in a boat, to sprinkle her ashes into the broad-breasted river. We had no priest with us, so Papa murmured what he knew of the Gayatri Mantra, and the broad-breasted Hudson rose to receive her ashes.

"All the rivers of the earth are one," Papa told me that evening as we stood by the garage, but as a helicopter flew high overhead he started coughing. The cough grew worse and Doctor Lakshmi, newly arrived in Gingee from Albany, treated him. He was charmed by the Indian woman doctor in her clear blue sari, and when he told her about his mother-in-law's ashes, she replied: "So it is that we maintain our traditions in the New World, where the sun will set on us too."

While this seemed to him an impossibly long sentence, it moved Papa to tears. Years later he would recall Dr. Lakshmi, her hands, her sky blue sari.

Black Water
(Draupadi)

"Without falling, no bridge, once spanned, can cease to be a bridge."
—Franz Kafka, The Bridge

A brilliant blue day. My legs felt heavy, weak. I felt little pulses, little jabs of electricity. Then *ping, ping,* I heard something inside me. Was it a double heart beating? I was by the stove. Right where Mama would have sat if she were with me. I thought of Mama in my growing-up days in Gingee, staring at the gas flame, watching it glow. My period just starting. The heavy pad between my legs. Warm stuff going *whoosh-whoosh.* Mama had set aside a pad and belt for me.

"Mama, Mama," I cried.

She was far away, lying in a hospital bed. I sat down on the stool, heavily, then dragged it to the window so I could breathe better. Staring out of my high window did not calm me, nor lull the stirring within.

I picked up a pot with black and blue stripes. Something Rinaldo found in Florence for me. I set it for an instant to my belly and then flung it hard against the wall. I crawled to the corner where the bits lay. Set my lips there. Head down I crept, a dog, a goat, a cow; wept into the broken bits. Crying into a place I knew nothing of.

Rinaldo, darling, I am not a child.

A little thing, a jot, a scrap of flesh and blood and air, a slight blessedness is stirring in me.

"Rinaldo, I am going to have this child."

He was there in front of me. He had returned from Saudi Arabia. He stood against my fridge. Nothing. Said absolutely nothing.

"Rinaldo, this could be our new life, our life together. Make a choice."

Nothing, he said nothing.

Because of Laura in her blue silken gown, you do not want this child. Laura, who lives in Perugia, who's been married to you for thirty years, would know about us, and your lovely son Mario who's all set to work for Fiat, hot, axe and all, against the Red Brigade, having seen their terrorist work close at hand.

It's the color thing, no?

Who wants a mongrel African-American-Asian child, by a woman who strolls through Harlem on full moon nights?

Harlem's an oyster, Rinaldo.

Glows in the night. The crack lights it up, the crack in the earth. Did you know about that? It runs down 135th all the way from the Hudson.

I shall go, my belly huge, and stand by the Korean grocery store. Look, look at my unborn child. I shall 'front the black men and women pouring in, I shall 'front the Asians. I shall paint a placard and hold it up.

I shall stand there, a living testimony. Look at all the cardboard I have packed in. I shall lift my skirts.

"Do not beware," I shall make out in sign language.

The nuns in Nyack taught me sign language, did you know that, Rinaldo? We have nuns in Nyack, too.

Lookie, sir, it's cardboard, not flesh, not my small stirring blessedness.

She, queen under the hill, mound of flesh and blood and skin you kissed.

A woman with one breast and no eyes, chin packed with hairs, stares back at me in the mirror.

Mama Marya, she cries, all lips and thighs, how shall I enter the kingdom of heaven?

Will the black virgin of Westbeth, she who is covered with condoms, will the red virgin of this native soil, bleeding with shrapnel, intercede for me?

Scissors in hand, Frida Kahlo turns in her grave toward Ana Mendiata. They wave crisp ribbons of flesh. I am their sister. Crying's not the thing to be done. Frida cries, though, lying through her teeth to Diego.

Crying. *Amor, amor* and all that.

I tore the bit about the mother who killed her dearly beloved child from the genius black sister's novel I was reading. Tore it out and stuck it in my dress.

O ghostly flesh of my foremothers. The slave ships are still in port. Did you know that? Docked right by the *Intrepid* where they take the school-children to teach them history.

O ghostly flesh of my black mothers, crying in me.
    I stuck the bit from that book in my dress. At the abortion clinic I lifted up the dress. I took it off. I hung it on a hook.

Amor, amor, she cried, and all that. Swallowing her sobs.
    I felt nothing. I swear I felt nothing.

Let our bodies be our playgrounds. You said that to me, two weeks before I could tell you about our child. You chucked me under my chin. Later you said,
    "A child needs a home, Dotti. I have no home for you."

I hung my dress with the bit of paper in it on a hook in the changing room. Wanted to hold the paper in my hand.
    No, dearie, no, they said. No, no.
    Saw the metal bucket at the foot of the bed.
    Metal lined with plastic the color of a cloud over the Hudson.

R, can you hear? I felt nothing.
    They tied my legs. Parted my sweet soft center.
    Slide, down, slide down, dearie. Lower, lower.
    Put out his hands with the rubber gloves, slid them in.
    You'll fall asleep. I promise.
    Slid the skin-thin gloves, up, up as the barbiturates strummed.
    Of course, it was my choice.
    Later I recovered my dress.
    I love you, you said, long distance from São Paulo, Dotti darling, my poor Draupadi.

Your Draupadi beats her head in the metal chamber of the new subway car imported from Japan. Against the shining metal she beats her head, over and over again. A stick-thin figure racing from the exit signs.

She claps her face against the sign that says: EMERGENCY EVACUATION PRO-CEDURES. LAS VIAS DEL TREN SON PELIGROSAS.

A week later she stands on the subway platform at Union Square, by the garbage dump.

Gazes there for her flesh. Her sweet, stirring blessedness.

S andhya, so thin and gaunt, walking by the pier, her face in shadow. Who was she with? Her cousin Chandu? I kept apart, hugging my arms.

Days later I visited Mama in Gingee. Saw the wasting flesh caught up in the checked robe Alma had sent. What passed through Mama's head no one could tell. She didn't know my name anymore, the name she had chosen for me, Papa had confided in a fierce moment.

"She wanted you to be named after the woman in the story your grandmother told her about. The one who had five husbands and triumphed over so many ills: Draupadi. She survived a battlefield too."

He paused, my papa, his sense of history shot through with the terrors of a time before his own imagination sprang into being:

"Draupadi loosed her hair to the wind, did you know? Divine winds that blew the Mongol fleet as they tried to attack Japan. Blew them right out of the water, destroyed them. The 'kamikaze winds' they called them."

He spoke as if Kurukshetra were everywhere.

"You thought kamikaze had to do with suicide fighter pilots in World War II?"

I nodded, proud of the knowledge he had packed into his head, carting the remains of the day from Dinkins' Soda Shop, his Japanese-American heritage, as he put it so proudly, via the pineapple fields of Hawaii, the internment camps of Arizona, something he was not willing to let go of. To have America at the heart, that is what he did, my papa, the red and white and blue of it, banners spangled with stars, blown into his head.

I had thought of Papa that hot afternoon when I stood facing Rinaldo. We were in my room. Rinaldo was naked, arms crossed. The taut energy of his body after making love vitalized my sight. I simmered in the aftermath of his arms and thought, yes, this is what I need to carry back into the street, into the street across which the garbage lies piled up. At that, a thought of Papa crept into me.

"I cannot bear it," I whispered.

Rinaldo had to move closer to me, to hear.

"What is it, Dotti?"

I do not remember anymore what I said. After all, I had not said Papa's name to him, nor mentioned what passed through my head. But that moment remained. Rinaldo's nakedness by the window, a flag flying on the pier outside for some festival or another, and my father's face up close as he told me about the kamikaze winds, his mouth trembling, hands busy with the bits of paper torn up, yellow ribbons, torn-up streamers the Lupos had scattered by the till in the Soda Shop. A gesture of disdain. The winds of Gingee picked up those scraps and blew them gently into my father's face.

Years later I found out about Draupadi's revenge. How she bathed her hair in the blood of the man who dishonored her in the court of kings. Her long black hair scratched the ice of the Himalayas. Draupadi opened Duryodhana's chest with her nails, washing her hair in his rib cage, the bloodied inner carcass of him. Afterward, as her mother, the goddess who looks down from the sun, wept for her, the roots of Draupadi's hair let the blackness drain out of them, little drops of darkness staining the soil, stippling the tongues of the tiger lilies that grew in the Vindhya mountains.

Overnight her hair turned white, pure white hair against her dark skin, drawing men from far regions, men who had heard the cries of a driven woman in their dreams: "When he threw me down, like a pawn, what right had he? Was he slave, or was he free?" "And Duryodhana, what right had you to strip me?" These cries she set to music, songs of her exile. And she turned away from them all, her five husbands, too.

It's hard to know what to do with the aftermath of anger.

Did the winds from the mountains blow her hair, making it rise like a wild blossom, each petal trapping sunlight, a bristling remembrance?

Or, as others say, did blood flow from the tips of her hair into black water for forty days? Was she born again, a girl-child, and did parrots from the Vindhya mountains flock to her arms, perch in her soft hair?

M y heart started to beat hard. A double beat, as if there were two of us there, inside me, all over again. And one of us so shadowy. Was it Mama and me? Or that little shadow, still inside? I was glad, so glad, when Jay came by. I spoke about Mama, her heavy breathing. I told him about the abortion. Had he guessed already?

"I think you'd better let go of Rinaldo," he said.

"Why?"

"You have to live your own life, Draupadi, breathe again. Aren't you the gal who was into the performance thing?"

He gave a wry smile as I got up nervously. I picked up the coil of rope I had bought for an installation and set it away. I wondered what had come over Jay. Couldn't he tell how hard things were for me?

That night I had a dream. Rinaldo and I were near Café Lalo, its wooden shutters sticking out of the red brick. He had his overcoat open and an old scarf flapped around the neck. He raced toward me, then dissolved at the first bite of sunshine.

In another dream there was a gull in the air between us, poised by the entrance to the Children's Museum. And above the gull, a shadow towering. Rinaldo was older, less hair on his head, overcoat so shabby.

Reeling made a vertigo of lips, arms, thighs. Over again, as if there were life only in repetition, we raced to each other. Rinaldo was so thin and old I could see his bones. How quiet I kept.

Rinaldo, I am holding you inside me, trembling as I stare into dark river water. What I see close to the bridge is water in which my namesake washed her face, her hands, her bloodied hair. After her exile.

Rinaldo, it comes to me how we stood together in a room, you behind me, holding white cloth across me, a shirt or undershirt, something white and fine so that my sex was covered. I stood in front, my body shielding your chest where the gray had started to sprout. I turned and we looked into each other's eyes as if for the first time.

There was a lull in the traffic outside, Manhattan, placid for once. Then the lawyer who has an office across from your bedroom dropped his files and yelled for his assistant and that alien voice, querulous, broke in as we stood, aware suddenly of nakedness. Two morsels of flesh, born of such different mothers, yet held now in the space of a heartbeat. How could I tear myself from you?

We walked down Sixth Avenue and I told you I was leaving. It was oddly quiet, a few elms swaying, a few trucks and buses, a movie theater showing a Buster Keaton movie with piano music drifting out to the street. We walked as if we were glued to each other, wobbling a little like a white-faced comic, his hat askew. Coming on a triangular wedge of land scarcely wider than the two of us, I stopped short.

A brick wall in front of us, chin-high: the second cemetery of the Spanish and Portuguese Synagogue. Lack of space moved them, those early Jews in the new world, to another allotment for the dead. Your grandmother might have been among them, that old lady you never saw, her devotions rimmed in black lace in your memory, her pain fantailed in your mother's Genoese heart. As we stood awkwardly side by side, I thought I saw her laid out on the stunted stones that marked out the spaces for the dead.

I felt my flesh flowing into hers. Saw you standing there, in the sudden light from the stiff grass by the yew tree. I was tiny, hard, I had a body. Wings blossomed on my gray body. I was a pigeon from Genoa, Gangotri, Jerusalem, perched on your arm. I was a pigeon hung in the window, as we stood naked facing the glass.

I was sheer delight, lift of thigh, liquid sweetness of an armpit raised for the lover's lips, freed from gravity that tamps in the gravestones, pours light onto the stone wall of the cemetery. I was freed of time that makes you twenty-odd years older than me, gives you a thickening belly, chest sprinkled with gray hair, balding head, makes you lever me down, down into my own exiled territories. Wanting it all. Is this what love is?

You did not have your wedding ring on your finger. I felt the bareness on your finger, no gold there. We both knew you could never leave her. You knew what I could not, the certitude of sorrow, the burden of attachment. All I could hear in my head was the boatman crying:

"Cross, cross the black river, before the water rises."

The body forces itself into a metal-bottomed boat and eyes stare out at the bushes packed with birds and wild beasts, all silent.

You stood next to me, thigh pressed to shoulder, our bodies packed against the wooden gate behind which the gravestones lay. The sunlight had dissolved. I do not know where your voice came from in that grayness:

"You want to be a wife."

"Yes."

"Sorrow, my sorrow," you whispered.

I felt your breath on my rib cage as you bent. There was something in your face I could not decipher, a taut argentine light, as if one of those bushes in the underworld were leaking into your flesh, transforming your flesh and bone into metallic substance. Later I felt as if you were looking into the face of your dead mother. That looking at me you were gazing into the eyes of our unborn child.

How softly the leaves turned, on the elms at the edge of the second Spanish-Portuguese cemetery.

R inaldo, I am in my old posture now. My belly empty, tight. I have stopped nibbling at the mound of peanuts I bought the other day. I am standing with my back to my half-finished installation.

You come out of the bathroom in your black-and-white robe.

"Ethnic cleansing," you say, raising your coffee mug. Your hair is wet against your head.

"Dotti, where will people like us be cleansed to?"

"The great Hudson River," I reply. "It is my river now, darling, you know that. I can always throw myself into it."

After you leave, I pick up torn threads from Mama's silk dress and wind them around my little fingers. I run my fingers through my dresser drawer and the silk catches on the hooks of my bra, on the sharp bits on my silver bangles, on the teeth of the tortoiseshell comb Elly gave me in school in Gingee, all those years ago.

"You want to be a wife," you said before you left. "Why? Why?"

"After all, Pocahontas married too. Doña Marina did the best she could."

"Sorrow, my sorrow," you whispered in my head.

Later I said to myself: Elegy doesn't become you, gal. You should have hustled him out, set out the three black barrows they need for the performance at the South Street Seaport, where you shall become the ancient Draupadi in the midst of the new world Columbus sought. You will trundle the black barrows crying:

"Ahoy. Niña, Santa Maria, Pinta, three ships a-sailing."

The three barrows are propped up against the wall as well as the black scarf I'll toss over my own head as I push them. I shall push them through South Street Seaport for the Diwali celebrations. Marry the two earths. Make myself whole.

Turning

Varki died quite peacefully in his sleep, Sosa told her daughter over the phone.

"He asked for you at evening before he slept. 'Wonder how our Sandhya is doing,' he said." And Sosa's voice trembled.

"No, my dear, no need to come for the funeral. It's all prepared. We live in a hot country, you know. We'll take the road by the river. Your father loved that road. We'll get to the churchyard from the back."

The calm in her mother's voice worked into her. She moved about the kitchen, hands poised over bread and butter and new potatoes, over the coriander she had bought in the open market. She must cook, she thought, what else could she do? Later, much later, she would call up Jay and Sakhi as she had promised her mother. Now she would stand there, musing on that road by the river where they would carry him. The phone rang again, shattering her thoughts. She was tempted not to pick it up, but forced herself to touch the receiver. It was Nunu.

Sandhya sat hard on the metal stool, listening. On and on her sister's voice flowed, a full complaint. They had already dug a hole in the church-yard for their father. Bhaskaran had told her. And did Sandhya know that there was another eruption of black snails, all over the orchids? Then Nunu started weeping, and it was the most that Sandhya could do to hold tight to the telephone and not hang up. Why not give their father into her arms to hold forever, Nunu cried.

"'The body will stink,' Ayah said. People who die stink."

"Oh Nunu," Sandhya whispered, but her sister wasn't listening.

She would have taken their father in her arms, Nunu swore, if they hadn't stopped her. Dug a pit next to the chicken coop. A mound of earth with a hole for an entrance. She would have curled there in the dark with her father's body.

When Sandhya called home a whole day later, her mother told her that Nunu had refused to go to the funeral, shutting herself up in her room, writing poems she said crows were dictating to her.

"Then she read me something from the Bible," Sosa told her oldest daughter, "and in a way it comforted me. I sat in the armchair your father used to sit in, listening to her."

"What was it?"

"Apparently she got it from some magazine she received. But it was a Biblical line."

And in her soft, mellifluous voice, Sosa intoned the lines Nunu had read out: *"And I saw a new heaven and a new earth: for the first heaven and the first earth were passed away."*

"Ahh," Sandhya sat up very straight. "Nunu read that?"

"She had it by heart, you know, and there's another line too: *'And there was no more sea. And the sea shall cease.'"*

"Oh Amma," Sandhya said, "if only there were no sea. I would pick up Dora in my arms and come right over to you."

That night she dreamed that she was in the garden of her childhood. Rashid was an angel, he was flying to her. And she knew he would come before it all ended. She could feel his wings brushing her face.

"The sea shall cease," he whispered in her ear softly as he crouched by her. And she, hearing her father call in the distance, sat quietly in the shade of the gooseberry tree. Ever so lightly she passed her hands over Rashid's black hair. His hair was moist.

"All that is left of the sea," she murmured, "is your damp hair." And in the dream she felt the sweat of her palm fuse her flesh to his.

Nunu stood in her grandfather's study, her face pressed against the bars of the window. Through the mass of mango leaf and twig flickering in twilight she saw the barbed wire fence and then the road.

On the road dogs were barking. She heard the sharp whistle of the train that came over Ashtamudi Lake where the accident happened, an entire train fallen in. No one knew why. The bridge was damaged and could not be used for many months. Whole carriages lay rusting in water till they were finally fished out. Nunu imagined herself underwater, swimming into a carriage, hooking her fingers into the metal bars. Someone should fish her out, she thought, drag her if necessary, out of this hole into which she had fallen. This house made her helpless. She touched her cheeks to the metal bars on the window, leaned her elbow on the windowsill.

She was a child again, racing through the compound, feet cut with the brambles by the mango tree. Tall as the window ledge in her grandfather's study, she could see all the way in. The room was empty except for the pile of books on the shelves against the wall, the rosewood desk with papers. She turned suddenly, on tiptoes, and caught sight of two girls crouched by the granary, examining themselves. Sandhya had her red skirt pulled up high over her knees. Nimmi was thinner, taller, with two braids pinned back over her broad forehead. The child Nunu squatted by the mulberry tree and stared hard. Nimmi had her hand under Sandhya's skirt. Nunu pushed a mulberry leaf off her eyelid. Her sister Sandhya's eyes were shut. There was sunlight on her face, though the rest of her body was in the shade. She seemed to be smiling a little. The bodies of the two girls were folded into each other. Nunu tore off the top of a mulberry leaf. She rolled it between her fingers. She kept very quiet.

Later when she saw her sister and Nimmi going to the river, Nunu flew into a storm no one could save her from. She raced into the chicken coop, picked up pellets of mud and chicken droppings, flung them at the house. She made low, growly noises in her throat that scared the hens, then raced around, flapping her thin arms like a make-believe rooster.

"Nunu, Nunu!" her mother cried in alarm, but Nunu did not stop.

So she had seen Sandhya there, with another girl touching her sweet flesh. Nunu pressed her face tighter against the bars. She should have gone to the river all those years ago with her sister. Splashed around in the cool water with her. Chased the golden fishes through the spray. But Sandhya had never paid heed to her. Now all she did was send postcards with pictures of the Empire State Building or the Statue of Liberty. The backs of the cards were filled with silly little details of what Dora was doing.

Nunu had burned two or three of the postcards in a wood heap at the back of the kitchen. She scooped up the mess of ash from the American postcards and scattered the soft flakes at the foot of the mulberry bush that stood by the granary. She discovered a soiled scrap of cloth folded into the roots of the plant, picked it up and shook it free. Dull red with those yellow flowers from Sandhya's skirt. The skirt, torn into shreds, had been used to wipe up chicken droppings or fish blood. Washed out again and again, it was lost finally in the earth. Nunu felt the wind tugging at the scrap and let it blow free.

That evening when the sun made a red glow behind the haystack and the dogs started their high-pitched barking, Nunu held up a piece of paper. She unfolded it carefully and noted the reddish glow it took on in twilight. There was enough light for her to sit under the mango tree and read the note from her new friend, Dr. Pirabhakaran. "Read Revelations," counseled the reverend. "A book that tells of a new heaven and earth ought to be the favorite book of any self-respecting Christian." The phrase "favorite book" had a nice ring. It was the sort of phrase Nunu had heard in the convent of Jesus and Mary in the Nilgiris. She could have stayed on forever with the breakfasts and lunches and dinners all laid out at the tinkling of a bell, life harnessed to birdcalls. Oh, the cries of calling birds that filled her ears, then as now, and left her little else to do. Just listen to those cries, write it all down, in a language no one else can understand. The language of the new world.

Only her father on his sickbed had smiled at her, so gently, when she showed him the poems she had written about birdcalls. And now he too was gone.

She clutched the paper from the Reverend Doctor. Right at the top was scrawled his favorite passage from Revelations:

"And I saw a new heaven and a new earth: for the first heaven and the first earth were passed away."

"What did that mean?"

Nunu did not know. Nor did she know who she might ask. She picked up the book that lay on the floor. She did not know who had sent it to her. *Alert on Red,* it said, on the cover in white letters, surrounded by spiky black signs. The book told of dangers that faced the world. Men who were dangerous: Saddam Hussein. Nunu read the name out loud. There was nothing much Nunu could tell about him except that he was president of Iraq. She didn't know anyone from Iraq, but it was not too far from India. He sounded bad, starving his people, building missiles, making war, as it said war would come, the very last.

Others too, in hiding, smaller devils, it said, making bombs. Men come from Sudan and Egypt making up bombs with fertilizer, rat poison, a real witches' brew. Men hiding the canisters in little holes in the ground, getting ready to blow up America. All Christians must check themselves, be on the alert. When Nunu had tried to explain all this to her big sister,

Sandhya had run away, all the way down the road to the Mission Hospital where their father lay on a bed. Why? Why didn't Sandhya ever listen?

Nunu felt her eyelids close with exhaustion. She would have to ask Jay. Jay lived in New York, he knew the Empire State Building. Once he had sent her a postcard with a picture of a tall building with a red, white, and blue spire pointing high into the darkness of the sky. That one she had saved. Softly, she started crying. She wished Jay would come soon, before it all ended. She could almost feel his wings knotted with leather strips and smelling of dead flesh. A bit like the smell of the cloth she had found under the mulberry roots. She shook her hair off her mouth. If only Jay would come soon. She would sit by him brushing the doll's hair. Berget, the blonde one, he had sent from Berlin. She could feel the brown wrapping under her fingers as the postman handed over the package. She was outside in the garden when she ripped off the paper and stared astounded at the brilliant mess of Berget's hair, white blonde like she had never seen before. What would it be like if each strand of hair were set on fire? It came to her with a slight jarring sensation: "A new heaven and earth!" Berget could help her reach the new heaven, the fiery new earth the reverend had spoken of.

Where was he now? It hurt her head even to think. Time and again Sandhya picked up the phone, only to let it drop with a clatter when she reached the answering machine. Where was he? Finally, late one morning, someone picked up. But it was a woman's voice at the other end.

"Draupadi?" Sandhya asked, almost not daring to breathe.

"It's Zeinab," the voice said clearly, "I'm Rashid's cousin. Can I help you?"

Then came days when Sandhya lay on her bed hardly daring to move, and Stephen, kindly to the last, took care of the child and brought his wife oatmeal in bed, with cinnamon on top according to his grandmother's recipe. Sandhya took a few steps, sat on a chair in the living room, and looked out at the blue awnings of the restaurant where in better times Rashid had taken her to lunch. And not so far were the smooth steps of the brownstone where Jay lived. She wished Jay could be by her, filling her with news of Tiruvella, Poonthera, Ayodhya, the world he was caught up in, so that her heart would stop beating so fast. So that some sense might fall into her life, as light into a room so disorderly that the coordinates of right-left, up-down have dissolved. The kind of room a painter might create to confound the viewer, to make one stop and think how hard it is to live, when the brush has no place on the dresser, the string of beads will not fit in the small wooden box, the apple lying in the corner will not be picked up and rinsed. And she who inhabited that room, glimpsed as a shadow in the painting, weakened beyond belief, turning toward the kitchen to let the dailiness of things stream into her, the black pot she had scrubbed and set aside a whole week ago, the sink, the white metal table, the shadow of her husband, laughing, tossing back his handsome blond head, his arm around her shoulders, their child in his arms. Later that afternoon, watching Stephen with the child, Sandhya felt relief, enormous, vivid, flood her. It was as if a burden of ugly parakeets borne on her shoulders, each bird crying out its gabble, had dropped off.

It was a shock then that night to feel she needed to hear Rashid's voice again, feel her body folding itself to a hand that caressed, gently, her pubic hair, the rough spot on her inner thigh. She rolled over, away from Stephen, imagining what it would be like if Rashid were with her, laying his body on hers so that the rolling lilt of flesh made itself felt in a pressure that built up to a delicious concordance, a burden that thrust her lungs flat till she was forced to hold her breath and finally cry, "Off, off with you, fat thing." And rolling over he would laugh, dip his head between her breasts. She shut her eyes, nuzzled against the gentleness of Stephen's arm, and lay waiting for the light to break on the street, for the lamppost to clarify, its white light dissolving into the greater radiance of the sun.

At times she puzzled over why Rashid's hands, his thighs, should pull her away from Stephen. "Be absolute for love." She had read that somewhere. Why could she not love two men? The story of Draupadi of the *Mahabharata,* who had five husbands and loved them all, came back to her, but Sandhya could not hold on to the image. The *Pandavas* seemed too large, too clumsy in their ancient lineaments to come any closer, the Draupadi they shared too lean a spirit to speak to her. Who knew what her real feelings had been, confronted with all five of them? Perhaps the delights they afforded her and demands they made were too distinct, too costly.

When she was a child, her father had told her a story: Draupadi turning to Bhima, the club-wielding husband, begging him for a flower that haunted her:

"Even when I walked the burning coals, the fragrance of that flower intoxicated me. O great Bhima, bring me the saugandhika flower, its fragrance bright as the sky high above the Nilgiris." Slowly, listening to her father's imagined voice, haunted by a mythic Draupadi, heroine of so many worlds, Sandhya fell asleep.

But as the days went by, her confusion intensified and she found she was having a hard time breathing. When the phone rang she started. But it was never Rashid who called. The sound of the keys in the lock made her tremble. When half-asleep she put out her arm to Stephen, to touch the coolness of his skin, it was as if an iron hook prevented her. Her fingers poised over his naked neck, clenched, and withdrew.

It was not the memory of Rashid that did it: his lips on her breasts, the way he parted her thighs with his hands. His hands in her dreams were small, tender. It was something behind the sensual memory. Her tongue licked steel. If she resisted—and she knew she never would—something would surely pull her back, hold her down as surely as the sandstone blocks at the mouth of the pyramid of Giza held down the earth, tamped it in.

It was not memory, but rather a force that sprang out of it and took root in her flesh, an absolute property, bare, anonymous, that seemed to say:

"Look, this is all there is, this clasp, this iron hold. And you cannot escape even if you leap into the mouth of the cooking pot, drop through the eye of the needle."

She put out her hand to Stephen's neck, but the fragile happiness that seemed within her reach grew brittle, turned into a metallic thing that wove water out of rocks and made it taste of burnt blood. Next morning she felt as if carcasses of animals lay in the acres of sorghum she knew from her childhood. And all of Broadway seemed deathly still.

A strong wind was blowing through Jay's hair, even his skin seemed caught up in the wind. He had no words left. His uncle was dead and Sandhya seemed to be taking it so calmly, no storms of tears, no scenes. Perhaps it was all spent in her. And her affair with Rashid? The two men had a drink at the West End Café and Rashid confessed to Jay that he felt quite out of his depth.

"Yes, I loved her," he said, his fingers tightening over the beer glass. The drops of moisture clung to his skin. Jay noticed that the past tense slipped so easily out of Rashid's mouth. So it was over, was it? Or was Sandhya getting too clingy in her need? Jay felt hot in his sudden confusion. How could he possibly mediate between those two? In any case, there was Stephen and the small child.

"You know about her father's death?" Jay asked softly.

"Yes, you told me. I did try to call."

Rashid seemed at a loss for words. He fumbled in his shirt pocket and held up a tiny black doll, its feet bound with crimson thread.

"She brought me this," he said, "the last time we saw each other."

Jay stared at the doll, propped against the wine list on their table. Its eyes were flat, shining bits of black painted on with the tip of a brush. He noticed the strands of hair, made of thread, hastily stuck on by the looks of it. The whole thing had a crude air about it. Jay sensed it was one of the pair he had seen on Sandhya's fridge that afternoon he visited her and launched into the tale of Uncle Itty. What had come over him, making up that narrative? Rashid was staring at him, and Jay needed to say something.

"She's a sensitive soul," he murmured, looking away from Rashid.

His friend stared back at Jay. "She gave me the doll. She said she wanted to live with me. Be with me."

Jay sat upright. His voice was harsher than he meant but it was a shock to his system to hear this. An affair was one thing, but to go that far?

"What did you say?"

"I couldn't do it. I told her."

Rashid sank back on his seat and mopped his face.

"'I simply can't,' I said to her. She was puzzled, mad. 'It's because I'm married, isn't it?' And then I shook my head."

Jay sat in silence, listening. Obviously Rashid wanted to unburden himself:

"I told her no. Not just that. I don't want to live with anyone just now."

Rashid leaned his chin on his elbow, picked up the doll, and placed it gently back in his shirt pocket. Looked straight at Jay: "You know something, old chap? I don't think she believed me."

"Probably not," Jay responded.

Suddenly he felt anxious. His cousin Sandhya Rosenblum had her back to the wall. What would she do now? There was no way she could turn back the clock, return to Hyderabad. Would she even want that? How happy she had seemed those first weeks with Rosenblum. What had gone wrong?

On his way back to his brownstone, the wind rose. Jay stepped over a pile of leaves the wind had blown to the side of the bus shelter. Old memories stirred in him. Gautam's eyes, his face, and another face, blurred, indistinct. He thought he saw Ahmed's eyes, but shook off the thought. Ahmed, his old school friend, Sandhya had even met him once, remarked on the fine high forehead, the curly hair, the pallor of the cheeks. It wasn't like Sandhya to make comments about a man, but she had mentioned Ahmed.

Jay shrugged his shoulders deeper into the jacket he was wearing. It was cold now, he was in another country. There were other lives, other obsessions. And still the past stirred, buried just beneath a mound of dead leaves, shifting.

The loss of Gautam,who had cut himself off so abruptly, must have been hard for Sandhya. And surely Jay had to take some responsibility. His mind swung back to the café on Nampally Road: Sandhya standing alone by the door. How shy she was, coming forward, newspaper in hand. It was a newspaper, wasn't it, she had in her hand when Gautam, courteous as ever, shoved back his chair and rose to greet her. When she joined them, he and Gautam stopped their jokes, something about the nawab's twin daughters and their bony maiden aunt, all hidden behind velvet car curtains, in strictest purdah.

Where were those twins now? Hiding out, behind a palace wall, in a rose garden grown dry with neglect? Jay had heard one of the girls sing when he had gone to visit Ahmed.

Time contracted, drew him in, and Jay seemed to hear that voice again, lifted in an immeasurably sad song of roses and dew, both bound to perish, a sun stained with blood. Wandering in the rose garden, Jay had searched for the source of the exquisite voice, but Ahmed called him on. Following, Jay saw a glimmer of silk in the bushes, started to race toward it, but as the leaves parted he saw a peacock, one claw raised a little off the dirt, and something red tangled in that bony sharpness.

Ahmed had pulled him away to the cupola at the end of the garden, to the fountain where he wanted to sit and play music on his flute. The very next day on his way to Gowliguda in a scooter rickshaw, for Ahmed had refused the ostentation of the chauffeur-driven car with curtains and personal attendant, the young man was stopped at the red lights by a gang of extremists.

"What is your name?" they asked him.

But the question, if he had heard it, was a mere formality. It was clear to his attackers, from the cut of his silk sherwani, his hair, and other tiny details of speech and gesture, that Ahmed was not just an ordinary Muslim but an upper-class Muslim, perhaps even a member of the extended family of the nawab. The young man was dragged out by his hair and stabbed repeatedly. The rickshaw wallah escaped to tell the tale.

When they trouped out from the palace with car and burial gown, they found the body lying on a pile of broken bricks, at the edge of the embankment. Ahmed's head hung, grazing the surface of water. They lifted him up, and sunlight reflected off his open eyes. His face was still beautiful, seemingly untouched by blows that had disfigured the back of his head, crushed the muscles of the throat.

At first when he heard of Ahmed's death, it was difficult for Jay to touch the mess of rage inside him. He felt as if his own bones were smoldering in the terrible light that shone out of Ahmed's dead eyes. A servant told him the story:

"*Saab*, when we lifted him out, his dead eyes hurt us with their light."

The old man had shut his own eyes with his hands as he spoke: "Two suns, *saab*, two suns burning."

There were streetlights burning above his head, just at the edge of Broadway, and Jay quickened his pace. He was almost at the road that led to his brownstone when he glimpsed figures crouched above the grating where the subway ran. He tightened his scarf about his throat, saw one of the men raise himself and stumble forward, clutching something sharp in his hand.

"*Nai, nai,*" Jay called out in Hindi, quickening his steps, but just as abruptly as he had risen, the man turned, suddenly irresolute, inching back to the grating and the small tent raised over it so warmth might waft up through the metal grille. When he turned back to look, Jay saw that it was a tent formed of bits of cloth and cardboard and shreds of a plastic bag, three sticks holding the whole caboodle erect in the stiff wind. Piecemeal shelter, housing made from detritus by poor, homeless men. He felt relief flood through his clenched fist. But, though thankful that a momentary danger had passed, the man's retreat troubled Jay. The old philosophies are dead, he thought bitterly. There is very little that can keep us warm. He clutched his jacket tighter about him as he turned back to gaze at the dark and ragged tent, its plastic flapping against the single, stoutest stick.

The wind had sharpened, lifting off the river as he hurried home. It was then he saw someone rising off the steps of the brownstone, uncurling as mist might, a body dark as stone. Another homeless creature, he thought, another derelict dogging me! At first he could not see the face, but glimpsed eyes, nose, lips, chin, the peculiar bent of shoulder. A cry was torn from him, sounding strangely in his own ears.

"Ahmed!" he heard himself moan and the sound echoed in the dimly lit street. High above his head someone lifted up a window and stared down at the foreigner in the baggy jacket, his arms stretched out in an alien ritual of mourning.

But it wasn't Ahmed who rose from his stoop. It was his cousin Sandhya Rosenblum. Jay stared, hardly believing the change that had come over her. Her hair was shorn close to her head and she was dressed in worn-out men's clothing. Perhaps men's clothing was wrong, but except for the silk scarf around her throat there was nothing feminine about her attire.

There she was, haggard in the street glare, waiting patiently for him. He raced up the steps, took her by the arm, and led her into his house. She was shivering and her hair, short as it was, was blown into tiny points by the wind. As she sat on his one armchair, sipping the brandy he offered her, he stared at her face, astonished at the resemblance to the dead Ahmed. How was it he had never noticed it before? Those high cheekbones, the fine bridged nose. What could he say to her, should he tell her what Rashid had said? But Sandhya didn't want to talk, didn't want to listen. She seemed content to sit utterly quiet. An hour later, when the wind dropped, he led her home, waiting as she rang the bell. Stephen, dressed in his cotton pajamas, his face blurred with sleep, opened the door. "I've brought her back," was all Jay could trust himself to say, and Stephen gulped out his thanks, taking his wife by her shoulders, leading her in.

That night in his journal Jay wrote the word DEATH and took a green marker and drew a box around it. Then he lay down on his bed and closed his eyes. A small child was calling from high in the Charminar, a child with dirt on his face and a flute in his hand. Or was it a girl-child with very short hair, calling out Jay's name from high in the four-cornered monument that stood at the heart of Hyderabad? Jay longed to put out his hands to the child, wave, call out. The child's face was so dark now, it made Jay dizzy. The child was Ahmed, no, Sandhya, Ahmed, then Sandhya again. How unstable the features were, melding, blurring in the dream. Jay's tongue felt like a bit of lead against his teeth. And his hands were so faint he feared his body had already vanished away like mist.

Finally he fell asleep in a tangle of bedclothes and dreamed of a little brown house. Rashid had said Sandhya wanted to live with him in a house.

It was dark outside the house till a woman's hand lifted up an oil lamp. Bangle-Seller's lane in Charminar, Jay recognized it instantly. A dark stain on the steps. The stain spread behind the closed door and he heard loud footsteps. Ahmed was running toward him, arms wide open. A thin man with an ivory cane was standing up in the police jeep, directing the chase. Jay had to get help. He pounded at the brown door with his fist. The door of the house blew open and she stood on the steps, his cousin Sandhya, arms pointed skyward. Jay pointed to a large bell that hung above the doorframe. Together they grasped at the rope, tugging it hard. The fumes of the jeep were so close now. Again and again they tugged at the bellrope.

R ough chimes hurled against the wind. A bell dulling itself with repetition. Jay sat up in bed, rubbing his eyes. The door swung open and there he stood, in raincoat and hat, a fistful of dollars in his hand, his big brother, Chandu! Jay stumbled out of bed, drew his brother into the house, and sat him down.

"Why didn't you tell me you were coming?"

Chandu, staring at his kid brother, took in his frayed shirt and *lungi,* thought of how disorganized Jay's life had become. But a rush of affection took hold of him. He clapped Jay on the shoulder, feeling the thin bones that threatened to edge their way out through the skin, then drew back instinctively. Chandu had never felt comfortable without a good padding of fat in his torso, or elsewhere on his body. How else to hold the world at bay? He glanced out the window at 113th Street. It had changed since his MBA days, more shops, more students sunning themselves, faster cars. But grimy, not like Paris or Munich.

He pushed his suitcases next to the futon and watched Jay put the kettle on to boil. Right away Chandu wanted to know about Sandhya. As delicately as he could, Jay spoke of Sandhya's affair with Rashid. What he knew was pale beside the dream of Sandhya outside Bangle-Seller's lane, tugging hard at the bellrope. Listening to his brother's mumbled words, Chandu found himself growing hot under the collar.

"Damn shame a cousin of mine taking up with an Arab. If it's true," he said, after a silence of immoderate length.

"It's true, all right."

Chandu sighed: "Well, I suppose I would have said the same if it were an Englishman or Turk."

Jay looked down at his hands, frail brown stalks, lying in his lap. He felt a weariness in his soul. "I need to go away," he said to his brother. "Return to Kerala. And you, my dear, can stay with Sandhya, but for God's sake keep your mouth shut."

"Taking more photos?"

"A travel piece, I think." Jay was hesitant. "I'll stay in Tiruvella a while, visit Nunu. Things must be hard there, after Uncle Varki's death."

"I'll say so. Nunu has gone quite crazy with all her religious claptrap. And Sosa aunty doesn't listen to me when I tell her to prohibit those magazines."

"Magazines?" Jay turned from the kettle he had just picked up.

"Yeah, all that wild Christian stuff."

"I didn't know Nunu had money of her own to subscribe."

"No need, sonny boy. They send it to her free."

Thereafter, Chandu fell silent and sat in the armchair Sandhya had sunk into just hours earlier. No, he wouldn't tell his brother of her, homeless, windblown, on his stoop. It would seem like a betrayal. But there were things he could say.

"Listen, Chandu, go gently on Sandhya, will you? She seems quite lost, what with Varki's death and all that ..." Jay paused, not wanting to enter into any more details. "Don't ask her about matters of the heart. She'll tell you when she's ready, I'm sure. In any case," Jay looked straight at his muscular brother as he said this, "it'll do her good to see you."

So it was that two days later Chandu made his way in a yellow cab to Sandhya's apartment. He had a knack of making himself feel at home and almost immediately found his way into the meager cache of drink Stephen kept. Ever the ardent cousin, he complimented her on her clothes, her new haircut. But Sandhya kept silent, as if it were nothing to be spoken of. She hadn't given up cooking, though, he was pleased to notice. As Sandhya worked in the kitchen, Chandu poured himself a jot of Metaxa. She pointed to Dora's little stool, assured him it was made of metal. So he perched there, glass in hand, sticking doggedly to what he thought of as his safe nugget of news: the failure of the LTTE.

"Thanks, Bachi, this drink's quite the thing. Reminds me of the JFK bar where I drank with my little brother. Now London airport's another story. Want to hear?"

She inclined her head politely, congratulating him on the new branch office he'd opened. He bowed his head, half in self-mockery:

"Nothing, my dear, just good Malayali capitalism."

She caught his tone and smiled back wryly. Three or four more days of

Chandu, she was thinking, and perhaps she could forget all she had gone through, thrust her old life out as liver on a spatula is thrust into hot oil. She poured sesame oil into the pan, sprinkled in a handful of mustard seeds, and waited for them to splutter.

Could she forget Rashid? "If I forget thee ..."

Chandu's voice sounded behind her, booming, slightly unreal. He often had that effect on her. She was gladdened by the muscular crudity he brought to words, deeds, even unspoken thoughts.

"The world is getting much smaller, my dear. So what does that do to our sense of belonging, eh? I took Air India as I always do. Must support our own. Colombo, Madras, London. Cold fog. Got off, bag in hand. British security agents raced in, dog and all, right onto the runway. They'd caught hold of a Tamil man just behind me, a thin, meek-looking fellow.

"They demanded his papers, but all he did was move his head about, quite helplessly."

Chandu coughed into his drink.

"One of the security men, a big strapping fellow, gave the dog's leash to the other and forced the man's mouth open. Imagine forcing someone's mouth open on the runway. Apparently they found what they were looking for, bits of messy paper, half-chewed. The poor chap—not so poor, an LTTE bastard obviously—had tried to eat his papers and somehow these blokes were tipped off."

She stopped cutting the onions:

"What good would it do, to swallow the papers?"

"Elementary, my dear. He could claim refugee status, couldn't he? Then and there on British soil, link up with the kingpin Prabhakaran, Kittu, all that unholy bunch, and plot more killings on Indian soil. Too much, eh?"

He stopped. Raising his glass to his lips, slowly added:

"I hear there are fanatic groups here, plotting things."

She was careful. Behind her the mustard seeds had started their wild popping, soft hearts thrust from the seeds, skins split:

"Oh that. They seem to have caught a few people."

She went on cutting the onions.

"So you've made new friends, eh?"

"New friends?" She was puzzled. Quite resolutely she kept her mind elsewhere: "You mean Draupadi? You'll enjoy her, I think. Quite a dramatic lady."

But Chandu wasn't listening. How peaked she looked, he thought, ready almost to faint. Things all around were bad enough, without her caving in. What was going on behind that sad gaze of hers? He fiddled with the knobs of the radio, needing to distract them both.

A voice broke through the static, a querulous voice complaining that religious fanatics were giving Waco, Texas, a bad name: "Religion should make you a nice, well-rounded person, not turn you into a nut."

"Nut?" the interviewer queried in a voice held too close to the microphone.

"Sure, nuts, those Branch Davidians."

"They must be right where Koresh and his group are holed up," Chandu said in a stage whisper as the interviewer described a small child hobbling out by herself under the searchlights. A child with her thumb in her mouth, saying nothing.

The radio voice faded, then crackled back into life: "When the Federal agent opened up the note pinned to the child's blouse, there was a line drawing. I will describe it for you: A man with a crown on his head, three guns pointed at him, barbed wire around his feet. DAVID KING OF THE JEWS, it says, under the image."

"Branch Davidians always give me a shock." Chandu stretched out his arms, turning off the radio with a clatter.

"I keep thinking they mean Dravidians. People like us, from somewhere south of the Brahamaputra. You know, Dravidians versus Aryans. But this was a madman from Waco. They put him on the cover of *Time* right next to the mad mullah of Cairo, Sheik Omar Abdel Rahman. I bought a copy in Hong Kong. Both ready to kill and be killed."

He shook his elegant foot free of the onion skin that clung to it.

"Tell me, Sandy, how is America-land going for you? I hear you've had your difficulties."

He said this last, in what for him was a sorrowful tone. But she laughed it off and made for the refrigerator. She called out to him, turning backward from the mound of vegetables she had piled into plastic bags:

"I felt so sorry for that chap they arrested. He looked faint, ready to pass out. It was Ramadan, too. And their van, it doesn't gel. If you wanted to blow up the Empire State Building, would you go back for four hundred dollars' deposit money?"

She drew out a plastic bag full of tomatoes from the fridge and returned to the chopping board. Her fingers stopped at the edge of the plastic. Such bags were difficult to come by in India and if she were Sosa, she would have washed and dried these thin plastic bags the vegetable shops gave away, hoarding them like treasure. She turned to her cousin:

"Apparently they saw it on TV in Tiruvella—'Bombing Planned, Culprits Caught in Nick of Time.' Building closed down. A group of schoolchildren stuck at the top. Amma was in such a state. It wasn't Dora's school, was it, she kept asking, over and over again on the phone. No, Amma, no, it was a school in Brooklyn and, in any case, Dora was fast asleep at the Purple Submarine at the time."

He sat up in mock surprise:

"Submarine? No! Not my niece."

"It's a daycare center."

She went on cutting, the tomato skins red on her fingers, juice oozing out.

"I'd go back for my four-hundred-dollar deposit, wouldn't you?"

Tossing this at her, he walked straight into the tiny living room. Soon enough she heard the strains of the Malayalam song he had put on the CD player. She wanted to stop, throw out her arms, let her other life pour through her, as she stood listening to the words: a girl with her long chain of flowers, singing in the forests, singing to Krishna.

The next morning Sandhya, in a worn Kashmiri robe, sat quietly on the carpet. Chandu was in his pajamas flipping through a newspaper. She looked over his head, through the living room window, and saw tiny houses, stucco and brick dotting the cliffs of New Jersey. Closer at hand, a balloon rose into the air above the New Khalsa gas station. What was Chandu chattering about? He had put his newspaper aside. She wished he would keep still so she could sit quietly, staring out. Her mind was on those houses way across the river. What would it be like to live in a little house with white walls, a small picket fence, a man who came home each evening with a bouquet of wildflowers in his hand? Her thoughts trembled and veered. She could not see the man's face. She heard his voice coming to her from a great distance. Something in French, a phrase Rashid had used about flowers, a bouquet of flowers. The word *l'absente* was in it.

"Think Jay will get to Tiruvella safely?" she called.

"Why not? Jay's a big boy now!" Chandu stopped short, then shrugged. He decided he didn't want to hear what Sandhya might have gone through. Nor did he like speculating on even a simple matter concerning his brother.

His photography, for instance—who would ever have thought that the basis of a career? He had proposed so many times that Jay enter into the chemical business with him. It would have been a family business then.

Chandu shifted in his seat, looking down at Sandhya, that firm set of her neck, the eyes clear yet troubled. What was behind them? And yet, he should follow Jay's advice, say nothing, wait for her to talk.

The next morning the sky was filled with an odd glare. Sandhya had to squint to make out the cars crawling over George Washington Bridge. What would it be like to be driven quickly over the bridge into New Jersey? Chandu knew how to drive. She called out his name, once, twice, and when he didn't respond, she walked briskly to the kitchen, poured coffee beans into the grinder. Good Mysore coffee she had brought back with her and hoarded for occasions such as this.

Drawing the chopping board close, she sliced onions and red chilies, readying them for a masala omelette. He came out, wet in his bathrobe, and she placed a cup of coffee in his hands.

"Storm, eh?"

She watched him lean against the window and suddenly knew what she must do. She would go with him to the meeting. Her voice was tentative, slow.

"Someone I know is speaking in the city."

He waited.

"Will you come with me?"

Her tone caught Chandu off guard. He set down his coffee cup and stared at her. She was growing confused, blushing a little. He could not resist the frail, feminine pleading.

"Where?" he asked.

"It's on Forty-second Street. An auditorium. Some students have arranged an antiwar meeting. I heard of it through a friend."

"My pleasure, dear Madam Rosenblum, to escort you," he said in an imitation German accent, and twirled an invisible mustache, bowing low. They set out early, just after lunch, but by the time they reached the building it had started to rain, and the sky over Bryant Park was filled with dark storm clouds penciled in gray over an empty white tent, the remains of a fashion show. Chandu and Sandhya edged their way into the crowd. As they walked down the steps to the underground auditorium, Chandu saw a poster with Rashid's name. He rubbed his eyes, tightened his grip on

Sandhya's arm. She seemed overly excited, catching his wrist and pulling him forward to a front row seat.

The lights dimmed. A man in a brown corduroy shirt came on. The lights glinted off his black hair. A slight man, this Rashid, not how Chandu would have imagined Sandhya's lover. He spoke well, that he had to admit. But it wasn't eloquence that had drawn his cousin. Suddenly Chandu knew he should drag her away, take her to Simla, Nainatal, for a holiday. But it was somewhere in the hills, surely, that she had met Rosenblum, and look what that had brought her to! Her eyes had a dilated look. She was staring at the figure on the platform.

How could he tell that other voices stirred in his cousin's ears, drawing her down to a rough basement—a dark, muddy place where syllables stirred their moist roots.

She heard her sister, Nunu, cry out in the Sanskrit her tutor forced on her: *"Aham patashala getchami!"* the singsong of recitation. She heard Arabic from the lyrics Rashid learned from his mother, a burial song, a woman with a swanlike neck, exiled in life, returned to her native soil in death. She heard voices from the streets of Bosnia, Rwanda, Sri Lanka, strange countries bruised as plums might be in a gunny sack. Voices too, from mats and torn mattresses stained with virginal blood, moans and sharp cries of pleasure, exhalations of delight, gasps as smoke is inhaled from burning cities where tanks rumble.

These sounds played within her in a ceaseless cacophony, struggling to become speech: the homeless voices of Sandhya Maria Rosenblum.

They are fixing the pipes.

Something dammed up, breaking loose. Water spilling down.

I gave him my breast. I pulled it out of my blouse. He raised his chin. Set his lips to my flesh and began to suck.

Buried his face, his mouth, his nose, his eyes, in my breasts.

I lay there, feeling him suck.

One of the workmen knocked at the door. I rolled over on the bed, fixed my blouse, smoothed my hair, stood up.

"Is it leaking?"

"Leaking?"

"Water, Mrs. Rosenblum, ma'am, from up."

I opened the door a crack. Green shirt, lean dark face.

"Okay, then?"
"Thanks."

Burnt into me.
    The blades of him.
    The sharp burning rose of him. I cannot come clean.

Voices: through the pipes, booming elegies for the dead. I was among the dead, a violet in my hair.
    He bought a violet from the Russian peasant woman and set it in my hair.
    The voices are trying Malayalam, Arabic, not quite succeeding.
    Little children never learn a language unless they are taught well.
    We need to be taught well so as not to degenerate into savagery.

He will come and bring violets for my hair, cover me in violets.
    Sita, Ophelia, Draupadi, Antigone.
    Must I become a dead woman so he will love me, as he loves her who gave him suck?
    In Beita the olive trees are blasted at the root. What will become of those trees in paradise?
    "I will take you to my homeland, Sandhya. You will understand the meaning of exile."
    He said this in Arabic. I did not understand and told him so.
    In heaven there is no need for translation.
    In heaven we find blossoming violets, tuberose, champa flowers, jasmine, the veliparithi that grows by Grandmother's well.

A woman leans over the stove. She has my hair, my face. The pot is mean, white. Alphabets seethe in the pot.
    "Come, come here, Dora, you little golden child," the *ayah* cries. The child picks up the letter *D.* A pasta letter.
    The *ayah* whispers to the child as she arranges her hair. No violets there. She whispers in a language I have never learned.
    The window shakes.
    Trees shake in the window.

They are bombing.
    He stands up on the platform and waves his arms in front of his face. "Ca, Caca, po, po," he sings, waving the crows away.

There were bits of grass in his hair and wildflowers, too.

I was wrapped up in my long skirt, pink silk with a brocaded edge and blouse to match. I crouched behind the pillars of the veranda so he wouldn't see.

"I am the snake princess," I cried. "The caca can't eat me. I am wrapped in pink!" I waved my arms, with all the bangles I had taken from Amma's cupboard. The glitter scared the crows.

Behind the tapioca patch Uncle Itty was burying something. Mud on his sleeves. When I looked next, the grass had grown over the little mound he made with his hands.

I saw her blood, the Muslim woman who lived in Bangle-Sellers Lane behind Charminar. After the *rath yatra* they took her out and raped her in the graveyard.

"We will show you," they cried, "you and all your sisters, foreigners in Hindustan."

Her small child, three and a half, was hidden under the bed. The child saw them tear the mother's clothing. The worst she was spared from seeing, but the child's third eye—like Shiva, children have a third eye— burned into the future.

"No oil for the oil lamp," someone cried in Bangle-Seller's Lane, behind Charminar.

"Hurry, bring me a rupee or two, so I can get the oil. Something terrible is happening in the graveyard."

They could not find fresh oil for the lamp. Some of those who hurried by shut their eyes, not wanting to see the young *goondas* rape the woman, who by now was begging for death.

What oil there was in the base of the lamp spread into the city and the city started burning.

Where his mother is buried in Cairo there is no marker. He carried her body, wrapped in the simple white cloth, and descended into the pit. He went down into the grave with the body of his mother.

The snake princess lives under the earth.

The earth made four walls and a roof for her.

The walls and roof fell in.

The cow tethered to the peepul tree fell in.

The moon fell from the cow's mouth and the heavens lit up.

A second sun was shining.

He stood on the platform under bright light. They are bombing and bombing, down into rubble, he cried.

Rashid was standing on the platform under the spotlights as he spoke: about red flares, cries of Iraqi children, young men from Oregon and Texas torn from their pillows.

He did say torn from their pillows?

He who was torn from my pillow.

Contra natura, he said, this taking of life, all the religions prohibit it.

He raised the hand I had kissed the night before, the night before all my nights, the hand with the mole at the edge of the thumb.

He touched soft flesh by his neck, earlobes with a tiny bit of hair, sharp nick of scissors there.

"I was cutting, cutting my ear hair," he said. "You don't have ear hair, do you?" Sweet sweet. *Halati. Nur el Ein.* Covering my eyes with his kisses, the blunt hair on his ear tickling me.

When you die, my love, I shall be there, the burning cities behind me. Amma there, Appa, a shawl over his shoulders, his dhoti crisp and clean, crying, "Infidel, what have you done to my child, my Sandhya Maria?"

Sir, I am not an infidel. I believe in the Almighty, in the Prophet, in the holy *Koran.*

Racism, he said, the firing of missiles, the contravention of international law. My head was hurting already. I wished he would stop.

War is erasure, he said. *Mémoire, mémoire que me veux tu?* he asked, as if reciting a poem.

Memory makes me up, I am a body of memory, quickened by his hands, his lips, his tongue.

His words come to me from a great distance. Tear gas wafts down from the streets of Delhi, Hyderabad, Basra, Baghdad.

I do not know how his words came to him.

Imagine, he says, walking along the streets of Manhattan on an ordinary day, climbing stairs in an apartment building, groceries in hand, crossing the streets as the ambulances race by, descending the subway. The mind moves out, pondering, then recoils in numbness.

What would it be like to live as an ordinary woman in a war zone: no water, no power, little food, and always the terror of a moment by moment existence?

What would it mean to flee? Across what border?

What if Manhattan were being bombed by an imaginary nation thousands of miles away? How would we manage in this city we love with its sharp river views, canyons of concrete and steel, broken subways, shattered beer bottles, wayside stalls and flower markets, bakeries, butcher shops?

No heat, no water, very little food, and always the falling bombs. What would we tell our children, tell ourselves?

The very first night of bombardment as much destructive power was hurled down by the Allied warplanes as was contained in the atomic bombs that fell on Hiroshima and Nagasaki in the Second World War.

In 1948 that American woman photographer in a pure white dress, I forget her name, went right up to Mahatma Gandhi and said:

"Should America stop producing the bomb?"

"Of course."

"Would you meet the bomb with nonviolence?" she asked.

"I will not bury my face in the earth," the saintly, quirky old man said. "I will go out into the open and gaze into the great bowl of the sky, let the pilot in the metal plane sense I will never hate him. And surely, even as he soars in the blue, his eyes will be opened."

A few hours after saying those words Gandhi was shot dead, at Birla House, by an assassin who was moved by precisely those streams of fascism that are coursing through India today. But Gandhi wished only for love, for the dominion of love.

His voice was making me ill.

What did he mean by the dominion of love?

After I licked his toe, he made me enter into his black djellaba.

When I came out again I was tiny, in a red basket made of Nile reeds.

He held me in his arms. "Wa, wa," I cried. In the way that my child thinks all babies cry.

"I want you to have another baby, Mami," Dora said. "I am so sick of seeing babies on the sidewalk and not having one for myself at home."

I was red, like the basket of reeds. Fleshy, formless …

A small bird sings in the night in Basra, in Baghdad.

It sings the story of corpses.

Outside the workmen are banging their fists. Water is rising.

I have crossed the black waters to come here.

My whole life is singing, swaying in me. He faces me. The lights make his pale shirt dark as indigo, Lord Krishna's color. He has a djellaba, a turban, too. His face is covered. He has a whip in his hand.

"This is the Theater of Cruelty," he cries. "Know what that means?"

I shake my head. Beside me there are two other women crawling.

"Lick me," he commands, "lick my toes."

Delicately, as if it were covered with too much salt, I set my tongue to his toe.

After we make love, he takes off his djellaba and puts on a black-and-white robe, Japanese style, with enormous wide shoulders and sleeves.

When I ask him about it, he says he never had a djellaba, that I was imagining it.

After the whip and the crawling, I could believe anything.

When I took the rope in my hand, I saw his face.

We were in the white room together.

The mask slipped down his throat and I saw his face.

My eyes were in his eyes and there was no space.

The room was painted white. Sandhya Rosenblum entered without knocking; she pushed with the flat of her hand and the door swung open. It was a simple thing, a door into the dark. By the window Draupadi was working away on a mound of crushed metal.

"Have you seen Rashid?"

There was an edge to Sandhya's voice. And that hair, so terribly short, made her look like a dark doll. The kind with shaved head and leather jumpers sold at F.A.O. Schwartz for huge sums of money. But Sandhya was wearing a sari, bound tight around her.

"You know Zeinab is here?" Draupadi stood up wiping her hands and instantly regretted her words. Sandhya had sunk onto the edge of the futon. Her voice was a whisper:

"Went to that antiwar thing with Chandu."

"How was it?"

"I heard voices in my head. All sorts of voices, and the odd thing was …"

Her words trailed off.

"Do you have something I could drink? It's terribly hot out there."

"Juice, tea."

"No, water, cold water will do."

"I've run out of the bottled kind."

"New York tap water is good, they say." Sandhya stood up, watching

Draupadi at the faucet running cold water into a glass, adding ice cubes. Draupadi handed her the glass, then moved away to stand by the unfinished installation, crushed metal glowing behind her.

"You were saying."

"I don't know what's wrong with me. But at that meeting, it was like I didn't have any skin. Just voices that clung to me. Burning hot."

Sandhya gulped down the water.

"It wasn't what Rashid said? Or seeing him?" How gentle Draupadi seemed.

"I guess," her voiced halted. "But all sorts of other things crowded in. Like a theater. Did Rashid call you? Afterward?"

Draupadi shook her head. "We don't really talk to each other anymore. Listen, Sandhya, you have to break loose of him. You have to take care of yourself. Look."

She held up her hands, scarred with daily labor, metalwork, paperwork, and the hard rub of the adz against wood.

"I'm doing a piece for the Diwali celebrations. Haven't a clue yet what it will be. But something to do with Indians and Columbus's misadventures. They have a new stamp now, have you seen it?"

Draupadi extended her palm, a gray-and-white stamp lying flat on it. "Well, take a look. It has a picture of a man. And the caption." She read it very slowly. "'The first Americans crossed over from Asia.' I guess we belong here, after all. If the postal service says so."

But Sandhya wasn't listening. Her eyes were fixed on the edge of the window, where the sunlight was fading. With her right hand she swept back her hair so that a slight welt on her forehead showed, a pale scar normally buried under the drift of hair. Her voice was faint and seemed to come from a far place:

"When Appa died, I sat down and imagined the rice fields they carried his body through. Rice stalks swaying, sunlight on the river."

She moved away from the window and touched the bowl of cut oranges on the counter, the white sailcloth Draupadi was stretching on a wooden frame.

"Such peace, Draupadi. I wanted that. I wanted to shut my eyes and get to that peace."

She sat down hard against the futon.

"Thought when I married Stephen it would all work out. New life, new memories. Instead all I have are these voices."

She moved forward, a new urgency in her voice:

"Tell me, do you think to be American I have to hear all these voices? I mean, is it part of being here, in this world?"

"Why do you say that?" Draupadi's voice was clear, firm.

"I don't know." She mumbled out the words. "I used to sit on a bench in Central Park wondering what it would be like to belong here. Dying to belong." She gave a little laugh.

She moved closer to Draupadi till she was right by the sink, facing a counter with knotted rope, axe, saw, scissors, pliers, steel wool, sandpaper, glistening hooks fit for a leviathan.

"Rashid told me a story about a monster, the bits of languages in his head, and bits of flesh he's formed from. He said immigrants are like that."

"Nonsense! My parents were immigrants."

"They didn't feel like this?" Sandhya lifted up her hands, making shadows against Draupadi's white wall. Draupadi stared at the flickering marks.

"Mama, perhaps. She was so unhappy, she should have been an artist."

"And your father?"

"He made do, I guess."

"But you do know what I mean, don't you? Those voices hurt so much. Squatting on me, burning through me, and nothing, nothing left."

"There, there," Draupadi murmured. She let Sandhya crouch against her side and then, wanting to free herself, said briskly:

"I know just the thing. A great woman singer, and she even changed her name. No, not to Rosenblum! Here, come over here."

She drew Sandhya forward to a stack of records. Draupadi hummed, then murmured the words:

> Southern trees bear a strange fruit:
> Blood on the leaves and blood at the root.

"Ever heard that lady?"

Sandhya leaned against the wall and shut her eyes. She seemed to see Rashid's face again, and then it vanished.

"Who's she?" Sandhya's voice sounded hollow, as if she had little strength left.

"Billie Holiday."

Sandhya Rosenblum straightened, smiling a little.

"Yes, of course, I have heard of her." She walked to the stove, fingered the pot in which Draupadi had poured milk to boil. Heard her friend say:

"It was a song Mama used to hum while ironing. Got it from her sister Sugatha, the rebel of the family, who sneaked into Café Society. Saw Lady Day in a black velvet gown, silk flowers at her shoulder, light flaming on her face, neck bent back, voice guttural, low, everything else, tables, chairs, glasses, chandeliers, in darkness:

> Black bodies swinging in the southern breeze;
> Strange fruit hanging from the poplar trees.

It's as if her voice were crying through all of us, Draupadi thought, as she watched Sandhya flipping on the gas, blue flames shooting under the pot. Sandhya shivered suddenly. "All that emotion, Draupadi, how could she bear her life?"

"Almost didn't."

As if Draupadi's response freed her, Sandhya drew herself straight.

"I am from the South, too."

"Not Alabama or Kentucky."

"No, Kerala. The first white people we saw were Portuguese who burned all the church records and conducted an Inquisition, stabbing, hanging, burning Indian bodies. So the souls might be saved."

Her voice was pitched high, a little too high, her hand trembled by the pot. Wanting to move Sandhya forward, Draupadi said: "Billie Holiday made up her own name. She was born Eleanora Fagan."

"Oh?"

"Her dad called her *Bill*. Maybe she took the name from Billie Dove, the film star with the smooth rippling hair, cut short, to her neck."

"Draupadi?" Sandhya moved away from the stove, her hand on the back of her neck, her fine cotton sari clinging to her:

"Why did you and Rashid break up?"

Draupadi stared at the brown arm, the fine hairs at the wrist, the tension in the fingers plucking at the sari, blossoms printed in pink.

"Why do you ask?"

"Just wanted to know."

Draupadi moved away. Next to the crushed metal she had strung up rope for her New World installation. Why couldn't she speak out, speak straight? Why this sense that slowly and painfully she must make up words afresh, without guidance or forethought, as the seconds ticked by, Sandhya her sole witness?

"Guess I wanted to get back to myself."

She tapped her own chest. "The part of me that thinks and feels. It was too hard, being so close to him and feeling he didn't really want me. So I cut."

She made a quick signal with her fingers. "Snip snap, as simple as that."

Sandhya was fingering the metal. Suddenly the rope swung off its hook. Draupadi saw Sandhya bump against the plaster cast of a bombed bunker, a jagged mess of simulated concrete. Its crudity seemed to frighten Sandhya, who crouched to stare into the hole in the concrete, an escape route out of imagined flames.

"Does Stephen know? About you and Rashid?"

Sandhya shook her head, picked up the rope, and handed it back to Draupadi, who used a chair to swing the coil back onto the high hook.

"I haven't a clue what I'll do with the rope. Hang the sun on it?" Then in a lighter tone she murmured for Sandhya's benefit:

"April."

"What?"

There was a slightly dazed quality to Sandhya's voice.

"Lady Day, born to sway, born in the green month."

"Her birthday?"

"Yeah, April seventh."

Sandhya touched the swinging rope and Draupadi saw tears fall free on her face. They shone on her clear brown skin. Sandhya faced her friend, mouth puckered, eyes squinting with the tears. She had never loved Sandhya so much.

"Why are you telling me this?"

"Because it's true."

"My mother's birthday. You knew that, didn't you?" asked Sandhya. Draupadi squatted down low by the bombed-out bunker she had fashioned with her own hands. Set one of the wire bits back in place.

"No," she said softly. "No, Sandhya. I know very little about your mother. Only what you've told me."

But Sandhya, right by the window, was staring out over the pier, at the darkened sky, waves brushing indigo against the light.

"I love him so much. I simply can't bear it. I can't tell Stephen. How can I?"

She stopped and went on: "Sometimes I feel there is an angel breathing down my neck. A creature of air. Born of shock."

"Shock?"

"Yes," Sandhya murmured. As she spoke, milk boiled over on the stove. Draupadi wiped it up with a wet cloth, feeling hot metal under her fingertips. Then Sandhya washed her face at the sink and some of the water splashed on her friend's eyes.

"Two hours," Sandhya said, "till I have to pick up Dora. I can't bear to go home just now."

"Stay."

It sounded cold, so Draupadi added, "Really, stay."

"Let me call Jay. I need to talk to him."

As Sandhya spoke on the phone to Jay, Draupadi worked at opening the gash where the smart bomb had cut through, short-circuiting the lights. She used a sharp knife on the plaster. She hummed under her breath:

> Here is a fruit for the crows to pluck;
> For the rain to gather, for the wind to suck.

She hummed till she thought her lips would sizzle with all that humming. She set the knife down and started kneading a bit of tinfoil in her palm. She wanted to spin a silver sun—or moon, she wasn't sure yet—above the scene of devastation, suspend it with a red thread. Then have the rope on the hook swing above it. Above the white sail, too.

Sandhya was flushed and excited when she got off the phone.

"Jay says to come over right now," she said, her words all in a rush. "Rashid is there."

"That?" Her voice dropped.

Draupadi held up the foil she had crushed in her hand. Sandhya nodded. So Draupadi made up her narrative, figuring it out as she went:

"It's the sun burning above Hispaniola where Columbus landed. Above Baghdad. Above Washington, too."

As she spoke the broken, sparkling words that Oppenheimer whispered from the Gita as he saw Hiroshima, the gray blossom of death risen above it, scented her breath. And she saw Sandhya Rosenblum standing utterly still, her eyes shut, breathing in her words.

Rope Mark
(Draupadi)

What could I have done to prevent it?

I see you hanging there. No wind in the room. Your body swaying as if the noose you made were touched by invisible fingers, a black cradle lulling the watcher. Was this the angel you spoke of? Were you trying to be that angel?

Above my rope your face contorted: tongue, lips, unlidded eyes, the physicality of flesh thrust to the front, the veil of sense gashed.

Your fingers were still clenched over a tiny doll made of string. Where was the other doll, Sandhya? The one bent in your hand was stuck onto white paper. Was there something you meant to write on that paper?

I cut you down.

Oh God, I cut you down, and then Simon Escobar came over, hearing me cry.

"You'll breathe, you'll breathe again," I whispered over and over, gasping for breath myself.

I did not know what was in my head and what was out of it.

What possessed you, Sandhya? What came over you?

Sometimes, still, I see you swaying. Twisting a little in the wind. As if I can't let you live, let you go on. Was there a slight wind? Had I left the window ajar? Summertime. I heard a child down in the street.

I raced in, cut you down.

Rubbed your poor raw neck. Your eyes were open. We hoisted you down, Simon from next door and I, to where the EMS men were waiting. You'll breathe. You'll breathe. I muttered the words in a mantra and started breathing for you.

Your sari came off in my hands. I had to tuck it back in. I looked at your skin, rich brown, darker even than mine. Nothing ashen about it. Only your throat had a rope mark. I called Stephen. He was in Greenwich. I got his number from Muriel, but I told her nothing, only "I must reach Stephen." She must have heard how quick my breath came. I think little Dora was with her at the time. I couldn't have borne the horror touching the child.

"I need Stephen's number," I said to Muriel. Finally I got him. I heard him choke as he listened, but the words that came out were quite calm. As if he had been prepared.

I didn't tell Rashid till much later. Saw him on Fifth and Fourteenth, right by the New School. Adjusting myself against the wall I said in a normal tone: "Heard about Sandhya?"

He shook his head. I believed him, told him the bare details. How I found you in my room, the rope mark on your neck, then added, "She'll be okay now."

"Okay, okay," he gulped. He was pale, paler than I've ever seen him. He clutched a book in his left hand.

"Class now?" I asked, to try to be kind.

He nodded. I left and walked into the subway stop at Union Square. I didn't have the guts to go down, all alone into that lower darkness. I felt my body trembling. I found a quarter and called up Rinaldo's office. "Mr. Montessori is in conference. Yes, indeed, he is back from Naples, but he is in conference," that cold voice shot at me. I stood by the pay phone, right where the platform curves and the number six crashed, and I waited.

Then I got out and paced by the Gandhi statue, stared at the wildflowers that had worked their way into the enclosure, the masses of pigeon shit dried by the wind.

I listened to the voices crying out, ordinary voices lit by the sun. Calling, calling your name.

Staying

Sakhi slept badly. She heard voices. She was in a marketplace, with vegetables piled up on wooden stalls, mounds of leafy spinach, green mangoes couched on straw, pale cabbages smooth as glass. She heard voices calling out in Malayalam. Seconds later stones started flying. The woman next to her bled from the nose all over her sari blouse. Sakhi was about to kneel by the woman when she saw Sandhya, her sari all muddied, racing forward. There was a welt on Sandhya's neck the size of a tiny plum, a dark, purple welt.

"Kal, Kal," Sakhi cried, sure her cousin had been struck by a stone. But at the sound of her own voice, the scene shifted. In place of the wooden stalls were the glass doors of a suburban shopping center and, in the middle distance, a car filled with skinheads speeding away. The youths were yelling "Hindu, Hindu go home." In response, her cousin ran hard, as hard as she could. Sounds flowed out of Sandhya's mouth, but Sakhi couldn't grasp their sense. She put her hands on Sandhya's shoulders, trying to calm her, but the torrent of words poured out. There was a lilt to them, though, an odd broken music.

It was six in the morning. Sakhi woke up with a start, picked up the phone, and dialed New York. Stephen answered, his voice low. Yes, something was the matter. Sandhya was better now, but she had tried to kill herself. Where? In Draupadi's room. Draupadi had cut the rope, rescued her. They were keeping Sandhya under sedation at the hospital. No, no one knew quite what had happened.

Feeling she was the closest Sandhya had to a sister, Sakhi convinced Stephen a short spell away in East Brunswick would be just right. She would drive down as soon as it seemed fit. Stephen was relieved. He was anxious, he said, to keep things as "normal as possible" for the child. So a few days later, taking matters into her capable hands, Sakhi drove over the George Washington Bridge. The waters were clear, yet black in their very depths. Sakhi saw trees at the edge of the Palisades turning color. Green leaves, burning with spots of ocher, crimson. She marveled at the changes that came over the natural world. People should be able to change as naturally as that. What if crossing a border one changed color, shape even? And if this happened to every single human being in the world? What if metamorphosis were built into the bodily system? Then who could one throw stones at? She trembled suddenly. There would probably always be that poor person who got caught in the middle, body half-brown, half-white, half-green, half-ocher, whatever was not the norm, skin and blood refusing to work a change. That person would be a target. But her cousin Sandhya had not really been a target. Of course, she'd been in the car in Elizabeth, and ducked. But stone-throwing, surely that wasn't all that ailed her? No, something deep inside her had quarreled with existence.

Sakhi braked hard, turning off the bridge. Before she saw Sandhya, she'd have to try to figure out a little of what had gone wrong. As the high apartment blocks surrounded her, and the river turned into a mere slip of gray, she tried to puzzle out what might have happened to her cousin.

The simple answer: passion—she loved another man, he didn't want her, she tried to kill herself—didn't pass muster. Immigrants always had their problems. Traveling places was hard, staying was harder. You had to open your suitcase, lay out the little bits and pieces into ready-made niches. Smooth out the sari, exchange it for a skirt, have your hair trimmed a little differently. Sometimes the air hurt to breathe, but oftentimes it worked well enough and lungs could swell with a slow inspiration. Then you tucked the suitcase under the bed and forgot about it, started accumulating the bric-a-brac that made you part of the streets around. If you were lucky, you had a garden, with a picket fence, a plot of earth you could plant, a patch of mint.

She coasted in front of the apartment building and found a parking spot, not quite in front of a hydrant; sat in the car for a few moments, allowing her thoughts to settle. Of course, you didn't have to have a patch of earth. People lived perfectly well in cities. But it was as if Sandhya had opened up her imaginary suitcase, taken out her little bits and pieces, arranged them carefully in an imaginary vault in her kitchen. Gold watch and silk sari she laid there, notebook and hairbrush, the little pacifier Dora had first used, her own wedding ring, a diaphragm she no longer needed. She shut the door. Gazed in through glass. Pressed HIGH and watched, astonished, as the bits exploded.

A child ran across the street in front of a passing car. The car braked suddenly, and Sakhi started. Her fingers jarred on the ignition. Then she raised her windows carefully, locked up, and crossed the street. No, consciousness blown up in a microwave didn't quite fit either. Sakhi paused, her finger on the bell that said "Rosenblum" in neat black letters. She ran her fingers through her hair, trying to rearrange it, fumbled in her purse for a comb. Too late, they were buzzing her in, she would have to forget all her theories, listen to Sandhya, help her pick her way back into a shared life.

As Sakhi drove over the metal ridges on the bridge, the car jerked and Sandhya clutched at the seat belt. She wished her cousin would stop chattering about the Diwali celebrations planned for the South Street Seaport: "Elephants to give children rides. We'll keep the cost low, and Ravi says they might get a flying balloon, to go as high as the skyscrapers." Sakhi mused on the food stalls they'd set up to raise money for the women's groups. Gomati, her neighbor, would make tofu samosas, imagine that! Draupadi Dinkins had promised to help them with a performance piece. "An Indian Woman's Life," she was going to call it. Hearing her friend's name, Sandhya felt as if she were dropping down through space. The water beneath her was clear and dark and she had to touch Sakhi's arm lightly with her fingers to restore herself.

"Okay?" Sakhi queried. Sandhya gulped, nodded. "That water," she said, "it's down so low. You know what I thought of?"

"No."

"The well, Sakhi, at home. We used to stare in. The water was so black. We could see our faces, you and me. In summer."

"How old were we then?" Sakhi felt her pleasure rising, the imagined waters stirring memories.

"I don't know, eight, nine perhaps. Your father was in Bombay all summer and when he returned he brought you those patent leather shoes. I was so jealous!"

As she listened, Sakhi rolled down the window and felt the cool wind against her cheek. Perhaps things would be better now, perhaps Sandhya would open up. And what better place than a car, moving at a smooth, even pace over a great bridge? But when she turned to glance at her cousin's face, she saw that Sandhya Rosenblum was staring straight ahead, her face a mask.

Sensations sizzled through Sandhya's skin. Even as she gazed at the metal span of the bridge she could feel the way the rope had itched in her palms; the crushing weight on her neck; feet breaking free of the parquet floor, the chair falling over. Then, quiet as a guava fruit on a thin stalk, her body swaying.

She saw her hands, neatly folded on her lap, thumbs locked together, each hand casting a shadow on the other. The choking feeling in her throat had been so harsh, unlike anything she had ever felt in her life. Worse even than childbirth pain, like iron rods poked into her back. And she had lain back, gasping for breath. All she had wanted in Draupadi's room was for a pure peace to pour through her. As she lay on the cold parquet floor listening to Draupadi's voice barking at the ambulance men, crying out to Simon Escobar, who was passing down the stairwell, she had wanted to say something just to signal that she was alive. But she felt her lips open and close on an emptiness.

Then in the ambulance, surely she had been delirious, hearing the newborn Dora, a cry slicing the air, her child's mouth pink and open. Two hands lifted the newborn, wet and naked, and set her to the breast. How chapped and sore her breast was, but milk colored like damp jasmine flowed into the child's mouth. The child sucked and sucked till the breast was emptied.

Then suddenly she heard Sakhi cry out, almost in triumph: "A sail, Sandhya, look at that sail!"

Could she bear to look? Slowly, Sandhya lifted up two fingers and touched her own throat. There was a slight welt beneath the soft fall of hair. She let her hand stay, touching the place where the rope had cut. Her eye caught the tip of a white sail as it passed under the bridge. She saw it poised, a harmonic of two elements, wooden hull against water. Sandhya leaned back against the car seat.

She had tried to seize time, that's what she had done. Wanting it all to cease. And she'd botched it. It wasn't in her hands anymore.

The image of Thoma's daughter, the girl who had fallen into the well, floated up before her, and she turned to her cousin.

"The well, remember?"

Sakhi cut short her mental notes on the performance piece Draupadi would do. Perhaps Draupadi could work in a moral like "Don't burn our sisters—marriage is not for burning women."

"Remember the well?" Sandhya repeated.

"Of course, who could forget, my dear? And the guava tree. And the two of us, both with long plaits, staring in."

"Did you ever see?" Sandhya stopped short.

"See?"

Sandhya spoke quickly, her voice stumbling over the words, almost as if she were speaking an unfamiliar language, racing through the phrases in an effort to get them right:

"I was thinking of Thoma's daughter. But perhaps it was the summer you didn't come. She jumped into the well. I sneaked out with Chellama and saw her just before the men came to fish her out. She couldn't have been more than sixteen. Skin puffed up like a lotus, belly huge, red skirt swirling in the water."

She stopped short and Sakhi, knowing she couldn't pull the car off the bridge, slowed down, took one hand off the wheel, and gently touched her cousin's cheek. She had to say something, make the words come:

"It's okay, Sandhya, it's all going to be okay, I promise you. And that poor girl, she jumped in because she thought that was her life, the only thing she could do with the shame they made her feel. But you and I ..."

"Yes?"

Sandhya's voice was so low, almost a murmur, hidden by the hiss of the car wheels, the sounds of gulls flying into the metal span of the bridge.

"You and I have to fight against that. There's no reason why women should pay this terrible price. A price for having been born, for feeling passion, for bearing life."

Sakhi stopped. They were off the bridge now, on the New Jersey tarmac, with the autumn trees just beyond to the right, and Sandhya was huddled in her car seat, weeping as if her body were nothing but a spring of ceaseless water.

A week later they stood together in Sakhi's garden, by the small patch of mint, and Sandhya turned to her cousin. "I'm sorry about that," she said simply.

Sakhi kicked at a piece of granite with her bare toe. It seemed a habit with her, this kicking against stones that were lying in the middle of her herb garden.

"Don't be silly," she muttered affectionately. "It can be a release, you know." Then she lapsed into silence, wondering at her foolishness in stating what must be so obvious. But Sandhya seemed glad of her statements. As if they gave her something to hold up to the light, etch herself against.

"I sat in your living room the other day," Sandhya said, her voice slow, as if she were drawing something difficult out of herself. "I thought of Amma in the old house in Tiruvella, all the darkness in those rooms after

Appa's death. I felt so close to it all, even to the mango tree outside Nunu's room, crickets near the well. I felt I was there and longed to live again. I think Rashid was like that for me." She stopped, trying to choose her words with care: "A passion that could simplify life."

"But he tore it open, didn't he?" asked Sakhi, whose eyes were fixed on a red car cruising slowly. It disturbed her somehow, that car. Why, she couldn't quite tell.

"We're all migrants," she added softly, "from the past. I guess that's the big thing."

But Sandhya moved on, unwilling to stop and listen: "See, I wanted a house with him. I wanted to wait for him in that house, so he would come to me. But it's all shattered now, that shining picture. And even the bright landscape of my childhood has cracked, cast me out. Sakhi, I can't go back."

"No one can, my dear, no one," Sakhi whispered, almost to herself, watching Sandhya scoop up earth from between her feet, let it trickle through her fingers. Fingers soiled with dirt. Sandhya glanced up suddenly at the red car. It had halted, its exhaust pouring smoke. Then it spun away deliberately.

When the car had vanished, Sandhya held up both palms to her face and blew a fine mist of dirt. "Gone," she said softly, as if making a plain statement. "All gone, my dear cousin!" And she turned away to stare at the street that was suddenly empty, at the pallor of the sky and a few clouds drifting above the low rooftops.

It was Sakhi's idea to take her cousin to a women's meeting in New York City. They were together in the kitchen, preparing the *lassi* Ravi had requested. Sandhya watched Sakhi's hands, busy whisking the yogurt, adding water and ice and a dash of rosewater. "Come with me," Sakhi coaxed her cousin. "Make believe you are going to another country. A different map is what you need. Well, what do you say?" Sakhi ran water over her hands, washing off the flecks of yogurt. "Yes," Sandhya said, with a show of resolution. "Yes, of course I'll come."

So she had gone back into Manhattan, a different city for her now that she was under her cousin's wing. As she sat in the large, ill-ventilated room at Columbia University, among many Indian women, Sandhya felt she had entered a country where she needed neither passport nor green card, nor any other signs of belonging. She sat back in the plastic chair to listen to the testimonies of the women on the platform.

There was an old woman from Lahore, partly blind in one eye, brought to New York as an *ayah* two decades ago, cast out onto the streets when she could no longer work. The woman had roamed the streets, sleeping on park benches, hiding her face in her *dupatta* every time she saw a policeman. Finally, through a kindly passerby, she had found a shelter. Her voice was low, resolute.

"I am learning to remake my life," she said. "At night I dream of Lahore. The small streets, the dusty marketplace. In my dreams I am always crying. Of late, though, it has turned to laughter. I am surrounded by small children and we are all laughing!"

There was loud clapping as she spoke. Sandhya wished she could run up to the woman, touch her on the forehead, feel all over her face. Then a younger woman came on, delicate, well-made, her body buttoned into a black sweater embroidered with roses. Voice brisk as she gave details of the sweatshop she worked in, she broke down as she came to her own life, a violent husband, difficult pregnancy, her flight into the night air, down the cold streets, the figure who kept chasing her: "I never even saw his face. I was so scared, could not tell if he was white or black. Or even a man from Lahore. Why should I care?"

Why care? Sandhya tried to phrase the question carefully in her head. It hurt her to ask it. All this awareness was coming with such difficulty. She turned to Sakhi, who sat quite still at her side. Sentences, Sakhi was thinking, welling up, out of hard lives. She lifted her braid off the nape of her neck, shifted in her blue plastic seat, watched Sandhya, who seemed to be listening intently. It was important to expose her cousin to other lives, but it wasn't just women, that was the thing. Men had to struggle, too.

Her mind slipped to Jay's friend Stu, who had fled Mainland China and worked near the Bowery. Each afternoon Stu would go out into the streets to pick up bits of scrap metal for his assemblages. One that he called "Asia," straightforward enough as a title, had moved her almost to tears. Metal cans, exquisitely piled up, lips of tin torn out. One afternoon, near where the old woman from Lahore had found herself, Stu was stabbed, over and over again. He bled to death on the sidewalk, right by a garbage can. For what? Three dollars and a pile of old cans.

Perhaps she would leave with Sandhya, walk to the Bowery, search out the spot where Stu had been stabbed, stand in front of the small memorial, a mound of stones and a dried flower or two, raised at the edge of the sidewalk. She could take Sandhya to see what was left of his installation. Jay had some photos in his room. One image came to her, Stu, eyes wide open, pointing at a pile of empty tin cans. Hope staring out of his eyes.

But hope was a calf born in the cowshed behind her grandfather's house, blind in one eye, the other streaming tears when the sun grew too bright. What was that song about the sun their grandmother sang? Eyes blurred with cataracts, their grandmother had held Sandhya's face in both her hands as she tried to form the melody. Sakhi had helped out by singing the words softly, using her cousin's name:

> We need it in sunlight
> on the high road.
> Amma hold the umbrella tight
> so Sandhya won't burn her eyes!

The names were interchangeable, but she knew, even then, that Sandhya was touched. Her cousin had leaned over and hugged their grandmother, burying her face in the old woman's shoulder. How long ago was that? Sakhi lost track. Other sounds cut in, growing in intensity in the hot, airless room. A discussion about the Diwali celebrations, and the contribution Draupadi Dinkins had offered. Should they accept? Yes, was the general consensus, even though she didn't have a direct link with India. After all, they were all part of the diaspora. Then came a debate about discrimination in the workplace, with two women lawyers, a woman from the hospital worker's union, and a fourth woman from a telephone company holding forth. The sounds melded in Sakhi's head even as the image of a black umbrella stayed. If only her flesh could be so fine, turning its own subtle substance into an umbrella to shield others. There might be some sense in that. She felt her cousin's hand on her arm and Sandhya's eyes, dark, enormous, staring at her.

"Shall we leave?" she asked in Malayalam, and Sakhi nodded. It was Sandhya's idea to take a bus to Hunter College, to see if they could find Jay. Perhaps at the back of her mind was the notion that she might see Rashid again, if only from across the street. Even a glimpse, from a great distance, might work for her. She had no idea that Hunter College was not in session. "I know the way," she cried out merrily, "just follow me!" Sakhi sensed her cousin was flushed, over-excited, but felt it was best to follow.

On Park Avenue a man approached them, a young man in his twenties, dressed in jeans and a raffish orange shirt. He had a black umbrella folded in his hand.

"Indian?"

Sakhi nodded, knowing from his accent in English that he was from Kerala.

"Vide evida?"

She noticed his fingers tightening about the umbrella. It had a plastic handle with little flowers embedded in the depths, the kind that hung by the dozen outside the market in Tiruvella, eight rupees at the most. So the man had brought the umbrella with him from Tiruvella. Discovering that his home was a mere twelve miles from Tiruvella, she launched into a conversation. Sandhya was content to keep step, let her cousin talk. She smiled when Sakhi pointed out that she too had come from Tiruvella. Sakhi could talk in Malayalam and cross the street with him and not be nervous. They spoke for the space of a block, and when family and children were mentioned, and the question of home and village, *"Vidu"* and *"Nadu"* came up, and a warmth flooded through.

It was fall, the chrysanthemums were in bloom, the crown of the Pan Am building was shrouded in smog. It seemed more than one might have asked for in an ordinary day: the fragrance of a far-off town wafting between two strangers on the sidewalk at Sixty-eighth and Park. The young man, Kurien, was a draftsman who had come from Chengannur. He started his new life packaging oranges in upstate New York but could hardly make ends meet, so he moved into his sister-in-law's place in the Bronx. Intent on the conversation, he did not look up at the sky that was threatening rain.

"The meat is good, the butter so sweet, but we miss home," he said softly as he descended into the subway, almost stumbling against the small tree planted a few weeks earlier, now shriveling in the stone pot. Next to it, a BEAUTIFY NEW YORK sign turned in the wind. Sandhya wanted to enter the subway but her cousin beckoned with her hand and drew Sandhya toward the double glass doors of the Hunter art gallery.

On the far wall was a triangle of green paint signifying a mountain, a trickle of dull red down its flank. Surely the style was contemporary Japanese. But that trickle? A stream of rusty water? As Sandhya straightened, the glass window caught her face and threw it back at her, fractured, unrepentant. There it was, a broken face on a woman in a sari clutching a leather tote bag, the whole burnished by a green mountain, lit by a bloodied stream, visible from a hot sidewalk in New York City. But behind that thin body was a dark shadow. As Sandhya moved her neck the shadow moved too, and then her arm, torso, thigh were all taken up in a quick step, a dark, marginal being basted to the reflection of moving flesh. She shut her eyes tight. Strains of saxophone music wafted up from the hole of the subway. She was tempted. She should turn back, go down into that darkness, never come back. But she was conscious of her cousin just behind her, gazing into the middle distance. Sandhya looked back at the glass window. It couldn't have been more than a moment or two, but the sun had moved behind a passing cloud. It was the angle of light, nothing more or less, but the shadow had vanished. And Sandhya Rosenblum stood there, the strains of music rising again, staring at herself in a bright mirror. There she was, intact and whole, no doubleness seizing her from behind. She felt the sunlight on her throat and relaxed, letting her feet increase their hold on the warm sidewalk. How long it would last she could not tell. Perhaps in a few months, a few years, it would all splinter again, and she would be seized by unknown passions welling out of her flesh. But for now, she would be, she would let herself be.

"Sakhi," she murmured, moving away from the mirror to where her cousin stood. Sakhi remained silent, but pointed her index finger high into the middle distance, eastward down Sixty-eighth Street. High up, far away to the left, was an orange swatch of fabric draped over the edge of a crane that swiveled slowly, thirty stories above ground level. The crane was set at the concrete tip of Trump's Pleasure Palace. A year ago, a bit of scaffolding fell, killing a young black man, a Hunter College student. Rashid had told her the tale. The lad was the only one in his family to go to college, the first child in the family to edge his way out of the subway stop at Tremont where they'll mug you at night for a few dollars, a few dimes tied up in red cloth.

Something started pounding in Sakhi's heart when she thought of the boy. "A dull ache, a saw severing my heart," his mother had cried, her head wrapped up in white stuff signifying mourning as they led her into the high hall her son had stepped through. At the thought of the unknown woman, Sakhi felt tears well up in her eyes and brushed them away, angry at this useless pity working in her. But there was her cousin Sandhya waiting for her, saying something. And gazing at Sandhya, Sakhi felt thankful for the gift of life. How fragile everything seemed from down below, the rough compact we make, thinking, Yes, we will live, we will live on.

"Come," she said, putting her hand on Sandhya's arm, comforted as Sandhya held her loosely round the shoulders. They walked, two women in unison, down the sidewalk that had suddenly become crowded with faces and voices, the thrust and pulse of an unknown future.

A week, perhaps two weeks, later Sandhya sat in Sakhi's living room, staring out the window at the yard next door. A woman in a short skirt was putting out the laundry. New neighbors, Sakhi told her, a black woman married to a white man. The marriage had caused comment in their old neighborhood. "Even here, even now," Sandhya murmured, wondering at the innocence with which she had leaped into Stephen's arms, a lifetime ago, on a hillside in another country. "They have a child, a little boy," Sakhi replied. "Lovely child. Couple of years younger than Dora."

There was a child's shirt in the woman's hands dripping water onto the lawn, a scoop-necked thing, and a pair of shorts with white stripes. Watching the woman's simple gestures Sandhya saw her own mother's hands, folding a sari, smoothing the *pallu,* then laying out a blouse, straightening the sleeves. Under her hands the plain white cotton of the bed on which Sosa laid the ironed clothes was clearly visible. If only she could reach back to that time, reclaim those moments, those gestures, she might slip into a lost life, be a mother again to little Dora. Yet how unexpected it was when Sakhi asked: "Shall we invite Stephen and Dora over? What do you think?" And Sandhya kept quiet. "They're longing to see you," Sakhi said. And all it took on Sandhya's part was a quick nod, a smile.

When the morning came, how eagerly Sandhya prepared herself. Her hands trembled as she smoothed down her skirt, examined her face in the mirror. The welt on her neck no longer showed. Hearing the doorbell ring, as if in a dream from which she might never awaken, she slowly descended the stairs.

Downstairs it seemed to her as if she had seen it all already, the white dining cloth with the bowl of fruit in the center, the chairs arranged around the table and, through the half-open window, the flowering tree whose scent had arrested her on her first visit to East Brunswick. It was fall and the grass was still green, the air still had a hint of warmth to it. A few hours after the hugs, the whispered greetings, Sandhya entered the parlor with Dora, held the child up to the window to smell the dogwood tree, and Dora, catching sight of the sprinkler on the lawn, pointed eagerly, calling, for there was a rainbow, she was sure, cast by the sunlight. Sandhya stooped, set her face to the child's level at the window, saw a multicolored glory, fragile, bending to the sun's ephemerality.

"Mama, a rainbow," Dora said, in a matter-of-fact tone. "I know how to draw a rainbow." Searching out the colored pencils she knew Sakhi kept in a drawer and handing them to the child, Sandhya felt that the whole of her life was passing in front of her.

It has all happened already, she thought, and she stood, watching her child reach out of the window for a spray of clear water. At dinnertime she sat next to Stephen and thought of putting out her hand and touching him on his thigh as she had done so long ago, but instead she held her hand flat on her lap. Sipping the wine Ravi had poured, Sandhya breathed softly, feeling as if her life were curving back in a torsion so perfect that past and future stood poised, apart, unequal partners in a hazardous game, the stakes immeasurably high. She gazed at Dora in the high chair that Sakhi had pulled out from a closet by the fridge. The child had a pink ribbon in her long hair. A long silk ribbon.

She heard music from the open window on the other side of the house. It sounded oddly familiar, a woman singing, a rich-throated melancholy sound. She wanted to push her chair aside, rush to the window, lift up her skirts and climb out. She imagined the hot stones underfoot, so like the stones of Hyderabad. Then, too, she wanted to catch hold of Stephen's hand, draw him out with her, show him how she could run into the sweet air, leaving the past behind. But it would have been rude to break up the group sitting around the table, with Ravi talking earnestly about cross-cultural living and everyone, even Dora, seeming to listen. If only she could have broken into speech, but Ravi was holding forth about plans for the Diwali celebrations and Stephen was promising to come, bring Dora and perhaps even Muriel.

"We will have elephant rides, and even a balloon in which Dora can take a ride, eh?" Ravi leaned forward, making cooing noises at Dora, who stared straight at him. "High, high up," he started singing and, watching him, the little girl giggled.

Then, feeling as if he were losing his audience, Ravi turned to his adult guests. "Both national anthems will be played," he said, sitting as straight as he could.

"And the flags of both nations, the Star-Spangled Banner on the right and the Indian Tricolor with the *charka* on the left. They will blow together in the breeze."

He said this softly, staring at Stephen and Sandhya. Stephen cleared his throat, trying to make a suitable response, but felt the color rush to his cheeks. And Sandhya, pretending not to listen, leaned away, fussing with the child's napkin.

The conversation drifted on. Sakhi brought up the episode in the *Maha-bharata*. She spoke of Draupadi in the banquet hall questioning her five husbands who had bartered her so shamefully in the dice throw, the Kauravas all set to tug at her sari, Krishna descending in a cloud, turning

Draupadi's thin cotton into a mystic fabric of a million threads that would never cease. On and on the sari would flow so that the woman was never naked. Sakhi paused. She hoped Ms. Dinkins might dramatize it for the women's group, for the Diwali Festival.

"She wants to." Stephen pitched in. "She came over the other day to see us. And to ask after you," he said, turning to Sandhya. "She wants to add an autobiographical flavor to her performance. Something of her great-grandmother coming over to Trinidad as a bonded laborer, her grandmother scrubbing kitchens in Port of Spain, her mother in upstate New York, chopping onions."

"How will she fit it all in?" asked Sakhi. "The mythic Draupadi and all these women's lives?" She paused. "Why not?" she added, her voice resolute, as she stood up to pass the fragrant dish of *dahi vadai:* "After all, each of these women crossed the black waters. And the mythic Draupadi, as we know, spent much of her life in exile."

Sandhya heard what Sakhi said. The word *exile* moved in her and she wondered what it meant, then cast it aside, as one might cast a shiny pebble. It did not make sense to her. Then suddenly she heard it again, wafting in through the window. Music that took hold of her, a slow, sad singing voice filling her head. Perhaps Dora was listening too, her finger in her mouth, screwing her head all the way around to follow her mother's gaze. Quietly, Sandhya excused herself from the dining table and walked to the far end of the house.

She heard Sakhi call after her, but did not stop. She found the window and raised it. On the other side of the picket fence was the child from next door, naked, splashing in water. The water that fell from the sprinkler shone on the child's dark body. The mist of water turned green, with the colors of the grass and bushes. The sky was blue sieved through aeons of air, no clouds there. In the bushes were birds Sandhya could not quite identify, peacock-colored, wings massed, fluttering. And behind the birds, visible through their wings, was a fresh row of washing: a small sheet that must have belonged to the child and next to it a woman's sweater with a pink line of stitching in it.

The music grew louder, the voice sobbing, of love, of loss. Sandhya could tell it came from the open doors and the windows of the house outside which the child played. Sandhya Rosenblum flung open the window and hung her whole body out of the house, her eyes two fountains all the salt in the Atlantic might have flowed through.

She did not know how much time passed, but it was as if her life, right from birth till that moment in Draupadi's room, when she hung a rope around her own neck, passed before her eyes. And she was left trembling with the rush of images. Then she felt Sakhi's touch, gentle on her shoulder, and Sandhya allowed her cousin to lead her back to the dining table.

"Where were you, Sandhya?" Stephen asked softly, and she could sense the panic in his voice.

"I heard music," she said, leaning forward so that only he could hear. "Music through an open window. Who knows, the mythic Draupadi might have heard it too." And she smiled gently.

She wanted to return to New York by herself when she was ready. So Stephen and the child had driven back. Then a week later, when it was time to leave East Brunswick, Sandhya took the train, switched to the subway at Penn Station. The route flowed into her so simply she was amazed. Right by 125th Street she got off the subway and found herself running, down to the river. The wind buffeted her hair, a woman running hard, and no one who saw her put out a hand or a foot to stop her. Not the women in the vegetable shops on LaSalle and Tiemann, not the men having their hair cut right under the elevated subway, not the small children with their hoops, not the larger children with stickballs, not the two mutilated soldiers crouched on the street holding up large signs. On and on she ran till finally she stumbled over asphalt, rocks, stones, a bit of broken fencing.

She was racing into America from the dark vessel of her past and she could hear it singing in her, ready to break free, the load of her womanhood, of the accumulated life, breaking free into an inconceivable sweetness. When she hit water—it was a broken hydrant on Tiemann Place spraying into the air—she started shivering and felt herself a cold, clammy thing, but she was weeping and laughing all at once.

"A Latino man passed by, a jaunty cap on his head, and pulled me out of the spray. I had slipped and fallen," she told Stephen when she found him in the apartment. "And guess what his name was? Colon, Colon, for sure." She recounted all this in great excitement, still feeling the cold spray on her. "Take the towel," said Stephen, pressing a little white hand towel on her, just thankful they did not have to hospitalize her for pneumonia.

"Nothing like that name, eh, old comrade?"

Hearing Stephen's voice again she turned, her hair all wet, so thankful he was still with her. With her palm she touched his cheek as if for the first time.

Later that week, after much thought, Jay visited his cousin. He brought her his poems in the hope that she would find some merit in them. That she might read a line and feel her emotions clarified, eased. As a leaf might, falling off a tree in Central Park, pierced in its falling by a momentary ray of light.

A golden leaf from the tree of life.

While this was his hope, he knew too that these particular poems had their own harshness. Some cruelty in their circumstance prevented the full illumination he hoped for. Yet syllables encrusted with Broadway grime—why not?

Why not let his poems be the fat, packed, resinous occasions of living, all their lives lived here? He thrust his hair back and paced by the window. Down below he could see the threshold of his small brown house. And on the steps he saw the burn left by the kerosene fire, the burst Molotov cocktail from the night after he had returned from a bout of drinking with Ravi at the West End Café. It was on those steps that he had seen the ghost of his friend rise. A slim body woven of mist, and Jay had put out his hands, filled with need. The mist had curled, blown into the streetlight. "Ahmed, Ahmed!" He had whispered the name, over and over again, as if it might serve to break down the nervous boundaries of loss, love's ephemerality. Weeks later the news came that another Ahmed was killed. A young black man named Ahmed Jabbar, who hung out by the Cotton Club doing odd jobs, shot to death for a gold chain, a pair of Nike pumps, two dollars in his shirt pocket. The police, arriving on the scene, had arrested two lads, passersby, innocent by all accounts. Roughed them up with their nightsticks, led them away, manacled and trembling. Sandhya had hung out her window, watching the police vans, the men in their peaked caps thrusting the two lads ahead of them.

Then came the rioters, the small fires in the garbage heaps, the cries of: "War, War. This is the Third World War. In your backyard, Boss Brother," till more and more police drove out from the precinct and the whole street was a chaos of sirens and bullhorns and cries. For days the small-scale rioting had spread till it came to the very edge of Central Park, right by 110th Street.

And for that, for all that, he had no words. Nothing.

Finally, his poems disgusted him. Still, he decided to give them to

Sandhya. He wanted her to see them. Perhaps she would even read them. She seemed so different since her "difficulty," as he called it. He felt that it would help him if she read them. Perhaps she would say a few words to him.

Sandhya sat on the metal stool in the kitchen and opened the sheaf of papers Jay had given her. The kitchen was filled with sunlight, so she moved her stool a little so the light would not blind her. Slowly, mouthing the words, she read four poems. The first two poems seemed contrived, too much outside any self she might imagine. The Draupadi poem was a piece of scrap metal with holes punched in it, lying in the waste, glittering by the side of the subway stop. It held her tight, made her uncomfortable. Why "Pariahs," she thought, about the title he had given it, why should we be pariahs?

It was "River and Bridge" that moved her. She repeated the syllables to herself, over again. Stopped short when she came to the line she had already borne in her mind: "a bridge that seizes crossing."

"That line I liked," she told Jay simply when she saw him next. Later she told him of her hurt when in response he had merely nodded and moved sharply toward the half-open window that gave onto the New York street.

Turning from the window, how swiftly he resisted the impulse to leap, Jay nodded to Sandhya, picked up his coat, and walked out of the room. At first in slow measured fashion, then breaking step, surging forward, he made his way to the edge of Central Park. Approaching the fence by Harlem Meer, he thought he heard singing. Pitched so high he was sure his ears caught only the smallest portion, the sounds filtered through the wild scrub and trees. "Manhattan Music," he whispered into the dark, still savoring the sounds, fragrant, subtle as flesh, countless voices singing.

The day of the Diwali festival was clear, cool. Sandhya made breakfast, flat white *dosas* from a packet of mix. Then she heated up the sambar she had cooked the night before and stood before the stove inhaling the scents of tamarind and *methi*. Fresh tamarinds hung on the trees by the kitchen in her mother's garden. And here she was, with her little store of dried fruit, its sour delight hoarded, used so sparingly. She shouldn't let the sambar bubble, a slight amount of heat would do. And she was sure Stephen and Dora would appreciate the care she had taken. It would be a change from the usual cornflakes or oatmeal. Right after breakfast she must make an exit, work her way into the city, do what she had to do. She promised though to meet up with Stephen at the festival. It was an all-day event, she knew, and Muriel had made plans to go, taking Dorris with her.

Stirring the sambar, Sandhya felt her mind slip back to the meeting with Draupadi. They had taken tea together, almost like old times, except that there was a fragility in her self she sensed now, a need to seek out harmony, avoid too much pain. Draupadi, too, while pressing on with her plans, seemed quieter. She asked Sandhya to help with the Diwali performance. A two-woman piece was how she figured it, and Sandhya would play the part of the immigrant women, four generations of women who crossed the black waters. She herself would act the epic heroine's part.

"We each have to be many women," Draupadi said, trying to coax her friend. "After all, how many lives did the *Mahabharata* lady have? Crawling through a tunnel to save her life, wasn't she someone quite different from the princess in the palace? And then, the woman bartered in the dice-throw between men, think of her shame, her rage."

But Sandhya, sitting with Dora, the window behind her giving onto a swift-flowing river, shook her head. At the back of her mind was the thought, no, no, I don't want to play the part she is giving me. Her hand hovered at the edge of the teacup. And there was Dora scrambling away, a chocolate bar half-opened in her hand. She would have to be stopped, the sweet retrieved, put high up, on top of the fridge. The dos and don'ts of her life as a mother thrust at Sandhya. But a minute or two wouldn't matter, and this was important.

"Draupadi, I don't want to speak your words. I have to find my own." How plain it sounded, blurted out like that, and instantly she was overcome with the desire to apologize to her friend. "Listen, it's just that I feel I need to be careful. You know?" Sandhya paused.

"Careful of what?"

"Not to be sucked in, I guess." She stood up, choosing her words carefully. "When I first came, you helped me so much. And then that awful business. Without you I'd be dead. But I have to find my own way."

Draupadi drank up the tea. She felt shaken. Sandhya was refusing her part. "So you don't want to do it?"

"It isn't that at all. Listen, why don't I help you with the sari, the mystic one that doesn't end, even when the bad guys keep tugging at it. I could do a Krishna behind-the-scenes bit."

"In the South Street Seaport? There's no behind-the-scenes there, you'll have to be right in front, my friend."

"Okay. We'll figure something out. Get someone else to do the immigrant women. Why not Sakhi?"

"You know she'd be wrong." Suddenly Draupadi saw the humor of it and began laughing. "You can see Sakhi, can't you, pulling out pamphlets: 'Stop battering women. Stop communal violence.'"

"She's a good soul," Sandhya murmured, pulling her child back from the doorway, the half-consumed chocolate bar dribbling down Dora's lips. "Ah, mess," she sighed, feeling an enormous contentment well through her as she picked up a tissue and started wiping the child's face.

"Dora's going up in a balloon," Sandhya told Draupadi, "up, up, and her papa and grandma Muriel are going with her."

"And Mama?" asked the child.

Sandhya drew a deep breath and Draupadi, watching closely, thought she saw a shadow pass over Sandhya's face. But Sandhya stood a little apart, facing her audience of two. Her back was against the door frame, her eyes seeking out the far river. It was as if she were making an oath, the words had that air of unreality:

"Dora, Draupadi, I do not want to be suspended in midair. No more, hung up, swaying," said Sandhya Rosenblum. "I shall stay close to the ground."

The ground was warm underfoot. Elm trees shifted light against their bark, as leaves ocher and beige spilled onto the paving stones of Union Square. The square was oddly empty and Sandhya saw how the green cupola of the subway stop caught the light. Here and there a pigeon fluttered, one passing so close it almost touched her hair. Right by the Gandhi statue she saw him and, in spite of herself, she felt her lips tremble. So he had not really changed, a little darker perhaps with all that summer sun. He was pacing quickly, in front of the statue, his arms swinging as he walked. It was that old restlessness that so attracted her. Then he turned, his face framed by the bronze of the statue, his head level with the old man's dhoti, and he saw her.

"Rashid," she cried, running toward him.

They stood there, shy as teenagers, skittish too. Her feet seemed to turn to water. They sat on a bench, staring at the traffic, at a red automobile, a speeding ambulance, a woman with roses in her arms, bushelsful it seemed, standing in an empty lot across the street. Rashid pointed her out and, gazing at the ample bosom, arms loaded down with crimson blooms, even the tiny thorns visible from so far off, Sandhya marveled at her own eyesight.

"Consider the roses," she murmured, and Rashid, bending close to hear her, felt his lips brush her cheek. He drew back sharply, his arm thrusting against her thigh.

"Sorry," he muttered, straightening up. Then he pulled back against the slatted bench and looked straight at her. She had lost that old gaunt look, he could see, put on some weight. But there was something tired about the eyes, some sentiment he couldn't quite decipher.

"Why, Sandhya? Why did you do that?"

"That?" Her voice was clear and strong.

"In Draupadi's room, I mean. Do that to yourself, why?"

How angry he is, she thought. Instinctively she touched her throat. On the other side of the statue a small child crouched, hands on the earth, a plastic ball under his knees. He was trying to balance his weight on the ball but kept slipping, falling to the ground. She was afraid she wouldn't be able to speak but the words bubbled out of her, perfectly formed, winged creatures.

"I guess now I know it's my life to live, but then I was so torn, Rashid. I felt you didn't want me."

"I do want you."

His voice was soft, stirring the small blades of grass under her sandaled feet, like a current of live air. Earlier she might have let herself drop, breathing in and out to the rhythm of desire. But she had gone through too much. Even tried to destroy herself. There was the throb in her forehead to prove it.

"But not in that way," she said, "not in the way I wanted. To take care of me." She watched his hands clench ever so slightly. "Anyway, I don't think that's right for me now."

She shut her eyes with the effort of speech. Heard the child by the statue cry for his ball, heard the mother running quickly, calling, "Wait, wait, I'll get it." Slowly she opened her eyes and saw the woman raise her skirts, jump over the low fence, and retrieve the blue plastic ball.

"I felt I was tearing up inside, and I was angry, too. You didn't want to speak to me on the phone. No, no, I understand."

She placed her hand gently on his trouser leg. Then her voice fell, as a stream might, into a shallow place, the water stretched fine, a shining surface skimming its own inexistence:

"I wanted peace, Rashid. Can you understand that? My father had just died. All I wanted was to shut my eyes and be in that paddy field, by the riverbank. Then be under the ground they walked as they carried the coffin. The paddy blades blowing above me."

"Oh Sandhya, Sandhya," he murmured. Then added: "But there was rage too, no?"

She breathed hard, deep. Her forehead throbbed, that spot she had struck on a window ledge, in a bathroom, in another country.

"Yes," she said, and stopped, nothing left to lose.

And still his face was turned away from her, staring at the empty lot across the street, the crumbling wall with faded alphabets on it. She followed his eyes. The woman with the armful of roses had vanished.

"Shall we walk a little?" he asked her, but she shook her head. "I promised I'd go to the South Street Seaport early. Meet everyone there."

"There's time, isn't there? At least let me walk you to the end of the road." He pointed ahead, feeling as if something in his own flesh was tearing. "Stop a moment."

And she, feeling the emotions in him flood her afresh, stood at the very edge of the sidewalk, and he was forced to draw her back.

"Here, open your hand."

She watched as he placed the tiny black doll in her palm. A thing of string and wood, it lay there, outlined in its own shadow. The red string that bound its feet was carefully wound around the middle, making a fine scarlet belt.

"Rashid," she murmured, "you've kept it all this while."

"Yes," he said, simply, wondering at the passion that held him there, at the edge of the sidewalk, facing the mad riot of traffic.

"I think it wants to go back into the dark of your pocket," she said, handing the doll back to him carefully. Then, just as she was about to step into the yellow cab that stopped by them, the words welled out of her. Old words she couldn't help. They had a new sense now, but still they mattered, so very much.

"Do you love me?"

"You know I do," he said, his voice cut by the honking cars. He held open the door for her, swung her in over the metal threshold. She waved at him, blowing a kiss through the cab window, wondering at the lightness that flowed through her, a current of sweet hot life, defying gravity.

But she wasn't ready for the festival. For the elephants and the skits and the speeches, the flags unfurled and the cornucopia of foods. Draupadi would be there setting up her scene, Jay with the photographs he had taken on his trip to Ayodhya, grim, graphic shots of the aftermath of the mosque torn down, Sakhi with her pamphlets and banners. They would each have something to do. Sandhya shut her eyes, imagined the seething square in the seaport, voices in Malayalam, Tamil, Hindi, Marathi, Gujarati, English, all calling out. She couldn't go there yet. There was something else she needed to do. Quickly she tapped on the glass, got the driver to turn the car around, drive toward Central Park. Once at the edge of the park she stopped the cab, thrust the few dollars she had into the driver's hand. He looks Indian, she thought, and she sensed he wanted to talk, but she didn't have time. Driven by a power she couldn't have named, she raced into the stand of trees.

Oak and chestnut and elm, they surrounded her, leaves tinged with red. Twigs crackled underfoot. She pressed her face against tree bark and when she moved away she could feel the ridges in her cheek, markings that had taken decades to forge. The trees sheltered her. She heard the murmur of crickets, the sharp whisper of tiny woodland creatures. In the middle distance she saw a bench painted green. Sandhya recognized the scene, as if from another life. Young mothers, their tiny infants popping out of slings and sacks, the sharp cries of toddlers dribbling milk. But the visible landscape, a fragile certitude, altered suddenly. Not in the details of tree or bench or sky but in a slant of light, a sudden shift of visibility, so that a fresh horizon opened up, and she wanted to plunge right into it. For the first time she understood how close to the edge she had been. Her passion had pushed her hard, and had it not been for Draupadi the whole business might have ended there. Now she couldn't just lean on others. She had to trust herself if she wanted to go on.

She stood on the flat of her feet, the street ahead of her, the copse of trees behind, undecided on which way to go. She had told Stephen and Dora she would meet them at the seaport, but the festival went on all day long. Then she heard the notes of a saxophone, that glory trying to rise, but the notes were whittled down, diminished. Through the trees he approached her, his eyes shut in concentration. She recognized the man instantly and was shocked at how his hair had grayed, just patches of black left, his clothes, once so shiny, torn, muddy, the crimson stuff hanging in tatters over ribs heaving with the effort of breath. She moved forward through the tall grass, and still his eyes were shut and he was walking forward, chin raised to the sky. She would have put out her hand and touched him gently on the arm, the cheek, but an inch away from him a stench enveloped her. It came from his body, the odor of flesh unwashed, of sweat, urine, tears. She backed away sharply, pressed herself against the trees and watched him walk on, as if some divinity were guiding him, an old man unhoused, his instrument drawing his pained, rasping breath. She felt compassion flood through her, the subtlest of recognitions. Then she turned and moved away.

Sandhya could not tell how long she wandered in the park in the midmorning light. Stumbling through the long grasses, her face streaked with dirt, it struck her that a few more weeks and she might be like that old man in tattered silks, only no saxophone. A woman with nothing in her hands. Finally, tired out and panting, she crossed the brambles by the horsetrack and found herself at the edge of a lake. How quiet it was. She could hear herself breathing. Birds hopped about on the flat stones by the water's edge. A tiny red flower caught in her toes. Like a wild thing, Sandhya Rosenblum crouched on a rock and stared into the water. There was a pinkish tinge to the light and, as she gazed into the water, she caught sight of two eyes staring back at her. They were liquid, those eyes, darkness tinged by color, the water burning in the sunlight on the lake.

My eyes, thought Sandhya, those are my own eyes staring back at me. The reflection quivered, pierced by a tiny fish that leaped out of the water, nose first, then dived back. A dragonfly, dark as a water weed, hovered over the place where her mouth was etched so delicately in water. She noticed another dragonfly on a water lily, struggling out of its translucent pupa, the large eye coverings left behind in the crumpling skin, the new body gleaming with moisture.

"Sandhya," she whispered, almost as if she were naming another being. In Sanskrit the name signified those threshold hours, before the sun rose or set, fragile zones of change before the clashing absolutes of light and dark took hold.

She felt rain on her cheek, a light sweet water. Still on the rock, she used hands and knees to secure herself on her perch, then pushed herself up, the hem of her skirt soggy with water. Her sandals were soaking. Plucking them off, she leapt lightly onto damp earth.

She was no longer fearful of the shadows in the trees, of the sharp cries of a strange bird with long tailfeathers. She thought she heard a creature snort near her. She stood her ground. There was a place for her. Slowly she opened her fists, releasing her fingers, letting the half-light pour through her, letting her hands lie quiet by her side. There was a place for her here, though what it might be she could never have spelled out. And she, who had never trusted words very much, knew she would live out her life in America.

She thrust through the copse of trees at the edge of the park and faced Central Park South. Perhaps because of the mistiness from the rain, the cross-hatch of asphalt, the streets ahead of her seemed whorled, as a snail's shell might be, in a shiny phosphorescence, but cast into flatness when the rain ceased, restored to earth she could tread. She heard laughter, a loud boom box, young men and women, a pack of them, approaching her. For a moment longer she stood at the edge of Central Park. Then, slipping sandals onto feet still damp with lake water, Sandhya Rosenblum walked quickly into the waiting city.

Coda: Four Poems
by Arjun Sankaramangalam

Brown Skin, What Mask?

Babel's township seeps into Central Park
I hunch on a stone bench scraping nightingale-bulbuls
cuckoo-koels, rose-gulabs off my face

No flim-flam now; card sharp, street wise
I fix my heels at Paul's Shoe Place for a dollar fifty
get a free make-over at Macy's, eyes smart, lips shine.
Shall I be a hyphenated thing, Macaulay's Minutes
and Melting Pot theories not withstanding?

Shall I bruise my skin, burn up into
She Who Is No Color, whose longing is a crush
of larks shivering without sound?

When lit by his touch in a public place
—an elevator with a metal face—shall I finger grief for luck
work stares into the "bride is never naked" stuff?

Against Elegy

Sick to death of elegies
where she swooned her flesh away
sick to death of the *Ubi Sunt Variations,*
ou sont les neiges etc.

She selected hot shot hockey players
with elegant thigh muscles
clean shaven quarterbacks in damp shirts
for her boogie-woogie dance in sneakers and top hat
and G-string made of a silken thing she tore
from a six-yard Kancheepuram sari.

At the West End Bar to catcalls, sodden roars,
heavy bellied, flushed, tin trident hurting her chin
she pranced: "Blood rings its own Thing"
she sang in honor of Shiva.

River and Bridge

Trees on the other side of the river
so blue, discarding light into water, a flat
white oil tank with HESS in black, a bridge
Holzer might skim with lights—*I will take her*
down before she feels the fear—no sarcophagus here:

I have come to the Hudson's edge to begin my life
to be born again, to seep as water might
in a landscape of mist, burnished trees,
a bridge that seizes crossing.

But Homer knew it and Vyasa too, black river
and bridge summon those whose stinging eyes
criss-cross red lights, metal implements,
battlefields: birth is always bloody.

Art of Pariahs

Back against the kitchen stove
Draupadi sings:

In my head Beirut still burns

The Queen of Nubia, of God's Upper Kingdom
the Rani of Jhansi, transfigured, raising her sword
are players too. They have entered with me
into North America and share these walls.

We make up an art of pariahs:

Two black children spray painted white
their eyes burning,
a white child raped in a car
for her pale skin's sake,
an Indian child stoned by a bus shelter,
they thought her white in twilight.

Someone is knocking and knocking
but Draupadi will not let him in.
She squats by the stove and sings:

The Rani shall not sheathe her sword
nor Nubia's queen restrain her elephants
till tongues of fire wrap a tender blue,
a second skin, a solace to our children

Come walk with me toward a broken wall
—Beirut still burns—carved into its face.
Outcastes all, let's conjure honey scraped from stones,
an underground railroad stacked with rainbow skin,
Manhattan's mixed rivers rising.

About the Author

Born in India, Meena Alexander lives in New York City. She is a professor of English and women's studies at Hunter College and the Graduate Center at CUNY, and a lecturer in poetry in the Writing Program at Columbia University. Her books include *Nampally Road*, *Fault Lines: A Memoir*, and *The Shock of Arrival*.